Happy Birthday

Love,

Anna

A NEST OF
SIMPLE FOLK

A NEST OF
SIMPLE FOLK

SEÁN O'FAOLÁIN

A BIRCH LANE PRESS BOOK
Published by Carol Publishing Group

First Carol Publishing Group Edition 1990

Copyright © 1989 by Constable and Co Limited

A Birch Lane Press Book
Published by Carol Publishing Group

Editorial Offices
600 Madison Avenue
New York, NY 10022

Sales & Distribution Offices
120 Enterprise Avenue
Secaucus, NJ 07094

In Canada: Musson Book Company
A division of General Publishing Co. Limited
Don Mills, Ontario

Manufactured in the United States of America
ISBN 1-55972-041-7

10   9   8   7   6   5   4   3   2   1

Carol Publishing Group books are available at special
discounts for bulk purchases for sales promotions,
premiums, fund raising, or educational use. Special
editions can also be created to specifications.
For details contact: Special Sales Department,
Carol Publishing Group, 120 Enterprise Avenue,
Secaucus, NJ 07094

CONTENTS

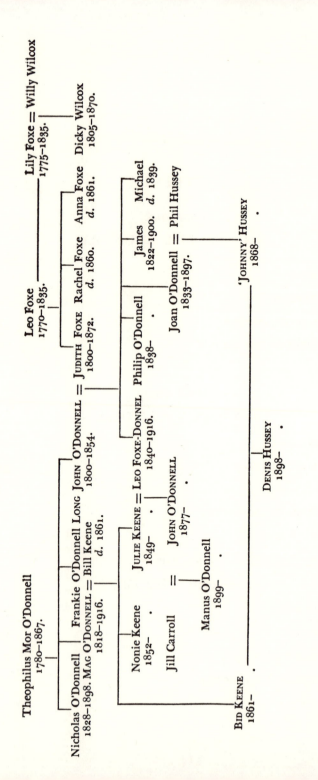

BOOK ONE

1854–1888

THE COUNTRY

1

The Will

1

OF his boyhood Leo Foxe-Donnel remembered only three things—his father's death, the day of the burial, and how, after that, he went for the first time to Limerick.

On that first evening, and it seemed to him as if it were always so, a frozen canopy of cloud hung over the plain. Far away, beyond the Shannon, its shaggy edges drooped down in a smoke of rain over the land, and there only could one see any movement in the banked mass, although the wind whistled in the alders that grew out of the walls along the muddy roads. That thawing cloud would gradually sweep all across the coloured plain, depositing its vapour in the already sodden fields and the browned thatch of the cabins, until after a slow journey of fifty miles its pall blackened into a downpour on the Kerry mountains. Until then there was nothing tall enough to scrape even the lowest cloud, and no shelter for the traveller if it burst too soon.

On that November evening in 1854 he was standing at the gates of his aunts' house of Foxehall, on its hill, midway between Ballyallinan and Rathkeale, both of them on a little tributary of the Shannon. Foxehall stood about a mile up from the road, at the end of an avenue of lindens. At a distance it was almost noble in its bare, square, limestone nakedness; at closer quarters it became a too-tall barracks of a building, outhouses on each wing, steps up to

the door, and not a trace of ivy or any other creeper on its
front.

In that house lived his two aunts, Rachel and Anna
Foxe, the last of the Foxe line, for at their death the house
would pass by entail to some Gloucestershire branch of the
family that nobody had ever heard of. The two old maids
had lived so long in that house, in a kind of waking sleep
of peace and comparative plenty, that as far as they were
concerned there might have been no world outside it.
Now that Boney was dead, and well dead, and they fervently hoped well damned, they felt that the whole world
would live in peace and plenty again for the rest of its
days. Vaguely they heard of other things, O'Connell,
Emancipation, Reform, new Poor Laws, political troubles,
but they lived indifferent to them all. In that great plain
since rumours of the Corsican devil had frightened their
childish minds, nothing else counted, because nothing else
happened. In that plain and that house nothing happened
from morning to night, and nothing happened from day
to day, and as they grew older and nearer to toothlessness,
even the years seemed to fall asleep like their paunch-tight
cats, life become more quiet for them in their age than a
perpetual summer dusk.

They were not to blame. Over all that rich land there is
and always has been a kind of sultry sloth, dead and over-
powering and drugging to all the energies of the spirit.
Hidden away from the tracks of peace and war alike, as a
glance at a map will show, this region of the Deel is a
meadowland of the finest heart caught in the loop of a
river that leads to a harbourless sea—all of it so drenched
in sleep that strangers to that plain fall into an apathy of
mind and will until time accustoms them to its too soft
air. History has reverberated only in the distance, and even
then but rarely and too far away to be heard, as when the
Williamite grenades burst all through one terrible winter

over Limerick city; it is a place into which news of the
world's calamities has seeped by rumour and dying echo,
and been felt in the end only for some small secondary
cause. So, before Waterloo, Rachel Foxe had stormed for
hours against the French because she had not got sugar
from Limerick for three weeks.

The two sisters had drunk in the essence of that place,
walking along and along in their youth by the toppling
river-banks of the Deel where it flowed beside them with
muted strings; along and along, facing the distant church
tower whose grey finger of silence rose faintly on the absolutely level horizon. If they visited that town, whose
decay had begun just before they died—in our day utterly
decayed—the silence was all the deeper for the presence
there of houses and shops and cabins from which, occasionally, an odd sound came to break it: the blacksmith's
anvil, a child's cry, a dish of water flung on the roadway.
If they climbed the hill, where there were only houses with
brass-knockers (and in their old age a Catholic nuns' convent from which no murmur was ever heard), there was
silence almost unbroken. And when once they entered from
curiosity, beneath that finger-spire, terrifyingly surrounded
by pock-marked crosses to its very base, dark and dusk as
the full tide of night, the quietness so resounded in their
ears that it came as a relief when, from some praying figure
wrapped in the black marble of a pillar, a sigh of devotion
rang out like a drop falling in a well.

Hemmed in by that silence, by those slow-moving, sedgy
rivers, by that plain, to leave which meant a long and
tedious journey, the two sisters, like everyone else about
them in that wide plain, accepted in all sincerity this only
life they knew. And as they accepted all they saw they
believed absolutely all they heard. They had been told
their father was a gentleman, when in truth he was almost
as much of a horseboy—an old man with soft features,

coarse fingers, no grammar, mainly interested in horses, a hopeless farmer and man of business, in whose hands the farm had gone to wrack and ruin; a man who thought as slowly and as carefully as he drank, in sips too brief to be felt by the palate, and with such long intervals that before the glass was drained, the night and his guest and the conversation were all gone. Of their mother they never heard; she had died when they were children, and their father never spoke of her. They had heard that Foxehall was an old and noble house, and they lived believing it so, generations after its last trace of nobility had dwindled away. A quick eye might have noted that the youngest portrait in the hall was at least two hundred years old, that the stables were empty and tottering, that the trees had disappeared without replanting, and that the crab-apples from the unpruned orchard were sold, at the lodge gate, to the tenants' children for a ha'penny the capful. The lodge itself was rented, the land all let out for grazing, cut by sod fences to the very door of the house, and every acre was so heavily mortgaged that the heir in entail would probably never bother to claim his liabilities, never come to live in that naked barracks with its half-naked rooms.

One thing only had happened in Foxehall, though a long time ago now. That was when Judith, the third and youngest sister, married into one of those white, thatched cabins that dotted the level plain about. The man she chose—he certainly did not choose her—was Long John O'Donnell, the eldest son of old Theophilus O'Donnell in Ahill, across the Deel.

"Great heavens!" old Leo Foxe had stormed at his daughter when she told him of the proposal. "But Ahill is nothing but a bog, a swamp. And old Theo and all his sons is nothing but born fools!"

"If it's a bog," retorted Judith, "why do you take rent for it?"

"To clothe and feed you girl," he replied, and hastened to go on with: "And that boy, Long John! He's the toughest, dullest clout of the lot of them."

"On horseback," cried his daughter, "he's like a statue."

And to anger him she quoted the *Limerick Dairyman's Ballad,* for he loved the old song:

"He's like Graycian Alexander riding to the fair."

Then she went on:

"I like him. He has the back of a thoroughbred. He has the neck of a swan."

"He has the hands of a swan," mocked her father, who knew those hands well from taking the sorry rent of the farm out of them on quarter-day.

"You'll be called Judie Long John," wailed Anna.

"Marry him!" shouted her father. "Marry him, then! I'll give you five fields—the last five fields I can dare to call my own. But if you marry him, I tell you, I won't talk to you again as long as I live."

"If you do marry him," said Rachel sweetly, from where she read in her corner, "I'll be glad to sponsor your tenth child, darling."

She did marry him. And Rachel sponsored her tenth child. And not merely did she marry him, but she turned Catholic with him. Why she did it nobody ever knew, and by the time she had borne her tenth she scarcely knew either. She had forgotten the fire of her youth, the sprightliness of her teens, the boredom of her majority. And the people of the place forgot that they had always called her "airy" and said she had a "shtreak" in her, forgot that they had jeered at Long John because it was his wife who courted him, and he had been proposed to by a girl. They never forgot how he had laughed back at them—as he could afford to. Five fine fields, all his own! And a woman with a tidy lump of money? And a jaw like a scythe, and eyes like a horse, and a cheek you could bleed with a rush-tip? And a pair of hips like a broodmare for a family?

"Oh!" he had smiled toughly. "It's a good bargain enough."

They were glad when they could prove that it wasn't, though it was too late then to prove it to Long John, for while he lived he had seen to it that the bargain prospered with him.

But if it was a good bargain for Long John it was not for Judith Foxe. For seventeen years her sisters never spoke to her, and her father died without seeing or forgiving her. People almost forgot she was a Foxe. She almost forgot it herself—until she grew big for the tenth time, and that child tamed her. She had shed her last tear of self-pity, she had lost all but her last shred of pride when, as she looked out one evening at a cold, rain-ponderous sky, she saw her sisters' old britzka swaying through the ruts of her boreen up to the house. The sisters, pinched in circumstances, and pinched in cheeks and doomed to virginity, had begun to feel, almost twenty years after their youngest sister, the loneliness of their life. Sick of dyeing their curls and painting their faces and pulling at their laces and inviting the one or two eligible men to cards or tea, they had decided, after about three years of wrangling, to visit their sister. But even then they refused to enter her house or step on her land, and they talked to her nervously from under the hood of their hen-roost of a carriage. "We just dropped in," they said (it was a mile of a boreen from the road), "as we were passing, to see if you were *still* alive!"

They saluted Long John where he stood at a distance, his cap in his hand, bowed partly with age and partly from respect, and they touched the dirty crowding faces of their little nephews and nieces with the very tips of their fingers, like a pair of cats touching water. And ever afterwards, in spite of that rutted, muddy, mile-long boreen, with its briers that reached out to scratch their faces, they always pretended they "just dropped in when they were passing."

So resolute were they not to as much as touch with the soles of their shoes the O'Donnell land, that once when they met a wain of hay in the boreen and neither car could retreat—these wooden-perch coaches never could turn in less than a barrack-square—O'Donnell and his neighbours had to lift them and their britzka bodily, lift them aloft like the Gemini terrified in constellation, and turn them, with much cursing and halloing in Irish, towards the open road and the safety of Foxehall.

It was just afterwards that the last baby was born. When they rolled into the farm-yard, dung-soft and stenching, Judith brought forward the old wooden cradle for the sisters to look down at their latest nephew. As it was a bald-headed, blue-eyed baby, Rachel went so far as to say it reminded her of her father, and had a Foxe look about it; whereupon Judith looked at her son like a mother who has heard a prophecy, and the sisters looked at one another in silence. She scarcely heard Rachel offering to sponsor the child. She only woke up when Anna said sharply that, naturally, the offer would not have been made if there didn't appear to be something rather attractive and, in fact, if she might say so, reminiscent about the child, with Rachel adding that if she did sponsor the child it must be called Leo, after its grandfather.

So the child was taken under the wing of the two sisters, and Judith said to her man that she wanted it called after the Holy Father, Leo the Twelfth, whose picture hung over their bed since they were married (and was turned to the wall on more than one occasion after it). It was the first lie she told him about the boy, and it fathered thousands. The child grew as a hedge between her and her husband, a cause of endless quarrelling, and if she had not grown tough and cunning with her years she would not have been able to protect him from the cruelty of the O'Donnell life. She pretended he was sick or ailing; she kept him out of her husband's way; she sent him to Nicholas O'Donnell, Long John's younger brother, the Master, to be taught Greek and Latin through the winter, and in the summer he went into Limerick city for music and drawing and deportment.

Here he was, then, this cold evening of cloud-reflected light, peeping about the corner of his aunts' gateway, his books under his coat, protected from the weather by a furry cap and a little Inverness coat with many capes, his little sharp nose pointed like a setter's into the wind. Suddenly about the corner of the road there came a light cabriolet, swaying in the potholes of the road, its leather hood shining with the last rainfall through which it had passed. As it came abreast of the gates he ran forward, and while the nag pranced and reared, he stretched up on his toes to speak to the driver. But the driver, a little red-nosed, ball-faced man, cried to his horse in a fury, lashed its belly and jerked at the reins until he had his nag quiet, if trembling. Then he turned savagely to the boy to curse him. Seeing who it was he halted and growled instead, "Don't you know better than that? What the devil do you want now?"

"My aunts said, Mister Normoyle, for to go with you to my mother's. And then for to go on with you to Bill Keene's."

"I'm not going next nor near your mother. Your mother is a mile off my road. I must go to Mag Keene at once. She's sick."

"My aunts," commanded the boy unmoved, "said for to tell you, that you are to go to my mother's first, before you go to Bill Keene's."

"What's wrong now? Is it the mare?"

"My aunts said, Mister Normoyle, for to tell you that my father is sick, and for to go to his house before you go to Bill Keene's."

"How bad is he?" growled the vet.

"My aunts said for to tell you, Mister Normoyle, that he's very bad sick."

"All right! Get in."

While the little ruby-faced man cursed under his breath, the child clambered in eagerly, and began gravely and slowly to deposit his books beside him and to tuck himself in with as much ceremony and care as if he were an old man. With a laugh the vet whipped up his nag, and the car swayed on its way. The child sat very straight, and the other stared at the horse's ears or glanced sideways at the drowned fields, his anger slowly draining away.

2

From his bed Long John O'Donnell looked out at the black tufts of the linden-tops, all moving slightly in the wind, all as black from the wintry weather as the rooks' nests still caught in their uppermost outermost twigs. When Aunt Rachel told Leo that his father was "bad sick," she did not tell him the entire truth. Yet even in his last, weakening moments of consciousness the old man murmured to himself with delight in his trees.

"They're great shelter. They're powerful trees."

For three years he had lain there in bed, in his timbered room, his beads in his lap, his stick by his side to tap on the floor if he wanted anything. The small, four-paned window, dust in its corners, damp on its glass, gave him his only view of the world, a quartered patch of sky edged by the linden-tops, where, apart from the budding or falling of the tiny leaves, there was nothing but an occasional whirling wing to tell the hours and the seasons. It was a swallow or a swift or a bullfinch flashing down in the spring, a speckled cloud of starlings falling on the trees for their thunderous orisons when the autumn evenings browned the sky, or in the winter the sparrows chattering because a lazily flapping crow or a farm-cat had frightened them. And then for the hours—a blackbird calling in the distance through the dusk, an owl screaming like a woman in pain when the dark fell. It was a world where the sick man was happy for a day if he heard, before anyone else, the reedy whistle of the yellow-hammer, or the first cuckoo, and then the winding, gyring lark that was silent when August came.

All that he had ever known in his boyhood and youth of the ways of birds had leisure in those three years to flow back to his memory, and make play for him in his final days.

But it was the lindens that alone gave him constant joy. The linden is a tree for a park, where it makes a tall, noble, hedge-like avenue, not only because it is smooth-topped as if cut with a shears, but because it is thick and bushy to the height of a man. As far as he knew, and he had inquired at every fair and market, there was not another farmer in the whole of Limerick with as much as three of them on his land—and he had not merely a line of them, but a double line. That night he held the title-deeds of the Linden Farm, or the Home Farm as he later called the five fields of Foxehall land, and locked them in the black tin trunk under his bed while his lovely young wife was preparing their first supper, he had tightened his mouth into a knot that grew harder and harder as the years went on. And when he ploughed between these trees and looked down between them at Foxehall, and then glanced athwart them at a neighbour's farm, his own poor shanty at Ahill where his

father lived with his sister Mag and his brothers Nick and
Frank, he would cry, "Hup!" to the horses, and dig the
share another six inches into the ground, and stay abroad
at his work long after sundown, ignoring the rain soaking
through the sack on his shoulders.

He made his sons hate him, because he was so hard and
pitiless on them. Old Leo Foxe had put an entail on the
land which left it to his daughter's male issue, and failing
sons, sent it back to the two sisters. It was the nearest he
could go to keeping the land in his own name. Why he
should be so hard on them, she did not realize for years.
Until once, when he lashed his son James with a horse-whip
across the bare legs and sent him to bed crying with the
pain of it, she stormed out at him in an utter rage. She
called him a clod. She called him a "shweep" and a bear,
and she almost frightened him with her burning eyes.

"Don't you see, woman," he had growled at her in a
corner, under his breath, in order that the children should
not hear, "that it's all for his good? It isn't my land, or
your land. It's his land. And if anything happened him,
where would you be then? It's all your father's fault—him
and his entailing. I want to have land I can own without
fear or favour to any man."

"Land! Land! You big fool, where would you get land?"

"Where, but by selling what I have to get more."

"You can't sell my sons' land."

"I can mortgage it."

"You cannot, then. You must have the boys' permission."

"Permission!"

He threw his whip in a corner with a look that seemed
to say, "Where is the use in talking to a woman like that?"
He had small trouble in inducing James to agree to a
mortgage. He merely told the young man one night to put
his name to a piece of paper, and without daring to ask a
question the youth signed away his birthright. After that,

Long John never even as much as discussed his plans about the land with his wife.

Actually Michael had been the first child, and the second James. Six daughters came in succession after that, every one of them unwelcome and unloved because she was not a boy. Michael died of pneumonia after a day's ditching in wet weather, and James, at the age of twenty-five, snatched the whip from his father's hands when he threatened to flog him again: he felled the old man on his own hearth with the butt-end of it, and ran out of the house to his old grandfather, Theophilus, at Ahill, neither expecting nor wanting to return as long as his father lived. On these two sons Long John had exhausted his ambition, and having mortgaged the Home Farm to buy the fine set of fields he called the New Plot, he began to slave harder than ever, and made his six daughters slave harder than ever, in order to work off the debt and possess completely his two farms. Long John's only hope now was in his small sons—Phil, and his last, born the year after Michael died, whom Rachel had sponsored and called Leo. He watched over these two boys like a mother, continually calling in the vet to attend to them, and his fear for them was one of Judith's great weapons to get anything she wanted for her favourite.

He became aged before his time with hard work and worry. An inherited palsy descended on him in his fifties. At the age of fifty-three, the year before his death, he grew half-blind, and then an ancient and terrible coffin-maker tapped at his side. A strange sore broke out under his arm-pit—a secondary cancer. Within a few months, far within his body, it deprived him of the use of his arm and he was hobbling about the farm with tiny steps on two sticks, aweing his children and his wife with his strange, soft smile, blinking his watery eyes at the sky as if craving pity of the sun. A few months more and the gnawing, inward-moving worm of death drew a paralysis on all his limbs, and he became a gentle child again.

Here he was, then, stretched on his bed, watching the swallows and the finches swoop and dart like dragonflies, and the nights succeed the nights, and the seasons follow one another in slothful procession—dead but for his memories of the fields and the work in the fields, his farm still encumbered, his work half-done, and his sons mere children. The lindens in the wet winds reminded him only, now, of the power of work he had done and the power of work that remained to be done, and as his beads passed through his roots of fingers, he would pause to hear his daughters' swift steps go and come in the kitchen below, and he would direct them eagerly in his mind, and his body would not respond to his desires, and he would fear that nothing was being done as it should be. Then he would look out at the sky, and that gentle smile of resignation loosen his lips as he prayed on through his rosary for pity and consolation of the God in heaven who decreed it all.

It was after his "stroke" that James returned to the farm, more as a servant than as a son. In Ahill he had become wild and lazy, drinking and playing pranks in the pubs, watching Phil and Leo growing up to take his place. Once he was in prison in Limerick for a month for hacking the tails from two of his father's cows. But the priest never ceased trying to persuade the father to take back his son, and when the old man took to his bed, he forcibly led the boy to the farm, and planting him on the kitchen floor, a sullen lump, ordered his mother to take and guard him from bad ways, ordering the stricken father to raise no word against her. Barely accepted by his mother, not as much as tolerated by his dying father, he lived in his parents' house, ignorant alike that he had anything to hope for, that the house over his head was his, and that all he could inherit with it was an encumbrance.

Once only the father asked for him, and that was when his mind was wandering and he was beginning to confuse the names of his children. But he recollected himself as the young man stood in his doorway; he turned to the partition, and the son went away.

Now, as the vet's car rattled into the yard, he stopped staring out of his pitiful eyes at the lindens. It was late, as he could see by the blackness of the tree-tops against the leaden sky—they are the blackest of all trees in wet weather. But he halted his hand as he was about to tap with his stick, and tried instead to listen. The vet's footsteps went into the rear haggard. That was to see the mare. That was why he came. They returned after a while to the kitchen fire. That was to prepare a bolus. He knew the mare wanted a bolus. If he was up, he could have done it himself. He heard nothing for a long time, hard as he listened. That was surely the vet talking about him, for they always whispered now when they talked of him.

It was really the vet talking about Judith. He was never long near Judith O'Donnell without throwing a swift, double glance over her body—a first glance of approval, because she had made such a good farmer's wife out of herself: a second glance, more long and searching, that always ended in perplexity and doubt. Then, instead of saying to himself with satisfaction, "She's made a good wife of herself for him," or, "She's made a good job of it, and no error," he would say with a sigh, "Ah, well! She's made her bed, and she must lie on it." Until he would catch her eye falling affectionately on Leo, and then he would frown, and go farther and say, "By Gor! Her heart is shtuck in that lad against them all"—meaning that the country people were right when they said bitterly, "The pack beginning to yelp at last. It's kind father for her to want to make an old fox out of a young O'Donnell." Whereupon, as if there was nothing on his mind, he began to roll the bolus between his palms, and threw her a merry wink that fell upon her glance as on a wall, and then cocking his eye on the child, he asked lightly:

"How old are you, Leo?"

"Fourteen years next December," said the boy, with complete assurance.

"Ha!" said the vet seriously to the mother. "Aren't we getting old? I'd say it was yesterday he was born."

"Oh!" interjected the child pertly, "but I couldn't be born yesterday."

"You could, young wisdom, in a manner of speaking."

Then he turned to the mother, eaten up like the rest of the country people with the desire to know what exactly the Foxe women were intending to do for the child, and he said:

"Fourteen years! Well, well, well."

Sadly he shook his head over the ball and clucked with his tongue.

"And you were married in twenty-one. We're the same age, you know. Thirty—what, thirty?—thirty-five years ago almost. Puh, puh puh! It's terrible!"

And he wanted to remind her, as he had never reminded her, the thing being worth no more than the passing honour of a sigh, that he had danced with her at a Hunt Ball, one of the last good nights Foxehall knew, barely a month before her wedding.

"Thirty-five years ago! I used to be going to Foxehall that winter," he went on, "to look at a filly of your father's, God rest him. I was only just out of college. Huh!" he laughed, and looked down at Leo with that memory. "She was a beauty, and no mistake!"

"Is it my mother, Mister Normoyle?"

The mother shook a warning finger at her favourite,

really more anxious to stop the vet's flattery than to correct the child.

"Plamaus," she said dryly, "never softened a hard tooth. What's too sweet can't be wholesome. Have you that bolus ready?"

The vet turned for safety to the child.

"He's a real Foxe, now, isn't he?" he probed.

"You're a real Normoyle," she parried.

He smiled foolishly, uncertain whether he might fish farther. He tried the boy again.

"Never anger your mother, Leo," he advised briskly. "She's a hard woman," he said warningly, "though she has a soft heart. But," he went on as if he were in her confidence, "keep in with her and she'll stand by you."

Judith rose abruptly.

"He can stand by himself or sit on his tail," she snapped. "Maybe you'd hurry up with that bolus. We can't sit here gosthering all night, and the man below ailing."

Normoyle rose hurriedly and shuffled off to the door. Out of the corner of his eye, like a mouse to a cat, he saw Judith's black eyebrows bent at him, and her horse's teeth bared. The rain sprinkled the flags of the kitchen as he sidled out, and when he was gone she sniffed and went anxiously to her husband's door. Long John leaned back his head on the pillows as she entered and sat on the bed-kerb.

"That's the vet," she said. "He'll look at you in a minute."

He did not reply. He saw the lantern rays wheel across the ceiling. They both watched them fade into darkness. Then she left him.

As the vet and Leo entered the stable, the smell of manure, straw, and hay-dust rose on the air. The mare did not stir even when the lantern flung a brilliant light on

the whitewashed wall before her eyes. Her head drooped
as if she were asleep, and her broad white flank filled the
stable. From time to time, as he bared his elbows and examined the mare, the vet glanced at the boy holding the
lamp, noting in him his mother's jaw, well rounded but
weaker at the chin, and how he had his father's eyes and
peered like his father, though far less cutely and intel-
ligently, and he smiled like his father, with a soft and
disarming smile, and he even had his father's large hands
like gloves—a queer mixture of the softness of the Foxes
and the softness of the O'Donnells. As he glanced at him
the vet decided too that it was a matter of chance whether
he turned into a tall, lanky weakling or a wiry image of a
fellow that would crown a horse, fish with the best, and
stride through the bogs in the rain with his gun levelled
and his nose out before him. His clothes were a strange
contrast with the "flitthers" on the young man, James, who
now came in to help him with the bolus.

"Hold the ball," the vet commanded Leo.

He coaxed up the head of the mare, and the brown-
furrowed teeth were bared and her lips curled away from
his fingers. He prised open the great jaws, firmly but gently,
and then, while James held them open without mercy, and
Leo lifted the lantern to let its light fall into the red maw,
he grasped the yellow-coated tongue with his right hand
and dragged it forwards and sideways from the mouth.

"Look at the dirt of that," he whispered, and soothed the
sidling mare with coaxing noises.

"Gimme the ball," he cried to Leo.

Deftly his thumb and little finger grasped it, and his
diminished hand dived to the bare elbow into the mare's
throat, and in a second was out again.

"Let her go!" he shouted to James. The mare's teeth
snapped within an inch of his fingers. The animal hardly
realized what they were doing, and her eyes rolled timidly

at them, and her head rocked like a toy horse as she snorted and swallowed. The vet held her by the mane, and ducking his head to the left side of her neck, laughed with satisfaction.

"Aha! There she goes!" he said, pointing out to Leo the sleek grey skin of the throat rising and falling where the ball slid gently down. Wide-eyed, Leo watched it, while the vet dived his hands in the warm water James had brought, and, drawing back, grinned at the child's surprise.

"Well, Leo? What about a little pill for you?"

Leo was timidly touching the travelling lump with his fingers.

"It's too big," he complained.

"Oh! But we'd give you a nice little fella. I always take one myself every morning. Look!" he said, pointing to his throat. "Mine got stuck last night."

The child looked doubtfully from him to his brother. Then he cried out excitedly:

"That lump's always there in you. James has one. And I have one."

"Oh. You're too smart. Give her a warm sponge, James. Just a rub. Not a wash. And change the straw. You say she's in foal?"

"I don't say that now. She was covered four weeks ago. I'd say she might be."

"But she'd be more sick if she took," argued Leo.

"Ho ho!" cried the vet, drawing on his coat. "We'll make a farmer of you, yet. Come on."

"Farmer?" mocked James, turning his back on them. "Farmer, how are yeh? He couldn't farm a window-box."

The pair returned across the darkening yard to the kitchen. The lad Phil was by the fire, and Judith was lighting the lamp. As she turned she saw her favourite in tears, and at once she rushed to him and, kneeling, gathered him

up in her arms. Her face softened, and she became a really
handsome woman again.

"My pet! My lanavaun! Who's been at you?"

The child drew aside, unwilling to be kissed before the
vet. James came in with the empty bucket.

"You're at the child again," she cried at him, and she
was like the mare in the stall—grinning at him.

"He's no child. You're keeping him a child with your
petting."

"Don't answer me back. I'll not have the child tormented.
Do you hear me, boy?"

The "boy" ignored her.

"Do you hear your mother talking to you?" she cried so
harshly and loudly that he faced her more submissively.

"Yes, ma'am."

"Then heed me."

He turned away again.

"Do you hear that? Look at me."

"Yes, ma'am."

He filled his bucket and went to the door. Nobody but
the vet saw the glance he hurled at his mother and Leo
as he went out, and with relief he began to fill his pipe,
and blow out his cheeks as if the air had suddenly grown
too hot and heavy for him. At the same moment they
heard the floor being hammered in the room below.

"Yes, John!" called out Judith.

To Leo she said in a whisper:

"Go to your books, until Mister Normoyle is ready for
you."

To Phil:

"Help the sisters with the calves, and give the doctor's
horse a gwaul of hay."

She waited until they were gone before she beckoned
the vet to the fire-corner.

"He's very sick," she said. "I've sent for Lawyer Dee."

The vet leaned forward eagerly.

"It's time he made his will, Mister Normoyle," she said sternly. "The man is sinking fast, and we can have no disputes and troubles afterwards. I want you to tell him it's time he settled about his affairs."

The floor below was tapped again, this time more feebly.

"The poor man," said the vet, looking at Judith expectantly.

She said no more, but led him to the sick-door. There she paused.

"Tell me the truth!" she warned.

He went in and she stood by the door like a sentinel.

The vet took the mottled palm in his hand, and he could feel the sweat of death on it. Two eyes, black as holes burned in a blanket, looked up at him.

"How's my sister, Mag Keene?" asked the sick man.

"I'm going over to her at once. She's all right."

"She was on the go for a while. I heard that. She'll bear a line of childer. There's powerful nature in the Keenes."

"John!" said the vet solemnly.

"How's Theo?" wheezed the old man.

"Your father is fine—fine out!"

"He's a powerful age," sighed Long John, and there was a brief pause.

"John!" said the vet again, in a still more solemn voice.

"Seventy-three years last Christmas—or was it seventy-four? He told me once he saw them lindens sot."

The vet leaned back, so as to let the candle in the window shine on the old man's face.

"He saw a power," he agreed.

"He remembers Boney," said Long John. "And French smuggling-men, in roundy hats, sailing up the Shannon to Saleen."

The vet's foot tapped the floor irritably.

"And Grattan's Irish Volunteers," said O'Donnell. "Oh! He saw a power."

In thinking of it he seemed to fall into a waking sleep.

"John!" said the vet firmly, leaning forward again.

But the old man did not remove his eyes from the window-pane that dribbled with shining rain.

"He saw 'ninety-eight. And he was flogged at the cart-wheel in Newcastle-west on the bare back."

There was another long pause that the vet did not break.

"And he saw the Union," whispered the old man. "He saw the Union."

The vet looked at him under his eyebrows, and caught one shifty glance at him from out of those watery eyes. Was the old man making a mock of him?

"He saw the Union, bedad! And he marched behind O'Connell. And he voted at the Clare election in 'twenty-eight. Would you believe that?"

His voice was so low, now, that the vet could barely hear it. As he leaned forward, the old man went on falteringly:

"And he lost his wife and every one of his childer but four only, in 'forty-five."

"About that mare of yours," shot out the vet suddenly.

"What about her?" asked Long John.

"Oho! You can hear that, can you?" cried the vet in triumph.

"Ah!" reverted Long John. "Theo saw a power."

"Blasht Theo!" cried the vet, slapping dust out of the red quilt. "Will you listen to me, man?"

With one skinny brown finger Long John motioned the vet nearer. Normoyle enveloped him with his shoulders, as he stooped his head to listen.

"Tam Normoyle!" whispered the failing voice.

"Aye?"

"I'll make no will."

The vet glanced curiously at him.

"It's time you did. Why won't you?"

The bones of the palsied fingers clutched the thread-worn blankets.

"Do you know what Theo said to me one time? *'Is treise greim an fhir mhairbh na Samsoun beo.'* " (The dead man's grip is stronger than Samson alive.)

"And what may that mean?" asked the vet, looking sideways into the eyes of his patient.

"It have a meaning," said Long John, gazing at the speckled pane.

The fall had grown heavier now, and they could hear it splashing on the pools in the yard beneath the eaves. Normoyle cursed under his breath at the thought of the foul roads, narrow and potholed, and the dark falling on them. He tapped the chest of his patient irritably.

"I'll tell you another saying: *Scaoileann an bás gach laincis.*" (Death loosens every spancel.) "Think on that, my man."

The palsied finger beckoned again, and the vet leaned hopefully.

"Theo," whispered Long John, "drank and travelled with the poets of the Maigue."

"Damn the poets of the Maigue," cursed the vet earnestly. "Lawyer Dee, in Rathkeale, has more knowledge in his *meirin* than the whole lot of them."

Judith opened the door inwards, and said in a low, harsh voice:

"How is he, doctor?"

Normoyle took the narrow wrist and counted the pulses on his half-hunter. Then he looked carefully at the sick man, and swiftly left the room. Closing the door, Judith came over to him, where he stood under the oil-lamp by the window lifting his coat from the deal table.

"Send for the priest," said Normoyle. "You sent for me too late. Get my cab ready."

"You must stand by me," expostulated Judith. "You must stand by the dying man."

"I must go to Mag Keene. She's in labour since the morning."

"But you must keep him alive for the lawyer."

He struggled into his coat—a barrel of a man.

"What will do you want him to make?" he asked boldly. "He says he'll make no will for you."

"I want him to make his own will."

"You don't. You want him to make a will in spite of himself. You left it go too long."

"He must leave his affairs in right order. You mustn't go, Tom."

She was pleading now. But he was irritable because she had tried to bully him, and would not confide in him.

"I can do nothing for him. It's the priest that man wants."

Leo was watching from the end of the stairs, and one of the daughters came in and sat by the fire on the settle. The vet smeared the window-pane and looked out. On the "tiger's" platform Phil was grinning at himself from under the hood of a sack. The vet went to the door and shouted at him:

"Come down out of that, you poltacawn!"

"Go with him to the master," Judith ordered Leo.

The pair went out, and left her with her man.

3

As the vet and Leo bowled in and out under the woven elms along the road the rain lightened and the west shone cold about the ears of the nag. On all sides the fabric of the sky fell apart and great clouds rose and sank through the windy air, so tangled in one another that only on the level horizon beneath them, ever so far away, could they see the pale light of the hidden moon. Presently the boy tugged at the vet's arm.

"Well?"

"My mother says I'm to be a farmer," he complained. The vet sniffed.

"Oh, but I mean a gentleman farmer," said the boy.

"Puh!"

"And what I do want is to be a vet."

"Is that so?"

"Then, what am I doing Latin and Greek for?"

"It'll do no harm to you. I knew a lot of it once."

"But what is the good of it to me?"

"Education. *Quadrupitantis*—isn't it?—what is it?—*quàtit ungula*—I forget—"

"There you are!" said the boy saucily. "You forget."

"Well, it was a long time ago."

"I'll forget it too," said Leo, and there was a long silence. Normoyle flicked the horse's rump reflectively several times during this silence, and looked from time to time at the boy beside him.

"The last time," he said suddenly, "that I saw your mother, she wanted you to be a doctor."

"Yes, but my Aunt Rachel wants me to be a farmer."

"Aha!" said the little vet with a bent head and an understanding wink. "Then, maybe your Aunt Rachel will buy you a farm."

"We have three farms of our own," said the boy proudly. "My aunts said it to my mother."

The vet spoke no more after that. He disliked the answer, and his face darkened on hearing it. Three farms? That meant the old farm of Ahill where Long John's sister Mag was married to the man of the Keenes; then the five dowry Home Farm fields that must go to James, encumbered though he heard they were. But the fine New Plot that by his sweat Long John had bought—*bought* when so few men owned any land but the landlords! Was that free farm to go over the heads of six sisters and two brothers to this last child who had never done a stroke of work on the land? The little vet flicked his horse incessantly when they came to the Keenes' gate, and he almost tore the jaw off the nag with the pull he gave the reins. There across a field was Ahill—a low, brown-thatched farm-house with a few scraggy elms on one side and the glint of a swamped field on the other. As he drove along the side of the field he sank in the deep mud-ruts, and the hedge had not been cut for a year. As he pulled into the yard the smoke seemed to tumble in a cloud over the roof of the farm-house, dimming the faint light in the narrow loophole of a window, and when they entered under the door all they could see at first was the same blue smoke whirling on the wet clay of the floor with the ashes from the hearth. For there was no light in the kitchen but the light of the fire, although there was a rush-light in the window of the lower room. Leo did not need light, however; he removed his little coat, folded it on a corner of the settle, and swinging the rain from his small furry cap, laid it on top of all.

In the fireside corner was a browned nook he loved well, and without a word he snuggled in there and began to warm his shins. He loved this ancient sooty corner of the Ahill hearth, where the white lime was always tawny with soot and moisture, and from which—since there was no chimney-stalk in the hole of the roof—he saw everything through a garment of invisibility woven out of smoke. To-night, so dark was it in that corner, as he looked up through the chimney-hole and the bit of box stuck in it by way of shaft, that he could see the moving clouds and the moonshot sky radiant behind them. And when he looked down, he saw, in the faint glow from the fire, nothing but the faces of old Theophilus, his grandfather, and Nicholas, the Master, his uncle, and a cluster of little children whom he only recognized by degrees. They were Julie Keene, his cousin, a wee thing of five, the first child of the Keenes, holding in her lap the baby of two, small Nonie, and struggling from her side was another child, clawing forward to reach the clay pipe that trembled in old Theo's gums.

He had completely forgotten the vet and was willing to sit, as he had often sat, for hours watching the curling smoke, thinking of nothing in the world, or listening to his uncle or grandfather arguing some point in history or literature, or, most pleasant of all, watching Theo carefully cutting a quid of tobacco in his fist, shovelling it tediously and patiently between his fingers into his palm, and from his palm into his clay pipe—one of those simple acts that, performed with so much care and ceremony, can suddenly reveal to a boy what is meant by age and life and reality. Old Theo had been a teacher, too, in his day, wandering from house to house in the autumn when the harvest was in, teaching under the hedges or in half-empty barns, or in dark outhouses, or when winter fell, about the cabin-fires, strange, useless knowledge for the most part, inextricably mixed with the rudiments of real learning and pedantically used to illustrate it, knowledge that he had gathered here and there in his reading, or inherited with increasing irrelevancy at each remove from his father and grandfather before him. His bottomless memory, linked with these in their turn bottomless memories, reached back so far that in that one decaying brain one might see, though entangled beyond all hope of unravelling, the story (as well as the picture) of his country's decay.

Leo did not like his grandfather. He was dirty. His hands

were palsied. His eyes were red and wet from hanging so long over damp fires and reading tatters of books and manuscripts under skies as dark and watery as his eyes. The lines on his face were as deep and as engrimed as the furrows of a bellows, or the corners of an old barn. When he talked he sprayed spits through his remnants of teeth. And he asked impossible questions, that nobody but himself could answer. Even now he was gathering himself for an attack, so that it was with relief that Leo heard Nicholas say:

"We'll begin with ode number five, Leo."

But already Theo's black hand was shivering on the page.

"What does it mean, young lad?" he asked. *"Cuir an casur ar an urlàr, agus tóg an billeóg as an casóg."*

Leo translated without hope.

"Put the hammer in the middle of the floor, and take the hook out of the coat."

From the room below came a sudden moan of agony, and Leo looked around in terror.

"Listen to me," commanded the old man, and Leo looked crossly at the fire.

"It means," said Theo, proceeding to break up the words into pieces so as to get a cryptic meaning out of his riddle, "it means for to put the fresh thwisht in the centre of the moist middle, and for to take the young leaf out of the young thwisht. That's its rightful meaning."

"That means nothing," said Leo.

"It has a meaning," said Theo solemnly.

"It's a riddle," said Nicholas, to keep the peace.

"It is not a riddle," cried Theo.

"It's a stupid old thing, anyway," said Leo.

"You don't know anything, boy," snapped Theo.

And then, so swiftly that small Nonie began to cry in Julie's arms, he asked:

"What was it Solomon himself couldn't do?"

"To square a circle," Leo tried timidly.

"It's not!" sprayed Theo. "No, but to find the square root of minus wan."

Leo's eyes dissolved.

"Whichever I said," he stuttered, "you'd say it was the other."

"I would not. I would say no such a thing. Solomon never thried to square a circle. And for why? Answer me that."

"I dunno," wept Leo.

"Because," snarled Theo, "he was too wise."

With that he shot a mighty spit into the fire, crossed his legs, and leaned into his corner.

Another shrill cry came from the back-room, and Leo turned in fright.

"We'll begin with this ode," said Nicholas gently, "to Thaliarchus."

Leo continued to snivel.

"Yes?" encouraged Nicholas. "*Soracte* . . ."

"*O S-s-soractus,*" snivelled Leo.

"It is not *O Soractus,*" interrupted Theo.

Nicholas threw him a few words of Irish, and turning away the old man spat once more into the glowing sods and did not speak again.

"It's not vocative," tutored Nicholas.

"*Behold Soractus,*" amended Leo.

"*Soracte!*" corrected Nicholas. "It was a mountain outside of Rome."

"Is it gone now?" asked Leo hopefully, while Theo sniffed.

"It is not," said Nicholas. "It is there always, and when the winter shnow falls on it and remains on the gable of it, the people in the houses at Rome can look out and see it shining in the far distance. So Horace says to his friend, '*Look at Soracte, now white with shnow.*'"

A woman ran out of the lower room, and opening the

back door flung a dish of water into the yard. Nicholas looked up fearfully, but all he could say was his sister's name.

"Mag?" he asked.

The woman rushed to the fire like a fury, whirling her elbows right and left in a flood of pity and compassion for the woman in the lower room.

"The girsha is all right, isn't she, Ciss?" spat Theophilus.

"Arrah!" she cried, as she filled the basin from the hanging kettle. "Lave me alone, God domn and blosht ye. My soul from the divil, but it's a great thing to be a man. When I sees ye there gosthering on yeer folbos . . ."

And she whistled away the basin with a red face of rage on her so that Leo fell prone from his little stool, and the children, even his cousin Julie, began to whimper at the sudden excitement. Nicholas half-rose, but Theophilus laid his stick across his son's breast.

"The girsha is all right, Nicholas, or she'd tell us. Or Bill Keene would come out and tell us."

"Are you hurt?" asked Nicholas of Leo.

"I am not," said Leo. "But there's no light from the fire." Theo thrust a bit of fir into the red core of the fire, and by its blaze they returned to the book.

"*The woods of Soracte,*" translated Nicholas, ever so slowly and quietly and gently, forgetting his duty to his pupil, "*are weighted down by shnow. The course of the river is dammed by the hard frosht. Therefore, O Thaliarchus, let us melt the cold.*"

In an antiphonal chant Theophilus raised his voice, his head lifted to the rafters, translating out of his bottomless memory:

"*Lave us,*" he intoned unmusically, "*heap the logs upon the fire . . .*"

"*Do not,*" responded the son, "*do not be for ever and always thrying to find out what tomorrow will give. But do you profit by phwatever turn the wheel of fortune may bring."*

"*A young man,*" intoned Theophilus, and his red eyes leered with a kind of satyr's joy in the amorous phrase, "*must not skulk away from the dance, or scorn the sweetness of love. It's where you should be,*" he went on, robbing the phrase from Nicholas with a snarl, "*it's where you should be is on the green or in the market-place, and by night in the parlours where lovely girls will phwisper to you as by foreordained agreement.*"

"*A smile in the dark nook,*" concluded Nicholas, with a little smile of his own to illustrate, "*betrays the hiding girl; and keepsakes are filched by cunning from the arm or the fingers that willingly surrender the little threasure.*"

The flame of the fir-splinter died to a glow.

"The fir is gone," said little Julie, and they all looked at it. Nicholas handed the book to Leo, and, disturbed by the moaning from the woman in labour, began to walk about the room.

"Translate that, now," he said.

Leo began, but nobody seemed to hear him.

"*O Soractus, thou art white with snow . . .*"

He blundered on uncorrected, and when he finished Nicholas was by the window and Theophilus nodding by the fire. Leo stirred the splinter-end with his toe, and it leaped into flame and then died out. A fir tree grew in his mind, tall and snow-clotted, waving in the flame. Then, sliver of a root, levered from its womb in the bog, it fell like all its ancient branches into a little dust.

The helping woman came out with a small white bundle, and laid it into a drawer under the dresser. After her came the husband, Bill Keene. Theo started up, and with Nicholas and Julie went forward: when he walked, Theo was bent like a gibbet at right-angles to his thighs.

"Ayeh! Mavrone!" said the husband, rubbing his great red poll with his palm. "Another girl."

"What matther?" comforted Theo. "What's old can't but be true. What are the three best things in the world? Will I tell you?"

His voice thickened with joy in the triad, as he squinted up at the foxy giant.

"Three lovers with land," he cried, "three roads to her father's door, and three daughters in a line."

And then he winked.

Uncorking the jar of porter that had been brought to celebrate the birth of a son, the men began to drink the daughter's health, and fell into a rambling talk about children and land. Leo tried to puzzle out the following ode, but even the first line was too much for him, and his mind wandered far from Mercury, the grandson of Atlas, to things and names more wonderful. There was the Arabian Darley, sire of all horses, king of the sires and stallions of the world, like Potooooooooo (called Potatoes), or Eclipse, the first of racers, "of whom, on May the fifth, seventeen hundred and sixty-nine, the memorable Mister Dan O'Kelly declared at Epsom in a well-known boast, fully justified by the amazing event, that it would be Eclipse first and the rest nowhere." His eyes saw the green book on his Aunt Rachel's desk. He smiled to see the cuts of famous horses and trainers. He laughed to himself, and banged his book to. For fifty years that night remained bright in his memory, the bit about snowy Soractus and Atlas and Mercury. Then, when he was a very old man himself, it suddenly occurred to him what a grand name Atlas would be for a horse, and what a powerful name Mercury would be for a racer.

He heard the doctor's voice, and his brother Phil answering him, and he jumped up to ready himself for the road home. But he saw Theo and Bill Keene and Nicholas getting ready too, and Phil came in to him to tell him that he had been sent for the priest, and old Theo was going in the cab.

"Is my father bad?" asked Leo.

"I don't rightly know," grumbled Phil. "My mother has us all in bed early so as to make no noise. I'd be in the loft, only for she wanted the doctor to come back straight, and she sent me after him and the priest."

"I can't walk all that way," complained Leo. "Is James within?"

"He is not then. He ran to the cross from her."

They were in the yard now, miserably watching Theo being lifted into the cab, and the cab lumbering away into the boreen. The night was clear, and the stars were arranged in the sky. Suddenly Phil gripped his arm and led him from the two men to a ditch near the duck-pond.

"Look!" said Phil, as he drew a sapling and a few pieces of stick from under a thorn-bush. "It's a trap," he whispered, and then he went on bewailing. "I was going after the otter when my mother said we were to be in bed for nine."

"You couldn't catch an otter by night," scoffed Leo.

They were so accustomed to alarms about their father that they made little of this talk of sickness.

"I could that," declared Phil.

"How would you shtick him?"

"For why I wouldn't shtick him. I'd noose him."

"You could in your eyeball," taunted Leo.

He always patronized Phil; but this time Phil grew angry at his mockery.

"I could catch him, 'faith! I—I—I watched that otter yesterday, and he making for his hole, and I heard him whistling tonight at the same spot."

"He'd smell you."

"I'd smoke the trap."

"You couldn't see him."

"Will you look at the moon and the stars?"

"He'd hear you."

"In my bare feet?"

"He'd ate you. You should have gaiters and cinders in them, so he'd think it was your bones were cracking in his jaws."

"I'd not go nigh him till he was caught. Will you come, and we'll set it?"

"My mother said for us to be home early?"

"You're afraid to come. You're afraid you'll be bet."

Leo looked at his grinning face, and then he dived over the ditch, followed by Phil. They raced bent over the field, and over every other field, whether ploughed or in pasture, until they reached the river's edge. A white mist lay under the moon over every field, and the flooded river swished by the edge of the grass. Down-river they saw the light of their home, up-river a few alders grew out of the darkness.

"Whisht!" warned Phil.

Over the gurgle of the river an otter whistled shrilly.

"Leave us smoke it now," said Phil. "Give us a page of your book."

Willingly Leo sacrificed a dozen pages of the *Odes,* and presently he saw again in the flame Mount Soractus, and after it Ulysses the son of Atlas. For the willow, which was the spring of the trap, and the cross-spindle, he yielded up the rest of his little green *Horace,* page by page.

"Have you the bait?" he whispered, crouching over the tongue of fire. Phil grinned, and drew a wad of it from his trouser-pocket.

"Now!" he whispered at last, and sitting on the wet clay Leo drew off his boots and stockings. Phil, who wore neither, shoved them for him into a rabbit-hole by the bank. Then stooping low lest the otter should see them, if he rose to vent, they crawled towards where Phil had seen their prey tunnelling to his muddy bed. He gripped Leo's hand. A grey thing scuttled, and halted by the river-brim.

"A rat?" asked Leo.

"Th' otter," said Phil.

There was a splash, and then a snout was raised in the middle of the stream.

"Down, you divil," cried Phil, and they lay on their bellies and peered at the swirl. They saw bubbles near the bank, and then nothing more. They could well have been flood-bubbles, but they *knew* it was their prey. . . .

4

In the Home Farm all their sisters were in bed, whispering under the bedclothes, entangling their limbs in the weariness of sleep. Below them the hearth was slowly filling. That phrase which makes the fields heavy with fear had gathered them in their pity to the O'Donnells' house.

"Is he bad?" each cabin had asked when they saw the doctor pass, and then the answer came, as old as death itself:

"The priest is called."

So they moved over the dim fields, like night-cattle gathering to a drinking-pool. All the small ends that made life real to them were diminished and denied by the endlessness of the grave. Seeing suddenly the futility and hopelessness of their lives, they brimmed up with pity for the man who had anticipated their common lot.

Yet only a few of those who walked towards the death-house entered it. They sat on their heels under the ditches and watched through the briers the lights in the windows of the farm, talking now and again on any of the old subjects that helped like an antidote to keep from them the poison of death. Long John's ambition, his plans, his will, the future of the three farms—the Home and the New and

Ahill on its bog—whether James would get anything—they knew all the questions that must arise around these things, as well as if they owned the farms themselves.

"It was never a right marriage," they agreed.

"Signs on it it's his childer will have the profit of it," begrudged another.

"The grandson went," said an old man, thinking of the boy Michael who had died. "And the son is going, and there's old Theo left after them all."

Somebody else started the usual litany of commiseration.

"It's an ease for him to die."

"There's a cross on the house."

"The poor man without a son or a daughter settled."

"And no natural end that has him whipped."

"Sure, nothing wrong with him but a pain in his inshides!"

In the silences they smoked and heard the cattle munching in the byre and the swine turning in their sleep, or the swollen Deel across the flat terrain. It was so quiet, that a foot stirring echoed in the night. The silence weighed down on them, spread out about them, sang in their ears. It was an ease to hear a man snuffle.

Inside the house were the husband's relations—old Theo; his sons, Nicholas and Frank (the two brothers); a cousin named Browne; and Bill Keene, the brother-in-law. There was only one woman, a third cousin, a puffy-faced, red-headed woman from Knockaderry, known all over the parish and into the next parish, and the next one after that into Rathkeale, and out to Newcastle as Norry-all-night, because her days were spent in bed and her nights in roving, from wake-house to wake-house, lamenting the dead and comforting the living. In her youth Judith had often mimicked her to her fathers and sisters. Now she heard the old litany poured over herself as fluently as a prayer. She sat a little apart, her mouth as hard as iron, glaring at the window and from time to time shooting a glance at the relations of the man she married. She was hoping for the sound of the lawyer's car, as she listened to the doctor's movements in the sick-room, where he watched over the sick man until the priest should come.

" 'Tis the hand of God," murmured Norry-all-night, with many shakings and noddings of her red mop, many blinkings of her eyes. "But God never sent a burden but He sent a back to bear it. God never sent a mouth but He sent a bird to feed it. Sure, God help you tonight, you poor woman you. The widow's lot is a hard lot to bear, but you must bear it. We can't fly in the face of Providence. It's the will of the Most High. You know, Mrs. O'Donnell, ma'am, it's known that if a woman sets her face against the will of God in the departure of a loved one, it's known he'll have a hard death."

"It's true," said Theo, with a spit.

"It's true," said Browne, uncrossing his knees and looking sadly into the fire. From the end of the kitchen Judith looked bitterly from one to the other of them.

"God helps the weak. He never shut one door but he opened another."

"He tempers the wind," whispered Judith to herself.

"He tempers the wind," said Norry, "to the shorn lamb."

"The ways of Providence," whispered Judith to herself.

"The ways of Providence," said Norry, "are inscrutable, and God sees reason in all things."

"Sure Mary herself," in Judith's mind.

"Sure Mary herself lost a Son," went on Norry, "and He the Son of God, and did Mary complain? She left it all in the hands of God and she trusted her only Son. The sword of sorrow pierced her heart and she didn't complain. There's a divine reason in everything. Your man is happy," she said with emphasis. "He's happy and contented. Sure his brothers and sisters and his poor boy Michael, that went before him, are calling him. John and Michael and Susannah and Bride and Caroline."

"May God rest them all," murmured Theo their father.

"They're waiting to receive him. He sees them. Didn't you see the strange look in his eyes, ma'am, a while ago? He sees things we don't see. What did he see now at the foot of the bed a while ago, and we all about him and he looking at none of us? Who was there that he saw? What name was he saying that we couldn't hear it?"

"He was," they whispered, as they crowded together and recalled, as the wife could never recall, all the dead people belonging to the old man, and all their own dead that he had known in his lifetime. Judith buried her head in her palms and ground her teeth.

"I looked once," whispered the gossip, "at the dark place beyond the end of the bed, and may God have pity on all wandering souls this night" (and here she and all of them blessed themselves), "I thought I saw a thing moving towards me. 'Michael,' says he, 'is that you?'"

Here she began to sway to and fro over the fire with a moaning that was taken up by Theo, and rose and fell tremulous from him like a man with a toothache. Unable to stand it, Judith rose and strode to the death-room, where she saw the stupid face of the doctor—he had been killing the long end of the day with her drink—and the eyes of her husband, closed and still, the lips pale and barely moving, the face grey with the ebb-tide of death. She was glad Normoyle was there, and that she did not need to keep looking about her into the darkness, and that she could keep her mind on all that she had planned for this night—planned so long and often since her child Leo was born. She had neither time nor wish for pity. Her mouth gathered itself into the firmness of a door-knocker. It was she and her son against him and his sons. She heard her daughters' deep breathing through the partition, and outside a flutter among the hens.

"What time is it?" she asked.

He peered at his watch by the light of the candle in the window.

"Near nine."

"He'll not come," she moaned.

"The priest? Of course he'll come."

"He won't come," she muttered, ignoring his assuring words, but so passionately that they heard her by the fire and looked meaningly at each other. She heard a horse stamp in the yard, and she ran to the door.

"Is that you, Mister Dee?" she asked.

The priest came in, a firm-jawed, rabbit-lipped old man. He comforted her with a grip of his arm, and ignoring the salutes of the group that rose by the fire, he hastened into the sick-room. As he went he produced his white and purple stole, colours necessary for baptism and fitting for death, and his silver pyx, and looking anxiously all the time at the dying man he began to whisper anxiously with the doctor. He stooped, and spoke in the old man's ear. There was no answer, no sign that he heard.

"He's low," he complained to the doctor, and in a fury he turned to the wife.

"Why didn't you send for me long before?"

"He's bad so long, Father," apologized Judith with a humble whine.

"Doctor!" cried the priest. "I'm surprised at you."

"Damn it!" said Normoyle. "He's been sick three years. How could I know he was going to go in a blast?"

"You've been drinking."

"Ach!" grumbled the vet. "It's a bad day, and I'm going every hour of it. If you were out since morning you'd be glad of a nip."

" 'Ssh!" threatened the priest, scandalized. "Do something for him now."

He turned on the wife and the red-haired gossip hovering behind her.

"Leave the room!"

Norry lit the blessed candles that stood prepared on a little table. He watched her gloomily, and when she was gone, sank on his knees and began to pray. Norry went back to the fire, and Judith sat by the sick-door glaring at them, hating their wake-house talk and their eyes humbled with fear. At last Theo glanced at her angrily, and with a spit that reached almost to her feet, he said crossly:

"Sit up to the fire, girl."

"No, Theo!"

"Sit and warm your four bones, girl."

"I'll stay where I'm put."

He paused.

"The lawyer won't be here for a long hour yet."

She looked at him in dismay.

"Don't you know," he sneered, and glanced at the others, "that a watched pot never boils?"

A step resounded on the causeway, and Judith rose eagerly to her feet. James entered.

"How is my father?" he asked in a low sullen tone.

"Bad."

"Why didn't you tell me? There was nobody at the cross, and I only heard it at Knockaderry an hour since."

His temper was up. She could see he had been drinking. She guessed they had been inciting him in the public-house.

"Didn't I ask you, boy, to stay at home and give him rest? Didn't I tell you he was sick?"

"You didn't tell me he was bad sick. Is that the priest's car without?"

"It is."

"Is my father in danger of death?"

"He is."

"Isn't it an almighty queer thing you wouldn't tell me that?"

He stood awkwardly in the centre of the floor, not knowing what next to do.

"Is the priest within now?"

"Yes."

His mind was on other things besides the priest. Like all sons on the land, apart from this one rebellion, he had been submissive to his father and mother, ignorant of their plans for his future. But now, within an hour, his life would be decided, and he would know whether by that blow on his father's forehead he had, or had not, thrown his rights into the lap of his small brothers.

"What other car is that without?" he asked.

"Maybe it's Lawyer Dee's?" suggested Theo maliciously.

"Is it?" the son turned on the mother.

"Sit down, boy, and don't be worrying me. It's Doctor Normoyle's."

"Is the lawyer coming?" he insisted.

Judith looked at him, but he faced her.

"Sit down, boy, and don't be troubling yourself."

"I will not sit down. If I'm troubling myself it's about what concerns me."

Her voice fell, low and threatening.

"Is that a way to address your mother?"

There was a moment's silence. The priest was murmuring in the room.

"Is that a way to address your mother?" she repeated angrily.

For several minutes they could hear the priest at his prayers in the room.

"I only asked a question," muttered the son.

"And a right question," declared Theo, glaring at his daughter-in-law.

"Aye!" said Keene.

"So!" said Browne.

The young man looked at them, hesitant, calculating. His mother rose and pushed him to one side with her palm, and stood over the group.

"Bill Keene!" she mouthed, with her iron lips and her big horse's teeth, and her jaw that was as solid as stone. "Bill Keene!" she said, and nobody looking at her smouldering eyes and hearing her rough speech could have thought that she had, first of all, come to that cabin in a silk spencer and a bonnet. "What question is it of yours to know whether or not there is a lawyer coming to this house tonight?"

Theo expanded his scraggy windpipe at her.

"I'll tell you," he said. "His wife, Mag, is your husband's sister. And she is my daughter. As he is my son. The farm she lives on at Ahill she pays good rent for to your two sisters at Foxehall—far too good of a rent she pays them, by the same token. But, as you know dom' well, she only has the interest in that land from your husband. And she only has it, what's more—and the more fool she not to have it better—by word of mouth from him."

"So you don't trust your own son, Theo, is that it?"

"It is not. The land is safe to her as long as my son lived. But you are too simple for us entirely," he mocked; and he held his hand out to restrain Bill Keene, who was trembling with anxiety to explain his own case for himself. "Too simple to live. What's to stop you from turning this man's wife here and his little children out of Ahill when your man is gone? God help us all!"

"Ah!" said Judith harshly. "She could buy another interest elsewhere."

"Oh, my God in heaven tonight," wailed Keene.

"You're very simple, aren't you?" sneered Theo.

Then his rage took him.

"But by Chrisht, woman, God forgive me for cursing and the priest in the house, if you was to do such a thing you would not do it for long. I never trusted you, and I never will."

He hammered his stick on the ground.

"Leave your husband ratify that interest this night to this man's wife and childer."

"I could never buy interest in a farm now," wailed Keene, as he rubbed his poll miserably and stared at Theo. "Where would I get the money?"

"My husband," cried Judith, "could never have given that Ahill farm to his sister if I hadn't brought him a fine farm from Foxehall."

"He gave it," said Keene, rising and wiping the sweat from his forehead. "He gave it, and what matter how or why he gave it. He gave it. He gave it."

"What a man have sure, he must hold," pacified Browne.

"Aisy, let ye, aisy on, now!" said Frank O'Donnell. "Sure Judie O'Donnell has no wish for Ahill. And sure she knows well," he added with a smiling threat, "that it would be going strong against the Tenants' League for to want it."

Frank O'Donnell was the great power of the landless men and the struggling tenants of that part of Limerick. It was said he had the brain of a lawyer, and would some day be arguing with judges in the Court at Limerick, where he owned a tavern.

"Ah, sure," repeated Browne, "it's only nature for a man to hold what he have."

"Is there need for a lawyer now then?" snarled Theo.

"I needn't be talking loud with ye," said Judith easily. "Ahill is John O'Donnell's farm—and it's not much of a farm. Let him do what he likes with it. And with any other little thing he had before he met me."

The group relapsed into positions of relief, but James stood forward.

"Then it's between what's left, mother! Tell me what am I getting?"

"Be silent, boy."

"Am I getting this farm, or am I not?"

"This farm is my farm, to give it or keep it. Keep a quiet tongue, for you'll get no more than you deserve, and what that is you know best."

"It is your farm—we know that . . ."

"Know it, and heed it."

She retired to her seat by the door of the bedroom.

"I want my rights!" cried the young man, and he almost sobbed in saying it.

"Your rights!" she mocked. "Your rights! And you cadeying about the country year after year. Sit down, and let us hear silence from you."

"I won't sit down. What am I working for? Do I get a penny paid for what I do? If I was a labouring man I'd get more. There's the New Plot. If you own this farm you don't own the New Plot."

His voice rose as she held silence.

"Who do you want it for? Am I to be denied for Phil and Leo? Who do you want it for? What are you aiming to do with it? Tell me that."

Her voice rose in reply.

"Don't pester me. You'll know in good time. Can't your mother manage this farm now, as she managed it for thirty-two long and lengthy years? You're growing very high and mighty in your skin all of a sudden."

"I want my rights," insisted the young man, as if he could think of nothing else to say.

He shouted it at them all and at her.

"I want my rights!"

"Aye, sure," encouraged Browne.

"Hush, now, aisy on!" warned Frankie O'Donnell, who was watching the pair like a man watching a prize fight.

"Didn't my sweat," sobbed James, "go into this farm and into the New Plot? Didn't my sweat make the pair of them what they are? Haven't I a right to wan or the other of them?"

"Aye, sure!" said Browne again, more excitedly this time.

The mother looked at her son, sizing him up. Her voice fell.

"Did I say you hadn't a right to one or the other of them?"

The son's lips moved and said nothing; his eyes wandered; he made a weak gesture with his hands.

"Did I?" she asked gently.

"No, mother," he agreed in a kindly voice.

Her voice leaped suddenly.

"Sit down, then," she bullied. "Sit down!"

Frankie O'Donnell rose.

"Sit down, James!" he counselled.

The round was over. He led the boy over by the corner of the table under the lamp, whose light fell on his yellow crown. The cheap clock on the dresser tick-tocked swiftly. Keene shuffled uneasily, and the *sugán* of his chair creaked. Norry sat up as stiff as a scarecrow, with her black hat like a frying-pan on the fire of her poll. Theo, older than all of them and twice the age of some of them, leaned with his stick under his arm-pit and squirted an occasional spit behind the fire; he gazed into the red turf out of his filmed eyes as unflinchingly as a lizard at the sun. He was the only one of them that seemed to be unmoved, not even interested. He had the deliberately calm air of a judge who will presently be called upon for a decision, and whose mind, in the meantime, is away on some problem that has occurred to nobody but himself. Nicholas, who had far more reason to be disinterested, kept moving continually on his chair, twisting his head and scratching his hands. At last Keene could keep silence no longer.

"I've reason," he whined, "to be throubled about them poor few biteens of fields I have. If it was settled long since I wouldn't be bothering you, now, in your great throuble, Mrs. O'Donnell."

"Oh! It's no bother," smiled Judith. "It's a great solace to me to see you there, Bill Keene, pitying me, and giving me consolation in my sorrow. You're no trouble at all, I can assure you. It's few enough of ye, as I can see, that came to visit me in my need. But I see," she mocked bitterly, "that it was yeer own need that carried ye hither, and not mine."

Browne leaped to his feet.

"I do not want one thing from you. If it wasn't a thing that I brought this decent woman to wash and lay out your man, and a fine decent man he is and always was, may God be kind to him, and a man," he said—with a look at the bare table—"that kept a good table for his friends when they came to visit him, I'd rise from your could hearthstone this minute and leave you."

"Leave me alone!" said Norry to the fire. "I've laid out corpses in poorhouses and prisons . . ."

"Ah! Then God blasht ye!" cried Judith, in a rage that made Nicholas hide his face in his hands for shame, and the colour to flood hot in her own face from brow to breast. "What call have ye, my friendly strangers, my dear neighbours, that I see once in a year, to be interfering in my affairs or my son's affairs? What call have you, Mike Browne? Or you, Theo O'Donnell?"

Her lips curled at them, and her jaws whitened the skin of her cheeks.

"But I know you," she flung at the old grandfather,

"with the look of you like a fox that sees a hen about to lay."

Theo's windpipe inflated again. Then he calmed.

"It's said well," he pointed out slowly, "of your name and fame and family, and said for two hundred years back, that the he-Foxe has a keen smell in his long gob, but the she-Foxe you could plough the crags with their eye-teeth."

He leaned forward, bent on his stick.

"Interfere? My buxom lassie, you'll see me interfere."

"I'd see you first out of this house, my *dradaire*."

The priest opened the door on them, his hairy finger in his breviary.

"What is it at all?" he asked gently and sadly, like a very tired man, as he advanced into the kitchen. "How is it," he went on, without waiting for the answer—too well he knew it—"how is it that I never yet came to see an old man or an old woman out of this world but the kitchen is always quarrelling over his bones?"

"Is he gone?" wailed Judith.

The door opened. They knew the lawyer's face as well as they knew the priest and the doctor. Dee was a powerful six-footer, with the eyes of a hawk, and the moustaches of a grenadier, and the manners of a general on campaign. With a regal sweep of his arm he flung his hat and coat on the kitchen table and glanced about the kitchen, like a giant out of a fairy-tale choosing among a flock of victims for the most succulent meal, and no less feared over the country-side. But the town, as towns always do, had him better "taped," and their measurement of him was in the nickname they gave him—they called him "Brainsy," or "The Iron Duke."

"Good night, Father," he said sternly and condescendingly.

"Good night, Mister Dee," said the fat priest, but before

he could say any more the doctor raced from the room and, gripping the priest by the arm, led him away.

"Now, Father! Now!" he said.

Everyone made a movement towards the sick-door. Everyone listened when Judith snatched at the coat-tails of the vet, and asked with a tremble in her voice:

"Will he last?"

The vet only looked at her, flung up his two hands like a man scattering grain, and then let them fall helplessly by his side.

She went to the dresser and took another bottle of whisky and filled a tumbler for the newcomer. But, as Dee raised his glass, with a gloomy face and a bow, and a courtly lift of his hand—

"Come without," she said.

Glaring too wisely down at her under his shaggy eyebrows, he swung his coat over his shoulder like an old campaigner and strode after her, while Normoyle sat into the fire with the bottle.

The plain stretched away on every side, dark under the clouds that hid the starlight and the moon. Out on the causeway it was cool after the heat of the fire, and as they walked up and down, the old scheming woman and the stupid lawyer, never passing the window of the death-room but each time coming near enough to see the priest's shadow on the pane, at one place the ducks cackled in their coop, at another the dung-hill was odorous, a rich stink, and when they reached the corner of the house the river murmured far away over the fields. The lawyer spoke to his client even more respectfully than the vet—he knew more; all the Foxe business, which meant the affairs of upwards of threescore tenants, was in his hands. In his office in Rathkeale there were a dozen black-japanned tin-boxes with the name of Foxe painted on their sides in white—Leo Foxe, Samuel Foxe, Gooddall Foxe, Rhys Foxe, Owain Foxe, Rhys ap

Owain Ffoulkes—back to the first "keen smellers," who were given grants of land by Ireton, here in Limerick, and shared the tall, square Cromwellian house of Foxehall that they had built on the Deel. Sipping his whisky he listened to Judith's hard, slow murmur. She weighed every word before she passed to the next, although she had gone over this speech so many times in her secret mind, as she sat by her fire with her brood about her, or on the edge of her husband's bed when he first fell sick, that she could have spoken it as smoothly as an actor's speech.

"First of all, there is this farm of Bawnrea, or the Home Farm, with its house, outhouses, stables, and barns, and the live-stock on the land."

The lawyer bent his flat leg-of-mutton head.

"Then there is the farm called the New Plot, with the stock on it."

" 'Mm," agreed the lawyer. "That's so."

"Then there is the farm, the house, the outhouses, but not including the stock, of Ahill."

"Which is at present rented by Margaret Keene, your husband's sister-in-law," he said.

He looked up then at the sky with a self-satisfied air.

"It is not," contradicted Judith. "It is rented by my husband, and he has granted the interest in the land to his sister."

He kept looking up at the sky.

"Of course. I meant that."

"And lastly, there is turbary in the townland of Knockfierna."

They were standing at the corner of the house, a light wind lifting the apron of the old woman. She drew her shawl tighter about her head, and kicked a half-turnip into the mud. The lawyer glared at it, and kicked it farther.

"I want Ahill, as it is, given over in proper legal form to Mag Keene—except that they continue to pay the rent as before to my sisters in Foxehall. And they, as you know, will continue to pay it to me."

This was one of the small secrets she had kept, and was profoundly glad to have kept, from her husband during all the years they were married.

"It amounts to a tidy sum now," said the lawyer. "Four hundred and twenty-two pounds, eight shillings, next Lady Day."

"It's mine," she snapped. "And remains mine."

She resumed in the same hard voice:

"This farm of Bawnrea—"

"Yes?"

"This farm of Bawnrea, called the Home Farm, its house, outhouses, barns, and stock, must go to my son James."

"It's his by law," said Dee.

"It's his by right," said the mother. "He worked hard on it until his father drove him beyond his power, and he ran from it. Aye! As he drove Michael that died before his time."

The lawyer had nothing to say to that. They were silent for a while, she cooling back into herself again, he listening to the river across the fields. A faint shaft of light lit the causeway behind them where the vet stumbled out with a dark-lantern to have a look at the mare. He saw the pair, but he did not speak to them, and he closed the mare's stable quietly behind him.

"Bawnrea to James," said Judith again, as she returned from her memories of twenty years ago. "I don't begrudge it to him, even if it wasn't his right. The New Plot," she went on more hurriedly, as if she felt they were wasting time with these excuses and explanations, "the New Plot, with all that's on it, outhouses and stock, must go to Leo."

"But, just heavens! Mrs. O'Donnell, there's six girls and a boy left before Leo."

"I said Leo."

He finished his whisky at a gulp, and laid the glass on the window-ledge.

"But—"

"James is strong, and able to fight to keep what he has. Leo can't."

"Bawnrea is a good farm, but it's a poor thing beside the New Plot. And the mortgage—"

"And the turbary in Knockfierna," went on Judith eagerly, "must go with the New Plot to Leo."

"Will Leo portion off the girls? What will happen Phil? How can your daughters ever marry if they're depending on this encumbered bit of land? James will never be able even to think of marrying. They will all be impoverished for life. It's a most unusual will," went on the lawyer, sternly feeling that, at this rate, he could well afford to lecture his client. And he went on, "Your husband will never agree to it."

"There was nothing I ever wanted from John O'Donnell that he agreed to. And little I ever wanted but I got it in the end. Is it a poor dying man to cross me now?"

"Is this your husband's wish at all?" questioned the lawyer.

"It's my wish."

The lawyer pulled his moustaches rapidly. Here was a nice situation to be in. She gripped his arm. The priest's shadow rose across the window-pane.

"I'm very much afraid," murmured the lawyer, "that—"

She hurried him to the door and lifted the latch.

"G'in!" she ordered, as if she were calling a horse.

She led him, for he was blinded by the sudden light, across the floor to meet the priest as he left the room. The relatives were on their feet. The priest was lifting the stole from his head, and his face, usually heavy and even coarse, was softened almost to tenderness by the emotion of administering the Eucharist to a dying soul. Unceremoniously the wife brushed past him, still holding the lawyer by the wrist, and looked down at her husband's face where, with his fingers manacled in the rosary that he could no longer number and scarcely felt, he whispered in an intermittent suspiration the words of the Hail Mary. His face, grey as dawn, his two peaked cheekbones standing up like hills, his forehead two vein-crossed ridges, his eyes amazingly bright with the vision that had entered by his lips, Father, Son, and Paraclete, made him like a deeply carved death-mask of a saint, lit, as a mask is never lit, by those eyes that glowed in the dusk like carbuncles. Already he was all but beyond his body. For a second the two looked at him, and listened to his lips that were as faint-murmuring as a parched reed in summer echoing the void of the night sky. Then as the lawyer took from his pocket the will-form he had already drawn up, with blank spaces for the names of the inheritors, the priest looked back sadly into the candle-lit room he had left. Turning, he signalled to the people in the kitchen, and they sank on their knees about the walls: clasping his crucifix in his great hairy hands, he began to intone the Rosary.

"Our Father who art in heaven—"

In the room Dee sat by the bed, and looked between pity and doubt at the still-ardent eyes and the ivory face. Behind her husband's head Judith stood and grasped the bed-post in her two palms. The lawyer decided it would be better for him to play into the wife's hands.

"It is time now, John," he said, "to say what you want done with your land when you are gone."

A wave of pain passed over O'Donnell's face, and turning slowly towards the lawyer his eyes gradually became hard and worldly.

"It's your will, John," explained Dee.

"I don't want to make a will," pleaded the old man.

"You must arrange your affairs, John. There might be

constant trouble after you go if you don't arrange everything. You must think of your wife and children and your
sister Mag."

It was with immense difficulty that the old man murmured his replies. He was already drifting towards the dark.

"What need? My childer will work, and my wife will
guide them."

In the kitchen, the voices were responding in a low, liquid
murmur. They could see Theo with his eyes on the door.

"—Give us this day our daily bread. And forgive us our
trespasses as we forgive them who trespass against us. And
lead us not into temptation, but deliver us from all evil.
Amen."

Judith's face, already in the shadow, seemed to grow
black with anger. Stupid as he was, the lawyer could not
help an internal shiver at the sight of it. It was clear what
she was thinking. The children will work, yes, and the wife
will guide them, yes, but who will guide the wife? The dying man had told the vet: *gur treise greim an fhir mhairbh
na Samsoun beo.* She would hold the land, and the land
would hold her. The children would hold her, the relatives
would hold her, the priest would hold her, the whole country-side would hold her, to that bargain of thirty-five years
before. She had become an O'Donnell, and an O'Donnell
she must remain.

"You must make your will, John," she said, like a ghostly
voice from behind his head.

"I'll make no will," he cried, and with the effort he began to pant, and they heard the first death-rattle in his
voice.

"If you don't make your will, John," she snarled, "I'll
not abide by one single wish of yours. I'll sell the New Plot.
I'll turn your sister from her farm."

Like a sigh of a gentle wind the prayers rose and fell outside.

"Mother of God, pray for us sinners, now and at the hour of our death. Amen."

From under the hedges the men and youths who had been waiting in the cold dark began to gather to the side of the house, knowing in some mysterious way that the end was near, and there they crouched under the shelter of the limed walls. Quietly then one of them opened the door an inch or two so that they could hear the priest, and they replied in unison with their prayer.

The old man's breathing came more and more heavily.

"You must protect your own, John," said the lawyer.

Keene was too excited to pray. He rose from among the kneeling group, and still half-responding, holding his beads in his hand, he approached the bedroom door.

"You must protect your sister, John," urged Dee again.

"No will!" gasped Long John, and the sweat glittered on his forehead.

Keene pushed open the door. Judith glared at him, and waved him away. He ignored her, and advanced to the end of the bed.

"Mag wants the Ahill land, John!" said Keene, in an agony of apprehension.

"The Ahill land to Mag Keene, John? Isn't that it?" coaxed the lawyer.

The hollow voice of the priest echoed in the kitchen: "Blessed art thou amongst women—"

Long John sobbed a cry of pain and misery. His pale lips tried to say, Yes, and the emaciated skull to nod. Judith rushed from the room and saw the doctor leaning in his drink against James. She dragged the stupefied vet to the bedside, and again the lawyer repeated:

"Ahill Farm to Mag Keene—your interest in it to your sister Mag Keene. Isn't that what you want?"

"Yes, John!" croaked Keene, his voice broken by excitement.

The old man's hand stirred like a broken wing, and with a great effort his lips said, "Yes." Judith and the lawyer and Keene all looked at the vet, and he nodded assent. The lawyer's pen wrote swiftly.

"Of course the rent goes as usual to Foxehall," he said, as he wrote.

"We'll pay the rent, never fear," said Keene eagerly.

The old man's eyes looked childlike into the brown hawk-eyes of the lawyer as if he were hypnotized. A candle fell over, and Judith blew it out and laid it on the limewashed window-sill, where its stench of candle-fat began to fill the room.

"The farm of Bawnrea, with its house and land and stock, you'll surely leave that to the eldest boy?"

"No will!" came, faint and cracked, in a moan from the dry throat.

"It's his by law," cried the vet drunkenly, and Judith shot a wild glance of fear at him; how did he know that?

"You couldn't keep it from him," said the lawyer. "Five hundred and fifty courts of law couldn't keep it from him. You may as well give your word to it. Bawnrea to James. Isn't that right? Bawnrea to James? Yes? Yes?"

Too drunk to speak, the vet pointed with hand and finger like a statue at the old man. The movement distracted his eyes from the lawyer's and they fell, fluttering with pain.

"The Home Farm for James," pleaded the lawyer. "Surely the Home Farm for James?"

"It'd be right!" panted Keene, as excited still as if the farm were coming to him.

"Get James," said Judith to him.

He stumbled out to get the eldest son. The little vet was still pointing fixedly into the dying man's face, leaning forward over the end of the bed, his lips mouthing dumbly like a paralytic, his eyes out of his head with the desire to say something. The lawyer struck the hand away, and it

came back as if it were on a spring. James came in and
stared in fright at his father's sweaty face. Behind him
Keene closed the door so that there was no light in the
room but one candle only, and no air because the window
was sealed with paint and dirt and wet.

"James is here," said Judith into her husband's ear.
"James is here," she said more loudly.

Would he never hear? Would they never get to the New
Plot?

"James is here," she cried. "James is here! Look at him."

The tired lids, crinkled as a hen's, swayed upward. The
vet's outstretched hand swung about and he shook the
young man savagely, but he could only stutter and gabble
at him like a duck.

"Speak to your father, James," ordered the mother. "Tell
him you want Bawnrea."

"I want Bawnrea, father!" cried James, bending down to
his father's head.

"Yes, that's right, isn't it?" whispered the lawyer right
into the old man's face.

He was rewarded by a tiny, surrendering, sibilant "Yes."

"You hear that?" Dee asked the vet.

The question seemed to loosen his tongue.

"I heard nothing," he said.

He began to pour talk into James's ear. He grasped his
shoulders. He put his arms about him. He implored him.
He fell stupidly over him, but all the while gabbling madly
at him.

"*You* heard it?" cried the lawyer to Keene.

"Bawnrea to James!" thrust out Keene. "I heard it!"

The pen scratched in a name and a word or two, and
another name. Suddenly, James, into whose ear the vet had
been pouring his flood of speech, cried out:

"I don't want Bawnrea!" he shouted. "I want the New
Plot."

"It's a cripple of a place," shouted the vet.

"Go, boy!" thundered Judith.

"I don't want Bawnrea," he shouted again. "I want the New Plot. Give me the New Plot. I don't want debts. I don't want debts. It's my farm bought the New Plot. Give me the New Plot."

The old man sat up suddenly in bed, and they all fell silent, amazed at his sudden vigour.

"Go," he said distinctly, and fell back.

The vet shouldered his way into him beside the lawyer, so that they both fought for position beside the dying man.

"It's not fair, John," he shouted. "Who's getting the New Plot?" he shouted. "You're denying your own blood. Give your own blood the best you have, John!" he shouted.

"Tom Normoyle," Judith turned on him in a fury. "Go out of the room, you. Go out of the house, you."

"It's no use, John," cried the vet, clawing the bedclothes.

"Give me the New Plot, father," implored James.

"The New Plot for Leo," cried the lawyer, lost in the excitement to everything but to win the struggle against the vet. "The New Plot for Leo!"

"The New Plot for me," cried James, shoving his way near his father's face.

"The New Plot for Leo," urged Judith in her husband's ear. "For Leo! For Leo!"

"No will! No will!" wept the old man, the sweat and the tears running down his cheeks, his head reeling for lack of sight, blowing like a horse for the last few gasps of earthly air.

The prayers below had ceased; the relations had risen and clustered into the door. To the old man the room was full of eyes, and it was hot and airless as a pit. The priest below still knelt by the table, his head in his hands, and as he prayed aloud the familiar litany came like a far-off echo to the death-room. Many a time since his childhood Long

John had heard it during the Sunday evening benediction
in the small church at Knockaderry.

> "Soul of Christ sanctify me.
> Body of Christ save me.
> Blood of Christ inebriate me."

The soft imploration ran secretly through his brain as
they shouted over him in the dark.

> "Water from the side of Christ wash me.
> Passion of Christ strengthen me.
> O Good Jesus hear me.
> Hide me within Thy wounds.
> Suffer me not to be separated from Thee—"

His failing mind lost the thread of the prayer. He strained
to listen to the priest, and recovered it again.

> "Call me at the hour of my death.
> And bid me come to Thee,
> That with the saints I may praise Thee
> For all eternity. Amen."

In the kitchen two wandering children crept stealthily
through the open door. They were stained with yellow clay
from head to foot, hands and face and legs, and Leo, who
had fallen into the river, was still dropping water from his
hair. Phil held a grey rat by the tail. Seeing the priest they
halted, and he looked up from his prayer at them. He
smiled, blessed himself, and rising took them to the fire,
whispering to them while they undressed shyly. In the room
their mother's harsh voice could be heard shouting at Theo,
and Theo saying, "A woman's excuse is nearer than her
knee." And above their voices, a great scuffling where the vet
and the lawyer and James struggled with one another for
the ear of the man who was all but left the world; yet the
lawyer, with arms outstretched like a wild bird, was keeping them all back and whispering incessantly:

"Leo for the New Plot, John. Leo for the New Plot. Leo—"

In the end Judith broke through them to the priest.

"Take away these people out of my house, Father Richard. Take them away. Isn't he my husband? Is it right? Or seemly? Or just?"

The priest rose wearily.

"I never take hand, act, or part in these will-makings," he said.

"Listen to them," foamed Judith. "They're killing the man before my eyes. That vet is as boozed as a lord."

The priest's brows gathered impatiently, and striding over through the press at the door he grabbed Normoyle by the shoulders, and hauled him out of the room into the kitchen and from the kitchen he pushed him into the yard.

"Leave these things to the sons and the parents," he said, when Theo and Browne followed, protesting.

The daughters were long since waked, and were peeping fearsomely out of their bedroom door.

"The lawyer is a cheat," complained the vet as he struggled to get back again, and the priest handed him off.

"He's a chate and a trickster," spat Theo.

In the room they saw that Keene was at the lawyer's elbow.

"Is my farm all right?" he was imploring him. "Have I it firm by me?"

"The devil take you," cried the lawyer in exasperation, "you have it for all your days, and your children's days."

And he turned back to the bed. But, still doubtful, still fearful of his patch of land, Keene came wandering out to Theo and Browne, and together they flooded back to the room. Judith halted in the swing of her step after them, and looked in amazement at the two half-dressed children.

"Where were ye?" she asked angrily.

"I fell into the dike," whined Leo, looking up at her out of one of his brother's coats, several times too big for him.

She glanced about her at the empty kitchen.

"Go to bed, ye!" she ordered the peeping girls.

The priest was on the lintel of the door pacifying the vet. The relatives were crushed into the room. In one last despairing hope, she snatched Leo's furry cap and fixed it on Phil's head, and on his back she dragged, so forcibly that he began to cry with fear, Leo's little brass-buttoned coat and his Inverness coatee with its many capes. Then flinging Phil's torn and muddy and sodden cap on Leo's head, she dragged the whimpering pair through the crowd into the room. With a kind of tigress strength and a wild look that for the moment terrified them away from her, she crushed them all back to the kitchen and shut the door on them. Besides her lawyer, only Nicholas the Master and James remained. It was all so swiftly done that none of the relations saw what happened. She drew James aside from the bed, and pushed forward the two terrified children.

"John O'Donnell!" she said so loudly and clearly that everyone in the kitchen heard her. "Which of these two children do you want for the New Plot? It must be one or th' other of them, or I'll sell it out on you!"

For the last time he opened his eyes, and in the dim light of the single candle he saw the boy thrust on him, the furry cap, the brass buttons of the coat, the many capes—and with his last ounce of strength he pushed the boy aside. She led forward the bawling Leo with his nose and his mouth wrinkled under the cap that was far too large for him.

"Which of the two?" she said again, firmly and clearly and in a dominating voice. "It's Phil," she added in a whisper for his ear alone.

James leaped forward, but the lawyer hurled him back against the little table. It crashed over, and with it the

last candle went. In the second's silence that followed Long
John spoke his last two words on this earth, faint but
audible, tender and fond.

"This lad."

At the crash of the falling table the gossips threw open
the door, and the light streamed in from the kitchen. The
dead man's bony, hairy arm hung heavily about the neck of
his youngest son.

"You saw that, Nicholas?" challenged Judith.

"Yes!" admitted Nicholas unwillingly. "I saw that."

James rose furiously, but Frankie O'Donnell held him
back from striking the lawyer, who was writing swiftly by
the light of the kitchen lamp. Nobody rightly understood
what had happened, but as they stared foolishly in the arm
slipped and fell, and for a moment it swung by the side of
the bed. Then it moved no more.

They blessed themselves and withdrew in a body, and
looked about themselves involuntarily for the priest to
reassure them. As by one agreement they quietened the
squabbling of the eldest son and the lawyer—there would
be time and time enough later for that. The man they knew
was already kneeling before the judgment seat of God. It
was as if in the deathly quiet, broken only by Judith sob-
bing bitterly in the room below, they could overhear the
rustling of the soul on its way through eternity. They were
afraid even to stir.

"Let us pray," said the priest.

After they had knelt, there was a pause while he chose a
prayer. Judith cried pitifully over her man. The clock
ticked with its faint double-note. Outside in the night dark
they heard the little sounds of the midnight that are inde-
cipherable and indescribable.

"O bright and glorious day which knoweth no evening,
and whose sun shall no more go down. O words of joy and
thanksgiving saying unto us: Enter into the joy of the Lord,

enter into life everlasting, enter where there is no sorrow, and all thy heart's desires shall be satisfied. O life, calm and tranquil, happy and secure, bring out my soul from its prison that it may give thanks to Thy name: in eternal blessedness, in happy eternity, for ever and ever. Amen."

They rose and straggled from the house. The priest climbed into his car and, leaving them to argue in a cluster in the moonlit haggard, rattled down the boreen. Near the cross to Knockaderry another trap bowled past him, and the lawyer raised his hand aloft in a magnificent salute. The priest sighed and turned his nag up the hill. When he looked back from the brow the whole plain was silent, unless the scuttling birds sought their prey in the hedges or blinked an eyelid as his horse stumbled past their nests. The whole plain slept unless in some other Ahill a wakeful baby was suckled at its mother's breast, or in some other farm like that he left, away out to the blinking lighthouse on the Shannon or east to the dark roofs of Rathkeale, they drew, by the candlelight, the brown shroud about the limbs of the dead, and comforted the children crying for the father they had lost. Even so, all through that night Leo cried in his mother's arms, where she moaned with him before a cooling hearth.

2

Gentlefolk

1

He had even better cause to remember the burial. It was a Sunday evening and that bright hour of evening when the fields, greenly luminous, and the ivy on the walls, and the bare beech trunks shone with a light reflected from below the flat horizon.

A hard wind whirled the manes of the cavalcade of horses as they sidled against the graveyard wall, and sent the mourners crouching behind the headstones with their faces behind their caps. Then the grave was risen above the level of the ground and the priest gone, and they were crowding into the shebeen beyond the churchyard. Before the turf fire they smoked and drank in silence, spitting heavily into the ashes, speaking hardly at all, letting their thoughts flow gently back to their own lives.

"He's planked," they said. "May God rest him."

"We gave him a great funeral," they said. "We respected him."

"It was a fine turn-out. The Lord be good to him."

They did not converse. They were satisfied to be answered by a nod or a spit. There was a ditch to be dug, or a horse lame, or they thought of the night falling and the road home.

As the children of the O'Donnells' moved in a cluster back to the two carts, a horse-cart and a donkey-butt, both tethered to a great ivy-root at the farthest end of the wall, their eyes were red from crying. But nobody saw Judith cry. With her black cloak drooping from her head to her feet she was a statue in figure and in face. As she waited for James, who was drinking in the pub, she stood by the horse's head, her jaws distended, her lips clamped, her eyes staring, indifferent to the wind that blew her grey hair about her face. But she saw that the women were watching her with pity, whereupon, taking Leo with her, she crossed at once to the well-field beyond the old ruined castle. One or two women were praying there under the willow that hung over the pool, but seeing her coming they rose and, shaking their heads with pity, they went away.

She stood down on the roots of the willow, looking into the pale green water, watching the bubbles of air rising endlessly in short gushes out of the sand. There was a time when she had made a mock of that tree, littered with rags and buttons and medals and beads and pieces of torn shift —like a servant's head in the morning. There was another time when she used halt her cart by the stile as she went into Rathkeale to the market, and come there to pray for guidance in her troubles. Then there was a time when she neither mocked nor prayed, but came there, as now, to think. The willow sighed and whistled as the wind rushed through it, and a little troop of spiders fled across the surface of the water to the darkest recesses beneath the rooted bank. She sat on the rough stone steps, and stared into the icy cavern where they lived.

Gradually the pub emptied and the mourners went home, and the grave-diggers took their last drink from James O'Donnell. But still the two carts remained tethered to the ivy roots and the children leaned together in a heap, too cold and tired to cry. Their Uncle Nicholas was with them, and at last he went back to look for James. He saw them in the farthest corner of the graveyard, a man and a woman leaning close together, dimly outlined in the falling dusk against the naked limestone wall. In pity of the pair of them, Nicholas sat on a gravestone to wait. He knew her, and knew that James knew her of old—the publican's daughter in Knockaderry.

The dusk turned to dark, and the two bodies became one. A boy's voice came through the night, calling out, "James! James!"—and then, "Nicholas? Are you there, Nicholas?"

Nicholas made no sound.

"James? Are you there anywhere? Nicholas, are you there, Nichola-a-a-as!"

"Halloa!" cried Nicholas.

Frightened by the dark and the wind in the grass, the boy ran stumbling over the graves. Nicholas looked down at him, and he looked up at his uncle's face that glowed in the night above his pipe. He liked Nicholas, with his sloe-black eyes, bright and jewel-like, his greying hair, his jaw that was long and pointed and appeared all the longer because his teeth were so big that his lips rarely met over them. He liked his mouth—that was red and round as a girl's.

"My mother," he panted, "is gone walking to Foxehall. James must drive us home."

"Lave us sit down for a while longer," said Nicholas, and the boy sat beside him on the stone.

James, thought Nicholas, would not be able to marry for ten, twelve, maybe fifteen years—if, indeed, he was able to marry at all. And yet, though he was not married and could not marry, he was spancelled. Behind him all his life would be his brother Phil and his five sisters forcing him to slave as his father had slaved so that the land should be freed of debt, and money made on it, and a dowry come into it that they might leave it. It was well for Long John to have praised the grip of death. The son was in that grip now.

"Is James here?" asked the boy.

"He's talking with someone. He's coming now."

"Where is he?"

"Beyant in the corner by the yew."

They could see the yellow light of a lamp in the pub window, down the slope beyond many tombs and tossing trees, and it comforted Leo to see it, for the wind was rustling terrifyingly through the last summer's dried weeds doubly loud because of the darkness through which its cold breath rushed upon them. The boy sidled nearer to his uncle and grasped his arm tightly and shivered in the storm.

"Are you cold, Leo?"

"Yes."

Nicholas opened his frieze coat, and stretched it about the boy's head.

"Is that somebody?" started Leo; and then—"I don't like to be here, Nicholas."

Nicholas held up a skeleton stem of cuckoo-pint, its pale cups still perfect at the top of each dried stalk. He shook it lightly at Leo's ear, and the little bells whispered faintly.

"That's the sort you hear," he said. "Or it might be any dead flower or wild grass at all."

"Can't we go away, Nicholas?"

"We'll wait another bit."

Then to distract him he went on:

"I saw how my uncle's gravestone is fallen down beyond there. He'd be a grand-uncle of your own."

"What killed him?"

To a boy's mind death is never inevitable.

"He was drowned in Foynes, in 'forty-seven."

"What drowned him?"

"Swimming after a grain boat he was. It set into Foynes to carry grain to England. He swam out to it with six other men to ask the captain for meal, for their childer were dying with the Famine."

"So he was drowned, then?"

"Quacky Quested from Limerick that owned the boat, and he cushed them off with flinging iron bolts at them. My Uncle Owen was pulled up after in the anchor chain, and his skull had seaweed in it."

"Who was Quacky Quested, Nicholas?"

Nicholas paused.

"I didn't mind that, now. He's a grand-uncle of your own, on your mother's side. I disremembered it, or I wouldn't have spoken against him, Leo. But, to be sure, there was no bond between your mother's people and mine in those days."

"Is all my people laid here, Nicholas?"

Nicholas paused again. He did not want to say some of them were laid under the slabs of Nantenan in the Protestant churchyard. The dry grass and the withered things rustled at their feet. Leo snuggled closer to his uncle, well satisfied with the smell of his frieze, the grip of his arm about his head, and the stink of his coarse shag.

"It'll be a wild kind of night before morning," said Nicholas, and his small mouth softened and his eyebrows trembled.

"The wind is queer, Leo. You'd think it had a life of its own."

Leo was always willing to hear his uncle talk like this—a bit daft, but odd, and maybe with a hidden meaning, if you only understood him.

"The wind, Leo, is of the nature of air. And because it travels over the land it is of the nature of earth. And look how, still and all, you cannot see it or tashte it, or smell it, but only feel it like cobwebs around your face."

Of a sudden he withdrew his arm and blessed himself and rose.

"James!" he called out, and as the wind drowned his

voice he shouted again, and Leo joined in. "James O'Donnell! Ja-a-ames!"

A voice hallooed out of the dark, and then two figures came up out of the nettles.

"It's time we were off, James. The mother is gone back the road to Foxehall. You must drive the childer home."

James looked at Leo.

"And what keeps him out of Foxehall?"

"Ah! Now, James, ye must be all together in the house tonight, and no father there before ye."

"G'wan ahead of me and I'll follow."

"The childer are starved with the cold, mind you."

"I'll follow on out after ye."

Nicholas drew the boy down to the graveyard gate.

"I think James is cross with me," said Leo.

Nicholas halted in the middle of the road.

"He is a very poor man," he explained. "Your father left you the best farm."

"Is it the New Plot?" asked Leo, hearing thus for the first time of his father's will.

"It is."

"Then am I to be a farmer?"

"It means James will slave himself all his life on poor land, and it in debt at that. Aye, and the poor fellow maybe never to bring a wife to bed with him."

"Yerrah, why so, Nicholas?"

"Because," said Nicholas, angered at the boy's stupidity, "he will have to portion off your sisters and your brother before he can marry any woman. And if he's not bent by then he's a Trojan. Come on, boy."

They found the girls asleep on the horse-cart and at once Nicholas untethered the nag and, leaving Leo with the donkey-butt, drew out on the road home. Presently James and the Frewen girl came and, putting Leo on the centreboards, the pair of lovers sat opposite one another on each side of the donkey's tail. In a few minutes they too rattled out into the dark.

After a mile or so Leo spoke.

"Jamesy!" he said timidly, and as he did not appear to be heard he repeated it. "Jamesy!"

As his brother made no sign, he crawled along the floor of the cart and tugged at his brother's elbow.

"Jamesy, boy!"

It was too dark for him to see his brother's face.

"Listen, Jamesy!" he said. "I don't want the New Plot. I don't want to be a farmer. I want to be a vet."

James lashed at the donkey's belly until the animal broke into a gallop. The girl did not move her head. Leo was thrown up and down like a cork on the timbers of the floor.

"Don't be angered with me, Jamesy. Sure what do I want with a farm?"

James spat into the ditch, and Leo did not speak again until the donkey had fallen into a jog-trot. The girl said something then, and James replied shortly. Thinking they were talking of his offer Leo tugged at his brother's elbow once more, only to be thrown backward roughly in disdain.

"Jamesy!" he cried. "Will you take the New Plot from me? Any hour you like, then you can take the woman to your bed."

With a tug and a curse James halted the ass.

"Get out!" he roared. "Get out, you bastard, you!"

With his whip he lashed at the boy, and screaming with the pain of the blow Leo tumbled from the cart.

"Jamesy!" he wailed from his knees on the road. "I want you to have it. I mean it."

The donkey-cart rattled off. The boy scrambled to his feet and began to race after it, weeping with pain and the injustice of the blow.

"Jamesy!" he cried after them. "Ja-a-amesy!"

Snivelling he ran forward, terrified at finding himself alone on the dark road, trying hard to sustain his tears until he should reach his mother and be comforted by her.

2

As Judith O'Donnell reached the top of the long avenue of Foxehall she wondered at the small size of the house. She had thought of it for thirty-five years as an immense place, and when she entered it now she found it small and naked and bare. Even her sisters, seen for the first time out of their feathers and bonnets and spencers, looked small, faded, and shabby.

Rachel was ill, and sat in the drawing-room over the smoky fire. She was wrapped about in all sorts of rags of clothes. Her hair lay thin on her scalp. Her cheeks hung from her like water-bags. And as she had not washed for a week, and had smoked herself continuously over the fire, she was as black and greasy as the black wrap she kept rubbing down over her chest with her palms, as if she was trying to rub her great bosom out of existence. And as for Anna—her hair was a horrible mixture of grey and henna dye; she was as thin as a crane, and she peered through red-fringed eyes with a perpetual grin of myopia on her foolish-looking face.

Judith looked slowly about her, and her hands itched to make the place clean and tidy. She saw butter in a paper on the sideboard, the trail of the quarrying knife deep in its side. There were chop-bones on the hearth-rug beside the cats' milk. Her face grew black as she looked, and she began to wonder whether her sisters could be of any help to her at all.

"I sah an ahful lat of caars returning fram the feuneral," wailed Anna sadly, as Judith dropped her long cloak and sat by the fire. Then she looked away and blushed at the blue dusk over the fields, sorry she had spoken.

"Two spoons and milk, I believe?" said Rachel, and without waiting for a reply she prepared the prodigal's cup, and then, from the black-spouted china teapot, shaped like a gondola, she poured out tea as black and greasy as herself.

"Give Judie some bread, Anna," ordered Rachel.

From a cut-glass salad-bowl on the hob—Judith remembered it came from Gatchell's, in Waterford, for one of her mother's birthdays—Anna spooned up the melted butter and smeared a slice of home-made bread.

"Deh air would make yeh hungry," whined Anna, but as Rachel looked at her over her teacup disapprovingly, she retired to her chair.

"I'm glad you came," said Rachel in her deep voice to Judith. "I hear his father left him the New Plot. That's as it should be. It was right that it should come back to the Foxes."

"The will isn't proved," said Judith cautiously.

"Puh! Who'd contest it?"

"James might."

"James? The boy daren't contest it."

"He hasn't the money," said Judith with satisfaction.

"I hear he got the Home Farm?"

"Yes. He did."

"I hear it's mortgaged?"

"It is."

"Huh! That will keep him to the grindstone," pronounced Rachel. "There's nothing like work for a wild horse. My father always said that."

"His father always said it, too," said Judith maliciously.

"It's different when a boy's farm is his own."

There was a pause, during which Anna half-rose.

"Will I light a candle?" she ventured, but they did not heed her.

"Well?" said Rachel. "What do you propose, Judie?"

"For what? For who?" asked Anna.

"For who but Leo? We must alter his way of life. And we must train him. It will take a great deal to knock him into some shape. He's wild. And I suppose the boy is rough in his ways, isn't he?"

Judith glanced faintly at Rachel.

"Aye! He's a rough, healthy, wild lad."

"He should come and live with us," said Rachel.

"For always?" asked Judith.

"Yes, indeed. Why not, too? For always."

"For always and always, do you mean, Rachel?"

"I said, for always. Until he becomes a man and can manage his own farm."

Judith spoke.

"I'll make a doctor of the boy."

Rachel looked at her.

"R-r-rubbish, Judie!"

"It's a good thing to be a doctor. It's a good trade. He can live by it. I'll set him up for a doctor in Rathkeale. I'd like him to be a doctor," persisted Judith, as if there was some magic in the word. "It's a respectable thing to be. He'd never get any good of the land. It's I that know it. Toiling and moiling and dragging and pulling."

"I said," argued Rachel, "a gentleman and a farmer. Do you think I want the boy to be after a plough? Our father"—she might have been speaking of the Deity—"made a living out of it."

Judith scoffed.

"There's no comparison. Father had lashings of land and a slew of money. Aye, and look how it dribbled away from him."

"The child," said Rachel, "will be like Tom Normoyle. Giving bottles to old men and horses. Out by day and out by night to pigs and cows and foals and infants. Does anybody," she demanded scornfully, "look up to Tom Normoyle in this county? To be sure, if the boy could be a surgeon in Dublin, with a house in Merrion Square, or in Limerick, with a house on Honan's Quay or Perry Square, I shouldn't mind that. But that means great ability. And though I don't wish to say, Judie—"

"Aye," said Judith, "it's a great thing to be a doctor. And maybe after a while he could set up in Limerick. But he must begin small. We haven't money to throw away. Rathkeale will be good enough for him to begin. He'll be respected there for his father's sake."

"For his father's sake? You mean, Judie, for our father's sake?"

"His name," said Judith, "is O'Donnell."

Rachel's face grew red under the grime of smoke.

"I want the boy, Judith," she explained, with an exasperated and exasperating patience, "to be a gentleman. Like his grandfather. I want him to take the name of his grandfather. He must be called Leo Foxe-Donnel. If he was Lord Wellesley himself he couldn't have a better name. I want him to have a house of his own and a farm of his own. I want him to live as our father lived, and to continue the name. I'll help him to do that, but I'll help him to do nothing else. He can come here and live here, and profit by good company and proper attention to his education. He can have his own room. In fact, it would be your room. I believe it was Anna's wish—"

Anna completed the sentence.

"It's just the way it is the day you left it, Judie. Won't yeh come and see it?"

She dissolved in tears at the thought of all the years it had been empty, but Rachel glared and went on, leaving her to snivel into silence.

"Anna liked to keep the room undisturbed, and so it is. It will be good for Leo to be here. It will teach him how to

deport himself. He can go to Nicholas O'Donnell for Latin
and Greek in the winter, and in the summer he should go
to Limerick for French and the piano, and lessons in danc-
ing and deportment. He can practise here when he comes
back each autumn."

That sounded well, Judith thought. It sounded as if
Rachel was prepared to spend money on him. To avoid
argument, and to avoid answering, she rose and ran her calloused palm along the rosewood of the old Southwood
pianino. She touched the yellow keys, and all the wires jin-
gled sympathetically as if the wind had suddenly blown
through them.

"I think it might want tuning?" suggested Anna.

Judith looked out of the window, down over the fields of
the plain, with its bare trees and its little cabins all bathed
in blue dusk, all vanishing smoothly into the darkening
northern sky. A gentleman? A coarse word, first learned
from her husband on the dunghill at Bawnrea, came involuntarily to her lips and she barely restrained it. She
wanted her boy to have a good living. It was a great deal to
wish him. Gentleman? she said to herself, and mentally
added the coarse word. Rachel went on munching with satisfied noises, enjoying the heat and the whining wind and
the dark falling over the whole wide valley below. She paid
no attention when Judith tapped a creaking key and no
sound came, and rapped it more firmly after, only to pro-
duce a dull thud and another internal resonance from all
the other strings. Judith's mind ran over all the people who
might help her, and as it did so her eyes roved over the
plain to where they might be found. The vet? He was a
toper and an old woman, and she was still furious with him
for his interference on the night of the will. The lawyer?
He was over there in Rathkeale, too busy with a long line
of children, and too stupid, anyway, to be of any use to her.
The priest? She dismissed him without a thought. Her eyes

were lost in the darkest night—blue in the north-west. In Limerick there was a cousin, Wilcox, who was a doctor. . . .

Suddenly she saw Leo's pale, frightened face looking up at her outside the window, and in her surprise she cried out an oath. She so terrified the sisters that they had no time to be shocked.

"It's Leo outside in the cold," she cried at Anna. "Leave him in to me."

The two of them opened the door to him, and could hardly close it against the thrust and whirl of the wind. His mother took him heavily in her arms and put him with his feet in the fender, for his clothes were thick with the greasy clay of the half-dried pools, and he had sprained an ankle. His tears came readily. His father was dead; his uncle had abandoned him; his brother had hit him; he had walked three miles in the cold and the falling night; he had hurt his foot; he was cold as ice and shivering with fear of the dark trees and the animals that shied from him as he tried to make a short way across the fields.

"Put the boy to bed," commanded Rachel. "In his own room. Light a fire in it," she ordered Mary, the old cook-servant. "Anna, give the boy a cup of hot tea and some bread with melted butter. Make rum for him and give it to him when he's in bed."

They gave him as much attention as if he had just returned from a battle. The servant bustled and fussed about the kitchen, and raced up and down the stairs in a state of excitement, filling the house with the smoke from the turf-sods in the warming-pan. His mother removed his boots and stockings. Anna wiped his hands and patted the sore places of his knees and knuckles. And then they set him up in a shawl before the fire and plied him with hot tea and bread with melted butter and home-made currant cakes. He took it all with a whimpering satisfaction, afraid to stop his tears lest he should lose their sympathy, answering their questions between forced hiccoughs and swallowings.

"Oho! Yes," said Rachel, with a shake of her head that set her jowls shivering like jelly and made Leo look at her in fright. "Oho! I think there's no doubt about it. The sooner that boy comes here the better for him. What good has he to learn elsewhere?" she asked, with a meaningful emphasis on the "elsewhere." "Wouldn't you like to live here, Leo?"

He heard the leaves scurrying along the paths outside, and the chimney moaned down at him, and the logs hissed up at it, and Mary tramped loudly overhead.

"For always?"

"Until you take over your own farm, Leo?"

"Am I to be a farmer, so?" he asked.

"A gentleman farmer," inflected Rachel, with the most subtle distinction in her voice as she said it.

He paused to gulp down a whole slice of cake.

"You mustn't eat like that, Leo!" warned Anna.

"Would you like to stay with your aunties?" asked Judith sharply.

"Would I be able," he bargained, "to hunt the otter with Phil? And could I go to Ahill to be learned? And can I go to the forge and see my sisters, and see Nonie—"

Thinking he might never see them all again, he thought there was cause here in plenty for further tears, and at once he began to weep again.

"Don't you ever want to see your mother?" asked Judith harshly.

Seeing her cross with him he redoubled the force of his tears.

"I do," he snivelled, so that she blew his nose in her petticoat, while he went on, "I want to see my mother, too."

"The boy should have a handkerchief," complained

Rachel crossly. "I don't see how you can make a gentleman of a boy without a handkerchief."

"I have wan," wailed Anna, holding hers out.

Judith looked at it and smiled, and seeing her smile, Rachel whisked it with a gasp of rage into the fire. Leo stopped crying suddenly, astonished at the green and blue flames.

"Oh! La, la!" said Anna, and retired to the window to sulk.

Rachel groaned with exasperation.

"Anna," she ordered, "will you go up and see if Mary has the bed ready?"

"Well, I see he must stay here for tonight, at any rate," said Judith. Then she smiled her crooked, hard smile because she had not needed to decide anything, and because she saw Rachel tapping her foot on the fender with impatience. She picked up her cloak and, draping herself in it, beckoned Leo up the timbered side-stairs to the old room of her childhood.

The turf-fire roared up the too-wide chimney with so hot a flame that Leo almost liked to hear the shutter on the window bumping in and out before the wind, and the gust under the door raising the rug inside it with a gentle flapping as of a stranded fish. And as his mother tried to fasten the shutter more firmly, opening it back for an instant to examine the bolt, there below, far, far away, were the lights of one or two farm-houses picking out the country-side, and overhead the stars, very bright and very high in the sky. Even his mother paused to look, she who had not seen that sight for thirty-three long years. She waited just for one half-minute until she saw the faint come-and-go of the Reeves Rock light, ten miles away, on the level Shannon. Then she closed the shutter and attended to her son.

She sat on the bed and held the blanket about him, while he sucked at his rum, and Judy and Anna bathed the sore foot as it hung out from the bed. There were the small boxes she had painted in blue and primrose flowers; there the sampler she had worked—with its date, October 1812; under it the chair where she used to sit and sew and look out at the plain. But she looked from them to her son as from a strange face to one familiar and more loved.

"Hurry, Leo. The rum will be cold."

Mary finished the foot and gave him "Good night, Master Leo," and Anna waited to kiss him again and again for Rachel, then going off finally and leaving the pair alone.

"You may say your prayers in bed," his mother said. "Hurry now and undress, like a good boy."

She looked at him while he undressed, but she did not see him. And when at last he was climbing into the bed in his shirt-tails, a little gasp caught her breath. Violently she blew out the candle, and by the flashing fire he saw her dark form go.

"Good night, mamma," he said, in surprise.

But she had shut the door and was tramping down the bare steps of the stairs. He lay listening to the turf-flames being sucked up the flue and the tree outside the window making moan. For a moment he listened carefully, for it seemed to him that what he heard was more than the moaning of the trees. Listening, he heard the wind, searching about the house for the slightest drop of moisture in order to suck and dry it up and leave everything as hard and desiccated as the frost-bitten bones of the dead. Because it frightened him he drew the clothes about his head. Tomorrow the land would be like iron.

3

Rising in the World

1

A<small>ND</small> then his third memory of how he went to Limerick for the first time. He often spoke of that when he was an old man, telling his nephews about it, over and over, but in the most rambling, tangled way, because it brought so many other memories in its train. Sometimes he would say that journey was the beginning of his life; at other times it was that first night in Foxehall; sometimes it was the following morning when he sat propped up in bed, scanning the land stretched below him, growing so tired and lonely as the day wore on that it was company for him to see a man at work two or three miles away in a field.

And at that he would say again how lonely it was for him during those weeks to be lying helpless and idle in bed with a sprained ankle, all through the short, dark days and the long, windy, pitchy nights. He went over his *Book of Horses* until he was sick of it, and when he had coloured all the pictures in the old *News-letters* that Anna found him, he had no more to do but sit looking over the millions of hedges at the pall of rain coming slowly towards him, or, when the evening dusk gathered over the plain, rising on his elbow to see if he could pick out by their light the houses he knew between Foxehall and the Shannon. Then one day beyond the linden avenue of Bawnrea he saw a man—it must surely be James—following a plough, and in the course of the week he watched that field turn brown, inch by inch, behind him. By the time two more fields had been upturned he recalled that Nicholas said James must work very hard now, and after that he watched with as much interest as if his brother were an athlete enduring the last rounds of a race. Once, on the wind, he heard the faint note of the bell his mother or his sisters always clanged from the hedge-top for dinner, but James did not halt. Not even when the coloured dusk fell and he was eating his own supper, gazing out through the window, did the plougher cease his to and fro. So that when it grew too dark to see him any longer he knew he was still there, hidden in the fog of the night. He would not loose the tackling and fling the chains aside until the next furrow was invisible in the dark. Only then would he walk beside his horse along the hoof-hammered paths to his house.

He did not pity James, and if he felt any inclination to pity him it was swept away by Nicholas, when he came daily to teach him his Latin and Greek.

"When is my mother coming for me?" Leo had asked.

"She's not coming, I'm told," said Nicholas gently.

"And why so?"

"Because James won't have you in Bawnrea."

"Why don't she tell him to have me?" he asked crossly.

"Leo! The farm is his, and he can do what he likes with it. Long enough he waited for it."

For a while the boy was silent, and then he said cunningly:

"Couldn't the priest tell him to have me?"

"For why should the priest interfere?"

"For fear they'd make a souper of me in Foxehall and I turn a Protestant."

"Is that the way of them?" cried Nicholas, horrified.

"No, no, no!" said Leo, frightened already at what he had said. "They make me say my prayers every night. Only I thought, maybe, you know, they might try it some day."

"Are they at you at all?" asked Nicholas sternly.

"No, Nicholas," he said humbly.

"Do they say any word to you?"

"No, Nicholas. Only every bite I ate they do be at me trying to make a gentleman of me."

"I hope," smiled Nicholas, " 'twill be fine weather for them."

There was no more talk after that of leaving Foxehall, and with Nicholas coming every day and passing the long hours in talk that the aunts took for work, Leo had small desire to go back on James's floor. It was fine to sit there listening to his master shanacussing about the Goban Saor, the king of all architects, who built the castles with bulls' blood and straw through the clay, or about Helen and Zeus and Hera who had eyes like an ox, and Hephæstus who fell out of the dawn, like a feather, Leo, sinking down with the sun, man, until he was tumbled in the Aegean Sea. A day was too short for his yarns about Aristotle and how he made his wife sit on her bareness on a cold flagstone peeling potatoes, while he gave her his knowledge against his will. "And inch by inch, Leo, the cold went through her until she fell dead, man, with the last drop of learning in her covetous head—and from that day to this day no woman has tried to be equal in learning with a man." But best of all he had a flute, which, after much beseeching, and because it kept him quiet in his bed, the aunts allowed Leo to borrow. In that way there were days when Nicholas came in the morning and did not go home until the nightfall; and when he was gone, Leo would squat in the dark bedroom practising old tunes, thinking of Zeus, who had eyes like a bull and fell into the Black Sea.

He remained in his room so long that, when he came down at last, Anna could show him the snowdrops drooping their heads on the lawn and a wren hopping among the crocuses, and he could smell from the steps of the house the tang of burning grass that is the true sign of spring. Leaning on a stick he went out to the nearest wall and, through a gap to the field beyond, watched the clouds float minute and many over the as yet bare and blackened trees. For he met nothing in bud until he came to a chestnut, and there he sat looking at the shine on the buds, and there Nicholas found him, and there he always came after that morning to be "learned" while the weather held fine.

But as the spring advanced and the chestnut's greenery bent over a meadow, there were days when Nicholas was too busy farming to come at all. On such days Leo found himself imprisoned in the drawing-room, under Rachel's eye. For an hour he was at the piano, sitting beside Anna, who, he found, had a strange smell at close quarters; for another hour beside Rachel, reading his history aloud and being questioned on it; for a third hour, writing an essay on some British admiral or general, on the "Glories of Summer" or the "Joys of Winter in the Country," always being encouraged with the promise of the effect on the other boys in Limerick when he went there to school in a few weeks' time. As a result he began to invent messages from Nicholas, and he would go off with a pile of books to the chestnut tree, wrapped up as if he were going to some polar region; then he would steal along the hedges down to the open road, and be away until lunch-time at the forge talking with the men waiting for their horses to be shod, or for a new tire, or a new felloe in their tumble-down wheels. Next to the hearth at Ahill he loved the forge. It leaned against the towering ruin of an old castle called Cashlawn Arawn Duv, or Blackmeal Castle, though why it was so called nobody, not even Nicholas, knew; the story of some siege buried with the centuries under the masses of fallen stone. He might even steal as far as Ahill, and run wild there about the yard, or if Theo was sunning himself under a ditch, play in the kitchen with Julie Keene, distracting her from the care of her three dirty-faced baby-sisters. There was a barrel in the kitchen where they put the older baby, Nonie, to stand, gripping the edge with its tiny fists. The small new baby they would put in the cradle to sleep or bawl as it preferred. Generally Theo had the third child. Then they were off romping about the haggard, with one eye cocked for the mother who was down in the fields working a spade with the men.

Even when Nicholas did come to Foxehall he often rebelled and scuttled away, with his master full-pelt after him, and if he was caught before he reached the cross-roads he would be hauled back, cursing and swearing all the English and Irish curses he knew. But if he once reached the forge he was safe because the men, who roared with laughter to hear him blaspheme—especially at his aunts—would plead for him with Nicholas.

But at night there was no escape. The doors were locked and chained and double-bolted, and he had to sit out the slow hours between his aunts, watching the sap oozing from the logs, reading listlessly, or accompanying on the piano Anna's playing on the violin of such gentle airs as the Larghetto from Handel's *Berenice,* which she dearly loved. At first it had been pleasant enough to pass the night with endless questions about the house and his grandfather's people. But these questions came one night to a sudden stop, and after that there was nothing but the oozing logs and the playing on the piano and the listening to the silence about the house.

That dreadful night when his questions went too far Rachel had produced a deed-poll, drawn up by lawyer Dee, showing that his name was now Leo Foxe-Donnel, and by way of making him realize the great honour of this new christening, Anna took down, one by one from the mantelpiece, the tin-plate daguerreotypes in their golden frames, the silhouettes painted on enamel, and the miniatures with their soft colouring, and went through them, answering patiently all his questions about his forbears. This was his grandmother, Anna Vaughan, who came from Jersey to marry their grandfather, and died when their father was born. This was his great-uncle David, who had sailing-boats that went from Limerick to Kilrush and around to Fenit with iron and timber for the Kerry merchants; he used to collect their grain and take it on to Plymouth and come back with a fresh cargo, until he was drowned off Ballyferriter on one of these return voyages. This daguerreotype of the man in a captain's uniform was their uncle, Carey Foxe, and that long-nosed man in the silhouette—with a tall hat and a wide cloak—was another great-uncle who never came to Ireland at all, but lived in the Quantocks, on a farm, and his children left it when he died and followed their mother to London.

"And will I see him?" asked Leo to each one.

"Oh, no. He died years ago."

"God rest him," said Leo piously, and they smiled at his goodness.

"But his children are alive still."

"Will I see them?"

"We are afraid they are lost to us. Though we heard they were doing well in business, and made a good deal out of the war."

"And who's that nice woman?"

"That's Charlotte Dunscombe. Was it a niece of our great-grandfather, Rachel?"

"A niece," put in Rachel positively.

"A niece, Leo!"—went on Anna positively—"of great-grandfather Rhys. She lived in Clare, and wrote an *Ode to the Shannon*."

"Show it to the boy," said Rachel, patting a log down in the fire, for the wind up from the plain was bitter and strong.

It was a large, flat, discoloured book.

"It's faded," whined Anna. "And it's no colour now, but it was green once."

"It's gogram-grey," said Leo cheerfully.

"There's no such colour," chided Anna.

"Of course not," said Rachel.

"Oh! That's the colour of cat's malacca!" argued Leo.

"Leo!" cried the sisters, shocked into unison.

"It's what my father used to say," pouted Leo. "Gogram-grey—the colour of Moses' tits. And my mother says it, too!"

For his mother's sake they said nothing, although Rachel's jowls grew rigid, and Anna, scarlet-faced, began hurriedly to read him the *Ode to the Shannon*. It was all about Tyre and Sidon and Sardanapalus, and the cities of the Nile and the famous rivers of the world on which British victories had been won, but there was nothing at all about Saleen and the smugglers, or Foynes and the silt where ships ran aground at low water, or Scattery Island where the saints lived; so that he soon tired of it, and returned to his great-uncle David, who brought iron to Fenit and took the grain to England, and to his other uncle, Carey Foxe, in his officer's uniform. For a long time he looked from one to the other.

"I know all about Quacky!" he declared at last.

"About who?" asked Rachel.

"Him!" sneered Leo. "Quacky Quested. Nicholas told me."

"Never mind Nicholas," glowered Rachel. "He never met David Quested."

"Nicholas said he took grain from Foynes in 'forty-seven."

"He probably did."

"And my grand-uncle swam out to it asking him for meal, for his children were dying with the famine."

"What nonsense!" cried Rachel, and she poked the log with venom.

"And Quacky," went on Leo, with his voice rising, "flung iron bolts at him so that he split his head, and he was drowned, and he was pulled up in the anchor and seaweed in his skull!"

"Oh! La, la!" cried Anna. "He belied our great-uncle."

"You had better show him his *Book of Horses,* darling!" said Rachel over-sweetly to her sister.

Then she turned on Leo.

"Your head is stuffed with rubbish by that man," she said. "And his head is stuffed by his foolish cripple of a father in Ahill."

"But Nicholas said it," cried Leo. "Nicholas said it."

Rachel leaned across and snatched the silhouette from Anna, who paled with fright.

"David Quested was a gentleman, Leo. You don't understand what that means, because you are an ignorant boy. You don't understand that a gentleman wouldn't do such things. Or say such things, as you have said, about a great-uncle of your aunts and of your own mother. Only a rough, country boy would say the like. Read your *Book of Horses.* You will learn later on to respect your mother's people."

To every sentence Anna nodded agreement, and at the end of the speech Rachel sent a thousand sparks up the chimney with the walloping she gave the fire.

"Will I show him Uncle Carey's epaulettes?" asked Anna, as if she were saying, "Will I silence the boy? Will I polish off the monster?"

"Let the boy see them," said Rachel.

Standing on a chair Anna took down the sword and epaulettes from over the door.

"There!" she said. "Your uncle carried them as a captain of the yeomanry in 'ninety-eight."

"The first man in Limerick to lead out his company," said Rachel with a smile of pride.

For a while Leo looked at them sullenly.

"My Grandfather Theo was flogged on the back in 'ninety-eight!" he growled with venom.

"I hope you don't say it was Uncle Carey that did it?" said Anna.

"Your Uncle Carey was a captain, Leo!" explained Rachel with ominous patience.

"Well," asked the boy, and his throat was heavy with oncoming tears, "who flogged Theo, then?"

"Oh! Some common soldier. Some common soldier."

" 'Twas that crokered Theo's back," he said, and his lip trembled.

"Crokered?" whined Anna sarcastically. "You mean crookened."

"His back is crokered," cried Leo crossly.

"Some Irish word!" snapped Rachel. "Talk proper English!" (She said it as if she were drawing corks.) "Talk proper English!"

"Oh! By Chrisht!" the boy flared up in tears. "His back is dom' well crokered!"

"Don't swear at me!" cried Rachel, losing her control over her temper at last. "You wicked boy! You are learning no good from that teacher of yours. I am sure his father got no more than he deserved in 'ninety-eight. A sound whipping"—she glared at him—"would do some people all the good in the world." She shook her jowls like a pair of tocsins.

This triple attack on himself and on Nicholas and Theo was too much for Leo. He almost spat into his aunt's face.

"You'd phwip him? Would you? With your big buck-teeth!"

He turned on Anna, who shrank back from him, and he imitated her doleful accent.

"And you, too! With the wahtery, ferrety eyes of you! And when you talk you whishtle like an otter."

Other terrible things he said to them that he had learned

at the forge, fortunately most of them in Irish, and kept calling them at the top of his voice, while Rachel took him by the collar and Anna put her hands to her ears and screamed for old Mary, and the three of them caught him by all his limbs and pulled him, kicking, up the stairs to his room, and bolted him in for the night.

In the morning when Mary came with his porridge she found the room empty, and when his mother came she told her sisters that he had crossed the fields to Bawnrea that night crying like a lost dog about the house. She had risen in her shift and opened the door, and at the same time James came down from the loft with nothing but his great-coat about him. She bade him go back to his bed, but seeing Leo he had come on the kitchen floor and ordered him out of the house, telling him, as he had told him the day of the funeral, that he was no son of his father's and brother of his. But she down-faced him, and led Leo in to lie by her-self. In the morning she had sent for Nicholas, and left the boy in his care.

It took a great deal of talking and arguing before the sisters would think of having him back again, but Judith gave them no quarter. She said she never regretted so much there was no house on the New Plot. She threatened to sell the New Plot to James ("More Foxe land gone!" thought Rachel) and send him at once to Limerick to live with his uncle, Dicky Wilcox. But she saw they were persuaded when she caught up the Limerick newspaper and read out sar-castically the change of name from Leo O'Donnell to Leo Foxe-Donnel.

"Is that all ye can do for my boy?" she cried. "Give him a name, and let me bring him up to it? With your D-o-n-n-e-l!"

With the dignity of a queen pardoning a regicide, Rachel said quietly that they could only be expected to consider giving him one more chance. But they were prepared to consider it. Provided, of course, that the boy came and apologized for his conduct. And promised to behave. Fortunately for her pride, Nicholas appeared on the gravel path just at that moment, and she was able to ring the bell for Mary and tell her to send in that man for one moment because she had something to say to him. When Nicholas came, however, Anna spoilt it all by crying out in one breath, to everybody's astonishment:

"Oh! La, la! Nicholas the Master, if you please. *Quis custodisis ipsis cistodises?* Tell me that, if you please, Nicholas the Master!"

"Leo," said Nicholas quietly to Judith, "is after running away."

"Away! Where is he run away to?"

"He's run off with himself to Rathkeale."

"Who told you that?" stormed Judith. "And if it's true, didn't I leave him in your charge?"

"How could I hold the boy?" asked Nicholas. "He has the legs of a hare. And as for who told me, haven't I my feet wore searching for him? Quirke the forge told me. He said he went back the road in a creel-cart."

"And what in the name of God does he want in Rathkeale?"

"In to the vet he said he was going. He said there's no wan wants him out here. Only his aunts tormenting him from dawn to dark making a gentleman out of him, and he aiming to be a vet."

Judith looked at Rachel for one dreadful second, and then, asking her to order the carriage if she pleased, led Nicholas to the door. It was a gesture that put the sisters in their place, and they knew it. Rachel bade Mary see to the carriage, and then, followed by the trembling Anna, stalked off to her bedroom.

It was Nicholas who suggested that they should take their time in arriving at Rathkeale, lest if they overtook him on the road he should take to the fields; it would be much better, Judith agreed, to catch him at the vet's lodgings, and on hearing her say, "catch him," Nicholas could not but feel pity for the boy. Actually, as they crossed the bridge and passed the town-pump, they saw from the carriage a group of loafers drinking outside a public-house, and in another instant, Leo, still holding a half-emptied pint of porter, dashed between their legs and raced up the hilly street. At once Nicholas jumped out and followed, while the loafers, who had been enjoying the boy's wild cursing talk, began to shout their delight in the chase, and Judith to shout at the serving-man to whip up the horses after the pair. Up the narrow, uneven lane they went, the carriage rocking in the ruts, Judith leaning forward like a charioteer, before them Leo with his streaming glass of porter, and Nicholas alternately shouting dreadful threats and wheedling promises to encourage him to halt. For a few moments the sleepy town came to life. A dog ran from the maw of an empty pub, and then ran back again in fright. From each doorway a head, or even two, protruded slowly, and one man actually ran out into the middle of the roadway to see better up the perfectly empty street. Then, at the turn out of Well Lane, the serving-man crashed his axle against the corner. The iron tire rolled down the street like a hoop, a felloe was broken, and the wheel collapsed with a crackling of wood. In the impact Judith was thrown heavily on the pavement. The driver kept his seat, and the horse was halted before it had dragged the carriage more than twenty yards. When they went to her she was pale as death, and there was blood in the corner of her mouth and a gentle dripping noise on the flag beneath her skull. Nicholas thought no more of Leo, but as he helped to carry the old woman into a public-house he found the boy weeping by his side. By night, when she regained consciousness, he was almost hysterical with terror and remorse.

They borrowed another wheel, and the carriage was walked back slowly to Foxehall. She did not speak one word all the way, and Leo, who sat opposite her, often said after that he was never so glad of the darkness as that night. They put her into her old room, where she remained, recovering the use of her limbs, until the summer was well advanced.

They said nothing to Leo about his rudeness to his aunts and his wickedness in running from them, except that Anna took him behind a bush one morning, and said:

"You'll be kind to poor Auntie Anna, won't you, Leo?"

Whereupon he said nothing, and sidled away. He resumed his old routine, except that now he almost never said that Nicholas was coming if he knew he was not. If he did tell a lie, it was merely to get away to the river for a swim or to steal along the farther walls looking for a wild bird's nest. When Nicholas came he never rebelled; if he even threatened to be naughty it was sufficient for Nicholas to say, "I'll tell on you to your mother," and he was on his best behaviour for the rest of the day. At his own request they made him a bed in his mother's room, and he was willing to sit there for long spells, talking with her, or reading slowly out of the *Iris* or the *Daisy,* or he played quietly for her on the flute.

The result of it all was that he did not go to Limerick in the spring when he ought to have (for Nicholas was always too busy during summer to leave the fields). But he was sent into Rathkeale to the tailor for a new suit, a waistcoat in colours, a shirt with a frill, a coat with two tails and two big buttons behind, and a pair of nankeen trousers. When he stood before his mother in this rig, every button in place, with an aunt on each side of him and old Mary grinning in through the door, Judith smiled for the first time since her accident. She took his hand and turned him about, and he leaned over the bed to be kissed, while Rachel went so far as to say:

"He's growing more and more like our father."

As he was—just as awkward with his hands, just as black about the nails, even worse in his grammar. But he had the long nose of the Foxes and a trick of holding his head apologetically on one side, which his Grandfather Leo used sometimes do, and he had learned to say, "aunt," as if it rhymed with "haunt." And that was a great advance in a few months.

2

Whenever he spoke of his youth he would speak of it in terms of that summer. He thought of a procession of hot, sunshiny days with the horizon wavering and all the plain below the house warm as fire. The waters of the Deel glittered beside the dry gravel, or flowed without sound, streaked with bowed rushes. The bog-pools glittered with masses of snowy cloud, inverted motionless in the dark water. Long after, when he recalled those days, it seemed to him he did nothing but lie under the sun for hour after hour among the reeds and the gorse, looking down into those pools, and listening to Nicholas, who lay on his back beside him, talking of the motions of the clouds or squirming around to look with him at their inverted cumuli passing slowly and magically, as in a dark lantern, from one rush-fringe to another.

"Ah, Leo!" the gentle lips of Nicholas would say. "It is the work of the Almighty. It is wonderful! And it is here you would know it, in this silent place."

They might have held a lighted candle in the air and the flame would not have stirred. If they raised their heads to look they would have seen no living thing, and if they listened they heard the faint hiss of a scythe far away.

"I like," said Nicholas, "to be in a quiet place like this, away from the noise of the roads."

Leo took off his coat and lay scanning the pool in vain for signs of life. Sometimes he could not pierce the refulgence of the clouds, and his eyes were lost then in the aerial distances below him. He scarcely heard Nicholas speaking.

"A cloud is a lovely thing, Leo. It is so fair and round. All shapes that clouds have are lovely, and yet, do you see, they have no shape at all, Leo. Will I explain that to you? It is because they are of the nature of water that is fluxive, and light that is everywhere, and air that no man has ever seen. That is why."

But Leo drew his flute from his pocket and dropped a great spit in the water so that everything shivered and was gone. Then, turning from reforming beauty, he would put the flute to his lips and the high-pitched notes would carol and float into the sky, maybe attracting a bird to sink down in its flight, so that Nicholas would halt the music and resume his odd alchemist's game of analysing all he saw.

"A swallow, Leo! Look at him! Will you look at him, man? Blasht you, look at the divil! Isn't he a fast fellow? Ah! He's gone—"

Leo's whistling would begin again and Nicholas at his strange talk.

"A swallow is of the three natures, and he is the only bird like that. He is happy on the land or flying low to it, on the water or skimming over it, in the air where he cuts it like a knife. A strange bird!"

So for hours that seemed to be endless, so slowly did the time pass. Then they would retrace their ways, Nicholas to the smoky, dirty cabin-kitchen of Ahill, where Mag would be suckling her young baby, and Theo wiping the smoke-tears from his eyes, and Julie preparing a small meal; and

Leo to meet his mother and walk out with her, holding her arm, and now and again wiping off the small beads of sweat gathering on her brow, towards the fields where her other children were at work. And in that dead heat, with the earth in finest heart, sweating under the fruit it bore, if the eight children suddenly turned their faces from the white clay to see the two leaning over a gate watching them, the eight, one by one, would lower their heads with no more sign of recognition than if they were a row of snails crawling under the mangold leaves from the flames of the sun. Or if, as they swung the scythes and the reaping-hooks in concert, they saw above the furze-tops the grey head bent low to the invisible boy beside her, as with one mind they would stop. Then James would stop and look where they looked, and take his whetstone, sharpen the blade calmly, and walk, with the rest following him behind, to the farthest corner of the field and a new stretch of meadow-grass. They made it clear in a hundred small ways like that how little they liked their youngest brother. It was as if he was no longer one of their family and had all but ceased to be of their blood.

His mother opened the fight for him immediately she returned to Bawnrea. She walked in the door as if she had walked out of it only an hour ago, and they in turn looked up at her as if it was only five minutes since they last saw her. James was mending a heims by the window and the girls were tidying the place.

"When will you plough the inch field?" she said to James, as she leaned up to hang her cloak on the wooden peg under the stairs.

"What inch field?" he asked.

"You know what inch field I mean. Are there two of them?"

"I have no inch field. That's Leo's field."

She rolled up her sleeves to prepare the feed for the hens.

"Well, it is time it was ploughed," she ordered.

"Is that so?" said James, tugging the waxed thread. "Then, begobs, it is time he ploughed it."

"You can plough it a' Wednesday," she said.

"I'll not, nor a' Thursday," he replied. "And if it's chicken-feed you're looking for, there's none there."

"Why isn't there?" she cried, bullying them at once.

"Because," he said, "we gave it to the pigs."

She stared dumbfounded at him. He rose leisurely and inspected the heims.

"Them hens weren't worth their keep," he said, over his shoulder. "I sold them to Mag Keene at Ahill."

She had the meal-stick in her fist, and in her anger she half-raised it and looked out of her fiery eyes at each of the girls in turn. They looked sullenly at her and at James. He pushed aside the heims and faced her.

"I'll plough no field for Leo," he cried.

"You'll do what you're told," she cried. "Get on with yeer work," she bade the girls. They might have been statues staring at her.

"This farm is mine, now," said James. "And I'll do what I like with it. Long enough I waited for it. And long enough ye drained me, and drained it on me, yourself and my father. And for who? For Leo."

He laughed bitterly and returned to the heims.

"Ha! That's a good wan surely," he said. "You to think I'm going to keep that *siófaire's* farm for him. After he robbing me? And you robbing me?" he cried into her face.

She spoke very gently then.

"I'll be talking to you in a minute," she said.

She laid down the meal-stick and the pan, and rolling down her sleeves she went to her room. They watched her as she opened the door. Her face was white when she looked back at them. Her bed lay dismantled against the wall, and the tick and the bed-clothes were tied in a bundle in the corner. Sacks of meal and flour were ranged along the wall. Harness hung on freshly cut pegs above them. The bin had been brought from the outhouse and stood where her bed had formerly stood. There was no more loud talk, but the low, strained voices of the pair of them trembled with passion and excitement.

"Who's doing is that?"

"It's mine," said James.

"So you want to hunt me from house and home?"

"What need have you for a room there?" he asked. "Haven't you room and leavings of room in Foxehall? You got on there very well without us. Never coming near us except to shpy on us over a ditch? And we got on all right without you, too. My father," he ground out the words relentlessly, "left this house, and everything in, and on, and about it, to me."

She crossed the floor by him and sat on the settle by the fire, her foot tapping the floor ever so gently, her eyes summing him up, and then each of the girls after him in turn. His eyes never flinched from hers, but the daughters looked away through the window.

"G'out out, girls," she said harshly. "I want to talk to this laddo."

They went in a drove. Her son sat down by the heims, and with trembling hands prepared a new fold of hemp, pulling it to and fro strongly across his knee, under the wax hot in his palm.

"James!" she said at last. "I'm staying in this house. I can pay for my keep, thank God."

"All right!" he said. "If you can, all right!"

"Have that room prepared for me tonight," she said.

"I'll not change it now," he said. "You can have the room you always had before my father took sick and died in it."

She capitulated again.

"Very well," she said.

"I suppose," he leered, "we can draw up a little agreement. With," he added venomously, "the help of your
friend, Lawyer Dee?"

"You'll plough that field a' Wednesday," she said.

"I won't," he said.

"And the lag field after it," she continued.

"I won't," he said. And, to let her know he meant it, he
repeated it firmly: "I will not."

In the silence that followed he tried in vain to thread
the bradawl.

"Will you do it next week?" she asked.

"I will do it no week. No, not next week, nor next month,
nor next year."

The thread and the awl trembled violently in either
hand.

"I will give you right of turbary in Knockfierna," she
offered.

"How many loads?"

"Two loads."

He hesitated.

"And if you don't take it, I'll draw down the priest—"

"All right," he agreed. "Three loads with the jennet."

"Plough them, and harrow them, and sow them after."

"Three loads," he countered.

She paused in her turn.

"Three loads or I'll not do it," he said.

"All right," she said. "On a' Wednesday?"

"A' Wednesday."

She rose and took her cloak, and went out to the haggard
to see what other changes he had made. He spied on her
through the window, threading and pulling all the time at
his broken heims, and when she had made her rounds he
went out with the finished tackling, where she had to pass
him on the narrow causeway. They looked at one another,
and for a second she hesitated as if to protest against what

she had seen. She passed on with her head held high; maybe a little too high and mighty, he said to himself, for wan entirely at her ease.

They made their bargain in Dee's office in Rathkeale a few days later. For two shillings a week he agreed to rent her the timbered room, two sacks of potatoes every autumn, a sack of meal twice a year, and two pounds of butter every month. She argued hard for three pounds of butter, or else one shilling and sixpence a week, but he said she was an old woman, and what would she be doing eating all that butter? For very shame of Dee she laughed and said he was an O'Donnell all out.

"And what does it all matter, anyway? Sure it's a thing of nothing, we'll never look at again."

"Aye!" said James. "What does sixpence here or sixpence there amount to with people like us?"

In silence they returned along the sunburned plain, shoulder jogging by shoulder on the seat of the cart, and in silence they parted at the gate of Foxehall on its hill. They did not even say good-bye. She walked through the gates and he jerked on the horse without a word.

In the fields below the house she saw how the wind blew the hay on the cocks, and they sank with their own weight or fell sideways, and how they cast cool, tapered shadows for all the length of the green field. It was time, she decided, that Leo went to Limerick, if he were to go at all that year. She found him sitting under a bush near the house, playing with one of the house-dogs.

"Would you like to go to Limerick to your cousin, Dicky Wilcox, for a spell?"

"I might."

"He's a doctor in Limerick—a high-up man—with a great house in Honan's Quay. Will you promise to work hard if I send you there?"

"I will."

"Pig?"

"I will, Mother."

She looked down at him for a minute, and then she walked on slowly to plan with Rachel for the beginning of the worldly education of Leo Foxe-Donnel, the first and last of that name.

3

So a few mornings later, when those long rick-shadows were pointing the other way, he stepped after Nicholas into the old britzka (it must have been one of the last journeys it ever made), and waving to his aunts on the steps and impatient of his mother's kisses, rolled and jolted and bumped down the drive to meet the mail-car at Rathkeale. Of that journey he remembered for ever the weight of the overhanging trees, moist with a night shower, the limestone roads heavy under the wheels with the sticky mud, and beside the roads for mile after mile the small, tumbling walls and the wilderness of high grass. There, too, to the south were the dark hills, low against the clouded sky at Ballingarry, on their sides emerald green patches shot with sun, and he saw everywhere how the ivy-berries were coming, the blackberries darkening, and the cattle sheltering, even at that early hour, under the inextricable hedges, or lying to their hips in grass so rich that they did not even need to lower their mouths to crop the stalks. And all the country about was so sleep-heavy and quiet that the dogs did not bother to bark at them, and once, when they halted to ease the tackling at the foot of a small hill, they could hear nothing but the little birds hopping in the hedges.

They halted at Rathkeale for a drink, the servant-boy promising not to tell, and then the mail-car man was call-

ing them and they were off, out of the silent town where
they had seen nobody in the streets but one old crone, who
came to throw a dish of soapy water on the road and looked
after them out of purblind eyes. From that on—the overhanging trees once more, the wild grass-edges dew-pointed
under the estate walls, the low walls of the unploughed
farms, the occasional heaps of road-metal.

At Adare they stopped for dinner, and while they waited
they had more drinks in a low-roofed taproom, daintily
curtained, where two fiery-faced cattle-dealers, with enormous paunches and chamois gaiters smelling of dung, sat
counting notes, whose edges they continually soiled in the
circles of their pewter-pots. With every careless cat-glance
they threw him, as they swilled their porter, Leo felt himself more and more a child, and all he could do was sit
with one foot treading the toe of the other, sipping his ale
out of his great pewter jug. When the dinner was ready
they almost jumped out of their chairs to the table, and
they reseated themselves there with as much shuffling and
blowing and arranging of neckerchiefs, and blessing of
themselves and manœuvring of knives and forks and plac-
ing of condiments as if they were a pair of generals planning the strategy of a great attack. And they did attack—
they ate as if they had not seen food for days, continually
putting out a hairy hand to the dish of spuds, scraping bits
of greasy cabbage from their chins with their forks, and
showering so much pepper on the corned beef that Leo was
hardly out of one sneeze before he was into another. Their
names, Nicholas whispered to Leo, were Jack and Tom
Wall.

He was too excited by the journey to eat, and when the
dish of potatoes was empty there were still two on his plate.
For a long time the younger, Jack, cocked his eye at them
and at him, and then he said:

"Young man, are you going to ate them spuds?"

"N-n-o, sir," said Leo.

"Then be heavens," he cried, shooting out his fork and spearing one, "I will."

"And I another," cried the elder dealer, spearing the second.

"Will you ate that cabbage?" asked Jack again.

"No, n-n-no, sir!"

"Gobble-gobble-gobble," said the cherub, and with his knife he swept up a lump of the cabbage into his mouth, glaring at the other who, with his knife, cleared the plate.

"Gobble-gobble-gobble," they mouthed in unison, and bent over the table to scrape their plates and wash down the food with a long, sibilant flow of black porter. Then they sighed and leaned back and leered at Nicholas and at Leo. Next they placed their fat hands on their fat thighs and, after licking their lips and sucking their teeth like a pair of man-eating tigers, they blew their noses and wiped their mouths with their hands and gurgled down another draught of frothy stout, and, side by side, fell by a series of nods into a sound sleep.

An hour later and they were all on the road, Leo between the two, who smoked all the way, spitting every ten yards, and nodding to almost everyone they passed on the road. Then the elder dealer began to sing a bawdy song in Irish:

> "Is fada an treimhse na rabhas ag snámh
>   Le cailin gan eadach bui sugach 's sámh.
>   Mar ba chóir di bheith bog bhi earball éisg
>   's in ionad suidhe ara . . . Ridle-um-randy-do
>   shuidh si ar pléasc.

> "Oh! Lately I went for a nate little shwim
>   With a lassie, was naked as nature, and thrim
>   As a fish, for her legs were all mackerels' mate

And you came on her scales when you thought
    'twas her . . .
        Ridle-um, randy, hi, randy, hi-ro!"

And so on for a score of verses.

At Patrickswell they saw the spears of Limerick rising above the trees and the great castles of the Shannon, like Carrigogunnel, on its rock. Within an hour they were passing the first low cabins of the city, and the churches and factories, and were cantering down George's Street, where long rows of tall, red-brick houses looked down on the wide and windy river. A donkey was rolling himself in the dust of a side-street. A drove of hogs was meandering slowly to the slaughter-house. A troop of red-coated soldiers were marching to the castle. The mail-car turned off into a side-street, and into another side-street and halted at a shop, on the facia board of which was painted the name Proinnsias O'Domhnall, and on one side, *Flour, Meal, and Bran,* and on the other, *Groceries, Wines, and Spirits.*

"Your uncle's, Leo!" smiled Nicholas, as Leo lowered himself to the pavement and stretched his stiff legs.

"Do you mean to say," roared Jack Wall, "that the boy is a nephew of Frankie's? Are you, boy?"

"He's my father's brother," said Leo.

Jack leaned over him, very solemnly, more from his toes, like a leaning statue, than from his hips, for there no bend was possible, and whispered, so that Nicholas should not hear.

"Listen to me, boy. I know the seed and breed of you for generations. But if you mention that potato, be jay, I'll out yeh!"

"No, no, sir!" promised Leo hastily. "I'll say nothing, sir."

"You should have told us, you ruffian!" cried Jack.

Leo laughed, and seeing him laugh, the pair laughed and slapped him on the back and aimed playful blows at him. Then they all crowded through the glass-panelled doors of the shop.

As they entered, the light of day was already growing weak and the day sounds of the city were dulled. They entered into a darkness filled with clamour. At the back of the shop, behind a bulbous wall of bags, was a beer-stinking lofty corner lit by a mud-spotted skylight, and out from this recess there came the shouting of a mob of men.

"A meeting, bejay!"

"Who is it?" cried Leo. "Who are they? What is it all about?"

"The Tenants' League," said Nicholas, hurrying forward.

Over the clustered heads a shirt-sleeve was raised, and a man jumped up on some kind of box and shouted loud enough to be heard above the babbling voices.

"That's Frankie!" Nicholas cried into Leo's ear.

Leo looked at the florid, merry face, with its small waxed moustaches and its hanging lower lip wet with the stain of porter.

"Look!" shouted Nicholas, again nodding and pointing furtively here and there. "Tom Fraher of Oola. Dick Mullins! And Lar! Timsy Danagher! Begobs, they're all here."

Leo strained up on his toes. He could see nothing but a mass of faces, shaven and unshaven, and all were raised to Frankie and cheering him like mad.

"Silence!" bawled Frankie, and he was like an auctioneer or a bookmaker on his box. "A song!" he shouted hoarsely. "A song from Old Tom Mulcaire of Kildimo!"

"Bejay!" wailed Jack Wall, "we won't get a dhrink for an hour."

"It's Old Tom, all right!" cried Nicholas excitedly. "Look at him, Leo. Look, man."

"Where? Who is he? I don't see him," cried Leo peevishly.

Nicholas raised him up in his arms, and he saw an old

man with a mop of white hair, a coat with greasy lapels, and a dirty shirt without a collar.

"A man suffered for the cause," shouted Jack Wall at Leo, in a voice fit to deafen him.

"Five years in Maryboro Jail!" cried Nicholas into his other ear.

Leo merely looked at the white face of the old man who had been in jail, and wondered why they put him there and what he had done, and what the cause was for which he had suffered.

"Come on, Tom!" cried Frankie O'Donnell. "Out with it, man. A good land-song!"

With his two hands he imposed silence on the crowd.

The old man looked about him quietly and then up through the roof-light at the warming evening sky. The bar-tender lit the swinging lamp over his head, and in silence they all watched the yellow light spreading about the wick. Foreseeing a triumph, the old man threw out his chest and glared about him.

"I won't sing," he declared, "but I'll give ye a little composition I heard last month in Castletown. It's called *The Divil's Address to the Merchants of Limerick*. Here it is!" He recited it in one breathless rush of words:

> "Well here ye are says he
> and ye didn't come far says he
> or need a car says he
> for the smell of hell says he
> is from Pennywell says he
> and out to the ridge says he
> of Thomond Bridge says he
> anyway I'm proud as hell says he
> to see ye so well says he
> but what makes ye so bold says he
> come out of the cold says he

and not be shaking and chattering says he
like a priest at a pattern says he
come in a bit nigher says he
and enjoy me fire says he
not like boys in a quire says he
wisha is that Sexton Perry says he
with lashings of sherry says he
and I suppose I can't avoid says he
taking wine from Lord Lloyd says he
or persuading Maggoty Quin says he
to go slow with his gin says he
and will ye look at Halpin and Speaight
    says he
behind each side of the gate says he
manufacturing mate says he
and Bateman and Hogges says he
with turf coal, and logs says he
to drive off the fogs says he
they're all here by dogs says he
Boyle, Roche, and Fox says he
the Halpins and Houghs says he
with every fish says he
your heart could wish says he.
We're the grandest variety says he
of Limerick society says he
and we'll make it a feast says he
to welcome ye east says he
call up on the trumpets says he
the best of my strumpets says he
the Countess of Clare says he
and Dame Castlereagh says he
King James and King Bill says he
can drink with a will says he
Cromwell and Pitt says he
and all that will fit says he.
Then rubadubdub says he
on the drum and the tub says he
drink lads and be merry says he

the finest of sherry says he
but what the divil is that says he
tastes like me ould hat says he.
I'd rather a kick in the shin says he
do you call that stuff gin says he.
Come on Mister Perry says he
out with yer sherry says he
here's a can for it says he
and I'm tha man for it says he.
Oh! may Cromwell then curse on ye says he
this stuff is worse on me says he.
And look at my fire says he
is it the way ye desire says he
for to make it expire says he
it's as could as a byre says he
what have I done says he
to ask ye to come says he
to my house was so spicy says he
ye Limerick lice ye says he.
I'll teach ye be civil says he
and not be cheating the divil says he
let this be yeer fates says he
ye Halpins and Speaights says he
for selling bad meat says he
both early and late says he
to sit on yeer rumps says he
under red-hot pumps says he
with boiling stout says he
into yeer mouth says he
and ye Boyles and ye Roches says he
ye Houghs in yeer coaches says he
and Maggoty Quin says he
with your gutrot gin says he
and fine Sexton-perry says he.
I'll make them merry says he
in Broad Street and Dock Street says he
and Bridge Street and John Street says he
and Clare Street and where street says he

to bate ye and rate ye says he
down West Watergate with ye says he
with yeer rumps in lumps says he
and harrows for barrows says he
boiling, smelling says he
bubbling, yelling says he
roasting, ghosting, toasting Limerick mer-
        chants to the Judgment Day says he."

There was froth on his lips when he ended. With a powerful gesture of a hand that once ruled the ploughshare he
stopped their applause, and concluded solemnly, his eyes
glaring in the lamp-light:

"And so, in after years at night should men inquire
What may it be that causes Limerick's smell,
Point down the Shannon to the ghostly fire
Of the fifteen Limerick merchants burning out of hell."

They had cheered every familiar name they heard, and
now they laughed at the mockery of Limerick city in the
last verse, and still laughing at it they returned to their
talking and drinking.

Frankie had spied Nicholas while the old man recited,
and he now leaped down.

"Ould Nick!" he said, thrusting out his long hand
through the press of bodies between them.

"And," greeted Frankie, "I believe this is our friend,
Mister Leo Foxe-Donnel. I am proud to meet you, sir."

The body followed the hand, and Frankie stooped to inspect Leo. It was quick of him, Leo thought, to recognize
me, and he was blushing with pleasure in the word "mister."

"And how's your awnts?" shouted Frankie, for every one
had to shout to be heard.

"My awnts are very well, sir," said Leo.

"And your dear mother?" shouted Frankie.

"She's very well, sir," shouted Leo.

"What'll you have?" bawled Frankie. "A glass of sherry? Sherry is the best drink for travellers, don't you agree with me?"

Leo smiled at the publican.

"Yes," he cried, "it's a very fine drink. I agree with you entirely."

He was now red in the face from shouting, but he said all this so seriously that Frankie winked at Nicholas and burst out laughing.

"You're a bit of a divil, I think," he shouted, and because of the compliment in the wink Leo did not mind his laughter. "Go outside," added Frankie to him and to Nicholas, "where ye can have a drink in peace."

They went out into the shop, and Old Tom Mulcaire followed them like a house-dog. Even here they had to talk loudly to be heard. Frankie came to them with the drinks, and again Leo was told, as he took the sherry:

"There's a man suffered for the cause. Five years in Maryboro Jail."

Leo shook his head in admiration and wonderment, but he asked no questions about "the cause."

"And all," said Frankie, "because he drove cattle from a landlord was crushing him with rent, and sending bums, if you please, to drive him and his family to the ditches. But he wouldn't stand for it. A brave man. Here's health to you, Tom."

"Thank you, Frankie," murmured Tom, and miserably he watched them drink.

"Yes, sir," he sighed to Leo. "Five years. And when I kem out not wan, blessed, single, solitary, square foot of my own to stand on. And my wife in the churchyard. And my childer scattered. I suffered," he said. "And I got little by it," he sighed, and looked sadly into the dark pool in the bottom of Leo's glass. "I never sings for money, though," he explained proudly. "No. But at a fair or a gathering I do sing to keep the spirits of the people up to the cause."

"Have ye no land-song, Tom?" asked Frankie, none too pleased with the old man's satire on the merchants.

"What's the land to me, now?" wailed the old man, "until I get my own land back. It's the merchants are my enemies now!"

Again he stared at Leo as if he were a figure of Age warning Youth.

"The merchants, young sir! They're my enemies. And the enemies of many besides me."

"And what about the lawyers and the doctors?" said Frankie, with a wink to Leo, because Dicky Wilcox was a doctor. "Aren't they a pack of rogues and robbers?"

But the old lad was too cunning.

"Ah!" he said. "There's a deal of people is rogues."

"I think you're a rogue yourself," said Jack Wall.

"We're all rogues!" said Tom.

They laughed, and Frankie turned to the Walls.

"Hard times in the country, I suppose?" he said.

"Hard as nails. Going night, noon, and morning, bejasus! Hadn't time to ate a decent bit of food. My clothes are falling off me. I don't know what I'll do about it."

"You're looking thin, too, I noticed," commiserated Frankie.

"Yerrah, what, man?" said Tommy Wall. "Sure we're ghosts."

"Too bad!" sighed Frankie. "That's too bad."

He gave Leo such a dig in the back at this point, that he upset his sherry and had to be given another glass.

"And all for what?" complained Jack. "For a few shillings of money. Prices are the highest they ever were. I tell you! What we want is another good war! This country," he declared as he rattled his loose money in his pocket and felt his breast pocket to see if his notes were safe, "this country is gone to hell!"

"Ah!" said Frankie, very serious now, "it's I that know it. This is the first time I sold sixpence worth in this bar for a month."

Here Old Tom Mulcaire caught Leo's eye, and he drew such a profound wink and made such a comical gob, that Leo had to laugh outright and, then, drain down his sherry to cover his confusion and save him from returning Frankie's peculiar glance.

Behind the sacks they were calling out for service, and shaking hands, a little more coldly, Leo thought, he bade them good night. They all shook hands all round, and Old Tom shook Leo's hand many times and said, holding it:

"Good-bye, young sir. There's the hand of a man spent five years in jail. I hope you're not ashamed to take it?"

"No, no, sir!" patronized Leo.

"I'll be seeing you again," said Old Tom, as he followed them to the door.

"I hope so, sir," said Leo.

"A man suffered for the cause you won't meet every day," said Old Tom.

"No, sir," agreed Leo.

The old man persisted no farther. They moved out of earshot, and the last Leo saw of him was his great hand erect as he gave his last benediction before turning into the pub-door.

"All he wants is money for drink," explained Nicholas.

"Is that all?" asked Leo.

"Frankie is a powerful man," said Nicholas.

"Is he?" asked Leo, wishing he had given a few pence to the landless man who had been in jail for the "cause."

But he soon forgot him and all of them, his eyes big with Limerick and the evening that was colouring the tall red houses and the muddy streets wide as a sea. After the reek of the bar the air of Clare Street, blowing up from the Shannon, was cold and sharp and sweet, and through the gloom it seemed strange that the lights high up in the office-windows and in the many loopholes of the murmuring mills did not waver under it, as, below them, in the last rain-pools on the drying pavements, the gas-lit windows wavered perpetually. They walked out to the quays where the river-shallows gurgled past, or the colourless deeps moved in slow, leaden swirls. Beyond were the fields, dark and wet; up-river the cylinder of the castle rising through the dusk out of the bed of the river; down towards the sea and the docks, where he could hear the rattle and rumble of unloading ships, an incoming sail raised its heavy brown triangle against the fire-ball of the sinking sun. They came to the steps and doorway of his cousin's house where they were to part.

"Don't let them make you so grand that you won't talk to us," laughed Nicholas, like one who didn't believe what he said.

"I'm as grand as the best of them," said Leo, "and I want to be no grander," like one who did believe what he said.

They shook hands and Nicholas turned away. As he halted to light his pipe and walk on towards the docks, Leo looked after him. Then, as he turned to the bell-handle and jangled it, he felt glad that Nicholas had not wanted to come in with him, for the door was very white and the brasses shone, and a maid in cap and ribbons and a high choker collar showed him into a hall of soft carpets and deep silence, and thence into a drawing-room, where he could barely hear the distant hum of the docks and the logs hissed in the fire.

At first there seemed to be nobody else in the drawing-room. Then from around the side of a saddle-backed arm-chair there protruded a head, small enough to be a boy's, except that it was bald above a faint fair fringe of hair.

"Who's that?" asked the head.

"It's me, sir," said Leo.

The head turned, and Leo saw a pair of cranky-looking faint-blue eyes, a peevish mouth, and two ears with whiskers in them. Still warmed by the sherry he would have laughed at this small image if he had not suddenly observed on the tip of the flattened nose a large wart, and in contemplating this he forgot to smile.

"Leo Foxe-Donnel?" snapped the little man.

But he snapped like a very weary or old dog.

"Yes, sir," said Leo.

His cousin jumped suddenly from his chair, looked at him for a second, and then seized him by the two shoulders. He turned him round and round as if he were a patient who had come to be examined, and then, still gripping him, he pushed and pushed until Leo felt his back flattened against the wall.

"That," said his cousin, "is the way to stand. Stick your chest out, boy."

Leo could see nothing but the wart, and staring at it his two eyes became round until he was as stupid-looking as a cow.

"Stick it out," commanded Dicky irritably.

"Am I right now, then?" asked Leo, shoving his chest forward like a pigeon.

At once he heard behind him the laughter of a pair of girls, and turning he saw in the shadow of the bellied window overhanging the quay two girls of about his own age, swaying in their long muslin dresses, their arms about each other's waists and their fair curls intermingling as they leaned their heads together.

"Children!" commanded Dicky, "behave yourselves. This is my daughter Felicité," he said to Leo. "Welcome the boy properly," he added to his daughter. "And this"—to Leo—"is my youngest daughter, Miriam."

They made a mock-solemn curtsy to Leo, but even as they did it he saw that their eyes still laughed at him.

"Phwat were ye laughing at?" he said, with a grin to show he was indifferent to them.

But they merely imitated his sing-song East Limerick accent, saying, "Am I right now, then?"—and went off into more peals of mockery, until their curls tumbled into their eyes, and Leo was red with mortification and shame. Just then their mother came in, a tall and lovely lady (or so Leo thought) and whisked them away to the window. She looked her poor relation up and down just as her husband had done, and with a sigh and a half-comical smile of resignation sank on the arm of a chair.

"So this is Leo Foxe-Donnel?" she asked.

"Yes," said Dicky Wilcox. "And what do you think of him?"

But he suddenly stooped forward as if to peer into Leo's eyes, so quickly that the boy leaned back as if expecting a blow, and remained like that after his cousin straightened his back and looked at him severely.

"Have you been drinking, sir?" snapped Dicky.

"I wa-wa-wa-wa—" stuttered Leo.

The girls in the window-recess stifled a laugh as they saw their mother's eye fixed on them. Yet even she had to smile. Slowly Leo resumed the perpendicular.

"What did they give you, child?" she asked gently.

"A glass or two of sherry," said Leo. "Don't you agree it's a very good drink for travellers?" he added, in one more attempt to assert himself before his new relations.

Mrs. Wilcox looked at her husband with a smile.

"Say nothing to him this time, Dicky-bird," she commanded, and rose to her feet. Leo observed that Dicky obeyed with no more than a long nasal groan of rebellion, and the warning:

"We're strict in this house, boy."

And he threw his hands behind his back and danced his coat-ends like a wagtail. Mrs. Wilcox did not look at all strict, however; she patted his shoulder and smiled at him more affectionately than anyone but Nicholas had ever done before.

"Come with me," she said, and added, by way of acknowledging the relationship, a very soft but warm, "Leo."

But as he left the room he saw out of the corner of his eye the two girls talking about him, with shoulders hunched in mockery, and Dicky staring after him with glum, disapproving eyes.

From his room they could see down the Shannon almost to the first islands, and with her arm about his shoulder Mrs. Wilcox told him that he could trace its course at night by the lights along the banks and the lighthouses in midstream. There was Woodcock, and the woods of Cratloe, and dark against the dim night-sky the side of Callan.

"Isn't it nice, Leo?"

"It is, ma'am."

"Hurry up, now, and change into your best clothes for dinner."

She finished brusquely, like a woman who has done her duty and has other things now to occupy her mind.

"But I have no other clothes, ma'am," he said.

Suddenly realizing that Foxehall had been bringing him up like any rough, country boy, he became ashamed of his new nankeens and his rough brogues, and his coat with the finger-fogged brass buttons.

"Nothing else?"

Her lower lip went out, and she looked at him in surprise from beneath her drooping eyelids.

"Oh, well," she sighed. "Wash yourself, at any rate. We'll see what we can do for you later on."

She said it kindly enough, but he knew that she said it in a voice of impatient, if not pitying, kindness.

He was almost ashamed to come down. The drawing-room was far more comfortable than Foxehall now that the candles were lit and the curtains drawn against the damp of the river and the fallen night. The last winches crackled down-river, and a milk-cart with churns rattled past on the cobbled quay. Then the girls came in with their hair in ribbons and flounced about with purple stuffs, and they all went in to dine. They were all very sedate now, and even tried to be kind to him and make small-talk for him, and he tried, too, not to give them reason to as much as smile.

"Well, Leo," said Cousin Dicky, as he carved the cold duck, "and tell us now, what sort of life have you out there in Foxehall."

"It's very nice, sir."

"Do you hunt?"

"No, sir."

"Oh? Fish, then?"

"Yes, sir."

"Shoot?"

"Yes, sir."

"Go around much? Visiting, I mean? Other houses?"

"Oh, yes, sir."

"Where do you go? Do I know them?"

"I go to Ahill, sir."

"Ahill? Who lives there?"

"Mag Keene, sir."

"Is that a gentleman's house?"

"Oh, no, sir."

"Where else do you go?"

"I go to the forge, sir."

"Oh? What do you go there for?"

He just prevented himself from saying "For a shmoke and a shpit."

"A talk, now and again, sir," he said.

"Don't you go to any other houses, Leo?" asked Mrs. Wilcox.

"Sure, no, ma'am."

"Well, what do you do on Sunday afternoon?"

"Ah, sure, I do go walking about the weirs or back to Ahill."

"And after you have done that?"

He, boastingly:

"Ah, sure, I might go east to the pub."

"Huh!" commented Dicky.

"Your nights must be very lonely?" said Mrs. Wilcox.

"Ah! Sure, no!" defended Leo. "We do have great fun sometimes."

"That's nice," said Mrs. Wilcox.

"What do ye do?" asked Dicky suspiciously.

"Ah, sure, we goes back to Ahill," tried Leo again. "And we walk the Bog Road. I once went for a swim in the moonlight!" he declared.

"Did you ever visit at Chesterfield?" asked Dicky.

"I know Chesterfield," said Leo.

"Oh, you've been there?"

"Ah, no, sir. But I do pass it often."

"Have you ever been to Dromard House?"

"I pass it, sir. But I never was in it."

"What in the name of goodness," asked Dicky peevishly, "do you do on a winter night?"

"Ah, sure, I goes back to Ahill, sir."

Cousin Richard gave it up.

"I believe your aunt is a great gardener?" suggested Mrs. Wilcox.

"Oh, a topper!" said Leo.

"How do you like my Paul Krampulls?" asked Dicky, with a backward nod to his geraniums that cluttered the window with a blaze of red.

"Well," parried Leo, "I haven't tried them for a while now, sir, but I have a great grah for Connemara Queens."

At this Mrs. Wilcox lowered her head and Dicky rubbed his chin, but the girls were pitiless and at once resumed

their teasing. They did not cease all the rest of the night
mocking him because he had mistaken geraniums for potatoes, and they never after allowed him to forget the joke.
They noted, too, how he stooped his head to enter the
room, how he had brought his hat into the dining-room and
put it under his chair, how he still clutched it after dinner
was over, and would have brought it with him back to the
drawing-room if Mrs. Wilcox had not taken it from his fist
and pushed him away from it to a chair.

"Ah! me dear boy," advised Cousin Dicky from where
he stood with his back to the fire, "you must go around
more. Those aunts of yours should take you out to see your
neighbours. Didn't ye ever go to take a cup of tea with the
curate at Nantenan itself?"

"No, sir!" confessed Leo.

"Leo is not of our persuasion," interposed Mrs. Wilcox.

"I don't know that part of Limerick very well, to be
sure," went on his cousin, as he took a cigar from his
smoking-cabinet and began to prepare it with a silver affair
he took from his vest-pocket. "Who is living at Beechmount, now?"

"Where is that, sir?"

"Don't you know Beechmount? Not know Beechmount?
This side of Rathkeale. A fine demesne. With a fine lake
and fine woods about it. A very fine house, Beechmount.
It's been in the hands of relations of your people for years
and years. There is a splendid covert behind it, on the
Ballingarry side, and the meet often gathers there. Oh,
a splendid property. And so you haven't been to Beechmount?"

Leo was weary and ashamed of his perpetual "No's," and
he merely shook his head.

"Were you there, sir?" he asked timidly, as his cousin
pulled at his cigar and regarded him with a large question
in his eyes.

"Oh! No! No! No! I haven't been there."

"Were you in Chesterfield, sir?" asked Leo.

"No! No! I confess I haven't been to Chesterfield. But," he explained testily, "I don't live in these parts. If you don't visit the houses of your own neighbours," he went on with the attack, "I really don't see, well—er—I can't see, to be candid—er—can you—er—Janet?"

"It's all very strange," said his wife, as she prepared the coffee. "Very odd!"

Leo turned his head from one to the other of them, and he found they were all looking at him curiously, as if he were an interloper or a pretender.

"So you don't go to the meet? Will you go this year? Cub-hunting has begun, hasn't it?"

"Yes, sir."

"Ah, you *will* go?"

"No, sir. I don't think so, sir."

"Where is this you said you visit?" asked Mrs. Wilcox, as she burdened him with a cup of coffee.

"I goes back to Ahill," murmured Leo, blushing as he said it.

The girls giggled, and with a sad "Ah! well!" his cousin abandoned him, and retired to his cigar, his paper, and his arm-chair.

"May I have a cup of coffee, dear?" he asked.

It was then Leo tumbled his cup of coffee all over his knees, and the snowy sheepskin rug was stained with a brown star. Mrs. Wilcox barely stopped herself from saying something cross and bitter.

"Ring the bell, dear," she asked her husband, in a cold voice.

"I'm sorry, ma'am," stuttered Leo, and began to wipe the rug with his hand.

"Let it alone, child!" commanded Dicky.

In silence the cup was taken from him by the servant,

and he could see the two girls glaring at him and his cousin
looking at his legs out of the corner of his eye. He could
stand it no longer, and timidly asked if he might go out
and see the city.

"Yes, boy!" snapped Dicky.

He stooped his head to leave the room, and the door
shut after him with a crash.

From behind the window curtains he saw the girls watch
him leave the house, and he felt they were grinning because he first looked up, like any country lout, to see what
kind of night it was, and as he strode along the quay
through a light mist, he felt they were following him
with their eyes, and doubtless giggling at his long steps
or his heavy boots, or the cut of his coat or the poise of
his hat.

He went straight to Irishtown and Frankie O'Donnell's
shop, only to find it empty, save for the barman and Old
Tom Mulcaire, now very drunk and making such a nui-
sance of himself that the barman was continually telling
him to behave himself or he'd get thrown out on his head.
Leo sat gloomily on a barrel under the hanging lamp, and
spent all the pocket-money he had been given for his stay
in Limerick drinking sherry and standing half-measures to
Old Tom. He listened dolefully to the barman's chatter or
Old Tom's occasional maudlin interruptions, so that the
night went slowly by, sprinkled occasionally by glittering
drops on the skylight, always clammy and dull and cold,
and here malodorous with the smell of dregs, in a medley
of words about otters and horses, and great houses built of
the blood and sweat of tenants, and cub-hunting that was
soon beginning, and sherry for travellers, and how many
barrels of Guinness the barman had broached in his time,
and the rent that you would be hard put to pay at the four
quarter-days, and it rising every quarter, and the Tenants'
League that was going to change everything, and how there

wasn't a finer city than Limerick, or finer people, in the whole of Ireland, once you got to understand them.

At last all his money was gone—it had seemed such a lot of money when his mother gave it to him the night before, taking it from her bosom and, with a kiss, thrusting it deep into his pocket—and the pub was closed on the pair of them. He wandered in the ceaseless drizzle about the streets of Irishtown with Old Tom, trying to be rid of him in order that he might face for his new home on Honan's Quay. But Old Tom insisted on teaching him a long song about Lord Castlereagh and an agent called Matty Fryer, making him repeat every line and every verse until he had it by rote. They leaned over Thomond Bridge, reciting down to the dark and smoothly flowing river until it was almost midnight and the whole city was silent with sleep. At last they separated at the corner of Honan's Quay after much handshaking and speechifying from the old man, but, to his horror, Leo found him at his elbow again, before his cousin's door, with another verse he had previously overlooked. Standing shoulder to shoulder by the area railings, they went over this verse too until Leo could recite it pat.

Then the landless man took off his hat and, raising his head to the windows, damned and blasted the Wilcoxes and the Foxes and all their seed and breed for generations, in every county in Ireland and out of Ireland, male and female, born and unborn, while from the steps Leo regarded him in terror of the door that might open at any moment behind his back. At last the old man spat at the house and thrust his hat on his head and rolled away, and Leo turned to regard the brass knocker and summon up enough courage to strike it.

"I'm all right, sir," he would say, and smile as he used to smile at his Auntie Anna when he wanted to appease her over something. Perhaps he would add, "I lost my way, uncle." Or he might say, "I hurt my foot—"

But it was Mrs. Wilcox who opened the door, wide. He sidled in like a dog expecting a kick, but she thrust out her arm to halt him.

"Where have you been?" she asked sternly but quietly.

"I'm all right, ma'am," he said, and tried his Auntie Anna smile.

She glared at him so furiously that he banged his head on the wall-rail in avoiding an imaginary blow. At that she laughed and then grew serious again.

"It's well for you," she said airily, "that my husband is in the country with a patient. Go to bed at once."

He almost ran to the stair-head.

"Boy!" she called, as he was half-way to the landing.

"Yes, ma'am."

"Where were you?"

"At Frankie O'Donnell's, ma'am."

"And who is Frankie O'Donnell, pray?"

"He's an uncle, ma'am."

"We appear to be a very large family," she commented dryly, and dispatched him with a jerk of her head.

As he went he heard the drawing-room door open and shut, and the merry sound of a man's laugh and hers replying. Then the girls' bedroom door was opened, and in their pink night-dresses they peeped out at him, and beckoned him with whispered invitation.

"Where have *you* been?" they whispered in unison.

"Ah, I've been out for a drink," he said airily.

"Ssh!" they warned. "We don't believe you."

He stood opposite them, and with his big gob he blew his breath in each of their faces in turn.

"Now!" he boasted.

"Blow again!" commanded Felicité.

"Pouf!"

"What is it?"

"Sherry!"

"Ooh. If daddy knew!"

"Where is he?" he said aloud.

"Ssh! Ssh! He's gone out the country to a sick woman."

"Who's downstairs?" he asked next, in a lower tone.

But they giggled and wouldn't reply. Then they began to complain bitterly to him—become quite friendly of a sudden—that their mamma had packed them off to bed hours ago.

"She always does when her friends come in. And always and always if daddy is out. He's her faithful flame downstairs," they giggled. "And we saw you come to the door with a blackguard man, and he said the most awful things up to us."

"Did he see you?" asked Leo. "Did you hear what he said?"

"Of course we did," they said—become cool and distant once more. "Nice friends you have! We'll tell daddy in the morning."

"Good night!" said Leo suddenly, and tramped loudly from their room, blowing his nose with his finger as he went.

There was a watchman's fire down the quay by the docks, and he slept watching a faint winking light in the blackness where the Shannon wound to the sea.

4

And as far as almost all the rest of his memories of Limerick were concerned he might never have woken from that sleep, so dim and faint were they. Every spring he went from Foxehall to stay there, but it was not Limerick with its streets and its houses and its quays that burned themselves into his mind, but the country-side to which he always returned when its crinkling alder-leaves were at their noisiest. It was that sighing land, wet above and wet underfoot, and that season between the last threshing and the first ploughing that became his land and his season, a world of brown hayricks wind-tumbled, birds fallen silent; low, lumbering clouds reefed with a chill that took the edges of the water in the lakes and the tattered spears about their strands. When he returned to the steps of Foxehall and looked out at the dark plain and those dark skies and they asked him how he liked Limerick, and what he was learning there, he would scratch his poll and mumble a few words of French with a stupid grin. His mind, to be sure, was filled with scraps of pictures gathered here and there in walks taken alone along the fields below the levees of the Shannon, the reed-clanking, the willow-edged, or with other images, properly respectful, of the elegant comfort of Honan's Quay, where he must have sat for months of hours in the bellied window, looking across the river at the night-hills of Clare—but he could not talk of them, and they would mingle and fade as he delighted in the sight before him.

But there were things in his mind deeper even than memories. He came to know better even than he knew the drawing-room of Honan's Quay, the damp and dusty and always rancid taprooms of Clare Street and Pennywell, their drovers and buyers and farmers that packed them as they packed his brain, men full of talk and argument, and always ready for a song about a landlord or an agent. From them he returned to the black water in the bog-fields, to the floods that ruined the always blighted and ragged bits of scran in the haggards, the cattle, with ribs like harp-strings, sidling about the ditches late at night, still unsatisfied, the sooty walls of Ahill, the sinking thatch with its roof-garden of weeds blown in the smoke from the chimney-hole. He saw these things as he had never seen them before, noted them even when he was out for the day with his dog and his gun, or sitting on his heels on a rock in the river, flashing his gut over the steely pools, a wiry young fellow, small of head, long of nose, all legs like a compass.

Such was his boyhood, idling in Limerick in the summer, in the autumn fields leading the men and lads to every new lair and covert and den he had discovered for them between the Deel and the Shannon, and of nights drinking clandestinely in the pub at Knockaderry; or, after the crossroads dance was ended and they all scattering to their homes, ruffling the girls with boorish shouts of delight in the damp and dark of the deepest ditches.

It was a very pleasant world, but to describe it would be like describing a dream that one has all but forgotten; it was the world of boyhood that can only be compared to the slow cloud-navy of an April day, glittering in its arrested motion higher and still higher above the fields, distilled from the earth; for all that earth-recusant, returning to earth only when it has sailed far from where it first began.

4

A Desperate Character

O F all those who saw his later youth, old Mag Keene was the only one who lived long enough to recount its strange story.

"Ah!" she used to say. "The time that goes fast for one it will go slow for another. Them years went with the wind on the poor boy. But, faith, if they did they were slow in their going for other people."

When she was very aged she would count her children's years by his, rather than by her own, of which she had lost count.

Already, when he was nineteen, his Aunt Rachel had died. Taking his hand in her cold hand, white and bloodless under its glove of dirt, she had smiled at him and whispered:

"I have left you something for yourself, Leo. But I have already given you more than money. The name of an Irish gentleman—I am sure you will be proud of it."

He was staring at her with big eyes when he felt a nudge in the small of his back. It was his mother.

"Yes, aunt," he said hurriedly.

Rachel smiled again, but she did not speak another word, to him or anybody.

She actually left him all she possessed, a few hundred pounds, on the condition that he spend it in the purchase of Foxehall. For weeks his mother raged against the terms of the will, but as she could do nothing to alter it she set about probing Anna to see if she, too, had money to leave her godson. Anna was not to be drawn. She grew morose and sullen if questioned, and if the questioning went too far, cross and tearful. In the end Judith gave it up as a bad job, and started instead to screw the last penny out of the rents. She might have saved herself the bother there; the following year Anna died, and the land and the house and everything in it passed by law out of her hands. Then only did she find that Anna, too, had left her few hundreds to Leo, and, as she feared, under the same conditions as her sister. Unwillingly she rented the house from its English owners until Leo should be twenty-one, and then she bought it for him. He still had the farm called the New Plot.

That winter in which they buried Anna Foxe, or Lady Foxe as half in respect, half in mockery they called her, Mag Keene suffered the birth of her tenth child, as always, a daughter, and the next year the death of her husband. So, she used to say, when Leo returned on his twenty-first birthday, he was in time for both a funeral and a christening in Ahill. But he went to neither.

"It's better not," his mother said. "There's a deal of money owing to me from Mag Keene this past five years. There's no use in being too familiar with her."

In the graveyard, Mag wept her last tear over her husband and returned swiftly to Ahill to do a day's work before nightfall. With the help of Nicholas and one serving-girl named Philly Cashen, she must bring up ten children, all daughters, until that time came when, one by one, they would be sent out to earn for themselves. As it was, she sent Julie, her first child, from her father's graveside in to Foxehall. She was only an urchin of just twelve years, but she could help at any rate to work off the arrears of rent, and maybe afterwards bring in a few pence to feed her long family of sisters.

That night of Julie's going from her was the night of Leo's birthday dinner, and from her cabin window at Ahill Mag saw the lights shining out of the bulky mass of Foxehall on the hill-top. She sat lonely in her kitchen, surrounded by her little brood, her face, though she was not really an old woman, already as lined as a Flemish portrait, a Van Eyck or a Memling, every wrinkle defined by dirt on her skin, her dewlaps beginning to sag below the level of her jaws like two withered potatoes, and her wearied eyes wandering under their lids from side to side of the open hearth where the long remnant of her daughters sat bare-legged, their arms around one another, watching the little flames leap in the turf-sods, whispering to one another their foolish gossiping talk. She was glad that Julie was bettering herself, would some day have a little house of her own, and surely she deserved it, for she was a good girl—they were all good girls. But she remembered, too, the night of Julie's birth, the date and the hour, her first child. She remembered her appearance when she was a little crawling, naked baby and her husband rocked the bumping cradle made from the half-covers of a water-barrel. There it was still, with her tenth baby sleeping in it. Julie was far more trouble than this little one when she was young, and the calloused fingers remembered the wonted services they had done when they were less like the twigs of a black-thorn, bent and gnarled. They remembered the dimples and hollows and creases of flesh in the tiny body, the soft clawing of hands, and the baby laughter that made no sound. As she thought of it she raised her body and shoulders and let them stoop again into her crossed arms. They had had their day. No heart would throb between them again. What they had bred they must slave to keep.

The country sent her in no sound. A leaf turning made a great whisper. She heard baby Bid draw a great breath in its sleep. She felt she must rise and take the delf cup from the dresser and in the dark of the night walk down the pathway to the well, above her the multitudinous stars, the empty fields around her, and no murmur of this world to break her thoughts. A child of her womb was gone from her, and surely the rest must soon go, one after one, even her youngest Bid, the weakest autumnal fruit of her body. At that thought she raised her eyelids and looked at her youngest daughters. One was looking into the red caves of the fire, picking her back teeth with a long lean finger, lost in God alone knew what hopeful dream of her life to come. One by one they would go, all of them but Nonie the Bull, the next after Julie, who must remain on the farm and, like her mother, slave the round of the years, growing heavy with each successive child until she, too, saw them go from her, "rising" in the world, as people say, as she dragged on to her end.

God knows it was a weary round of life, and if the good God in heaven did not requite them all in the life to come, surely it was a cruel life as well. It was a cruel world and there was surely little reason to it. But the good and kind God had His own end in view and it must surely be a good one. His name be praised and blessed; she was near the end of her trials now and it would be a relief to everyone when they laid her under the sod. But she had a good deal of work to do yet, and she hoped she would be spared for it. The lower field that must be dug, and the barn that was falling, and the dairy needing to be roofed, and the debts in Rathkeale and Knockaderry to Jack Frewen the shop, and the girls to be portioned or sent to business, and Nonie that would want to be marrying and bringing in her own man. . . .

Then Julie ran into them, her little fat legs muddy from

the bog-pools, to tell all about the dinner-party at Foxehall,
and all about the glories of the house.

From attic to basement, every room had been prepared
for the homecoming of Leo. The attics had been scrubbed
and brushed and then closed up because the floors were
too bad to be patched. All the upper doors had been
pasted with paper to keep in the winds from the empty
fireplaces. New iron bedsteads had been put in place of
the old wooden ones, and the whole house filled with new
printed tray-cloths and trays, tin candlesticks, brassy picture frames, stamped fire-irons, metal ornaments, table
utensils, knick-knacks. "Mother, you'd be blinded by them!"
There were lace curtains in every room, scarlet bob-tassel
valances to every mantelpiece, door, window, and bedside.
The well, which used to be slimy and clay-fouled by the
side-walls, had been filled in. The outhouses had been
locked up. The gravel drive had been turned into grass,
which (Julie repeated the cook's words, who had repeated
Judith's) was "much cheaper to keep." Every door and
window and every inch of the panelling had been painted
a lovely yellow.

As for the dinner—the lawyer was there, and the vet, and
the parish priest. There was porter and whisky punch, and
Leo Donnel—they never called him Leo Foxe-Donnel—sang
a land-song about Lord Castlereagh and Matty Fryer. And
the vet told the mother that the last time he was in that
house was forty-one years ago at a hunt ball, and how they
were stopped in the middle of a dance by old Mister Foxe
—God rest him—telling them how he had news that Boney
was dead. And the fiddlers played up a song, a French song,
and they all did a set to it, and then the cows were mooing
at them in the dark, over the ditches. Then the priest said
he had christened six of Mrs. O'Donnell's children. Then
the lawyer said he and his father, and his father before him,
had watched over the Foxes, and he got up and made a

great speech. He said Leo Donnel had a wonderful, fine, grand name entirely, a powerful name that was in Irish history and story, and how he was joining the orange and the green, and they were all going to be one from Malin Head to Cork Harbour, and how Leo Donnel was a fine Irish gentleman, and he knew it by the cut of him and he in the cradle. And then Leo Donnel got up to make a speech and they all clapping at him, but the poor boy got sick and puked in the fire, and the lawyer and the vet carried him to his room.

"And I went up the stairs after them with the candle in my hand, mother, and they put him into bed. But he was all right, only too much drink he had taken. Then I went down and brought him up a cup of tea, and I said, 'Is there anything else now, sir, you want for the night?' And he said, 'Put the pot near me for fear I'd get a sick on me again.' And I shut the shutthers in the window, mother, and I looked out and I saw the light of our home away down from me, and I got terribly lonely, mother, and I wanted to be home with my mother and my sisters again."

"Arrah, don't be making such a cry-babby of yourself, Julie. Run away back now and attend to your work, for they must have great clearing after the feast."

But Julie cried all the more at having to return, until her mother slapped her face for her and told her to take that puss down off of her, and packed her back to Foxehall over the fields. Julie went crying, and she had to leave an apple and a piece of cake and four sweets to her sisters.

She sent her flock to their beds and went down to the well, beyond the flooded haggard, to drink cold water in the great silence. The light was bright in the hill where Foxehall stood, and she looked at it for a long time. She went to and from between well and house, sleeping only a short snatch in the dead middle of the night, until in the end she was sitting by the cold water watching the dawn come slowly up, east of the house, and the stars growing fainter. Then she saw the dome of the sky fading from the dark blueness that had met her eyes when first she stepped from her doorway, so that if she covered her eyes for a moment she would uncover them to a new day. Her brood slept in the cabin, an arm flung across a sister's breast, an arm hanging over a bed-kerb, a bare thigh white where the heavy red quilt had slipped off during the night—Joanie and Moll and Kate and Lil and the rest of them, each at her own dream, maybe of the school or the fair, or the time when she, too, would go earning in the great world.

The woman had enough thoughts to keep her there for hours, wrapped in her shawl against the cold of the morning, and for years she came there like that whenever her troubles became too heavy to carry about without sitting down to ponder on them. But life went on always, and rising wearily she moved back to the house to call the elder ones to the milking. The dew cleaned her old whitening boots, stiff with clay and dung, the drops fell on her head as she brushed past the shivering willows over the well, and as she halted for a moment by the browning hay in the shed, her mind began to stir once more, eagerly, avidly, in its habitual round and race-around, searching for ways to live and not starve, not to be turned on the side of the road by Foxehall or Judie O'Donnell from the land she had put her blood and sweat, and the blood and sweat of her dead husband, and the blood and sweat of her children, and all her people before her. She became in that second the hard-faced, hard-minded, hard-fisted, tough old woman that the shopkeepers of the town and the village knew as "Mag Keene back in the bog."

Ah, but it was growing hard to keep a grip on herself. In the dawn-light the hulk of Foxehall looked down coldly at her. Between her and that grey house was the grey ruin of the castle near the graveyard and the holy well. Her eyes sought out the dark patch of the yews in the grave-yard with deep and unconcealed desire. The donkey-ass stamped to hear her pause. The pig grunted in his sleep. She forgot the cows waiting with swollen paps to be milked until Nonie, waking of her own accord, came out into the yard. Then, with soft sounds, she called the cattle to her hands, and "hoigh-hoighed" the heifer out of her way and cursed the barking dog.

2

When Leo came downstairs late that morning, with a tongue like a carpet and a head that had petrified during the night, it was good to stand on the steps and look over the well-known fields, drinking in the cold autumn air. The clouds had parted for a space so that the stone balus-trade was warm under his palm. There, before him as always, between the fading trees, were the brown cocks and the green after-grass and Knockfierna away to the left, and the low rise—one could not call it a hill—behind Newcastle, and of all that wide country-side just one bright field held up the pillars of the sun. Beside him was his mother. He felt in his pockets a letter he had brought her from Dicky Wilcox, and handing it to her he went in to breakfast.

He found her on his return just as he had left her, but when he began to fill his pipe and talk about Limerick, she interrupted him brusquely.

"You're not going back any more to Limerick," she commanded.

"Why so, then?" he asked.

"Cousin Dicky says—what he has been saying to me year after year—that you'd never make a doctor. Not if you lived to be as old as Moses. You haven't the head for it, he says."

"I'd as soon be a vet, I think," he suggested, and lit his pipe easily.

"No more would you be a vet."

"Then what am I to be? I never wanted to be doing French and Latin and the piano. I always wanted to be a vet."

"You can't be even a vet if you haven't the grey matter, boy. You must settle down to it. You can't be fooling like this for ever. I haven't the money now to keep you at it."

"Then what am I to be? I must be something."

She drew a long, unhappy sigh.

"Your mother and your father before you—"

"Ah, that's it. A farmer? You always wanted me to be a farmer. A gentleman farmer, my aunt used always say."

"Them that hasn't it in the head," she said, "must have it in the back. I haven't the money, I tell you. I spent shoals of it on this house. You must put your shoulder to the wheel."

"I never wanted this house."

"And where would we live?"

"I could live in Limerick."

"And I would go begging to James, I suppose, that doesn't want me. Let me tell you, boy, I scraped and scraped for you. I had to mortgage four of your fields at the New Plot to buy this house. I denied your brothers and sisters to buy this house. I left James portion them off with his own money to buy this house. I turned my own again' me to buy this house."

"I never wanted the house," he persisted.

"You can sell it when you're tired of it," she said bitterly. "While we had the money," she cried, "we spent it on you. And if there's no return from it, then it's no fault but your own, you idle lastar. Wasting your years that you had your chance. If you were the stupidest gomach in the whole of Limerick you'd do more than you did. There's

Michael White's son gone for a priest, and what was his father but a herd on my father's land. There's Browne's son setting up in the Medical Hall in Rathkeale with a shop would dazzle you. And my son can't even pass an examination to begin being a doctor. Only in and out and up and down with boozy publicans in Clare Street."

"Frankie O'Donnell is my uncle," he cried. "And the President of the Tenants' League."

"What do I care if he was the President of five thousand four hundred and forty-nine Tenants' Leagues. What do I care who's ating my money this day, but to know it's gone down the sink of a pub, from me, and no return from it?"

He turned on her.

"Did I ask you to make a doctor of me? Did I ask you to send me to Limerick? To be shaming me before my fine cousins? Did I ask you to make a gentleman of me? A lot you know about being a gentleman. I never asked you for a thing but to give me my due and let me go my way. If I haven't the head—"

"You haven't enough head," she mocked, "for to hold a sup of rum-punch. Aye, and you talk of your due!"

She laughed bitterly, and went on:

"Aha! Wisha! and aha again! Your due? If you only knew the due you got and the more than due! Your due, indeed? Well," she said sarcastically, "there I leave you."

She turned and flung her hand up to the face of the house and out to where his New Plot could be seen across the river.

"There's your due. You have a fine house. The besht in the land. Furnished to the height of finery. You have a fine farm still. As good as the besht into Kerry. You got all the chances of education the heart of man could wish for. There's your due, boy, and take it and work it."

He heard the door slam behind him. For a while he stood glaring over at his fields and then he entered the house, took his gun, called up his dogs from the kitchen, and strode down across the weirs to the bogs.

Twice his setters ran to one side and pointed with iron tail, once at a black-cock, once at a quail, but as he strode on unheeding they raced barking after the vanishing game. With his gun held aloft he leaped the widest canals. He went into the heart of the marshland, where even the dogs thought best to follow in his footsteps over the narrow paths. There were one or two patches where the scythe had been at work on the thick stalks of the meadowsweet, and here the stubble crackled like wire under his foot. The air was cool about his face, tanged with autumn and the soft odours of the myrtle and the mint and the wild thyme that he crushed as he walked. At last he came to a small covert among outcroppings of wet limestone rocks, and here he crashed a way through the willows until he found a bank, where he flung himself down to smoke and take his ease. For a long time he smoked, enjoying as much as he dared, one of the loveliest autumn mornings he had ever known. Then his pipe fell from his hand and he dozed and slept, while his dogs rambled off, nosing the ground to their content. Clear and distinct, though it must have been very far away, he heard the bleat of a sheep and the fall of stones as if it were clambering over a wall.

He woke to a distant halloing, and rising he saw a girl on a rocky knoll against the sky. He recognized her for Philly Cashen, a serving-girl who, he had heard, was now at Ahill; he had rolled with her more than once in the ditches after the cross-roads dance. He went towards her.

"It's a heifer," she cried. "Did you see a heifer any part?"

"I heard a sheep crying back by the river and stones falling. I thought it was the sheep. But maybe it's the heifer gadding."

"Ah, then meah on it. I must get it, blasht it."

She descended and came stepping on her bare feet towards him, light and quick as a running goat.

"I heard you were back," she shouted, as she leaped.

"You heard quick," he said.

"Ah!" she scoffed. "We hears things."

She came up to him, panting.

"Though I suppose you won't talk to us at all, now that you have the Big House. And maybe I shouldn't be talking to you like this either?" she mocked.

And not being quite sure of herself she cocked her head proudly at him, as much as to say, "A lot I care!"

"Yerrah, stop that, Phil!" he cried, and took her by the waist, so that she wriggled away from him with her mouth agape in the loose smile of country courtship. With a laugh of delight he chased after her and caught her again.

"There's no high notions about me," he said.

"Ah, but you're the great man of the place entirely now," she scoffed, leaning back from him.

"I am, and so is Kelly," he said.

"That was a great speech I heard you gave last night," she taunted, still in the crook of his arm.

"Blast yeh!" he cried, and squeezing her tightly, kissed her with wet lips.

"The divil take you what cheek you have!" she cried back, wiping her mouth. "Do you think my face is a grazing ground for every donkey in the land?"

"Don't be so cross with me," he said, "for I'm in no humour for it."

"Yerrah, what's wrong with you?"

"Amn't I to stay here for the rest of my days? I'm not to be a doctor after all."

"Yeh, why so?"

"Because I haven't the brains."

"Oh, jay! Then what will you do, Leo?"

"I'm a farmer from this day," he said miserably.

"And what will you be farming? Foxehall?"

"Foxehall? I don't own a foot of Foxehall but them five fields there west of the river. But what matter—it's the best of land, a king of land, and I'll make a go of it."

He laughed suddenly, throwing his troubles from him.

"The divil a care I care," he cried. "I'll be seeing all the more of ye."

He pulled her to him and kissed her again. There was no mistaking that his blood was up, and this time she did not pretend anger.

"Come and let me see, are you a pillar of salt?" he cried. He tumbled her suddenly on the grass, while she implored him to let her go, to let her go, Leo, and find the heifer, for Mag would be waiting for her, Leo, Leo, be quiet, to be quiet. Not now, not now . . . He held her close. He quoted the *Limerick Dairyman* to her, and she surrendered and laughed at it.

" 'To animate the crayture, sure, he laid her on the primrose bank.' Isn't that it, Philly?"

"You divil!" she whispered.

They heard the dogs splashing among the reeds beside them, and in the distance stones fell with a strange gurgling sound from a wall.

He stumbled back over the fields to Foxehall under the moon, as drunk as a lord. His mother and the cook carried him to bed, his long legs dangling out of the crook of their elbows, his head lolling, Julie tramping before them up the stairs with the candle blowing.

It was two weeks before he could be got to think about his land, but when he did he set about selling the hay with vigour. He returned, after being out three days with his horse, and laid a bundle of notes on the table before his mother. She counted them slowly, while he watched her with anxious eyes. Finding he had made a good bargain she nodded her head, and tied them up in a purse she wore about her neck.

"Who did you sell them to?" she asked.

He went through the list of buyers, but for the life of him he could not remember the last one. She looked at him and rose from the table.

"It's well he paid you," she said.

He had been so proud of making a good bargain with the hay that her word and look annoyed him. All the day he kept trying to recall the last buyer, but it was not until he was clambering into bed that it suddenly flashed on his mind. At once he climbed out again, and with a stub of chalk wrote the name on the back of the window shutter. Then he returned to bed and fell asleep. In the morning he met his mother at breakfast and faced her triumphantly.

"That last buyer!" he said. "I remembered him after you went out yesterday. You know, if it was to save my life I couldn't recall it. It was funny, you know!"

"Who is it?" she asked.

"Yerrah, that man there east—"

He had forgotten again. She laughed outright at him, and in a rage he ran upstairs to his room to read the name on the shutter. Racing down he burst out with it.

"It's Jim Mullins of Cappagh."

"Yerrah! Where did you find it since?"

"I wrote it on the shutter for fear I'd forget it."

His mother could not restain herself, and even little Julie Keene had to join in her mockery at him. They laughed all the more because he grew red with fury, and flung down his knife, and threatened to go out of the house without a breakfast if they didn't stop. They could not stop. He raced from them to Ahill for a cup of tea and a cut of dried bread.

Julie bell-rang the story about Ahill, and from Ahill it went all over the parish and out to Newcastle and Rathkeale, until it became a legend from one end of Limerick to the other. He might be walking the road and a farmer would greet him from a cart, and then turn to shout after him:

"Have you me up on the shutter yet, Leo?"

To this day you might hear it spoken without understanding, as the people speak of Jack Wall's shirt and Bradley's gander, long after they have forgotten the story. "Mark that down, now," they say, "like Donnel and the shutter long ago."

The upshot of it all was that he would not do a hand's turn on the farm for months after, telling his mother that he always knew he had no head for farming.

"No!" she mocked. "Nor a head for anything else either. It's a nice how-d'ye-do for my son to be a laughing-stock from here to Magherafelt."

So another quarrel began, and he took to the bogs and his gun and the pubs in revenge. In her chagrin she blamed it all on Julie Keene, and packed her off home to her mother, and as a result turned the rent-screw even tighter still.

3

All that winter Leo kept going and coming between Foxehall and Ahill. He saw a great deal of Mag and her brood, and of the old sooty chimney-corner, and of Philly Cashen. Nicholas had built himself a herdsman's hut with sods and clay and thatch near the river-side, and here, too, he often went. Sometimes an animal might be sick or a cow calving, and Philly would take turns with Nicholas to stay in the hut with it, for between Mag and the children and the dog and the hens there was no room in the cabin. At all hours

Leo would go down to keep Philly company. It was a quiet place for the pair of them.

By the spring Mag noticed her condition and charged her. There was a dreadful scene when she mentioned Leo Donnel's name.

"You throllop!" cried Nicholas. "You're belying the boy."

Philly opened her mouth as wide as a horse.

"Aw," she cried. "I'm not belying him. Sure he's known from one end of the parish to the other. But it's idle for you to stand up for him when there's no wan else will defend the blackguard after you."

Nicholas almost struck her.

"I'll crewsht the face of you if you say a word again' the poor boy."

"Be aisy, Nicholas," warned Mag. "There should be no such talk before the childer. Come out here," she beckoned to Philly.

The three of them went into the stable, with a dim lantern to give them light.

"Every girl tries to find a well-off father when she's in trouble," said Mag quietly.

"I don't," wept Philly. "If I did wouldn't I say it was Sir John Philpot up in Beaconsfield, or Colonel Bickley over at Ashville. There's more childer than mine fathered on them. What are the two of them doing from year's end to year's end, but playing into one another's hand filling their lodges with their gets? I say the true name of Leo Donnel, and let him deny it. And he's not rich or well-off. Why should I blame my misfortune on him, but for that it's his fault."

"It's your own fault," persisted Nicholas.

"Arrah, have sense, man," retorted Philly. "You're protecting a dandy man."

Just then steps sounded on the flags outside. It was Leo

sent after them by the children, when he came visiting the house.

"Is it a calf that's coming?" he cried, stooping his head eagerly to enter the stable.

They looked at him in silence.

"What's this? What's it all about?"

"Let him deny it now!" said Philly, facing up to him and them. "Now let him give me the lie."

He was prepared for this, however—too well prepared.

"Maybe it's charging me the slut is," he cried. "Nicholas! Surely to God you don't believe that wan?"

Nicholas collapsed. He thrust his way out into the dark.

"How did you know," Mag went to the bother of saying, "what we was talking about?"

"The childer told me," he lied. Mag turned away. "Sure that girl would court a haggard of sparrows. That wan would run a mile after a scarecrow if it only had the britches on it. Is it charging me you are?" he cried in amazement at Philly.

"Oh, no!" mocked the girl. "Not at all!"

The lantern sank down the length of Mag's drooping hand. It cast its light on her blue apron and Philly's red petticoat. It threw ugly shadows into Leo's face.

"Go out, girl!" she said.

"Where'll I go to?" asked Philly.

"Go wherever you like," said Mag. "I can't have you here, where there's ten little childer to be thought about. Go away from me, and don't let me see you ever again."

The girl broke down and began to weep. Leo stood at the door looking at the night-sky.

"I have no place to turn," she wept. "Who would take me in? I have no place to go. Can I be walking the fields all night?"

"You can go to Nicholas's house."

But when she had packed her few rags of clothes Nicholas would not have her go to his hut. He told her she could find a barn or a stable to sleep in. Through the dark she wandered down the long boreen from Ahill, weeping to herself, until a man stepped out from the hedges and thrust a ball of notes and silver into her fist.

"Walk into the poorhouse in Rathkeale," he said.

It was not until by the light of the moon she saw his long legs raising a mist over the fields that she recognized the father of her child.

She went then to Browne's farm-house; but he knew her of old, and turned her from the door. She went back to Nicholas's hut, but it was locked, and she had to leave it in the end. In a rage then she turned her steps to Foxehall. There Leo had locked the doors and turned loose the dogs. His mother heard their fierce barking, however, and knew by his face that there was something afoot. She went to the door and called the dogs to heel, and saw, down the avenue, cowering against a beech tree, the figure of a woman. She went to it and saw it was Philly, and after half an hour of low, bitter argument between them, Leo saw her lead the girl to the door. He met them both there, standing at the top of the steps, and told her that if she brought in that girl—believing her against him—he would not stay in the house.

"You can do whatever you wish, boy," said Judith. "I am going to give the girl a bed until the morning. I am going to Bawnrea myself, and I will never come back from it."

She led Philly in, and locked her into a room for the night. She saw Leo go; afterwards she heard he had slept at the pub. Then she went herself back to James. They made up the old settle where her daughters used to sleep, and there she lay down. She lay there all night, watching, on the raftered ceiling, the last flames of the hearth, her mind so rancid that she was still awake when the dawn in the kitchen lit the falling mist.

4

For several years that settle-bed was kept ready for her. She came to it without warning and went from it without warning. For she both had to make up her quarrel with Leo, and when a new one broke out have somewhere to go from him. Between the quarrels there were many joyful days when she and he would be seen again, walking his fields, arm in arm, a tall, soft-lipped young man and a bent, white-haired old woman, their heads bent close together for secrecy, his curls tossed by the wind and her hair blown in thin ribs from her starched and ironed cap. Then James would see her coming over the fields, and he would mutter:

"Ha! They're at it again. The foolish set of them."

And she had cause in plenty to quarrel. Year after year his farm went in grass, and the land gave such heavy hay that he lived easily on the sale of it. He would not even save the hay, but sold it standing. In the winter and spring he fattened a few cattle. He had sheep on Knockfierna, and he made a few pounds by their wool. But work he would not. He had a cook and a man-servant, who had to be paid dearly to stay with him. Once he kicked the man-servant out of his bedroom because he had failed to polish the soles of his boots. On another occasion, shortly after, when the same servant was waiting on him at table, the pudding so displeased him—he was after a bout at the pub—that he flung it into the fire, and when the servant went to gather it up, he laughed at him and cried out:

"Aye! Scrape it up. It'll make a plaster for your broken behind."

The poor man told the story in bitterness to the village, but the village, accustomed to Donnel's mad pranks, only laughed at him, and the name Broken Bottom clung to the fellow and remained in his family for generations.

Several times the priest came to talk to him, for before he was twenty-six it was abroad that Philly Cashen was not the only girl he had laid a bad hand on. But if he saw the priest's dark coat down the avenue he would dodge out at the back of the house and race from him, like a bold school-boy, over the fields. If he met the priest coming towards him on the road, he would turn his horse and gallop from him. Finally, it was in the little village of Knockaderry that the priest raced out suddenly from a cabin and held him before the eyes of the women, leaning like ships' prows over their half-doors. He merely hung his head sullenly, and traced figures in the dust with his riding whip.

"And Minnie Mulligan, too"—the figureheads heard the priest thunder—"says she had a child by you."

"Does she?" replied Donnel. "She might," he added. "She's bad enough."

The priest shook him as if he were shaking an empty bag to see if there was anything at all in it. All he shook out of him was a growling, "Yes, Father," or "No, Father."

In the end the priest threw him from him in disgust, and "read" him from the altar at Mass on the following Sunday. He was not there, however. To recover his dignity after that shaking and questioning, he had gone straight up to Frewen's and drunk himself into a swagger. But as he rolled down the hill, lashing at the drooping berries on the side of the road and chasing after the gadding donkeys like a wild fellow, he saw the fine sturdy lassie who had served him in the kitchen of the pub pass him by on a cart, and he real-ized suddenly that it was Julie Keene.

That Sunday the priest "read" him he went out for a day's quiet fly-fishing to soothe his pride. Then he pomaded his curls, put on a new cravat, and made up the hill for Frewen's. This time the women drew back into the shadows as he passed, and then peeped after him as he entered the pub. It was old Frewen who met him, however, and warned by the priest not to allow such a ruffian inside his pub, compromised by receiving him in the snuggery. There Mrs. Frewen served him his drinks, and talked at him for hours about his aunts and his grandfather and all his people. As he went out, the glimpse he got of Julie's dark eyes in the shop and the sound of her bell-like laughter only told him what he had been missing all the night and overlooking all the time he was going-and-coming to Ahill after Philly Cashen.

He began to wait for her on the short-cuts to her home, for since the affair of Philly he had not dared enter the house. At last he met her, and for an hour she dallied with him and he went home well pleased. The following day, after watching until Nicholas should leave Ahill, he went in to Mag and explained to her that he needed a new servant at Foxehall, and wouldn't her daughter Julie do? She listened to him civilly, and when he was done she thanked him. She even prayed God might bless him for the kindness of his thought.

"Ah, but sure, Leo," she said, "I always liked you. I always knew there was great goodness in you. And your mother is a good and kind woman to have Julie back after the little upset about yourself and the shutter."

Not entirely comfortable about this speech he bade her good night, and went away with her blessings in his ears.

She closed the door after him and looked after him through the loophole window.

"And does that cripple think," she cried to her children, "that I'd send my little girl into his house again. The cesspit! The dunghill! The walking divil! My little girsha to go into that house again, that has the blood squeezed out of me and mine, and laid my poor man in the grave with slavery? The shly eel! The long pillar!"

All day she kept muttering at him, and when Julie ran in before dark, she at once seized her and dragged her on the floor. Poor Julie, thinking it was known that she had stopped to talk to him, stuttered out her defences, only to find her mother horrified the more by what her child told her. Mag shook her as if she wanted to hear her bones rattle, and shook her again until she had every word of the truth out of her. Then she grew quiet, and taking her cloak went slowly down the boreen and along the road to Bawnrea where Judith was living at the time.

As she entered the door Judith was knitting in the corner between the table and the window. She rose and settled a chair for her visitor. She still thought of Mag as her tenant, but after glancing at her face this time her eyes darkened and became troubled. She returned to her knitting, and a silence fell between them.

"I understand," said Mag, "that you were thinking of having Julie back in Foxehall?"

Judith shot one glance across the fire.

"Ah?" she said. "Is she wanting to come back to Foxehall?"

"It's for me," said Mag, looking into the depths of the fire, "it's for me to say that."

"And what do you say?" asked Judith, knitting rapidly.

"It's Leo was asking her to go there," said Mag, her breath coming heavily. "Do you think Julie would prosper there?"

Judith's needles clicked ceaselessly. Then she stopped suddenly and looked up at Mag, and Mag looked across at her—four stony eyes in two hard, stony faces.

"Foxehall is a fine place, thank God," said Judith.

"Supposing she did go there," said Mag, "would you have an eye to her?"

Again they looked at one another. Nobody could have told by those looks but that they were good friends, and their children the best of friends.

"Let me put on the kettle for you," said Judith, rising. "A cup of tea after a walk is a great thing."

"Still, as I say," said Mag again, "you would look after her, wouldn't you?"

"Yerrah, nonsense, woman!" cried Judith, in a hearty voice. "What looking after she wants? Is it a bag of salt the girl is? She'll look after herself. She's a fine girl now, too. When will she be going?"

Mag threw her such a strange look that she halted in the middle of the floor, her hands—one clutching the ear of the teapot—on her hips, her belly stuck out, and her mouth puckered up as if it were tied inside with a running string.

"Glory be to God," she cried, in a pretence of sudden rage, "do you think there is need for me to be looking after your child? What's wrong with the child? Or is it something you would say is wrong with my son's house in Foxehall?"

Mag rose before her, a pillar of black, her face on one side warmed by the fire, lit on the other by the evening sun through the window.

"Let me tell you this," cried Judith, in her roundest, harshest voice, as if she were calling the cattle home, "let me tell you that Foxehall is the home of gentle people, and was the home of gentle people for long before you or your line came hither from beyant the Shannon. And my son Leo is a gentleman, and he have the breeding of a gentleman, and he have the education of a gentleman. He's fit to walk the world and talk to the highest in the land. He have the height of education. He's a credit to me. I spared no penny on him. Remember that, if you please."

Mag replied in a low, quiet tone.

"I said no word against Leo. And I said no word against Foxehall. You misunderstand me."

"I do not misunderstand you."

Swiftly her manner changed.

"Yerrah, sit down there, Mag Keene," she said cheerfully, "and have a cup of tea and shtop your blather."

She leaned over the teapot to pour a handful of tea into it from the caddy on the hob.

"What I said," Mag went on gently, "was that Leo wants my Julie to go to Foxehall. It will be a nice home for her."

Judith's hand poised over the teapot. She did not turn. She did not move.

"She'll make a good daughter-in-law for you," said Mag.

Judith straightened her back and looked into Mag's face.

"What was that you said?" she asked, almost in a whisper.

"I said that my Julie will make a good daughter-in-law for you."

The kettle spurted on the fire. Neither of them heeded it. Mag's breath was coming heavier than ever, but she looked straight at Judith out of the dark hood of her cowl.

"She will not," said Judith.

"Well," said Mag, "if you say it, maybe she won't. But" —she ground out the words like grain between the mill-stones of her teeth—"it's the only way my daughter will enter beneath the rotten roof of Foxehall. And," she went on, grinding out each slow word, "if any harm comes to my girsha, inside of Foxehall or outside of Foxehall, there's somebody will leave a mark on Leo Donnel he will remember to his dying day."

"Psha!" scoffed Judith. "Is it threatening Nicholas on us, you are?"

Mag went slowly to the door, shutting out the fields and the faint sun. There she turned and took a few steps back to Judith.

"If my own hands," she said, and stretched out her ten

bony, wrinkled fingers, "have to leave a mark on that white gullet—"

Her hands shook and her voice broke in a sob. Then she turned and went out. Slowly Judith replaced the teapot and let the tea drain out of her palm into the caddy.

A week later Judith O'Donnell found a place for Julie in a pub at Ballingarry—ten miles east along the ridge of far hills. When she met Mag at the chapel gate the following Sunday the two women looked at one another and nodded their heads.

"A grand day, thank God!" said Mag.

"A fine day, thank God!" said Judith, and passed in.

5

So went his years between twenty and thirty, those years when most men learn by experience, hoping in the ten that follow to learn by thought. But he seemed unlikely to learn in either way, or in any way at all, until at last in the spring of 'sixty-seven, a soft-dripping, blackbird singing, odorous spring, the thunderbolt fell on him.

One heavy Sunday after a day with the East Limerick drag he came ambling slowly back from this side of Croom, up through the little village of Knockaderry. His horse's hoofs sucked the mud at every step, and he, too, was tired and cold. Without the reins the nag drew in beneath the dripping rose garland of Frewen's door and, stooping, Donnel looked through the moist fanlight. To his surprise there was not a soul in the shop, but through the spyhole from the kitchen beyond a bright chink of light fell on the unwashed glasses on the leaded counter. It took a great deal of knocking before Frewen came out to him, and when he did, Donnel thought he saw a strange, frightened look in the publican's eyes. And when he had entered and was making for the fire in the kitchen, Frewen halted him in silence, and lighting a candle on the counter gave him his whisky in the cold snug.

"Oh! But I'll go in to the fire," said Donnel.

"No, Mister Donnel," lisped the publican. "I have vithitors with me."

"Psha!" grumbled Leo, trying to push past him, "I won't ate them."

But the fat publican stood in his way, refusing to budge, and growing angry when the other tried to thrust him aside. At last, in high ill-humour, he had to sit alone in the uncomfortable snug with his drink and the single candle, staring out at the low evening star above the farther valley and the clouds passing dark beneath it. Then when Frewen had left him he began to cock his ear to the sounds in the kitchen, and, rising, he stole to the end of the counter and peered in by the side of the little spy-window at the "visitors." He knew every man sitting before the fire—farmers' sons from about the place, and Nicholas among them—but he did not know the little burly man with his rump to the fire, a black stump of pipe between his teeth as he talked in a high voice to the men circled about him. Well he and all Ireland knew him after—James Stephens the Fenian. At every word his voice rose as if he were making or repeating a speech.

"I'd say," said the little man, "that there were twenty thousand men that day marching out to Glasnevin. That's the cemetery outside of Dublin—Dan O'Connell is buried there. Four after four—twenty thousand men—and they were so long in coming that the night fell on us while we waited at the grave, and they were given torches to light as they crowded in. If you saw them, as I saw them," he went on in his deep, hoarse voice, "with their faces lifted eager to hear me in the flaring lights, circle upon circle of them, climbing on the headstones and the crosses, staring up at

me so that you would think the stones themselves had eyes
and ears for what we had to say of Terence Bellew Mac-
Manus—"

As he spoke in the silence of the soft spring night that
lay about the little house, mile upon mile of silent country-
side, the firelight flickered on the faces raised to him.
Vibrating from throat to toes with hate and triumph and
pride, he repeated, his teeth still clenched on his pipe, what
he had said that night of the dead MacManus, and what, he
probably felt, would one day be said also of him. Donnel's
face was pressed to the glass to hear.

"And I said to them," he flung out, "I said to them: 'A
little while ago this man, whose body we are about to lay
in the earth, lay dying beside the waters of the Pacific. He
was wasted by disease and broken by despair. He was
doomed from the day he left Ireland in a convict ship to
die an exile's death. And yet, though all his thoughts were
of Ireland, year after year of Ireland, he threw back with
scorn every word of intercession made on his behalf. Here,'
said I, 'we have raised him from the grave with feelings
such as no king has ever inspired and never could command. We have borne him over a continent and two seas.
We have restored his body to the mother that made him.
Tonight, look out over his grave at that motherland. Our
people are melting away. Our homesteads levelled to the
ground, our enemies gloating at our ruin. Even a cardinal
has said that the famine was a hidden blessing, because it
scattered our people to carry the faith to the ends of the
earth!' "

At this the speaker took out his pipe and laughed with
such hate and bitterness that Donnel drew back his face
into the darkness of the shop.

"A blessing?" snarled the man by the fire. "A few months
before he died Terence MacManus wrote to me that the
city of San Francisco was a pure city until the Irish work-

houses began to pour into it the unfortunate Irish girls
with which they teemed. And that is what our cardinal calls
spreading the faith? Well may Kickham call this thing a
holocaust to hell, when Irish girls sell themselves in America to buy bread. But what help," he thundered at them,
"have we ever had from the priests of the Church? They
stood by O'Connell against the Young Irelanders. They
stood by Keogh and Sadlier against Gavan Duffy. They
stand against this dead Fenian whom you have borne
through the streets of Dublin under their averted eyes."

The lisping publican, carried away completely, forgot all
about Donnel, and Donnel forgot everything as he listened
to the envenomed passion of this man, and stared at him
through the heat-dimmed glass. He had always disliked the
priests; now he could hate them. Those pubs of Irishtown
had set in him, year after year, a seed of interest in his
people and his country; at last it burst through him like a
well. For it is not the sudden storm that slants the sideward tree but firm winds blow often and in the end
prevail.

Suddenly the speaker pointed with outstretched hand
straight at him, and, as the men turned in fright, Donnel
strode into the kitchen.

"Is this the visitor I wasn't to see?" he asked Frewen.

Then to the stranger who was almost a foot below him:

"Stay at my house for the night," he said.

The other looked him up and down. Then he looked at
the publican inquiringly. Frewen shook his head.

"Why should I?" he asked.

"I'd like to have a talk with you," swaggered Donnel.

"Where do you live?" asked the stranger.

"Foxehall," said Donnel. "I am Leo Foxe-Donnel."

"I heard of you. Frankie O'Donnell spoke of you to me."

"He's my uncle. Nicholas O'Donnell there is my uncle,
though he won't know me at all now, I suppose."

The small dark man looked at him for a long while. Then he smiled slowly.

"I'll come with you," he said.

The stranger stayed that night at Foxehall and the following day he passed on; but wherever he went he left behind him a slow fuse that blazed in the south a month later and set the heart and mind of the foolish Leo crackling like a fiery furze. Once more he was to be seen with Nicholas at the cross after dark, or in the forge, where, behind the bolted door, they beat out pikeheads in a little penthouse made of the stones of the shattered castle above their heads; they talked in low voices there while the night fell heavily and the dark was soaking with its dew the bog between the castle and the sweeping road, softening the dung-hardened floor of the roofless shell beneath whose bulk they hid, moistening the cotton on the rush-stalks and the faint-blue bog-flower with its barely pulsing scent. They blew the dull heap of ashes to a bursting, spark-mad glow, and late into the dawn they hammered at the old cart-springs that were to become pikes. A yellow pot of black porter sustained them while they worked, heated in body and flaming in mind, in that confined smithy. Outside they might hear the trot of a sidecar or the rattle of a cart returning late to Knockaderry, and, after ceasing until it passed from hearing, begin again to hammer and rasp and file until their eyes were closed with the great heat and the desire for sleep. Or, if there was no work to be done in the forge, they clustered and talked excitedly, the same eager group, in the herdsman's hovel hidden by the mist rising from the Deel, or about the fire in the drawing-room at Foxehall, with its daguerreotypes on the mantel, its epaulettes and crossed swords over each door, and its pianino in the far corner that would never play the softness of *Berenice* again.

From that to April they talked and worked. And then

one wet, blowing, bitter-cold night he and Nicholas led a handful of serving-men and labouring boys up the furzy sides of Knockfierna against the police-hut at Ballingarry. They divided their small band in two, Nicholas approaching the hut from the west, Donnel scrambling about the lower base of furzy Knockfierna to the east. After the climb his men were so cold and tired that they craved a drink before the attack. Willingly, Donnel knocked up a tavern-keeper at the end of the village, and in the barn behind his house they drank jorum after jorum of whisky, so excited that he did not see that the serving-girl was Julie Keene. Since she came to Ballingarry she had been "walking" with a peeler, and in terror for the safety of her man she rushed off to tell him. Without a thought, she slipped away to the police-hut, and in five minutes the door of the barn was burst in, with a sergeant at the head of his men shouting that every man there was under arrest. At once Donnel fired his pistol into the black mass at the door, wounding one. Then flinging himself at them he fought like a tiger, with six black-coats on top of him. His fellows escaped in the mêlée, but he was marched, his chin and nose streaming with blood, to the hut. There Nicholas was blazing away like a fool and calling on the unanswering walls to surrender. The police took them and him in the rear with ball-shot, and the farming boys broke and pelted for their lives down the hill-fields into the dark. Nicholas was found later, behind a ditch, his throat torn by a gunshot wound and almost dead from loss of blood.

They took them, handcuffed to each other, out along the old familiar road to Limerick; from there to Richmond Prison; after months of trial and retrial, across to Millbank, from Millbank to Dartmoor, lastly to Portland. There, for fifteen years, they promised to tame the Irish wildness from the blood of the pair of them.

Yet it was not any of the ordinary humiliations that broke Donnel's spirit—not the terror of judges and juries and staring courts, warders and policemen, and armed detectives chained to him—"Left wrist. Right wrist—you bloody Fenian!"—not the strippings and washings and searchings and threats, not even the blows; not starvation itself, although there were times when he joined with the convicts scrambling to pick candle-butts from the ordure heaps in order to wipe and eat them. For his first six months they left him by himself in a cell, and it was the silent hours that broke him. He often recounted it afterwards to his wife, how he had to sit and look at the barred sky and the puff-clouds of spring where the winds of the Channel blew them slowly past his window far out to sea. "Oh!" he would say, with scalding tears and twisted mouth, "but prison can break a proud heart!" He thought of days spent hunting on cloud-topped Knockaderry, and the little furzy hills of barely rolling Limerick, and thought that worst thought of all for a prisoner, how for fifteen long years he was blotted out of existence. So he began to live solely in the past. When the cold October rain came, dripping from the upper window-ledge, he remembered how he hunted hares of a day when the fallen leaves were pasted to the wet road and the drops fell from the sickled chestnut boughs. The summer sun sank in the track of the moon and the miracle of the evening star shone between them in the pure white air, and he wept at it because he had told the hour many a time by the moon grown too heavy to drag herself along. Or it was the chill wintry dawn-light waking him to prison labour, but first reminding him how he had watched the cattle being driven from the byre with a lantern in the herdsman's hand, and he had turned from its yellow flame to see the east greying from its blue to a new day. On such occasions he would insult the warders, and they would insult him; and he would strike them, and they would fall on him; and while he tore and bit at them they banged his head on the floor, and dragged him away to a low cell and tied him up there with buckles and straps, and he cursed at them and cursed at himself and wept with rage and misery. With mouldy bread and stale water they tamed him. They got him so that when they sneered at him he knew better than to sneer back, for if he as much as looked crooked at them they tore the clothes from him and searched him in the most disgusting way. The blood would rush to his head, and his eyes diffuse, and his breath fail him, and yet he would not reply to their taunts. But it was the silence of the dammed volcano, the silence of a tide swelling and swelling against the levee. They knew, but they did not care. There were fifteen years to go.

"Ah! I would say to myself"—he used to confess after—"wouldn't it be well and well now to be edging along the crumbling banks of the Deel under the sifted light of a watery, morning sky; to be walking with myself through a solid curtain of moist light to where I knew the ash and the willow hung over the wet islands of gravel."

Free as the swallow, fishing and lying at his ease, smoking and dreaming to himself until the summer evening turned to rain, and then back with him to Ahill or the old forge, listening out of the sooty chimney-corner to the drip-drip of the eaves. He grew to know how true it was what old Theo used sometimes to quote him from Bœthius: *Fuisse felicem et non esse, omnium est infelicissimum genus;* to have been happy at one time and then to be unhappy after, isn't that the greatest unhappiness in the whole world?

And yet why should he have any love for that place, or for the people of it—dead, lazy, lifeless wretches, as he called them. But he would chuckle like a madman to himself at that; remember that it was not love for them, but that little

burly fury in the pub at Knockaderry that drove him to what
he did. Aye! First it was his mother, forcing him to what he
had no wish for, then it was his aunts, then came Frankie
O'Donnell, with his smooth tongue, sending Stephens on
his track; and then Stephens himself who, so a warder
taunted him one night, had dodged jail like a hare, and was
now drinking in the pubs of Paris. While he—here he was,
in a British jail, in England, in Portland, for the best fifteen years of his life, and for all his imprisoned youth he
would have to try to keep his body and his mind and his
heart from rotting, for the beggarly pleasures of a premature old age.

He received letters now and again from Foxehall, letters
in which she reproached him, blamed him, praised him,
flattered him, upbraided him, taunted him, loved him. He
never realized what it cost her to hand in those oddly addressed envelopes over the counter of the little post office
at Knockaderry. He read them over and over, although
they never told him more than that the crops were promising, that his horse was getting fat, that his sister had another
son, that such and such weather had come and gone over the
great plain of the Deel. She never told how many times she
had gone before his trial to Mag Keene in the dark of the
summer fields to try to confer with her about closing Julie's
mouth, how Mag had received her with a hard pride—
secretly ashamed of Julie, and tormented at the thought of
Nicholas—and how after every visit she had returned head-
bowed to the empty house, her long cloak sweeping the dew
from the grass. She did not tell him that James had eyes for
nothing but the New Plot, hoping that it would fall to
rankness with the years and he would buy it for a song.

Then one winter the letters stopped. He got none for
weeks. He got none for months. He felt as a man must feel
who wakes to find himself marooned on a piece of rock in

the middle of a shoreless sea. One day he found himself near Nicholas in the hemp shed, and he whispered:

"My mother?"

Nicholas glanced as near him as he dared, and whispered, "I'm sorry."

Again Donnel whispered, "My mother?"

Out of the corner of his jaw Nicholas dared a louder whisper, "I'm sorry."

Donnel muttered, "My mother!"

Nicholas said, "God pity her."

Donnel stood up and stared at Nicholas, and said aloud, "What are you saying?"

Down the shed a great brown-bearded warder roared at them:

"Silence there!"

Leo gripped Nicholas by the shoulders, and in a voice of agony he cried out:

"My mother? My mother, Nicholas? My mother?"

The warder rushed on them, but was thrust back by a long whirling arm. Again and again and again that one word rang through the shed while Nicholas stood silent and stupid, not realizing that there was nobody to tell him the news. The convicts ranged along the benches under the pale sunlight falling through the roof looked at them without interest. Four warders fell on him and dragged him to the cells.

He did not see Nicholas again; a change of government brought an amnesty to most of the Fenian prisoners in British jails, but he was thought too dangerous to be released. He remained in Portland for ten years, and from the day of his mother's death he might as well have been in a mine for all he ever heard of the world he had left. He became so, that when the warders would see him pausing in his work and staring vacantly before him, in pity they would pretend not to notice him, winking at one another, with a shake of the head, as much as to say, "Poor devil! He's well christened 'Mad Paddy from Ireland.'"

6

Sometimes, as dreamers do, he would drug his mind by wondering what the people of the plain of the Deel thought of him now—what they said about him in Frewen's or in Browne's; whether in the pub in Clare Street Frankie O'Donnell ever spoke to the Tenants' League about the man who was suffering for the cause in Portland; or whether James ever shook his head pityingly over him by the fire in Bawnrea. Sometimes Frankie did, indeed, talk about him in a frightened whisper over the counter to Old Tom Mulcaire; or in the Knockaderry pub they might, with a cautious glance about them, boast of how they went with him to attack the police hut, though they would always end by cursing him for a wild fellow that nearly got them all into trouble. But James never thought of him. His back was bent with troubles of his own.

For ten years, while his brother was frittering away his boyhood and early youth, he had worked as he had never before worked to get rid of that mortgage on his farm. Every fair day you might see him halting his ass-cart outside the bank in Rathkeale, his face hard and sour, shouldering his way without a by-your-leave up the steps and in through the crush of dealers and jobbers until he had his elbows on the counter.

"I want to see Mister Barlow," he would say.

There might be six people before him. But it was all one to him. And if the clerk did not attend to him, he would stretch forward his ash-plant and rap him impatiently on the arm, and nod his head and wink with another cry of:

"I want to see Mister Barlow, young fellow."

"He's busy," the clerk would say, and if he were a new man, who had not been told about James O'Donnell, he might say it crossly and haughtily. O'Donnell would grip his teeth together—a face on him just like his father used to have when he wielded the whip over his sons—and say:

"Cock of the walk, do as you're bid."

"I tell you, he's busy," the greenhorn would say again, getting red in the face because the rest of the clerks were tittering at him.

"Busy! With your four eyes, you shkinny lump. And your backside falling out of you with the hashte that's on you. Busy? Wisha, where did you come from at all? Busy? I suppose you didn't have time to ate your brekusht this morning? Or wipe your little shnoteen of a nose? Busy? My jacadandy. You're so busy that you can't attend to your business. Will you tell Mister Barlow that James O'Donnell wants to see him?"

He would shove his body and all his nose and face forward under the scarlet face of the new clerk.

"Or," he would snarl, "will I tell him how busy *you* are? Will I? My little calf from the city?"

For half an hour he would be inside with the manager, and then out with him again, bruising his way through the throng to his cart. There one or other of his sisters would be waiting for him; they, like him, hard-faced, though not yet old. They did not need to urge him to his work; urge him to get rid of them by portioning them off in marriage. He muttered at them almost hourly under his breath, knowing that when the ten years were up and his farm clear, he would merely have thrown off one chain to take up another. For during those four or five years before his brother in Foxehall went, as he said, "wild against the law," one by one he was sending out his line of sisters, each with such a miserly portion that it merely flung her from one slavery into another—for herself and her children, now, as before for herself and his sisters. The only time in all those years that he had been known to laugh, was when he heard of Leo's arrest. Then he threw up his head, and clicked his finger before his eyes and gave one wild guffaw. But, the second after, his face was serious again. He was standing at the door of his cabin scratching his chin with his finger, and picking at the point of his long nose, and biting his nails, as he looked long and peeringly across at Foxehall on its hill.

From that on he was for ever nosing about the fields of the New Plot after dusk, more and more ready, his mother found, to plough and reap it—though always at a consideration, for he was grown hard as a miser. The year after she died he was turned fifty, and had got free of all his sisters. No barrier remaining between himself and marriage but his brother Phil. The girl of the Frewens whom he had embraced in the graveyard that evening of his father's burial was still waiting for him, though she was now forty, and the fiddle-strings had begun to appear on her neck, and her legs were growing thin and her body large. And yet he would not give Phil his money; or marry his woman. Phil did not matter so much; he was growing into a fat, cheery-faced man, with a hearty laugh and a big hand out after the girls. And for the present he was content to wait—too content, James found him.

"The end of you," he warned his younger brother one night as they sat alone before the empty hearth at Bawnrea, "is that one of them lassies will put her comether on you. And then you'll be running to me for your twenty pounds, I suppose?"

Phil laughed good-humouredly.

"Twenty pounds, if you please?" he said, and held out his hand. "Twenty for a first instalment, you mean?" he said less pleasantly.

"Maybe," scoffed James, "you'll be expecting fifty sovereigns from me?"

"When I want my money," said Phil, "I'll demand it. And it won't be fifty pounds I'll demand, either."

"I'm glad of that," said James, deliberately misunderstanding him. "But why should we talk of such things? You've time in lashings to spare before you think of marriage."

"Do you say so, now?" smiled his brother to torment him. "How old am I?"

"You're sixteen years younger than me, and I'm not married yet," snarled James.

Phil threw a sod of turf on the fire. James kicked it off angrily.

"Is it roasting us you want to be?"

Phil replaced the sod. James spat on it, as if he would prevent it from burning.

"What I think," he said slowly, "we ought to do with our money is for to buy more land with it."

Phil looked at him.

"With twenty pounds?" he asked maliciously, and James squirmed with discomfort at his brother's cunning.

"Arrah, what nonsense!" he cried. "Do you think I'm saying to buy the land?"

"Where else would you get land?"

"Where, but where my father got the New Plot?" suggested James more calmly.

Phil looked at him again, and then he leaned back.

"I'll sign no mortgage on this farm," he warned.

"Ah, there you are. I suppose you want to be throwing your few shillings into the lap of one of them slipeens that do be running and racing the road after the cross dance. A man of your years, you ought to be ashamed of yourself."

"Ha! A minute ago I wasn't old enough to be married."

"You're not old enough to be weaned," cried James.

"What the divil do you want with more land for?"

"Money brings money," said James.

"And debts bring debts," said his brother.

They paused at that. Phil puffed at his pipe. James never smoked, unless he borrowed his brother's pipe now and again for a puff.

"You'd have a betther portion in ten years' time," said James, "if we waited and worked for the Foxehall land."

"Puh! I'd be near by fifty. And you'd be old enough to be a grandfather. I suppose you don't think I'd let you marry before me?"

"Five years' time would do you to marry. You'd be a young man of forty years then. A nice tender age."

Phil rose, and went out to the door as if to spit into the yard. He looked across at Foxehall. He went out then for the night, but he did not go to the dance. When he came back James was still there looking into the tiny fire.

"If I asked you," questioned Phil, "for my portion of money in five years' time, would you agree to give it to me? Even if you had to mortgage the New Plot for it?"

His brother said nothing.

"Give me a shmoke of your pipe," he said.

"*Sho gal,*" said Phil, offering it.

With his palm over the bowl to get the better suction, and the stem half into his mouth, James puffed slowly.

"I'd give you half of it," he said, without removing the pipe.

"You can keep it," said Phil.

"Wouldn't the three-quarters of it do you?" demanded James.

"It would not."

"And I'd promise the rest of it within the year."

"I don't want it," said Phil. "Give me my pipe."

James took a last deep drink of the tobacco, and then

squirted a great spit between his lips into the fire. He rose and looked at his brother.

"All right," he said.

A shadow crossed the window. The two brothers looked at the woman passing to the door, and then Phil went out by the back. The latch lifted, and the Frewen girl entered. James lifted his hand to her and smiled with joy.

"Ah! Molly, will you come in, girl," he said. "Come in, my brightness."

7

By the time he was in jail ten years, Mag Keene had sent all but three of her daughters away from her. Nonie, "the Bull," was at home on the farm; she had brought Julie back to Frewen's in Knockaderry to keep her under her eyes; the baby, Bid—now sixteen—was the last to go. All the rest were scattered. Mag and Joanna and Bridie were gone to America with ten golden sovereigns, their birthright, stitched into the hem of their red petticoats, and a jug of freshly churned butter and a pair of wheel-cakes, hot from the bastable, under their arms for the long voyage out. What happened to them in the end no one ever knew. One is said to be buried in Boston, Mass., killed in an elevated-railway smash; another is supposed to be still alive in Brooklyn, New York, married to a Protestant Scotsman; but after the old mother died those at home never heard from them. They did not even have their addresses, for, as they said at home, the Yanks knew they would be writing out for only one thing, and that they were too tight-fisted to give. Then as the years went by and the other girls came each in her turn to sixteen or seventeen, they went their way, either to business in Cork or Dublin, when the premium could be paid for them, into a boot store or a drapery store, or again, like Kate and Ellie, to the States, or, like poor old Moll, all by herself, to Australia. These Mag never laid eyes on again from the morning Paddy Frawley or Rich Hickey whipped up his horse outside the farm door, and the children went bawling down the long boreen to catch the morning train at Rathkeale for the Queenstown boat. Each one broke a new heart-string in the old mother. Each sent her snuffling alone by herself in the kitchen, or drinking cold water down by the well. Until at last the time came for sending Bid away, Bid, the shakings of the bag, the weak-legged lamb, and her she could not bear to send far from her like all the rest.

"Bid is such a frail bit of a thing," she used to say. "I can't send her from me. Not like Nonie, 'the Bull,' that has no more heart than an ould dog."

She managed to find a place for her in Madigan's grocery shop in Rathkeale, where, on Sundays, the child could walk out the short-cut across Reens to the farm, and be with her mother and Nonie again, as if they had not been separated at all. So there was one more last early-rising in Ahill, and the mother and daughter went into the town, jolting and bumping, on the ass-cart, Bid with her back to her mother, her Sunday straw hat very straight on her head, and the heels of her new laced boots rattling on the planks. She was a big-eyed, frightened lump of a girl in her early spring, her faint invisible crescent, the best loved of the ten. As the donkey walked the hills, and Ahill and Foxehall and last, Knockaderry Hill, drew out of sight, and the cold spire of Rathkeale came nearer, much of the mother's talk was of that love between them.

"Ah! Sure, Bid, 'twas always you were the soft-hearted one of the flock. Wasn't it you would always creep in to me from the settle-bed on the floor of the kitchen below, and come in your little shift and your bare shins into your mother's bed in the back-room to ask me did I want e'er a thing, I was crying so? How well it wouldn't be Nonie,

snoring beside me on the bed ever since poor Bill died,
God rest him! She wouldn't as much as turned her head
to say, 'Mother, what ails you?' It's no harm to call that
one Hardy Arse the Gribbero! But you'd rise up from the
spread settle and come pithher-pattherin' across to me, and
creep into me, and say, 'Wisha! Mother, why do you be
cryin' like that?' And you'd be with me for an hour, but,
you poor craytur, you'd fall asleep in the end, and I'd rise
and carry you back to the settle on the floor, the way you
was—between Joanie and Moll. And if it wasn't too far
from the dawn, I'd put on my old muddy brogues and go
down the grey dew of the grass, and drink cups and cups
of wather, like a body had the toothache and couldn't sleep
with the pain of it—"

Then there would be a silence, during which they would
hear the rattle of the linch-pins and the bumping wheels,
and the mother's great indrawings of snuff. It was market-
day in Rathkeale, and when they came to the town they
had to wind slowly through the carts in the street up to
Madigan's door. There she saw Bid taken upstairs and,
after ordering her goods, she went on her business. When
she returned Bid had her parcels ready for her—the first
task at Madigan's—blue bags of sugar, brown for cereal
and white flour, the silver tea-packets. Packing them into
the cart she handed the reins to her mother, kissed her, and
stood back in the door of the shop while the donkey
ambled slowly away up the street, through the crowds, and
rounded the corner of the hill-road to the chapel.

Whatever little bustle might be down in the street, here
there was always perfect quiet. Not that Rathkeale isn't
quiet enough, goodness knows. To sit in the back-orchard
of one of those houses on the main street, is to feel a silence
such as one can never feel in the loneliest mountains. But
to kneel, as old Mag knelt in the perpetual dusk of the
too-roomy chapel, is to feel a silence in which the small

breath of devotion sounds like the moaning of the wind.
Once in her corner she began to mutter to herself about
Bid and Julie and Moll and Joanna and the rest of them,
her thoughts shuttling to and fro until she had eased her
heart and could think of her donkey waiting outside in the
falling dusk. Then she would rise and move about the
chapel, halting at the grotto of the Deposition to murmur
in sympathy with the afflicted Mother; shuffling on to the
pious picture of the Sudarium, where the eyes in the blood-
streaked face seemed to open and gaze out at her as she
looked; pausing at last before the great altar, where she
would bow and bless herself. Then, peering right and left
and all about her in pure human curiosity, she would move
up the main aisle murmuring the last anthem of her pro-
cessional prayer:

> "Oh, God help us,
> God rest us all.
> A hard and cruel world!
> God help us all."

A dark figure, bowed on his hands, knelt at the end of
a bench on her way, and as she peered at him she seemed
to know him. Hearing her pause he raised his head and
looked up at her.

"Leo Donnel?" she whispered, and her thoughts flew at
once to her daughter behind the pub counter in Knockaderry.

"Is that Mag Keene?" he whispered.

She whispered back at him, "Are you out?"

He nodded weakly. She stared at him, half in fright for
her child, half in a smother of pity for the drawn face and
the hollow temples of him, the grey hair, and the eyes that
had lost their fire. Then compassion for him overcame her.

"When did you come back, my poor fellow?" she asked, and knelt in beside him.

"An hour ago. I landed on the mail car, and I didn't know where to go next. So I came up here."

"Are you going home?" she whispered.

He looked at her sideways.

"Is Foxehall there always?" he whispered. "I heard from no one for five years."

A groan broke from her and she patted his hands, clasped on the back of the pew in front of them.

"To be sure it is. If we only knew, Leo, that you had no wan to write to you, sure, we would send you a letter now and again."

"Nicholas never wrote to me," he complained.

"Ah! Sure, Leo!" There was a world of pity in the way she said it.

"Where is he?"

"He's at home, Leo. He's only back a few months."

"Back?"

"Of course, you didn't know, Leo. The poor lad was in the asylum in Cork for four and a half years. He lost the light of reason after he kem out, and in the heel of it we had to send him away. He's at home now and he'll be all right, maybe, with the help of God. Every day before he went he used say he was writing to you. Then we met James, and he said you'd be all right. We thought your own would write to you, boy."

Donnel looked before him at the cold marble altar.

"I heard from no one for five years," he whispered as to the faint red light before the tabernacle. "From no one at all."

"We'll be going home," said Mag into his ear, and she took his rough hand. He rose and went with her. He neither genuflected, nor dipped his hand in the holy water, nor blessed himself. Below the long steps of the church the donkey stood as motionless as stone. They sat opposite one another on the corners of the little cart and ambled down the hill, through Well Lane and past the last white cottages out to the familiar fields. All the way they never spoke. At the little hill which is beyond Ballingarry Cross the donkey fell into a walk. Below them men and girls were turning the hay; beyond stretched the sunlit plain.

At the gates of Foxehall they turned up the grass-grown avenue. The shutters were drawn on every one of the fourteen windows. He knocked many times, and then went around the back; after a while he returned.

"There's no one there. I can't get in.

"And for the last ten years," he smiled wanly, "I couldn't get out."

"Sit up," she said. "We'll go on to Ahill, and have a cup of tay and a bite to eat. Broken Bottom might be there, and he'll come back with you."

The donkey raced all the way out of the long avenue, eager to be home.

In the kitchen at Ahill, not so sooty as it used to be and much larger looking with nobody in it but Nonie, he sat in his old place by the fire, until Nicholas came in. For a moment they did not recognize one another, and then they were side by side in the middle of the floor in a warm handshake, crying like children.

"My God! Nicholas!" said Leo.

"Leo! Leo! So they let you out!" said Nicholas.

In a few minutes they were talking wildly and excitedly, like boys freed from school, laughing and crying with delight. They let loose all that had been tied up in them for years, because nobody would have understood if they had spoken.

"But that foxy fellow?" cried Nicholas. "He had a mouse."

"Bulger!" said Leo.

"He was there for because he killed his mother," roared Nicholas. "He was a joker. I seen the warders laugh at him when the mouse stood on his head."

"Oh, but I warrant you he had a tongue," said Leo.

"Oh, my heavens," wailed Nicholas, with a face of terror. "He had a tongue."

"But he loved that mouse," said Leo.

"It was the funniest thing you ever saw," cried Nicholas to his sister Mag, who stood listening in delight, because they were so gay.

"He's there still," said Leo quietly.

"He's a lifer," said Nicholas. "But he was funny, you know. It wouldn't be the same place without him."

"He lent me a book once," said Leo. "And do you know what it was? It was a *History of Greece*. Nicholas! Do you know the story of the horse had wings?"

"Ah, yes!" smiled Nicholas. "It's an old story, surely."

"I tell you," sighed Leo, with deep delight. "I tell you."

They sat to the table, the boiled eggs and the tea with milk, and there was actually butter on the bread.

"That day I got that book—" began Leo, and then a shadow fell on the door. Julie stepped across the threshold and looked at him. She did not know him, he had got so thin and haggard, and she sat on the settle in silent respect of the stranger. Then she saw how the man was looking across at her, taking her in from head to toes, and she knew him. He saw the flush of shame and fear on her face, and suddenly he realized that she would be for ever despised in the parish as the girl who sold the Fenian. It might have been some feeling of the rake of one family for the rake of another that made him rise and take his hat from the window, and say:

"I'm glad to see you well, Julie, and I bear you no grudge, girl."

Before they could stop him he was out in the dark fields, crossing by the short-cuts to his house. He sat for a long while on the horse-block by the steps, listening to the far-off cuckoo. Then he saw Broken Bottom coming hurrying towards him on his game-leg, rattling the keys, and praising God for the master's return. He sat for a little while in the cold house listening to the old servant's talk of the farm and money affairs—they might have been far worse if he had never gone to jail—but his mind was riotous with the excitement of home, and he went early to his bed. Sleep did not come to him for hours, and then it came and receded in waves, and he was awake before six, as he had been for the last ten years. But this time he saw green trees rising out of green fields, and the smoke of cabins faint against the last stars. He lay looking at it all for over an hour, unable to believe they were the same stars.

For two weeks he enjoyed all that he had promised himself to enjoy. There they were—the clouds roofing Limerick, the wind crawling over the sunken river, the bogs spice-laden, the hot sun on the furze of the hills, his pipe and a jug of punch out on the steps in the cool of the night. But after that he grew irritable, and he was soon quarrelling with Nicholas—strangely enough over Julie Keene.

"Is Julie still in Frewen's?" he asked.

"She is," said Nicholas.

"Is she married?"

"I wish she was. She's a wild piece with no breeding in her, though she's a niece of my own. I'm in dread she'll soon be out of the parish, and we won't be able to keep an eye to her."

"Why so? Where would she go?"

"Why so? Do you ask me that, Leo? Didn't she put myself and yourself into jail? And aren't all the people on our side now?"

"I don't want them to be on my side. Every time I meet

one of them they whisper at me, and crouch over me, and
ask me questions in corners, and draw me under a tree to
talk to me behind their hands. But if they meet me on the
open street in the village they pass me by—the cowardly
mob."

"Never mind. Didn't your own mother, God rest her,
ask the priest to move her after you were arrested, and she
came back to Knockaderry?"

"If she did, I didn't ask her to. And I hope you won't
say the priest is on my side, too?"

"He's not on her side, anyway," evaded Nicholas.

"Then there's something in the girl," mocked Leo.

Nicholas unwisely lowered his voice to speak of the priest.

"He's the priest, Leo. He knows the world. And he's a
great friend of the inspector of the police."

Leo scoffed. The word "priest" was always enough to set
his blood boiling now.

"Aye! The cockroach and the greenfly. They're the pair
that have the run of Ireland. The cockroach praying for
the greenfly."

And in spite of himself he found Stephens's words coming back to him.

"What good were the priests ever to Ireland? They were
again' O'Connell—"

"They were not again' O'Connell!"

"They were again' O'Connell!"

"They weren't!" cried Nicholas, who knew better.

"Stephens said it!" cried Leo.

"He did not say it! He couldn't say it. They were again'
the Young Irelanders."

"Well, it's all the same. They were again' Gavan Duffy."

"That's so."

"They were again' the Fenians."

"That's true."

"The cockroaches!"

"I won't hear you say that, Leo."

"I say it. I say it. The cockroaches!"

Nicholas took his hat, and left him with a sour mouth. He watched him go, and then flung his saddle over his nag, and passed him out on the road to Knockaderry and Frewen's door. When he strode into the pub the girl behind the counter went white, and with trembling fingers gave him the bottle of whisky he asked for, and the glass and the water-jug, while the country boys stood about like statues.

"So the peeler didn't marry you?" he said.

"No," she replied, in a low, terrified little voice.

He liked the strength of her back, and her firm chest, and her healthy skin.

"You were handsome enough," he said. "Here's to you, anyway."

He threw back a glass of neat whisky.

"Why didn't he marry you?"

She stared at him.

"Would you have him?"

Still she looked at him and said nothing.

"Well, here's to him! For a damn fool!"

He leaned over the counter and whispered to her:

"You must come for a walk with me some night."

As she did nothing but stare at him he leaned farther forward, while she drew back a little and looked questioningly into his eyes.

"Wouldn't you? Come on, wouldn't you?"

The girl's eyes shifted all about her and returned to him, as if she were a little child frightened by strange company.

"Do you hate me, girl?" he asked gently.

She shook her head ever so faintly. He laughed and drew back, and looked about him at the country lads.

"Fine night, men!" he said.

They growled indistinctly in reply. He turned back from

them and smiled at Julie. He took his whisky bottle and bade her good night, and went out and galloped away.

It was her misfortune to meet him alone the following night by the weirs, and he began his old game of courtship all over again as if he had never left it ten years ago. Within an hour he found himself lying under a willow in an old rath, trying to dispel the last timidities of the girl beside him. The night was thick and the dun moon was trying to struggle through a cobweb of clouds. The dogs were barking at it. The grasshoppers sang, intermittent, elusive. The smell of a shrub fell about them. The light of a distant cottage shone on his left. He laughed aloud with the very joy of it all, so that the girl screamed when he squeezed her about the waist.

"You little divil, you," he said. "You're worth ten of them."

When they parted he walked the fields by the river for two hours, trying to persuade himself that he must be done with that, have no more of that, cursing himself as every man does who is a man of passions and fearing his passions is divided against himself by perpetual temptation, failure, doubt. Yet he met her again the following night, and for many nights after. He drank far more than he could carry, trying to forget that he could not keep on postponing for ever the act of rejection and reformation.

Then, at last, she came tapping at his window one night, and behind his stables she besought him not to let her mother at Ahill know of her disgrace, to do something for her, not to let her sister Bid know; above all, Nonie "the Bull," and Nicholas. He sent her off to Dublin to have her child. It was farmed out there in one of those little hamlets outside the city, whose seed and breed for generations had been the bastard blood of every wealthy rake in Ireland since the days of the Parliament bucks and the Hell Fire dandies. She returned as gay and light-hearted as ever, happy because nobody knew but the two of them—and, of course, the priest. In his hurry to get some ready money he mortgaged the house, and then spent the capital that accrued since his imprisonment in paying off the interest.

After that he decided to see no more of her. He made up his quarrel with Nicholas, and the two of them spent days accumulating and poring over the newspapers of the years they had lost. They began to make out lists of dates and columns of events, from the smallest to the biggest, as a list of the meetings of the various political organizations in Limerick, a list of the men jailed in and after 'sixty-seven, and other lists, over longer periods, of all the men deported or hanged for political crimes. On his farm he never did a stroke of work, leaving all to Broken Bottom, who was getting far too old to do anything properly, so that by degrees less and less came in, and if he did not soon bestir himself, as the people said, "He would be over the border and never return." They were right. His ruin was not so much a descent as a fall.

8

The year of his release Parnell was leading the Irish Party. The year after that, Davitt came out of jail, and when he came to Limerick to organize the Land League, the first men he naturally came to, east of Rathkeale, were the two Fenians. Davitt and Nicholas stayed a night at Foxehall, and when Davitt went the two Fenians went with him. The pair became familiar figures on the Parnellites' wagonettes, Leo, with his long black beard streaked with premature grey, up on the driver's seat; here his hair would blow up in the wind like a cock's comb, and he look down proudly at the people cheering him whenever the speakers made a reference to the men who had fought for the cause of freedom and liberty. But though he eagerly wished it they would never let him speak, and as a result the people began to have a profound respect for him as a desperate man who did not believe in wasting time in words. Except, that is, in his own home parish, where the tough Deel-side farmers knew him for a boy who had wasted his substance and his strength to no purpose. Nicholas, on the other hand, became such a favourite speaker at these meetings that he travelled farther and farther abroad, and Leo began to see less and less of him every year. When they met, Nicholas would seize on Leo's newspaper cuttings for his speeches, and over them they would quarrel like two paupers in a poorhouse over a ha'penny.

All this time his brother James was watching him like a hawk, with one hand appeasing Phil, restraining him and advising him and encouraging him to have patience for one more year, and one more year, before he should marry, and on the other hand, meeting his Molly night after night under the hedges, telling her that he was only waiting to make her a home fit to house her, and joking with her at the foolish young people who rushed into marriage before they had enough to support themselves, let alone a family. His plans about the Foxehall land he never mentioned to her. They were the early 'eighties, when for a succession of years the crops were battered by blight, almost total failures, and only the careful farmers survived by keeping their bellies to the ground. If he had mentioned it to her he knew she would have made him marry her at once; and yet, as he told Phil over the fire at night, the harder the year the better for them who had no care but for themselves. Those 'eighties brought Donnel to the brink of ruin. A mortgage on the fields, to the agony of James, who wanted to buy the fields from his brother and not from the bank, followed the mortgage on the house; and then, just when he was beginning to realize that if he didn't do something to save himself he would be bankrupt, Leo was arrested again—this time neither he nor anyone else knew for what. In a few months he was free, but the spring and summer was gone, and his last chance with it. James refused to help him, and his old servant could not. The autumn crowned his misfortunes. Parnell was in jail, and in rage Davitt's League raised a cry of "No Rent." At once Donnel flew into a fury, and driving into Rathkeale to the bank, called imperiously for the manager, just as his brother used to do years before.

"Ha!" said the old clerks under their breath. "Here's another of them."

"I've come," he cried to Barlow's successor—as if he were delivering a speech from the dock to him—"I've come here today to tell you that the farmers of Limerick won't pay you a penny more interest on any mortgage you hold on their land. You may take that from me."

The manager sucked gently at the tip of his pipe with his soft lips, and his eyes smiled up at his visitor.

"Come, come, O'Donnell," he began.

"Mister Foxe-Donnel to you," cried the Fenian.

"I beg your pardon," bowed the other. "You mean," he went on, "that you refuse to pay us any more interest on your mortgage?"

"Not a penny."

"You know we should have to foreclose on you in that case? You are, I believe, somewhat in arrears even as it is. Shall we see the books?"

He half-rose to call his accountant, but Donnel waved him back.

"I want to see no books. I speak for the Land League. We'll break you if you dare try to foreclose on our property."

Gently the manager caressed the corner of the table with his pink forefinger, his eyebrows raised, then falling to a frown, then smoothening back to his professional twinkle.

"I'm sure it won't come to that, Mister Foxe-Donnel. You'd better write to us."

He rose to show him out.

"I'll write it now," said Donnel bravely.

"No, no, no! Best think it over again. We don't want any trouble."

"I never withdraw," said Donnel bitterly, "what I have once said."

He left the business man staring after him through the glass door and then down at him on the street, where he climbed into his saddle and trotted away through the town, proud as a peacock at having had the last word. And it was his last word, for when the bank finally did threaten him with foreclosure and eviction he had nothing left to say.

That Sunday he went to the League Committee in Rathkeale. The room was empty; they had deserted him. He swore at them for traitors, not in the least understanding that there was nothing else for them to do. He had kept aloof from them too long; mocked their priests; lived differently from them—wildly, incontinently. They were fighting for the merest right to live, and they had no time for spendthrifts. They had met in another house, and were going through their business there as he rode home in a black fury, and with his one and only faithful servant—his old Broken Bottom—barricaded the house to resist the bailiffs. They prepared pots of boiling water, red-hot pokers to thrust at them if they came through the windows; and with his own hands—it was the first time since Portland that they had done a stroke—he carried huge paving stones to the upper stories to fling at anyone who should dare approach underneath. But two men could not hope to hold so large a house against twenty helmeted police with carbines and a battering-ram, grappling-hooks, and ladders. The "greenfly" threw the two defenders on the grass of the avenue, removed the doors from their hinges, unroofed half the house, and smashed every window and shutter. Then they carted away whatever furniture and stock they had left, telling the two that they were lucky not to be arrested and given five years in jail.

He was glad of the night, and he disappeared into it. There was a herdsman's cottage on the farm, empty for years now, and to this shack Broken Bottom dragged a few sticks of furniture that the bailiff had not thought worth removing. The moon was up as the old man crossed the beaten meadows with a bucket or a kettle in either hand, calling out as he went:

"Sir! Sir! Mister Leo! Sir! Sir!"

Many times he went to and fro, resting often because the battered bed or press was too heavy for his aged hands. The mist was about his knees as he went, and he had made a furrow in the high grass. He stuck a stump of candle in the window of the hovel and waited for hours. Once more he made the rounds of the fields, calling like a night-bird:

"Sir! Sir! Sir! Sir!"

He peered through the windows of every farm-house for two or three miles about, hoping to see his master by the fireside; there were people at every hearth, but never Donnel. Exhausted, he halted by a pollarded willow, and there below him at the river's edge, where there was dry gravel under the aery roots, he heard the voices mingling with the murmur of the water. He could hear his master crying like a child, and the girl comforting him like a mother. He withdrew, and waited patiently until they should rise and come towards him, and then as if by chance he met them, and led them to the hut and the dying warmth of the fire.

There for a while Julie tried to make the place comfortable, while the moon rose and night went far to meet the morning.

They heard feet outside, and with a sudden crash the

door was flung open. They saw the priest, and behind him Frewen, the publican, peering over his shoulder like a hen. The publican's wife had been overcome by pious scruples, and insisted on her husband routing out the priest to go after her missing servant girl.

"Is Julie Keene here?" roared the priest.

"Good night, sir," said Donnel. "Come in. Take a chair by the fire."

"Have you Julie Keene in this house?"

More than ever like a hungry hen, Frewen kept peering about the dark corners of the hovel.

"There'th a light in the room, Father," he lisped.

Striding to the partition the priest flung open the door.

"Come out," he cried to the terrified girl, and by the wrist he dragged her to the outer door. "Take her home," he ordered the publican. "Go out, you!" he ordered Broken Bottom, and the old man went, and waited shivering under the eaves.

What he said to Donnel that night nobody ever knew, but ever after it the two lovers met in snatches of darkness like any guilty pair fearful of being caught by parent or priest.

Once or twice again he went to the League Committee, but the priest was always in the chair, and they would give him no real help, and he would break out at them and abuse them, while the priest swore to have the law of him or drive him from the parish if he did not behave himself.

And so back to his hovel, from whose door he could see the police patrolling his farm and the tarpaulin bellying over his house. Soon the last shopkeeper gave him the last shilling of credit, and Broken Bottom was hard put to keep a bite of food in the house. If Julie had not secretly given an odd shilling to the old servant and persuaded her mother, Mag Keene, to send him a few pounds of flour or a peck of potatoes he might have died of hunger. In the summer Broken Bottom died and was taken out to a pauper's grave, while Donnel stood in the corner of the hut without uttering a word, motionless as a scarecrow.

The next spring James O'Donnell was ploughing the fields of the Foxehall farm—he had bought in the mortgage both of the land and the house from the bank—and Leo Foxe-Donnel was working on the public roads, mending the gutters and the potholes, with his shovel and his brush. The people would have liked to help him now, but he was always so "high in himself," so near his temper, that they had to leave him alone in the end, calling him an old bear—he was really under fifty—until in the eyes of the children pattering to school, the county councillors driving past in their cars, the clerks in Rathkeale and Newcastle in charge of the public works, he became like any other poor labouring man. Twice he was before the magistrates—once for threatening the police who were guarding James, "the grabber," and once for threatening James himself. But before he left that place he had the satisfaction of seeing James pay dearly for his land-greed. The Frewens realized immediately he took Foxehall that he could not marry for at least another ten years, and already he was sixty-four or sixty-five, his Bawnrea farm was mortgaged, and he was working merely to pay off the interest on that and a high rent on Foxehall. They took him before the court at Limerick for having deceived their daughter by repeated promises of marriage, and they made him pay her a hundred pounds and high costs. Worst of all, the rumour came to him that Phil was now thinking of marrying her for the sake of that fine dowry. But yet he held on to his two farms, and for all his threescore years set out to work himself free and rich once more. His life became a torment to him, with Phil badgering him for his portion, the bank after him every month for their money, the police living in the one house with him and their cost having to be shared with the rates, and always the dispossessed Leo crossing and re-crossing his fields to his mud hut, taunting him and sneer-ing at him and mocking at him for being a barren man.

"Will I lend you my britches?" the Fenian would call to him across a hedge. "It would help you to grow up, James."

Or:

"That's a great family you have up in that house, God bless them. Great strapping boys, entirely. How on earth do you feed them so well?" (Referring to the police guard.)

Or:

"What about doing the rounds at Nantenan? There's great nature in that water for men like yourself, James. Will I bring you a sup in a bottle?"

Until, in his turn, the Fenian was caught. Once more the publican's wife, who hated the whole line of the O'Don-nells impartially, came galloping to the priest with the wind through her skirts. This time, the priest went straight to James—more for the sake of his parish than for the woman.

After a long argument he returned with fifteen pounds. He went to Donnel's hovel and put the notes on the table, adding to it ten pounds of his own.

"Donnel!" he said: "You have ruined that Keene girl. No man will marry her after what you have done to her. There's twenty-five pounds. You are a man of some educa-tion. You have nothing to gain by living like this. The man who has your land can't live in peace with the dread of you. You're keeping the police in the parish protecting him, and their cost is on the rates. I have noticed a little shop in Rathkeale that you could open and sell papers and any other little thing you like. Marry the woman, and I'll give you that money to open that shop, and my blessing will be on you, and the blessing of God that you seem never to have had."

For weeks the priest badgered and implored him alternately. In the end he agreed, and with his twenty-five pounds and a few pounds Julie had saved, and a few more her mother gave her, the two began their married life. They found a little three-cornered house, wedged in the corner of Well Lane, off the Main Street of Rathkeale, one window to the lane, one to the street. For Julie he wrote on a card the word *Dressmaker,* and when her baby was born, unhappily dead, the queer pair settled down there to the business of beginning life all over again.

The town, like all towns, had a malicious wag—one, Constable Wintermann, in the police barracks, who christened every new inhabitant that arrived. It was he who had called the lawyer the Iron Duke, and the vet, Sthripoff, because these were his first words to all his patients; he had also christened the priest's dog Metamorphosis, because nobody could tell its breed. He at once named Donnel —Count Spider, and his wife became Jolly Julia, or Julia of the Strong Men.

BOOK TWO

1888–1898

THE TOWN

1

Rathkeale

1

IN a little town like Rathkeale all the joy of life is in its changeless ritual. Everything that happens is so familiar and so long foreseen that the days become inseparable in the memory, and the years weave themselves into immeasurable periods of time. The body is altered with a tender slowness and the mind remains unchanged.

So for the fifteen years during which Bid Keene grew tall and slim and womanly, her mind was as smooth as a mountain lake, and her life so simple that if she had been asked to describe it she could hardly have found anything to say. She might, perhaps, have spoken of the church on the hill. That was always open to her, and it filled her heart with the greatest ease and rest to kneel there for long hours before the candles of the Virgin, praying for her mother and father and her sisters that were scattered from her, so that the other shop-girls in Madigan's used to say she was the holiest of them all, and would surely be a nun if she didn't marry Johnny Hussey, on the Hill. At night, too, she would take repose from the bustle of the town, praying in her attic-room before the altar she had made with soap boxes, and filled with pictures and blessed statues, her prayers and her little courtship filling almost her entire day. Sometimes there would be a walk by the telegraph poles towards Knockaderry or out by the commons. Once a year, or even less often, she would go in all her finery to a travelling theatre or circus. But most of all she enjoyed a foray across the yard into the egg store, where Johnny Danagher was spying at the sun through a brown egg in his fist as he culled for the market. There they would laugh and joke in the straw—about what?—something so near to nothing that one could scarcely put their fun into intelligible words—an egg with green spots on it, a straw on Johnny's tail, a bit of dung on an eggshell. And yet, long afterwards, she used to say what great fun they used have in Rathkeale, and in Madigan's, and in the egg store! But by then the ritual of her youth was broken, and she had begun to feel the passage and the power of time.

That breaking began and her life to form when, as she was praying before her gilt-framed pictures one night in the quietness of her attic, she thought of Johnny Hussey with a sudden fingering of the little red lamp, and thought there in the quietness of the night how if he married her she would have children and a house like Julie's, and thought, on the other hand, whether she would really prefer to be a lay-sister in a convent. At that moment her young face grew small and hard, and her eyes dilated as if the strain of calling up all the hard-gained wisdom of her fathers and her forefathers had transformed her suddenly into a woman before her time. She was ready, she said, to bear and rear her line, to help to "further them on," "to push them up," "to improve theirselves," "to rise."

If there is any beauty in being alive, in simply being, this girl was intensely beautiful, though never again so much so as when she sat back on her heels that night in her attic above a sleeping town, fingering the wick of her lamp, that glinted on the sides of her biscuit tins, lovely as she smiled into its ruddy light at the life that lay before her.

She was even lovely to look at, tall and slim as a poplar, so tall that when she laughed she always swayed over to one side like a reed, so slim, so very slim for a country girl, that there was not a corset in town small enough for her, and that she had—ordered specially from Limerick—laced more tightly than any normal woman could bear. Then she was so slim that Johnny used in game make as if to grasp her waist in his fingers, while she skipped from him in laughing and shocked evasion, bent in two like a hound in chase or a drawn bow. Then, because she was shocked, she would stand straight up and look sternly at him out of her watery blue eyes. But he would only laugh at her because she was blushing, and look at her cheeks, pink, fresh, fair, and her soft lips that were never closed, and rush for her again. She blushed easily, but when would she if not then, in her early love, in her courting day, in her virginal prime?

But at night along the shadowy roads she did not blush when he caught her in his strong hands to kiss her. She wasn't bold and forward like her sister and wouldn't lie in a ditch, nor would Johnny want her to, for he was a respectable man, but when she prided out of him and out of herself—she knew there was not a finer pair walking out in Limerick—she would return his kiss with the best of them, would kiss him many times, shyly, gently, fondly, and even warmly if her blood were up. She would not think then of nuns or convents or lay-sisters, but she had many a thought of a home and a family, and the pride she would have in her husband and in herself and in the blood of the pair of them.

When Julie married and came to live in the town she had another place to go of nights, and, knowing nothing about Leo except that he was a Fenian, or about Julie except that she was a bit wild, she used to boast of them to the other girls. She was too innocent to guess that, behind her back, they made fun of Leo, and talked of his shop as a "hole-in-the-wall that hadn't a square room in it."

Leo shared some of her innocence and knew even less

than she how bitter the tongues can be in a small country town; how little there can be there of the warm, generous feeling of the country-side. He was so simple as to think that the town and his little shop were a haven where nobody would bother about him any longer; so that as he sat behind his shop-window in his narrow, hollowed street, or of sunny days before his door, biting his nails, gazing idly up and down, it pleased if the man on the water-butt selling water at a halfpenny a bucket, or the flour-white baker on his ambling van, threw him the merest, " 'Day, sir!"— or, better still, took no more notice of him than if he were the pump at the end of the lane. He took it as a sign that they had accepted him without question. Whereas for a year after he came there, if he passed ten times a day through the silent empty street, apparently not a soul awake in it, in the course of his procession a hundred curtain-corners rose and fell, and if he had turned his head as he passed some dark and empty shop doorway he would have seen an effigy draw back into the gloom, staring before it like a waxwork as it disappeared.

He thought they knew little about him, when they had actually found out everything within a month. So that if he met one or two of them down the Bog Road, or coming from the station, and spoke distantly and condescendingly to them, the townsmen would say, "Yes! Mister Donnel," or "Oh! That's a known fact, Mister Donnel," as if he were to be respected as a man of substance, but when he was gone they would look after him with hard, questioning eyes, and then wink at one another with a wise, slow smile. They took heed of his white collar, and his shirt-front that, from this on, he always wore, and his fine suits of black clothes, always brushed and pressed with care, his white handkerchief tucked into his white cuff, his beard with every rib finely combed in place; and knowing well how much of Julie's sweat and labour went into those clothes

and that linen they said it was terrible pity for a fine woman, what matter if she was a bit of a streel itself, to be
spancelled to an ould cock-of-the-walk like that. So they
watched him with a sneer in their eyes sitting there all day
long with his nose stuck in a book, stroking his lovely
beard, rising only to go to the station when the noon train
from Limerick brought the morning news, and they made
a great joke of the way he would not even go the rounds
with the papers, but paid a halfpenny a day to a small
boy to do it for him.

"That fellow has the life of a lord," they said, as they
leaned against their jambs, looking across at him, or watching the child come slowly zigzagging up the street under
his eye with the *Gazette*.

It was little wonder that for years the only people in the
place he knew were his wife and her sister, and, strange
visitor for such a house, the policeman Johnny Hussey—
accepted because he was "walking out" with Bid, and was
a relation of his own; actually he was his sister's son,
though which sister—it was really Joan—he never asked,
for he had no interest in his relations, and wished only to
forget and be forgotten by everyone that knew him in his
youth.

All that distrust of the townspeople Bid never guessed,
but they never hid from her that they liked her sister
Julie. She was so fat and jolly and coarse, and she worked
so hard at her dressmaking that, although nobody ever got
a dress back from her in time, they all went to her for the
sake of her stories and her loud, doxy laugh. They liked a
woman who was always ready for a foray down the street
to a crony, of a night of poll-talking in the back-kitchens,
for a game with the girls at Madigan's or Dooley's, or the
girls in the hotel, or the nurses in the poorhouse. There
were even some gay nights in her own three-cornered parlour over the shop in Well Lane. But they were few: no-

body could be gay with a lone man, stroking his beard with vanity, in the middle of a bunch of women.

But Bid's greatest pleasure of all was to return home every Sunday along the white road and across the dried brown grass of the bogs, the pollen of the wildflowers dusting her shoes, down over the stepping-stones of the Deel to Ahill Farm. There Nonie, the eldest of them all after Julie, had married, and was bringing up her line of children. Long before Bid arrived at the haggard somebody—Nicholas if he were at home, or even the old mother—would call out that she was approaching, so that when she did step under the door-tree they scarcely raised their heads to welcome her, and she, knowing how they had welcomed her long before, would merely take off her hat and loosen her boots and sigh out, "Glory be to God, it's hot," as if she had only left that kitchen an hour ago to climb up the hill to mass. Then she would sit in the cool gloom looking out through the open door at the wavering mirage over the fields, picking from them and giving to them, bit by bit, as if they both grudged it, the news of the week. She would exchange a word about the sermon at Rathkeale mass for a word about the mass at Knockaderry, news of Madigan's for news of Frewen, news of Julie for news of Nonie. Then they would wander on to Phil O'Donnell who, at fifty, was marrying a young girl from Croom, and had got the house and two bog fields in Bawnrea from James as his portion; and they would tell her as a great mock how James was gone living all by himself in Foxehall in two rooms, and how the roof was falling in, and he wouldn't mend it, and how he was known now in the pub at Knockaderry as Sir James O'Donnell—and how it was said, too, that for all his sixty-seven years he had his eye like Phil on a young girl of twenty or so, in Newcastle-west, with a bit of money under the bed and a squint in her eye. Over that they had great fun, and Nonie would say that a

man needn't mind what he had in a bed if he had something good under it, whereupon her husband would make
a run of scandalous jokes with many a side-glance at Bid's
blushes, that were his delight, and his mother-in-law's eyes,
that were his warning.

Then the country dinner with the spuds on a plate because it was Sunday, and then a walk over the fields to see
the improvements, and a talk under a hedge with her
mother, and a look at Nonie's baby, and in the cool evening the long slow return to Rathkeale, where every shop
was closed and the street like a plain. It was a good exchange—news of Ahill told in Rathkeale, news of the town
in the country; and always her secret courtship to be told
to no one.

Johnny Hussey's particular friend was Wintermann, the
wag who had rechristened Donnel as Count Spider. Wintermann was a tall, red-headed lank of a fellow, with red-
fringed eyes. Minor wags agreed to call him The Cock. The
pair were always together, because they were both studying
for the acting-sergeant's examination—"Orthography, Bid,
and caligraphy, Bid, and ar'thmetic, and geometry, Bid,
and the geography of the British Empire." As he regarded
himself as a man who would "rise" his nicknames were
never kind, and he had earned many enemies by them: but
since no Rathkeale can do without its wag, he had also
become famous to the very uttermost limits of the town.

The two of them spent all their free hours, either in
studying the police code, probing the dictionary for poly-
syllabic words—and using them in their speech—or asking
one another questions about the chief towns of the world,
or, by way of recreation, in Madigan's shop, where Wintermann would throw his long body across the counter, and
leaning on his elbow gaze up into the eyes of one of the
girls, "alleviating," as he said, "the toil of the day by my
racontations." Madigan hated the sight of him—he had

been called Cinderella by him, because of his large feet—
but thinking it better to keep in with "the Force," he
merely grumbled ineffectually at them through the girls.

Johnny Hussey did not pretend to be a wag, and though
he liked to make his careful jokes, they were never personal.
They were so carefully stripped of intention, that they were
often innocent of all meaning. They consisted of parodies
on the unknown, and were universally acceptable because
they came home to nobody. Suddenly, and without any
warning, he would sing out:

> "She is far from the land
> And she can't swim a stroke,"

ending with a great guffaw. Others of his collection, always
given out with the same irrelevancy, were:

> "This is a most auspicious occasion."

> "The king was on his throne,
> The rat-traps thronged the hall."

> " 'Hurroo,' she cried, and down she flopped,
>   and waved her wooden leg, and shouted,
>   'God save Ireland.' "

> "Lead on, Macduff, and cursed be him who
>   cries—three fine oranges a penny."

> "The boy stood on the burning deck,
> His trousers wanted mending."

> "Are you casting nasturtiums on me?"

> " 'I see,' said the blind man, when he couldn't
>   see at all!"

"God helps those that helps themselves, but God
help those that I catch helping themselves."

To these Bid never failed to respond, bending sideways
as if the laugh had contorted her whole body. Wintermann
she did not like, and she wished that Johnny was not a
friend of his, and said so. But as Johnny found him too
useful as a help in his studies to quarrel with him, the two
continued to try to arrange their beats together, to do their
month of night-duty together, to take their holidays at
the same time. It was while they were on night patrol that
the bank was found one morning with a notice, "TO LET,"
pasted on its front window, and the canon woke to see a
notice, "APARTMENTS," dangling from the handle of his hall
door, and Madigan's numbers, turned upside-down over-
night, read 91 instead of 16. Madigan went so far after that
as to say sarcastically to Wintermann the following day:
"That was the grand pathrollin-o ye did last night."
"Yerrah, what are you thinkin' now, Mister Madigan?"
asked Wintermann innocently. "We were the whole night,
and we sitting on the pump steps discussing the palin-
genesis of the body from the mausoleum!"
"Ye were on yeer . . . Grr!"
Speechless with anger Madigan strode back to his office
and sent Bid Keene packing eggs with Johnny Danagher
because he caught her laughing at him behind his back.
In time Wintermann joined Johnny in his visits to Well
Lane and, apart from Bid, these two men were the only
people in Rathkeale who ever came of nights to the musty
little parlour over the paper shop. There, summer light-
someness or winter dark, the five would sit, Leo with his
pipe, the two policemen studying their books, their green-
black uniforms unbuttoned, their belts broken-backed
across the chair rail, their little boat-shaped caps on their
knees, and the two women quietly sewing. Summer or win-

ter the nights were very long, since for hour after hour
there would be great pauses in which no one spoke except
by snatches. Only at odd intervals would any sound break
the silent weaving of the night, as when into the rain-
emptied streets the boys would come out from the temper-
ance hall, and tramp resoundingly home. Then they would
hear again the rustle of Leo's paper, or of the paper over
which Johnny and Wintermann would be leaning on the
table, or, if no one was reading, the rain dripping from
the window-ledge, or the cracking of the old man's joints
—the night slowly drawing over their listening ears and
drooping eyelids all she had so far woven of the dusky
fragments of the warp and woof of sleep. Sometimes the
silence was broken for a long period, maybe for the whole
night, if a chance remark of Johnny's set the old man talking passionately of Portland, of the rights of the people to
the soil, of the speeches of Parnell or Davitt or John Bren-
nan or Scrab Nally or Gladstone. Or a word of Leo's might
set the policemen talking of the depot, or of evictions.
Then an argument would start that grew hotter and hotter
as the night advanced, with bitter words and bad tempers,
and it would be as much as Julie could do to part them
and quiet them and turn it all to a laugh. It was here that
Johnny's humour came in useful. No matter how warm he
got he could not deny himself the chance of his joke. They
would be squabbling about the Women's Land League and
Fanny Parnell when Johnny would guffaw and cry, all in
a breath, " 'Hurroo!' she cried, and waved her wooden leg,
and down she flopped, and the band played *God Save Ireland, said they, proudly—*" Here he would imitate a fife and
drum band playing lugubriously, so that even Wintermann
would relax and grow cool, unable to resist the women's
laughter. Then once more the silence, and the little rain
that dripped outside and the cold wind whisking like a
mouse across the floor.

Perhaps that silence would not last long, perhaps it would last an hour. In these long patches, so characteristic of country folk, Johnny would wink secretly at Bid, or even nudge her while he stared solemnly at the fire, or smirk at her with a cock of his eye at Wintermann or Julie or Leo. Bid would throw one warning glance at the others, and then give him a smile of so faint disapproval, with falling lids and head turning away, that he would at once give her a jerk under the ribs, leaning forward with a great cough to cover these secret ciphers of his love.

They were quite happy because in every house in the town they knew it was the same—people sitting before a fire in the back-parlour or a kitchen, silent, resting after the hard or idle day, talking maybe in snatches if somebody dropped in for a while to sit with his back to a far wall and his cap on his poll or dangling from his fingers between his knees. Indeed, if they stretched the circle wider it was the same silent night for miles about, far beyond the town, in the cabins glimmering among the moist fields, always the same for mile after mile through the whole length and breadth of Ireland, a gentle, dim night where only the small sounds murmured in the grass and the dark and oncoming sleep muffled human speech.

"Aha!" Leo would burst out, startling them all by his sudden memory of a point he had forgotten to make maybe an hour ago. "Aha! It was well for me I was in jail, was it? Aye, then, my laddo, but it was well for you that you were in the depot when there was trouble in the country."

"I was in the depot," Wintermann would reply—always calling it the "deepot"—"when there was trouble within a stone's throw of it. Wasn't I in the depot of the evening of May the sixth, at half-past six in the afternoon, in the year eighteen hundred and eighty-two, when Lord Frederick Cavendish and Mister Under-Secretary Burke were murdered in the Phœnix Park? It was a lovely, salubrious

evening, and well I mind it. And I listening to the water
splashing in the fountain and looking at the flowers in the
beds and the metropolis of Dublin, all red and blue, lying
down in the smoke below me, hummin' like a hive at the
end of the day. It wasn't flowers we were thinking of then.
Only closing the gates and questioning the promenaders,
and doubling the guards on the vice-regal lodge. Oh, that
was nice doing. Two lovely gentlemen. Perfect gentlemen."

"Ah! 'twas a shocking crime," says Johnny, very serious
now.

Leo would have burst out against the dead men, but
Julie held him by the arm.

" 'Tis done. 'Tis all over. For why do ye be dragging up
what's gone and done with? For God's sake aren't we all
together here, fine and fat and comfortable, and what call
have we to be bothering our heads with the past."

In such a case as that, where the memory was salt and
bitter, the night would end with an unbroken pause.

There are some things which cannot be described. There
are certain such hours in the late evening when all the last
loveliness of day moves briefly across the sky. There are
such hours, too, at the end of an old man's day when he
does not so much live as breathe in sleep, moving towards
his rest like those clouds that darken imperceptibly until
all the world below and above and around them is dark
too, and dead. The ten (or nearly ten) years Leo spent in
that town were so tranquil that they can scarcely be spoken
of at all, of such a calm that—in the way of all old men
by whose garrulousness we are amused—he would talk
afterwards with emotion of the small breaths, of no interest
to anyone but himself that ruffled it. Like his aunts before
him who dated all their lives by their childish fears of
Boney, he dated all his life now from his coming to Rathkeale, and since, like them, nothing else happened because
nothing else counted, he was content, like Bid, to see the

years pass over his head. Once or twice one summer Johnny
rowed him on the slow-sliding Deel in an old flat-bottomed
boat of the doctor's, and he trailed his gold-ringed hand in
the water or over the tips of the flat reeds. He might seem
to some watcher, so intent was he, to be hearing the deep
internal motion of the river that waved within its dark
womb the invisible cords of the lilies on their leaves. With
a tag of Virgil he pulled the white cups up from—so he
spoke of it—the omphalos of the river god, and held them
in his pale hand and looked at them. Then he walked
home along, smoking a cool pipe, and stopped at the first
pub in the street for a cool drink, and walked out of it back
to Well Lane wiping his lips with his white handkerchief,
rattling his few pence and his head in the air. Of that
summer he spoke for years. He never forgot it indeed; and
he used to match it afterwards with a summer he once spent
on the Ahill bogs with old Nicholas O'Donnell. And yet,
it sometimes maddened him to see Bid and Johnny so
leisurely in their love.

"Good God!" he would say to his wife. "Have they no
fire in them at all?"

"Aye, sure," she would say dryly, looking up from her
endless sewing. "And look at the way some people have
enough for ten."

And when she said it, she made a secret mow to herself,
and threw him a half-glance of fear over her shoulder, like
a wicked child. To her he was always "the boss" or "himself," always at a distance from her. Even those forays down
the street she had to make in secret, and was continually
fearful of a reproof for her slovenly ways. She had plenty
of them; he hated the way she threw her slops from her
saucer under the grate, gave him his meals on a newspaper,
because she couldn't be bothered preparing a cloth, and
more often than not he slept not merely without a sheet
under him, but on the uncovered tick—and always alone.

Privately she mocked at that to her "bosoms," as she called her cronies.

"It's a queer world, surely. Before he was married to me he was after me every night of the year, and now, be-jiminy—"

With a scandalized laugh the cronies would hush her, whereupon, like an old cat laughing with fat, she would stick her tongue between her teeth, and splutter, with leaping eyes and hunched shoulders, at her own wickedness.

2

One night in the little three-cornered parlour over the shop when only Bid and Julie and Leo were there, silent about the fire, Bid cried out with a sudden remembrance:

"Oh, sure, Leo—I was up at the barracks last night."

At the word "barracks," Leo put down his book and looked at her strangely.

"What took you up there?" he said.

Julie tried to signal a warning to Bid, but the girl failed to see it. She did not realize that although Johnny and Wintermann were allowed in the house, the rest of the barracks was as hateful as ever to the Fenian.

"Johnny that asked us. He asked a couple of girls in the shop to go and see it. And we seen the guard-room and the cells and the carbines and the lock-up and the handcuffs and the strait-jacket. Oh, we seen every bit of it."

"Did they talk about me?" asked Leo.

"Wisha!" she scoffed. "Why would they talk about you?"

"They're always asking questions about everybody up there."

"Not at all, Leo."

"Did they talk about anyone in the town?"

"They talked about Johnny Danagher, the shop, and

how he likes his drop. But sure, Leo, they're all nice men there, and it's only laughing at him they were."

With a sudden passion that amazed the simple girl, he burst out:

"I know them better than you. They're spies on the people."

The girl's blood rose in turn.

"Johnny Hussey is no spy."

He quietened down.

"Johnny Hussey is a decent man. He's our own blood. You picked a decent man when you picked Johnny. And that gom of a Wintermann, has no harm in him either. If he had, I wouldn't have him inside my door. They're not all like Johnny Hussey."

Scarcely mollified, the girl tossed her head.

"But I wager some other of them greenfly had something to say about me?" he persisted.

Again Julie tried to warn her sister.

"Leo! You have a set on them. They—"

She blushed. Leo pounced forward like a bird, his nose ready to hook the rest of the sentence out of her.

"They what?" he snapped.

"Nothing, only—"

This time Bid saw Julie's eyes wide with fright, but it was too late.

"Only what?" thundered the Fenian, rising from his chair.

"The Acting . . . Nothing at all, Leo."

"What was it, Bid?" asked Julie.

"It was nothing at all, Julie. The Acting said, 'Leo Donnel was a foolish fellow to be cadeying around with foolish people like himself.' I said, 'Leo Donnel can look after himself.' And he said, 'I suppose he can, and anyway, he ought to. But, then,' says he, 'you can tell him that from me, all the same.' 'I won't,' says I, 'tell him anything.' 'All right,'

says he. 'But he might be thankful to you in the heel of
the hunt,' says he. 'Ah, sure, the past is dead now,' says I,
'and for God's sake, let it be dead. It's what Julie always
says,' says I. And I suppose he had no right to be dragging
up old scores—"

Neither of the other two were listening to her. She saw
it, and became frightened, and wondered what she had
said, and whether there was any deeper meaning to it all.
She began to talk in a rambling way of the cleanness of
the barracks, part of it whitewashed every month, of the
tar at the base of the wall, the rows of boxes with each
man's name on the side of his own box, the great leather
straps and steel buckles of the strait-jacket, the bare cells
with the sloping wooden shelves on which the prisoners
slept. All the time Donnel glared at her, as if he were hypnotized. She faltered and finished. He rose, and they heard
him on the landing take his coat and hat and stick and go
downstairs into the sleeping town.

When the door banged Julie leaped at her sister.

"Mother most high, Bid, in the name of God Almighty,
where is he gone to, and the night down? What are you
after doing to us, Bid? Bid! O Bid!"

Bid scarcely knew. She had once or twice, yes, twice,
as she and Johnny were walking the Bog Road at night,
down by the canal from the lake, over by Ballingrane—
"where there's trees across the road, in a hollow part of the
road, Julie, it does be wet there most often"—thought they
saw Leo leaning under a hedge with a man. And one night
at Ballingrane they saw Leo open the carriage-door to a
stranger, and raise his hat to him as the lighted train
moved away from the dark platform. At the railway gate
they met Leo, and she asked Leo—"It was Johnny prompted
me to ask him, Julie—'Who was the man?'

" 'I didn't know him, did I?' says I. 'Ah!' says he—and
he passed us in, and set off home with a wave of his hand

—'Ah!' says he, 'that was a man I knew long ago in Limerick.' I said nothing, Julie, but do you know, I take my living oath it was my Uncle Frankie O'Donnell."

It was enough for Julie. She sent Bid home and knelt by the little, low window, waiting for his return. Hours later she heard the familiar step, and saw him coming down the street, under his wide black hat. As he came to his own door who should come around the corner at that very moment, but two policemen, taller than human men in their round, heavy night-helmets, frieze-coated to the short stubby leggings on their ankles.

"Good night, Mister Donnel," said one of them.

He halted for a second, and looked up at them under the brim of his hat. Then, without replying, he shoved the key in the lock.

She drew in her head, and sat by the little fireplace, with its one dead lump of coal. In the darkness, for the lamp was gone out, he did not see her, until her figure came between him and the dim radiance of the night through the window. At the same moment she spoke. She could see him start, and his hand move to his breast.

"Will I get you a cup of cocoa, Leo?" she asked. "It's a raw, damp sort of night."

He sat as he was, coat and hat still on him, his stick in his fist, before the cold grate.

"I'd like a cup of hot tea," he said.

When she returned he was still there. They made no more sound than if they were in a morgue, except that he drank with a sucking noise through his beard.

"Why do you stand there?" he asked of a sudden. "What are you staring at?"

She said nothing.

"Why don't you light the light?" he asked. "What are you at? I can't see you."

She bent down, and whispered timidly in his ear:

"There's two peelers with their backs to the bank opposite!"

It was that whispering, secretive tone he had always hated since he came out of jail. It kept him a prisoner, a man outside the law, to be spoken to in a way different to everyone else. He put down his cup, and strode to the window. A chair fell. A china ornament broke on the floor. He rattled up the blind, and leaned out to look—to stare at them. When they saw the whitening beard and the glittering eyes of the old Fenian glaring at them in the nightlight, they stared back at him. He said nothing, but continued to lean out and look insolently at them across the sloping street. At last the two policemen moved slowly away. Donnel lowered the blind quietly. When he turned, Julie spoke in a tremulous whisper.

"Johnny Hussey—" she began.

"Don't whisper at me, woman!" he cried.

"Johnny Hussey must never come to this house again," she murmured.

"Why so? Johnny is a decent fellow. There's no harm in him."

"Bid must never go to the barracks again," she said.

In the dark, she could hear him finishing the tea at a gulp.

"Bid," he said, "is your blood and not mine. You can do what you like with her."

"But mightn't Bid let things out of her? She shouldn't go to the barracks, Leo."

"Are you trying to probe me, too?" he snapped. "Bid can go to the barracks as often as she likes, for all I care. I think you went often enough to the barracks at Ballingarry in your own day."

She lowered her head at the cruel jibe. So he had not forgotten that dreadful night, thirty years ago, when she sold him to the peelers. He turned at the door.

"I met Casey, the chemist, coming from a card school. He said his wife told him get that dress from you, but he forgot it. I said you'd bring it around in the morning."

When he was gone, she sank into a chair and began to cry. The dress was not ready for Casey's wife. It was a small thing to cry about, and any other time she would have laughed at it, and said Casey's wife could fish for her dress. Though it was well past midnight she went to the work-room, and, lighting a lamp, began to whir and pedal at her machine.

Her tears fell on the dress. If Leo Donnel had suffered (and she knew only too well how much he had suffered), life to her, too, had been neither gentle nor generous. She had been living in her own way up there in Knockaderry, and afterwards in Ballingarry, when he crossed her path each time. It was a simple life, but it was a happy one.

She heard his boots fall on the floor overhead. The lamp began to wane, and she rose to fetch the oil. He had often complained bitterly to her that other people had always been interfering with his life. Hadn't he ruined her life, not once, but twice! Her tears fell into the oil in the lamp-bowl. For the first time in twenty years she thought of her child that she had not seen since she bore it. In filling the bowl the pungent liquid overflowed and rushed across the table, and ruined the precious silk of the dress. Her tears came redoubled by rage as well as self-pity. She heard a chair stir upstairs, and in a gust of anger she rushed up the little crooked stairs and into his room.

In the candle-light he looked ten years older than he was, sitting on the red-quilted bed, pulling off a trouser-leg; his chest was narrow and ribbed, his cheeks were hollow. She stalked over to him and stood over him.

"What call have you to talk to me like that, Leo Donnel? You that were the first man to put a hand of misfortune on me. What did you ever do to me but destroy me? I that had to go my two knees to you to make you hide my child from the priests and people of Knockaderry."

Again she thought of her lost child, and how she would never have another now because she was grown too old.

"And where is my child? Where, and what, is he? Is he alive, or is he dead? Is he a pauper, or what is he? My God, it was never good for me to cross my decent blood with the mad, black blood that is in you."

"Go to bed, woman," he said gently and quietly. "You're forgetting yourself, I think."

She threw her hair back out of her eyes with a wild gesture.

"Oho! You're very fine," she mocked. "And you're grand. Very grand. My Lord Donnel, if you please. My gentleman from Foxehall. But what use is your grandeur to me? Where is my child, after it all?"

Her voice rose at every word. His eyes darkened with misery and discontent, but she mistook that look for anger and contempt.

"Look at my shin!" she cried, and lifted her skirt to the knee to disclose her red flannel drawers, hanging loose about her thin shank. "I've worn it to the bone for you. From the day you were thrown out of your farm I slaved for you."

He looked at her in silence, still holding the loose trouser-leg in his hand. To infuriate herself the more she clapped her hands together as if applauding him.

"Give me my child, Leo Donnel. Give him back to me. Get him for me to be company to me, while you and your secret friends are skulking in the shadows of the ditches out by Ballingrane. Waiting for the darkness to cover ye like the owls."

He shrank up a little at the knowledge that they had been talking of him and spying on him.

"Ah!" she cried, "there's a curse on me since the day I

met you, and a curse on all ever met you, and your curse is on them and their curse is on you, and may God light it down on you. Where's your mother? Where's ould Bottom? Where's the house was bought for you? The land was given you? Where's the girls you ruined? Where's Philly Cashen? And Min Carey? Oh, I know all about you. And I'll tell the people about you. I won't stay with you. I won't stay. I won't stay."

"Very well," he said softly. "You may go."

He had spoken with the polite, almost foreign, intonation his aunts used to affect, and try to teach him. It drove her beyond herself. She flung out of the room and down the stairs, and he heard her fumble at the chain. The chain rattled loose. The rusted bolts squeaked as she drew them. He pulled on his trousers and pattered down after her, and as she stepped on the damp, starlit flags he caught her arm.

"Woman!" he whispered to her. "Where are you going?"

"What is it to you?" she shouted, deliberately shaming him. "Let me go."

"Come in, girl," he flattered. "Come in," he cajoled. "Come in and talk it over."

"No!" she screamed. "No! No! No!"

Each negation rang in the empty street. She was having her triumph over him now. She tore away from him, and ran towards Madigan's shop. A prowling dog ran from the gutter, and ran forward again when Donnel came after her, his bare feet slapping the pavement. A window was raised. Up the street the two policemen came thundering on their steel-tipped boots. Another window was raised, and Julie crouched by the wall, terrified at what she had done.

"What's up here?" panted one of the policemen.

For a minute an old terror fell on Donnel as he looked up at them, enormous in their long, black-belted coats, their great domed helmets, on the front of each the hateful dark-shining medallion of the harp beneath the crown.

Across the street he could see somebody in a white night-dress peering down at them through the window-pane. The other policeman's question took a different form, and Donnel noticed that.

"What's he up to now, my good woman?" was what he said. "What are you doing to her?" he growled at Donnel.

"Nothing at all," said Donnel.

"We'll see about that," he said truculently, and he took Donnel by the shoulder. "What's he doing to you?" he asked Julie. "Are you hurt?"

"No," said Julie, not daring to look up.

She was quiet now.

"Come home, Julie!" he implored.

She turned home, rejecting his hand when he wished to lead her.

"What's wrong with her?" asked the first policeman.

The Fenian tried to be friendly and jocular.

"Ah, sure!" he smiled. "The women do be always getting into bits of tantrums."

He hated them and hated himself for that speech. They had dragged him to their level. He had spoken to them as to friends.

"Good night, men!" he said lightly.

They let him go unwillingly. Over his head he thought he could hear an unsympathetic murmuring as he went, suddenly feeling the cold flags under his feet and the cold air through his shirt.

Julie was gone upstairs when he reached the shop, and by the time he had locked and bolted and chained it she was in her room. He went wearily to his bed, and began to undress again. For a long time he sat there, his head in his hands, and then he heard her steps come slowly upstairs to his door. She came and stood beside him, and whispered down to him.

"I disgraced you, Leo. But you rose me."

He said nothing, and she turned to go away.

"I suppose," he said quietly, "I suppose—"

She looked at him.

"I suppose," he tried again, "we could have him here."

"Who?"

He would not acknowledge his bastard.

"Your son. He'd be near twenty, now."

"He'd be twenty-one next December."

"We could say he was my nephew from behind Limerick."

She came and sank beside him on the bed. They were shoulder to shoulder as they sat looking at the candle. Her hand reached out slowly and fell on his bare thigh. She stroked it a few times, and began to weep again. He took her wrist and shook it assuringly.

"Come to bed," he said.

She undid her clothes and crept in beside him—the first time since they were married.

From her attic window in Madigan's Bid had seen the little group clustered on the pavement, and after they were gone she dressed herself and went down the cold stairs and across to Well Lane, but the quiet street and the moon glittering on the damp slates calmed her, and she hesitated to knock at the sleeping house. She stole back timidly to the shop, only to find the door locked; so once more she went to Well Lane and began to whisper and call through the letter-box, and fling pebbles at Julie's window. As there was no reply, and she could hear the tramp of the patrolling night-police around the corner in the main street, she flitted away down the lane, and so out to the first fields beyond the pump. The white muddy road was cold and dreary as it stretched in a perfectly straight line—it was a military road—off to Ballingarry. She walked beside the hedges for a while, past one or two cottages all dark and silent, until presently the sudden grunt of a sow behind the ditch frightened her, and made her realize how lonely it was wandering alone in the open country at night. She turned and faced the cold roofs of the town, a little beneath her, since the road was on a gentle slope to the distant hills. But as she approached the straggling, intermittent beginnings of a street she thought how she would have to stand knocking at the hall door of Madigan's, and perhaps be questioned by the two police. There was enough shame down on the Keenes for one night, she felt, and at the cross to Beechmount she turned to the right, remembering suddenly that the morrow was a fair day, and the cattle would early moo their way into the streets, and the morning carts begin to rattle early in to the creamery.

But then the walls of Beechmount began to rise up on each side of her and the trees arched overhead, so that there was first a gloom and then a second night. She halted. Then she moved ahead, hoping to hasten out of the pitchy tunnel into the brighter night beyond. The road turned and she saw a faint, dim glow ahead of her. An animal suddenly hammered down on her, and she crushed against the ivy of the wall to let it go by. A man shouted, and she heard a woman's voice cursing, and she turned to run. They were tinkers camped on the side of the road until the dawn would let them in to the market-place to sell their crooked-hoofed donkeys. The man came up with her and grabbed her.

"Blasht you!" he shouted. "Is it you loosed my dunkeys?"

She screamed with terror. The woman ran to the pair of them, ready to strike a blow for her man if he needed help. She could see at once, even in that darkness, that Bid was not a tinker or a walking-woman.

"Lave her go, Rich. That's a dacent woman."

The man released her.

"Go after the ass," the woman commanded. "It's only the way her bloody spancel broke."

"May hell roast you," he snarled at her. "It was you put the laincish on her. I'll wallop·the face off you when I catch her."

He raced off after the straying animal, and the tinker woman cursed after him under her breath.

"It's late you're out," she said to Bid.

"I was locked out," said Bid.

"Who locked you out?"

"The shop locked me out. I can't get in until the morning."

She could feel the tinker-woman trying to see her better in the dark.

"Come and sit by the fire, if you want to," said the woman.

They moved to the red glow of the banked fire, and Bid was given an upturned bucket to sit on. A small, dirty-faced boy was peering out at the pair of them. They could hear the breathing of other children on the straw under the cart, and the shuffling of a group of donkeys farther along the road in the lee of the wall.

"I think I should go home," said Bid.

"Arrah! Don't be frightened," said the tinker woman. "We won't harm any dacent girl like you."

"Mother," whined the boy, "where's my da?"

The woman swiped at him with her shawl.

"Go to bed, you little bastard, you. Will you go to bed," she cried, "when I tell you?"

He sank down on the straw and continued to look at Bid.

"That's your eldest child?" asked Bid timidly.

"Yes," said the woman. "That's my first misfortune."

Then she sniffed as with contempt of him.

"That's young Leo Donnel," she said. "And his brother," she mocked, "is young Sir James Quirke."

Bid stared at her across the glow of the fire.

"What staring you have!" said the woman. "What's your name?"

"Bid Keene."

"Sweet God!" whispered the woman. "Is it from Ahill?"

"Yes," whispered Bid.

"You don't know me?" asked the woman.

Bid looked at the hollow tawny face, the greying hair thick with dirt falling about it, the eyes soft with drink, the teeth dark as from decay or tobacco smoke.

"I don't recognize you," she said.

The woman laughed a deep, throaty laugh of scorn.

"So you don't know Philly Cashen?"

Bid said nothing.

"Did you ever hear of me?" asked Philly.

"No," said Bid truthfully. "I never heard tell of you."

"Ah!" sighed Philly. "I was before your time."

She poked at the fire.

"How's Leo Donnel?"

"He's well."

"Is he in Foxehall always?"

"No. He's in Rathkeale."

"Cripes! Is it living in Rathkeale he is?"

"Yes."

"So he sold Foxehall?"

"He lost it. A grabber took it—his own brother, James."

"Hell's cure to him. What big house has he in the town?"

"He has no big house. He has a paper shop in Well Lane. He lost all he had when he came out of jail."

"Out of jail? For God's sake, what put the—in jail?"

"He went to jail for a Fenian. He was in jail for ten years for near killing a peeler."

Philly laughed out so loud that the donkeys were hustled together in a heap. Then she stopped suddenly, and leaned over the fire to look into Bid's eyes.

"Begobs, then, I'll go into that paper shop tomorrow to

see him. I'll bell-ring him all over the town. I'll sing a song
for him. Ha! Won't he get the surprise to see me!"

Bid looked at her in horror, vaguely beginning to understand the connexion between this woman and Leo. She
could see the fair gathering about the door of the shop, the
half-drunken woman waving her shawl in the air, the foul
words of abuse. As she looked, Philly clapped her hands
with delight.

"But he's married," was all Bid could say.

"What gom married him?"

"My sister Julie married him," said Bid angrily.

Just then the tinker came back with the gadding donkey,
and tying it by the neck to the wheel of the cart, he hit the
woman a blow on the side of the head that knocked her
into the mud. At once she rose, and scraped about for a
weapon to hit him with. Bid raced from them as they quarrelled, and presently their shouts and the crying of the boy
faded behind her, and she was again in view of the dark
roofs of the town. She stole in, her mind turbulent, to Well
Lane, stealing, like a criminal bearing some dreadful secret,
along from door to door. Again she called and whispered
through the slit of the letter-box; she tapped, and then
knocked at the door; she threw small stones at Julie's window. At last she began to aim higher still, at Leo's window,
always looking guiltily about her to see if the police or
some waking person were watching her. The window rose
creakingly, and Julie looked down.

"Are you all right, Julie?"

Julie answered crossly.

"There's nothing wrong with me. Go back to bed. Go
back to the shop."

"I can't," she whispered up. "I'm locked out."

"Oh, by dog," muttered Julie. "What a night!"

The two went into Julie's bed, and, as they lay side by
side, Julie curled against her young sister's flanks and be-

gan to weep softly on her breast and confess her troubles to her. It was a comfort to Julie to tell her sister of that sin she had never confessed to anyone but the priest. Staring up at the dark, Bid heard her in a kind of terror at the ways of the world.

"Shouldn't I have my son?" asked Julie through her tears.

"Yes, yes, Julie!" comforted Bid, as if she were a mother herself.

"Oh, Bid, I wants him," said Julie.

"Yes, yes," murmured Bid. "Husha now! Husha, Julie, now! Sleep, like a good girl. Husha, hush! What's the use of crying?"

Julie slept and Bid lay awake, her mind going back and forth over what she had heard that night. She knew more of Leo Donnel than she had ever known or suspected. She thought of Philly Cashen and other names she had heard spoken in a sideward way when she was in Ahill. She wondered if her life could ever pan out in that crude and cruel way, and if she had not feared to wake her sister, she would have broken into tears at the thought of it. All she could do was to turn her head from time to time to the window to see a patch of night-light, and keep herself from being maddened by the impenetrable dark. Towards dawn she slept, and then the sisters wakened to the mournful lowing of beasts beneath their window. Disentangling their limbs, they stretched their unrested bodies and listened to the rain falling on the fair.

3

Donnel crouched by the shop stove all that morning, in his fist a crumpled piece of paper, on which Bid had written a message and a warning about Philly Cashen. He poked the fire from time to time, leaning forward as if to hide his head in his own shadow.

Outside the door the pent cattle thrust their tousled fur through the red bars and the blue bars of the creels under a drizzling rain, their mooing and bleating passing from cart-creel to cart-creel, and from dawn to noon, weaving in the wet air with the crying of men's voices, linking cry to cry in ceaseless lament. Only in rare moments did an astonishing silence fall, and then the deep moaning of beasts that had waked the town in the rainy dawn rose again and again over the dung-sodden streets. In that brief moment, while the beasts seemed to halt for breath, he heard the human voices, hoarse with passion, shouting in argument or dispute.

"They're good calves, and I won't deny them, and I won't belie them, and I won't decaive you, my good man. The woman didn't shtint the grain on them calves that never had wan day's ailing. Am I bumming or boashting to you, my good man, that I would tell you a lie on them? My sworn oath I would not, nor thry to, nor could I. Now lave me talk, I tell you, lave me say my say on them calves, my dacent man, and I am telling you the truth about my lovely calves that got the besht of feedin' and atin'. By Chrisht, may God forgive me for the cursing, but you will go farther and fare worse, but I won't press you. Oh, no! I won't press you or thry to influence you—"

Yes, but in Quain's and Ambrose's and Neville's, and the other five-and-forty pubs in the town, the voices would be milder and more sibilant as they talked of his wife and him. As they stand swaying and leaning, sideways and forwards, to drop great brown spits on the damp floor, the frothed pints of porter before them on the lead-covered counter or the cross-legged tables, or around the ledges of the walls, they probe delicately for his intimate history.

"The money's in them calves and you're the lucky man

to see them go to your haggard this day and I'm loth to
lose them, the lovely craytures sure, that got the feeding of
childer. If you saw them calves, and they suckling milk
and they shwelling with fat, then, by my hand, you'd have
them without a word. You can feel it in them; for God's
sake, man, you can feel the blomach of them. I'm glad to
sell a good thing. Tell me. Will you have to dhrive them
far? Phwat might your name be now? I'd like to know
where my dotes of calves is gone to. Didn't I know I
thought I knew you! Do you know them Keenes of Ahill
west? Did you hear what happened last night? Well, now—"

And later, in some other snug where man and wife meet.

"I did sell them"—dragging off his grey wool socks—
"and there you are. As good a price as was got at the fair.
I heard no price betther. I'd liefer bring the calves back
home than take less; and I told the man so, a man of the
Brownes, west by Knockaderry, that bought them from me;
and, by God, he was a tough man, but I was a match for
him. 'Will you shplit them?' says he. 'I will not,' says I.
'Fy would I?' 'If you will make a divide of the animals,'
says he, 'I will give you the price you ask.' Do you see what
he was up to? 'Will you make a divide of the animals?' says
he, and he knew dom' well I would not do such a thing. 'If
you will do so,' says he, 'I will give you your price.' But
I was able for him. Do you think I would let him pick a
choice of my bashtes? We had a drink in Normoyle's on it,
and do you know what he told me about them Keenes of
Ahill, and that ould divil down by Well Lane—?"

In every snug it was the same, where the voices would
rise with the body-steam and the blue and grey tobacco
smoke, and with rounder, quieter voices the women sipped
their whisky or their stout, and kept a hawk's watch on
their mates' handling of the new-found money; and, again,
upstairs, where these voices penetrate like the rumbling of
a weir to the parlours, and the voices are lower still. The

women, stuffed creaking into their best Sunday black, touch
heads over his wife's name and his name, and, maybe, other
names like that on the piece of paper in his fist, that he had
hoped Rathkeale would never know.

And so, too, every shawled figure that entered Madigan's
made Bid look up with fright, lest it should be the tinker
woman of the night before. She had been lucky enough to
see her with her husband in a far corner of the square, and
had managed to speak with Johnny—he was on duty in the
streets—and implore him not to let "that creature with the
bandaged head" go next nor nigh the shop in Well Lane.
"Arrah, for why?" asked Johnny. "I can't tell you, Johnny,"
she said. "I'll tell you another time. But she have a spite
for Leo Donnel. I can tell you that, and she'll disgrace him
if she sees him."

All day Johnny hung about near that cart and its drove
of shaggy asses, waiting for a chance to move the woman
and her man out of the town. By noon she began to get
slightly drunk and noisy, and he found her abusing another
tinker woman in foul words. On the spot, he threatened
to put her in the lock-up if she didn't behave herself. By
the afternoon, when he came back from his dinner, she
was drunk, and he took her by the arm and, bidding her
man follow him, led her out to the edge of the town and
ordered her go about her business—for if he found her on
the streets again that day, she'd not leave the town until
the petty sessions sent her to Limerick Jail. To lead her
the quickest way from the streets, he took her down the
deep, crooked side-alley that leads to Well Lane and the
open country. As the little group, the woman shouting, the
husband protesting, the children crying, and Johnny silent
but stern, turned into Well Lane it passed Leo Donnel,
where he led his mother-in-law's donkey into the cooper's
yard by the pump. Nobody took any heed of him but
Johnny, 'and he shot him a hard, contemptuous look. The

old man halted until they passed, and he was white and trembling long after they were out of sight.

As he turned the donkey loose in the backyard of the cooper's to crop the grass between the cobbles, he could see the old women, after shriving, sitting in their frilled bonnets in the back-kitchen, gossiping with one another while they peeled the potatoes with stony fingers, and dipped in the fat bacon on their plates for a piece that would not need munching by rotted teeth or empty gums.

He heard the voices suddenly fall, and looking in he saw them eyeing him, as he thought, curiously. He broke from the stable boy who was talking to him, and hurried back to the sanctuary of his shop.

There he found his wife and Mag Keene standing waiting for him, and he could see by Julie's face that she had been crying.

" 'Tis in Quain's, the cooper's," said Donnel, and he poked the coals in the stove, and turned down his coat collar.

"I must talk with you, Leo Donnel," said Mag.

"Talk away," he said to the red fire.

"You should have told me," said Mag, in a cold voice, "that my daughter had a son by you."

Julie closed the door of the shop. He put his hands behind his tails and faced her.

"It wouldn't be any good to you to know."

"It would. My daughter would have married you twenty years ago, or she wouldn't have you at all. She'd have married you when you had a bit of substance, and not when you were beggared and she has to work for you. And do you think if I knew of it I'd have let my children go from me to the ends of the world, if I knew the sort of thing could happen them at my own door? Ah, but if my husband, God rest him, was alive now—"

"I wasn't afeard of your husband, or of any man."

"Don't rise me," she threatened, and her bleared eyes grew pointed and her face flushed.

"What is it you want of me?" he asked.

"That boy must come back," she ordered. "I know you don't go to church or chapel, Leo, and may God and His Holy Mother forgive you and soften your hard heart, and I suppose it's all equal to you whether the boy is being brought up a Christian or a Protestant. But back he must come, and be given the rearing he deserves."

"I'm thinking he's well reared now, if he's alive at all."

"Maybe you'd wish he wasn't?"

He walked to the dingy window and looked out at the thinning fair. "There's no need for your talk," he said. "I'll see about it. But it's because Julie wants him, and for no other reason."

The old mother nodded with satisfaction, and turned to Julie.

"I'm going up to the chapel. I must lay my troubles before the Mother of God. I have no wan to live for now, Julie, but yourself and Nonie and Bid. Don't deceive me again, girl."

"I won't, mother," cried Julie fervently. "I won't, mother."

"Don't, Julie. Nor you, Leo."

With the toddling steps of a child she moved to the door. Leo opened it for her. The gabble of the fair and the moan of the beasts was still deafening.

"That will be done, Leo?" she asked.

But, as it was less of a question than a command, he would not reply, and they left it at that for the time being.

2

An Ambitious Man

THAT night—it was in the April of 'ninety-eight—put a
stop to the meetings in the little parlour over the paper
shop. Johnny and Bid quarrelled because she would not,
after all, tell him the story of Philly Cashen, and Wintermann suddenly declared that he couldn't stand listening
any longer to that old devil of a Fenian blathering against
the Government.

In June, however, Johnny and Bid made up their quarrel, and he agreed to meet her one evening as she left the
shop, and walk with her along their favourite path by the
river. But as he lay on the blanket of his bed in the barracks dormitory, studying the fat blue book of the police
code until it would be time for the appointment, the Head
entered. He glanced at the book, and nodded approv-
ingly.

"You couldn't be reading a better volume, Hussey," he
commended.

Then he drew a long envelope from his tunic and held it
out.

"Take the trap, and deliver that at once to the district
inspector's house in Mount Massey."

"Now, sir? Tonight, sir?"

"I said 'at once.' I know you aren't on duty, but it's im-
portant."

Johnny buckled on his belt and perched his forage-cap
on the side of his head and hurried out to the stables. If he
was quick he would still be in time for Bid. He rattled

quickly about the rear of the town, and within half an
hour he was cantering under the trees of the Mount Massey
woods; many a time he had poached there as a boy, and
seen many a fox break covert there and head for Knockfierna. The inspector's house was a tall, red-brick house with
a white portico, and Johnny almost feared to lead the
horse on the clean, winking gravel of the drive before it.
He was wondering whether he should stand to attention
before and after he rang the door-bell, when the inspector
himself appeared about the side of the house. That simpli-
fied things, and Johnny stood like a statue while the letter
was being read; he was entirely at a loss for the correct
routine of behaviour, when, after reading through the letter, his officer glanced keenly at him and, turning on his
heel, said over his shoulder:

"Come inside a moment."

Johnny almost scraped the soles from his boots on the
iron scraper, and he sidled about the picture-laden hall like
a shop-walker after a customer. And when he found himself
in the study, and, in response to his superior's invitation,
sat in an arm-chair, he still kept the upper portion of body
so rigidly to attention that he could scarcely breathe. The
inspector offered him a cigarette from a silver case.

"No, sir, thank you," faltered Johnny. "I don't smoke at
all, sir."

"Well, it *is* a foolish habit. But I have such a lot of work
to do—er—it keeps me—er—you know—"

"Yessir," said Johnny with vigour.

"Just forget for a moment, will you, Hussey," said the
inspector, as he leaned back in his desk-chair, "that you are
in my house."

"Yessir," said Johnny, like a rifle shot.

A little frown passed over the inspector's face.

"I mean—er—just forget that you are on duty, would
you?"

"Yessir," said Johnny, with equal precision and greater respect.

"The head constable tells me," said the inspector, with his hand on the letter on the desk, "that"—he paused to blow a smoke ring—"you are a very efficient constable."

He smiled inwardly at Johnny's blush of satisfaction.

"Thank you, sir," said Johnny very mildly.

"How long are you out of the depot, Hussey?"

"Just over four years, sir."

"I see. Tell me. You're a Limerick man, aren't you?"

"Yessir," smiled Johnny. "I come from five miles west of Rathkeale."

"Indeed? Oh? I don't know that side of Limerick very well, but it's rather nice there, isn't it?"

"Oh, it's nate, sir."

"Good hunting?"

"The best, sir. Great for fox and snipe, sir."

Johnny was gradually becoming dog-loyal to this man, who was so natural and condescending, and yet kept all the correct manners and the proper distance of a gentleman and a superior talking to a policeman.

"It's very quiet, too, isn't it? I don't believe we have had any trouble at all there recently, nothing worth mentioning, I mean."

"I never remember wan particle of trouble in the place, sir, since I was a boy. Ah, they're very decent people in Limerick."

"Though there was, about ten years ago, wasn't there, I have a vague recollection of it, some kind of land trouble? An eviction. And we sent men on special protection work. What was the man's name? Connel, or Donnel, or something?"

Johnny's heart jumped.

"Leo Donnel, sir. Foxehall. A grabber that took his land."

"A grabber?" asked the inspector sternly.

"I mean, sir, that's what the people called him."

In land matters, for all his four years in "the Force," even Johnny was still more on the side of the people than the law.

"By the way," said the inspector suddenly, "this Donnel man was in jail, wasn't he?"

"Yessir. Ten years in Portland Prison, commuted from fifteen years' penal servitude. He took part in the 'sixty-seven troubles, sir. He was a Fenian."

"Was?"

"Ah, there's no harm in him, now, sir."

The inspector rose and filled a glass from a decanter.

"Drink?" he asked Johnny in the mirror opposite him.

"No, thank you, sir. I don't drink at all, sir."

"Yes. A foolish business, drinking. But—er—medicinal. After dinner especially—er—I find it quite, what you might call, soothing."

Drinking it slowly, he turned, and then he suddenly shot out:

"How well do you know this Fenian, Hussey?"

"I—I—I know him well, sir."

"How well?"

"He's, he's my uncle, sir."

The inspector halted in the act of raising his glass, and looked in a peculiar way at him.

"Indeed? Your uncle?"

"My mother's brother, sir," said Johnny, trying to minimize the connexion. "He was always the wild one of the family, sir," he explained timidly.

The inspector tapped the head constable's letter in an absent way, and smoothed out some wrinkles on the paper; the constable's answers agreed with everything in the Head's report. Johnny twisted his forage-cap around and around on his knee, feeling far from happy at the turn the conversation was taking.

"Ten years' penal servitude—that's a stern sentence?"

"It is, sir."

"He must have been a dangerous man, Hussey. There's no getting behind a sentence like that. I think we can agree on that, eh?"

"Oh, yes, sir."

It was an interview that Johnny would never forget—the importance of it, the condescension of it, the impressiveness of it, the unexpectedness of it.

"And," went on the inspector solemnly, "he's probably a very dangerous man yet. Why did you say there's not much harm in him?"

Johnny wished he hadn't said so. After all, if old Donnel was only a foolish old lad, he could do dangerous things in his foolishness. He remembered the fair day and the tinker woman, and the night before it, when the town said he chased his wife all around the streets to cut her throat. Johnny decided that it was none of his business to protect him.

"Maybe . . ." he faltered. "Well, I have no reason, sir, only his being so quiet of late years."

"Ah! Quiet? Still waters run deep."

"Of course," Johnny hastened to say, "he's no real connexion of mine, sir."

"No, no, no, no!" The inspector was equally quick to agree. "Quite! I quite understand your position. Every family," he condescended further, "has its black sheep."

"Yessir," said Johnny—much relieved.

His relief was brief. Once more the inspector shot a surprise question at him.

"You visit him very frequently, I understand."

The question gave Johnny exactly the same feeling as the sight of the two night police had given Leo Donnel when he saw the might of the law towering above him. Johnny felt the same immense and pitiless forces closing about him; he saw he was being watched and reported on. He began to suspect every one of his colleagues, especially Wintermann.

"Y-y-yes, sir."

Seeing the inspector considering him, he thought he should add some explanation. He gave the true one.

"I think, sir, if you don't object to my saying so, sir, it's on account of his sister-in-law, sir."

The other smiled benevolently. He actually raised his glass to Johnny. Johnny could have gone on his knees with gratitude.

"Ah!" smiled the inspector, as if he were sincerely relieved. "That's it. Now, I understand."

"That's the way of it, sir." Johnny smiled foolishly, nodding his head many times in a kind of maudlin shyness. "And to be sure, sir," he resumed very seriously (if Bid could have heard him!), "if it's against the rules in any way, I'd not be—"

"No, no, no, no!" interrupted the inspector. "Not at all. A man's private life is his own affair. The Force does not, to be sure, meddle with politics. But apart from that, a man's private life is absolutely his own. You understand?"

"I understand," sighed Johnny obediently, as if he were equally willing to believe or cease to believe at a moment's command.

"I hear," said the inspector—and Johnny wondered what was coming next—"that you are having a shot at the acting-sergeant's examination?"

"Well, I *was* thinking of it, sir, but—"

He had been so humbled that it now seemed a presumption on his part to aim so high.

"It's in July, isn't it? That's next month! You know they always ask me for my opinion of the man?"

"Do they, now, sir?"

That "they" was filled with awe.

"Yes. Of course, I just go by the reports of the head constable. Unless I happen to have met or known the man in some other way."

"Yessir."

The inspector rose.

"I need hardly say that counts for a lot."

What "that" meant Johnny was unable to say.

"Well, good-bye, Hussey. I wish you luck."

He held the door-handle, for so long that Johnny looked up inquiringly.

"I was wondering whether I ought to tell you," said the inspector. "Yes."

He considered for a second—or seemed to consider.

"I think you ought to know that Leo Donnel is still a Fenian."

"Aren't the Fenians all done and finished with, sir?" asked Johnny innocently.

The inspector sniffed.

"He is a member of the Irish Republican Brotherhood— a secret society, as you know. Condemned by his own Church."

"Couldn't he be charged with an offence, sir?"

"It's not easy. Or advisable. Certainly, if any man commits a criminal offence, that sort of thing would be taken into account in considering the seriousness of the purpose. But Donnel is, as you say, very deep. I just tell you so that you shouldn't be taken in by him. It might prejudice your career, you know."

"Certainly," thought Johnny, "this was the decentest man he ever knew." The "decent man" led him to the hall.

"He won't take *me* in, sir," he said warmly.

"Of course, I know he is your uncle—"

"I don't care, sir, if he was fifty and forty times my uncle."

"Well, good-bye."

At the hall door the inspector left him with a final word.

"As a conscientious member of the Force, we naturally expect you to report anything suspicious you may observe."

"Yessir." (This a little weaker.)

"Write directly. to me."

"Yessir." (Weaker still.)

The inspector turned on his heel. The glass door closed. The hanging beads on it rattled. In the half-dusk of the trees Johnny felt his brain all tangled and dark; easily he untied the knots in the reins. In a dream he let the horse walk down the avenue. He saw alternately the bland face of his inspector, the cunning grin of Wintermann, and old Leo Donnel in his black hat, smiling foolishly at him over his pile of yellowing newspapers; but he saw now, as he had never seen before, a cunning in that smile and a secret in those small, peering eyes. Under the trees of the main road he halted the nag, to think over all that had been said within the past hour, and so intent was he in trying to find his own profits in that conversation that he forgot all about the passage of time, until a flake of night whirled before his eyes and he heard the squeak of the frightened bat. At Beechmount Cross he took the long way round, knowing that Bid would have given him up, and he could not see her until she returned from her angry, solitary walk to Well Lane.

It was only nine o'clock, and the summer dusk was yet tenuous and aerial when he stabled the horse and changed into his best uniform and walked down to Well Lane. He got no reply to his knocking, however, and inserting his hand in the letter-box he drew the wire tied to the lock inside. Nobody replied to his hammering on the counter, or his calls as he went upstairs, step on step. There was nobody in the parlour, but he could hear a deep snoring from the workroom, and there he found Julie lying across the machine as if in a faint. When he raised her head she opened her eyes faintly, and muttered something through lips dribbling with saliva, and he could smell from her breath the sweet fume of whisky. He had carried her into the parlour and laid her on the one-armed sofa, just as Bid's light step raced up the stairs. He met her at the door, and his strange look silenced the angry reproach on her lips.

"What is it?" she cried in fright, looking past him.

"She's all right, Bid. Come in here."

He led her to the workshop, and there they both saw in the same instant the bottle and glass beside the machine.

"Just a drop too much," soothed Johnny.

She sat by the machine, and overcome by this climax to the smaller sorrow of the night, broke into a fit of childish weeping.

"Oh, so that's what all the talk is about," she wept.

"What talk?"

"Oh, the town is talking. It was Leo three months ago, and now it's Julie. I hears them in the shop, and they shuts up when I come near them."

"I heard nothing, Bid, only—"

"What?"

"Well, I heard Wintermann call her . . . what?—The Jolly Jailor."

She overcame her tears at the insult to her name, and went into the parlour. She tried to make her sister comfortable on the sofa, and sent him to get a greatcoat to throw on her.

He went upstairs to the bedrooms, the first time he had ever been in that part of the house, and knowing she was in no hurry for him to return, he sat on the edge of Leo's bed and looked about him. There were old coloured supplements tacked to the wall all about the room. On the dressing-table lay a pile of newspapers, a row of books, the combs and brushes that Leo used for his fine, long beard, the paper spills for his pipe, the dozen odd objects that an old man loves to accumulate. The greatcoats behind the door startled him; in the dim light they were like effigies of their owner. Idly he drew out the drawer of the dressing-table: a couple of old coins, a skin of orange, a clasp-knife, a bundle of letters, a miniature of a beautiful woman.

"How he loves to collect old rubbish," thought Johnny.

Then he dived his hand into the bundle of letters, and at random he drew out three or four and stuffed them into his pocket. He took down a greatcoat and went back to Bid.

They covered her, and went down to the shop to wait for Leo. He came in almost at once, and telling him Julie was "a bit sick," they went out, without speaking or thinking, along the white, dusty, empty street to the river and a brief walk. It would be dark in half an hour.

By the river the old walls of Castlematrix and the high flour mills tower side by side where the shallow water breaks over the gravel shoals, or about rocks bedded in the middle of the stream. The flowering chestnuts, milk-white and rose-pink, drooped down to the grass that rose, rank from rain, to meet them, and deep in their gloom white cattle lay, munching in fat-throated ease. As the two walked by the river's edge, Bid confided at last to him what her sister had told her that night before the fair—the secret of her unacknowledged son—and then told him also the story of Philly Cashen and how she had met her, and what she had discovered from her about Leo. She told it all to excuse her sister, and she was glad to find him ready to agree with her in everything she said in her bitter anger against Leo. Yet, when she had exhausted her pity for the sister, she was sorry she had been so harsh on the old man.

"We're hard on the old divil tonight," she sighed, half in mockery of herself.

They were sitting in a deserted corner of the river, where the reeds covered them and they could hear nothing but the gurgling water. They were very happy in their renewal of love after so long a quarrel, and they leaned against each other and were ready to be more confiding than they had ever been before.

"No," Johnny said, "we're not hard on him. Look at all the harm he done in his lifetime. Didn't he ruin himself? Didn't he ruin his mother's work and his father's work, that bought him a house and a farm that's all gone for nothing now?"

"It's what Julie told him, Johnny!"

"And didn't he ruin Philly Cashen, so that she's a dirty tinker's woman now, streeling the roads, and in and out of the police court? And is she the only wan? And from what you tell me, didn't he ruin your own sister, too? No. I haven't a spark of pity left for him. And what's more, he doesn't deserve it. What!" he said sternly. "He's my own mother's brother, and he's your own mother's nephew and a cousin of your own, but I have no soft words for a man the like of that. The lazy old highcockalorum! The tree grows the way of the young shoot, Bid, and mark my words, there's badness in him yet."

"Ah, his day is done, now," said Bid. "And a hard day he made for himself, too."

"Hard? What hard? Did my mother have a hard life? Often I heard her tell of it, and no soft words she had for him that helped to make it hard. Did I have a hard life? Did yourself? Did your own poor old mother? Did Julie?"

He pointed his finger at the root of a thorn tree that grew beside them.

"What was it made your mother's fingers the like of stick? Are Leo Donnel's hands like that?"

She saw her mother's hands. She saw the body bent in two, the hair so thin that you saw the scalp beneath it, the chin grey with outcrop, and the two eyes red and bleared like a wintry evening.

"Ah, yes," said Johnny, he also seeing his own mother's face, wrinkled and furrowed, and the two eyelids white and wrinkled like an old hen's.

" 'Tis true," she sighed, and the life of Ahill flooded back to her, and she saw herself as she had been on that sorry farm, her thin legs unprotected from the thistles and the shale, her fair weak hair tied with a bit of red shift, and falling like a horse's tail down her hollow back.

The lovers rose. The dew was thick on the grass. The night was about them.

The last glimmer of day was falling out of high, passing clouds, so vast in their shaggy shapelessness that they covered west and earth and east with their glow. In that last strange moment of light, thrown back from the fields, livid as ivy, Bid's dress gleamed like marble, and the brass fittings on Johnny's belt cast a sheen of verdigris on the black leather of his belt. She would have turned back, but he led her farther and farther into the fields, and as they went the air grew more still and heavy, and the leaves on the chestnuts hung motionless and ponderous from their branches, and it was already thick night beneath them. In that heavy air she could scarcely breathe, in that hot aqueous gloom, and as he drew her nearer to him, she almost allowed herself to be carried along bodily in the crook of his arm.

He saw that she was crying softly to herself, and he drew her under a hawthorn tree from out of whose dark, sweet heart a robin or a wren, or some small field bird, came fluttering like a mouse.

"Let us sit here, Bid."

The great drops fell, and they sheltered deeper still, and he began to talk of love to her until she was ready to sink on his breast and fall there into a swoon. As the sky flashed with white fire, and after a second the thunder rumbled over their heads, she curled closer and closer to him and he drew his body about her as if it were a cloak, so that by the time the downpour was hissing around them and the storm passing in its swift flight and the last night-pour ranging over the deserted fields, they were lying in one another's arms by the tree trunk, their knees locked and their lips one. It was a long time before they rose, shy and awkward, and as yet unused to love. Silently they went back the path they had come, until they came to the last field by the bridge.

The water of the river was louder now and the tall bulk of the mills dark above them against the last glimmering of the sky. They held one another by the hand and paused in their walk.

"Bid," he said, "if it was a thing, now I could make a home for you, would you marry me?"

She leaned against his shoulder, her mind filled with the scenes of her harsh childhood, her empty, lanky girlhood, all the miseries and the small precious joys of home that were gone for ever because womanhood was fallen on her and she must begin her own life. She and Johnny had enjoyed the days and nights as they came, and as surely came and went again. She had asked no more than that they might go on like that for ever, though she had waited eagerly, too, for this question, thinking fondly that when it came it would open a new world to her. But now he had asked it, and she saw no new world beginning—she did not even see the continuance of the old. Instead, with Julie's troubles, and this talk about Leo, she saw that her life was linked as by a bridge to the harsh life of Ahill she had for so long forgotten. Her tears returned, and she made no reply.

"Would you, Bid, girleen?"

Through her tears she said then that "She would indeed, Johnny." He kissed her, and for a long time they sat there, she with her face buried in his shoulder calming herself, he looking into the dark, listening to the falling of the stream, very near to tears himself.

That was all. When she was calmed she rose, and they went slowly through the fields, arm-in-arm, joined to one another for life.

They crossed the railway to where the road was white, and the dust clung to their boots. There was a dim light in the windows of the church, and as they came nearer to it they saw the women, in twos and threes, hurrying down the steps from their sodality.

"I'll tell you a secret, Bid," said Johnny in a low voice. "In return for the secret you told me. But you must promise not to tell a living soul, Bid."

She said nothing.

"I know you wouldn't tell anyone, Bid. But it's a great secret—that I know only in the course of my duty. I don't know should I tell you at all."

"I don't want to know it," Bid whispered. "For what we don't know don't trouble us."

They walked on in silence.

"What is it?" she asked.

"You promise?"

"You can keep it," she snapped; and then— "I'm sorry, Johnny," she offered humbly.

"Well, then, it's this. Leo Donnel is being watched up at the barracks by somebody. He's a man, it is well known, that's likely to make trouble again for himself and others. That's why I say to you, Bid, that there's no pity lost on the old fellow."

"Is it Leo?"

"Bid!"

He held her by the arm.

"I was told it this very night by the D.I. He's in a secret society. He's out to do harm."

She turned to him in terror.

"But, my God, Johnny, we must tell Julie. We must tell himself."

"Tell what?" cried Johnny. "After you promising me to tell nobody? Do you want to ruin me? My getting the stripes depends on nobody knowing."

He was sorry he had said so much. But she did not appear to make anything of it at the moment.

They halted on the second railway bridge and looked down at the few dim lights of the town.

"Oh! The old fool," she said crossly. "The wicked old cripple. Isn't it enough trouble he caused? I wouldn't care what happened him only for Julie."

"You can't stop the tree from growing, Bid."

She turned, and looked at the last few old women toddling out of the church.

"You promise not to tell anyone, Bid? Not even Julie?"

"I'm going to the chapel," she said. "I lost my sodality for you."

"You promise me faithfully, Bid?" he persisted, leaning over her.

She nodded.

"Bid!"

He held her cool hand for a second; then she ran from him. He watched her climb the long wide steps, and disappear into the great door of the nave. He wondered whether he should have told her, but he felt it would be for the best later on. Turning, he saw the last train for Tralee and Kerry draw in by the platform under the bridge. The passenger got in and the passenger got out; the postboy flung his light bag into the van; there was a clank of milk cans, and the guard waved his flag. The white clouds of smoke evaporated in the dark beyond the bright signal-box, white in the dark, and the great domes of the crowding trees. There it clustered for a while and was gone.

Johnny turned to find a stranger by his side, a low, fat, dark-haired young man, with a pair of deep-burrowed eyes staring at him from under a peaked sailor's cap. In his hand he held a black duffle bag such as sailors or soldiers use.

"Do you know a gentleman, mate," asked the stranger, "called Leo Donnel?"

"I do," said Johnny, and he looked curiously at the sailor.

"Maybe," suggested the stranger politely, "you could direct me to locate his dwelling-house?"

"I could," said Johnny. "I'll go with you. I was going that way," he said, as the stranger began to expostulate. "Did you come far?" he asked next.

"A bit," said the stranger.

"It's a grand night for travelling, anyway," said Johnny offhand.

The other said nothing.

"Might you be a relation of Leo Donnel?" asked the peeler politely.

"I might, sure. As a matter of fact I'm his nephew."

Johnny looked at him. Nephew? As Leo's own nephew himself he knew every cousin he ever had. Then, as he remembered what Bid had told him, he asked, to be certain of his man:

"I see. You're really a nephew to his wife—he's only your uncle by marriage?"

The stranger looked crookedly back at him.

"He's my uncle," he said shortly.

They walked on silently, Johnny stealing glances at his cousin—Leo's son of how many years ago? Twenty? The fellow looked more, browned and wrinkled from staring the sun.

"This isn't a bad town," said the sailor.

"The population is six thousand five hundred," said Johnny absently. "It was better, but it's going down the slope."

"God help us," said the sailor. "All Ireland is going down the slope."

"I wouldn't say that," protested Johnny uprightly.

"Yeh what, man!" cried the stranger in such a boisterous voice that three heads popped out at once from the pink-washed cabins lining the hill. "Yeh what? Don't I see it with me own two eyes? Every time I come back to Ireland she looks dingier and shabbier than ever before. Look at Dublin!"

He halted and pointed with his stick back up the hill. "Tanneries shutting down. Mills shutting down. The bottle factory at Ringsend on half-time. No wan can persuade me. Down the slope—that's the only word for it."

He resumed his walk.

"You come from Dublin, I see," hinted Johnny.

"Maybe I do," growled the other.

"You're a travelled man," commented Johnny. "I suppose you've travelled a great deal?"

"I've travelled enough," said the other shortly.

Johnny fell silent. To gain time he led him by the longest possible way about to Well Lane. At every door there were people taking the last breath of air before turning in to their kitchens for the night.

"I don't like the cut of this place," complained the stranger, as they came about at the rear of the town. "I think I'll go back to Limerick by the next train."

"There's no next train," said Johnny. "You came by the last one."

"What sort of a bloke is this Leo Donnel?" asked the stranger, halting by a fallen wall, and spitting into the nettles behind it.

He cocked his eye at Johnny as if it were Johnny who were trying to lure him on.

"Ah, he's a nice old man," Johnny said. "Are you related to him?"

"Are you a policeman?" asked the stranger suspiciously.

"What makes you think that?" asked Johnny.

"You asks so many questions," complained the other.

They walked on a few steps. It seemed to Johnny that he wasn't going to probe anything out of this fellow.

"Is he odd?" asked the stranger.

"Odd?"

"Yes, odd? Soft? Off his trolley? Daft? Gone up here? Looney? Batty? *Is the man mad?*" he explained with exasperation.

"Ah, no!" said Johnny. "He's old, to be sure, but he's not mad. And he went through a lot. He was in jail for a while."

The other stopped dead.

"In jail? What for?"

"For being a Fenian."

"A Fenian?" roared the sailor.

A donkey inside the wall raced away into the dark.

"Yes. He nearly killed a policeman in 'sixty-seven."

"Begod! So the old cock had something in him!"

Johnny did not fail to note the delight with which the other said this. They were at the town pump. They turned up Well Lane in silence, and halted by the paper shop with its empty dusty windows, and inside by the light of a candle stuck on the counter Leo Donnel reading a newspaper, a long dribble falling from the cold bowl of his amber pipe.

So deeply was he buried in them that when he raised his weak eyes to peer over the flame at the pair he was too far away from Rathkeale and from that night to recognize Johnny or guess who the other was. A strange look in

Johnny's eyes—a look never to leave it when he was in the Fenian's presence from that on—made him straighten up slowly, and look from one to the other.

"Herself isn't too well," he explained. "She's in bed. And Bid wasn't in tonight."

"This man," explained Johnny in turn, "asked me to show him where you lived."

"Good night, Uncle Leo," said the stranger timidly.

Those peering eyes, the lovely greying beard, the long hair, the black wideawake had all impressed him. He held out his sunburnt and tattooed hand with a smile. Leo took it slowly, with a stern look.

"So you are my—"

At that instant his eyes fell on the wrist of the hand he held in his, and his lips softened in what was almost a smile. Johnny noticed it, and looked, too; he frowned to see on the wrist, incised in brilliant green, the figure of the harp above the crown.

"Would you take them papers up for me, Johnny?" asked the Fenian politely.

The policeman lifted the pile of frayed newspapers and went unwillingly out of the shop up the stairs. On the landing he stopped to listen. But with an exaggerated gentleness the Fenian closed the door at the foot of the stairs. Johnny did not need a great deal of imagination to see him, then, turn eagerly and swiftly to his son.

In the little parlour the lamp was lighting dimly, and he turned it up to put the papers away. Below, he could hear the excited murmur of talk from the pair in the shop, and he had no other fear of interruption at that hour. He drew out the letters he had stolen from the Fenian's drawer. The first letter was from Nicholas O'Donnell, and was all about the forthcoming 'ninety-eight rebellion centenary celebrations. Only one sentence seemed suspicious. "But," it said, "they won't throw it at Limerick this time that we took no part in the cause, no more than they could, thank God, in 'sixty-seven. I'll say no more on that score here." The second letter, of a later date, was from Frankie O'Donnell in Limerick, and as he read it Johnny grew red with excitement and delight. It ran:

"Dear Leo,

"The days of pikes are gone. I'm ready to do my part, as I always was, and others can't say the same. I and all of us look to you for the lead, and we know you won't let us down. If money could fill breeches, you could mow down every policeman and soldier in Limerick. But money is as cheap as talk, and I'm no talker. We will either have to take the things by force, or bring them into the country secretly. Sure, it was done before, and can be again. Anyway, if it's not done nothing else can be done. And I may tell you I'm not done. All we want is the man. You will hear from me in a week.

"Yours in the cause,

"proinnsias o'domhnall."

The third letter was brief.

"Dear Leo,

"Is my black pants in Well Lane? I haven't a stitch on me behind, and Callan white with snow!

"nick."

Johnny put the letters in his pocket, and went down the stairs. The uncle and "nephew" were leaning across the counter, side by side, deep in talk.

"Good night, Leo," said Johnny. "I must be off."

"Good night, Johnny," said Leo, and he showed him out, and locked and bolted the door on the night.

3

Johno

1

WITHIN a week there wasn't a soul in Rathkeale who had not seen Johno, the Donnels' nephew from Dublin. He showed himself willingly in every pub in the town, where they knew him as Sindbad or the Young Garibaldi. He remained for two weeks, while his ship was undergoing minor repairs in Limerick, well pleased with summer in the fields and the slow routine of the town, so pleased that even in the broad noonday he would raise in the cool, shadowy pubs a roar of song while the publican stood stolidly behind the counter with an occasional wink to keep him in good humour and avoid trouble.

Johno would be sitting on a porter barrel sipping his Guinness when all of a sudden he would see a cork from a wine bottle on the floor, and picking it up and smelling it, he would break off his gabble about this or that or the other to cry at the wide-eyed man or woman serving him:

"Where am I? Where am I now? Ah! Tacking by the mouth of the Douro, in by the quayside at Oporto. There it is—the smell of the casks on the quays, and they brown and red from the wine. That's a smell, I tell you."

"Mind you that, now!"

"Smells! What smells? Three miles away across the Pacific I'd smell a fruiter. The Spice Islands at five miles, and a timber boat at two miles, if the wind was with her. Ah! But

Madeira at night. To be anchored off Madeira at night, and the smell of the oranges in the summer air!"

His voice trembled with emotion to recall it. Then, if it was a man was serving him, he'd drop his voice and whisper across the counter:

"Madeira! All the English swanks goes there. All the high-up ladies. Why so? Ah, why so? They goes there to have their babies—that's why they goes there. And then they comes home as fresh as paint, and who hears again—?"

He would tap his nose and wink, and the publican would feel a strange delighted satisfaction in hearing of a wicked-ness that, thank God, Rathkeale never knew, and never would know.

Or he would recite for the publican in his empty pub all the wonders of New York and San Francisco and the ports of the Argentine and the rigours of the Horn. He didn't care whom he talked to, or when or where; all he asked was to be allowed to talk.

But it was in the parlour of Well Lane that he loved best of all to hold forth. There Leo and Julie and Bid, all so accustomed to holding their peace, were perfect listeners. On a few nights, because Julie entreated her, Bid actually brought Johnny to the house again, and then Johno's cup was full. A dozen bottles of stout stood to attention on the red plush table, and a bottle of port captained them at the ladies' end. With their aid Johno demonstrated every story, the lay of the land, the position of the captain and the first mate, the points in his plot.

So:

"Terrier? Have you a terrier?" he interrupted somebody to ask Johnny.

"Oh, no," explained Johnny. "It's the canon's terrier they're talking about."

"Ah!" sighed Johno—and at once they all leaned forward.

"I had a terrier once. And where do you think I found that dog—an Irish terrier. Just where?"

They would smile, and nod, and shake their heads.

"Odessa! Odessa!

"The chief ports of Russia," Johnny would intone, with a glance of pride at Bid, "are Odessa, and Nikoleyev in the Black Sea, Riga and Saint Petersburg in the Baltic, and Archangel in the White Sea, but the latter is closed for several months in winter.

"I was in them all," Johno would lie—though not from envy or spleen at the policeman, whom he had accepted because the Fenian had accepted him before him.

"Odessa, you know, is a terrible place. There it is"—marshalling the bottles of Guinness—"a black cliff at night, rising up over the ship. But with the moon up and the snow shining, it's like a wall of an iceberg." (*He throws his handkerchief over the bottles.*) "And there we were moored down at the wharves, and not a man aboard but the captain and myself. Every man-Jack of the crew up in the town sousing vodka. I was down in the engine room keeping up the pressure so as to be ready for the high tide, and over me head I could hear the captain tramping out on the plates of the deck like a madman, and he cursing the crew for not being aboard for the tide. Down he comes to me." (*A bottle of Guinness marched over to Johno.*) " 'Paddy,' says he. 'Sir,' says I." (*Another Paddy Bottle of Guinness—very like Johno in appearance, stood up to the Captain Bottle.*) " 'Go up, Paddy,' says he, 'and tell those bastards'—saving your presence, ladies—'that if they're not aboard in half an hour, you and me'll sail for Nikoleyev without e'er a crew.' 'Well, now, Captain,' says I, 'that's all very well. But after all, now, what authority have I,' says I, 'to order that crew to come aboard. I'm only the donkey-man,' says I, 'and these men,' says I, 'are all soused with vodka. Supposing, now,' says I, 'that I said to them, "Men," says I, "come aboard at once, men, or we'll cast off without you"— 'those men would pay no heed at all to me,' says I. 'Never you mind,' says he." (*Here Captain Bottle danced with rage.*) " 'Go up, and do as I bid you.' 'Aye, aye, sir,' says I." (*And Paddy Bottle marched off to the heights of Odessa.*) "Well, the moon was out, and it racing in and out behind the clouds, and when it was in I'd stop for I couldn't see a stim, and when it was out I'd move ahead, for I must tell you that the region of Odessa about the wharves is no nice place, what with warehouses, and drinking-houses, and low-down lodging-houses, and other kinds of houses I make no mention of; and where the snow was melted the ground was as black as if there was a hole through it to South America. I may tell you I was wishing I didn't have to go up that hill that night. Anyway, all of a sudden, as I was passing a dark hallway sort of a place, didn't a door open and a flood of foreign lingo come out of it, and a man and a woman arguing like divils, and the next thing I knew I was on the flat of me back in a lump of sooty snow, and an ould black string of a mangy dog manœuvring about me, and whinging with the kick out he got and the fear of the next kick in that he'd be sure to get if I could only reach him with me boot." (*A torn brown cork began to circle around Paddy Bottle on the red table.*) " 'Oh! Yeh black *siofaire*,' says I to him, 'what a time you chose for your exit. Go away,' says I." (*The cork raced over at Bid, so that she screamed with fright. Then Paddy Bottle threw out his chest, and tramped on and on like a grenadier up the hill. After him tripped Cork. Suddenly Bottle turns. Cork flies backwards in terror.*)

Bottle. " 'Is that you after me? Go home out of that, will you, yeh heathen mongrel.' " (*Bottle marches on in disgust. Cork slinks after Bottle. Bottle turns again.*) " 'Are you there still? Go home to hell out of this, will you?' "

Cork (*its nose in the air*). "Weowwwuuuh!" cries Johno.

Bottle. " 'It's no good for you. You picked the wrong

man, when you picked John O'Donnell to tie your tail to.' "
(*Bottle marches away. Cork circles about and follows at a safe distance.*)

"Well, I found the crew after searching about four taverns, and when they seen me, yerrah, they raised such a racket they'd be heard from here to Limerick. They put their arms about me, and it was, 'What'll you have, Paddy?' And, 'Give it a name, Paddy.' And, 'Have a this, and have a that, and have a the other.' 'I want no drink,' says I, standing up to them, as if I was the captain myself. 'I'm here,' says I, 'to tell you,' says I, 'that if yeer not down at the docks,' says I, 'in quarter of an hour,' says I—I shortened the time for them, because, yeh see, I knew them fellows better'n any captain—'within quarter of an hour,' says I, 'we'll sail without ye, and pick another crew at Nikoleyev.' Yeh, sure, they cursed me, and they cursed the captain, and they cursed the boat, and they cursed Russia; and their language was such fo'c'sle language I blush to as much as think of it in the presence of the ladies. 'All right, mates,' says I. 'I told ye,' says I. 'Ye can't say I didn't,' says I. And off I went, and they blaspheming after me like black Protestants." (*Bottle marches down the hill taking no notice of Cork, who marches at its tail. Bottle suddenly turns. Cork takes to flight, and then halts at a distance.*) "Out I came— there he was, beating his stump of a tail on the snow, me bould laddo of a dog. 'Oh,' says I, more in sorrow than in anger, 'you Russian bitch,' says I, 'if you don't get out o' me sight,' says I, 'I'll lay yeh out.' But it was no good." (*Cork follows Bottle implacably.*)

"What could I do? Did I want that dog, do you think? Down I went, and I seen to my boilers. But didn't that ould dog set up such a hullabaloo that the next minute the captain was roaring down at me to shut him up, or hunt him away, or get rid of him by any damn way I liked.

"Well, up I goes, and I cushes the ould dog away. 'Get away from out of me sight,' says I, and I throwing lumps of snow and ice at him. No good. I was hardly down, when he begins to whine and meaouw all over again. Up I comes and I takes him up in my arms and I puts him under my coat and I takes him down to the engine-room and there I kept him, feeding him with bits of meat all the night long, until he was so full he just lay down at the back of the boilers and began to snore with comfort and a fat belly.

"Well, of course, I forgot all about the ould dog. That is, until we were well out to sea. And, glory be to God, what should the mongrel do, but go lolloping up the following day to the captain on the bridge."

" 'Who,' says the captain, 'brought,' says he, 'that dog,' says he—and he holding up th' ould dog by the scruff of the neck—'aboard this bloody boat?' And he give an almighty roar that shook the ship out of the sea.

" 'Paddy, sir,' says the crew like one man.

"Well, I needn't tell you, I was in fear and trembling, and I going up the deck to stand aforeninst the captain. But, would you believe it, when I seen him and he about to swing the poor ould baste of a dog out into the Black Sea, me heart went out to the poor mangy brute.

" 'Don't drown him, sir,' says I. 'Don't drown him this time, and I'll get rid of him at Naples. I promise it, sir.'

"Well, his heart was touched. He let down the dog. 'Well,' says he, 'I'll allow that. But, mind you, now,' says he, 'that dog,' says he—and he leaning over the bridge to me —'if that dog,' says he, 'was to bite wan of my crew, I'd be responsible.' 'Well, of course,' says I, 'I sees that.' 'Oh, that's a fact,' says he. 'Mind you, now,' says he. 'Aye, aye, sir,' says I, and off I went.

"I took that dog. I took him, and I fed him. And within a week didn't I discover when the dirt was washed off him, and you couldn't—what you could when I got him—play *The Harp that Once* on his ribs, didn't I discover, bejasus, that he was an Irish terrier. By the time we reached Naples that dog was reborn. Reborn, I tell you!

"Well, sorry as I was to have to part with him, I dressed myself up and I went ashore, and my fine wire-haired terrier at my heels. I went into churches and out of churches, and I went into taverns and out of taverns, trying to give my boyo the slip. I climbed towers and I came down out of towers, until me legs was aching. I went into museums and out of museums, but ever and always there he was grinning up at me when I'd come out. I used to go in one door and come out another door half a mile away, and yet he'd be around there waiting for me as if he could see right through stone walls. In the end, he angered me, mind you. Much as I liked him before, I began to hate the sight of him now. 'All right!' says I to him, 'I have a trick will finish you, my bucko.' While he was looking after a lady dog was passing by, I hops up on a tram, and from the top of it I could see him below and he sniffing up and he sniffing down and in and out and east and west wondering where the hell I was gone to. 'Good-bye to you,' says I, and I raised me hat to him as the tram goes off around a corner. That finished him. I spent the rest of the evening in a part of the city a mile and a half away from where I left him, and when I approaches the boat late that night I had put him clean out of my mind. I got to work at my boilers, and we took the tide, and off we sailed for the Port of London, and I turned in."

Here Johno faces the company dramatically.

"I was awaked in the middle watch by being flung out of my bunk on to the floor. Yerrah, man, the storm was something terrible. There can be most fearsome storms in the Mediterranean, you know. The rudder was near torn out of its sockets. The bridge and the compass and everything about it was swep' off like a matchbox. A matchbox!"

He seizes Johnny's forage-cap, shaped as it is like a child's paper boat. Into it he lays the bottle and the cork and shakes it up and down, heel and toe, as if it were being flung to and fro by the waves.

"Can I have my cap?" asks Johnny quietly at this point.

With a frown Johno hands it to him. (*Bottle draped in a handkerchief looks very like what Johno might look like in his nightshirt.*)

"We ran before that storm like a leaf in the wind. All night long we were helpless, and when the morning broke there was a thick mist over the waves. We had no more idea where we were than if we were in the middle of the Atlantic. We might be off the coast of Morocco, we might be off the Balearic Isles, we might be driving for the rocks of Corsica. Then all of a sudden up breaks the ould dog from where he was hiding in the boiler-room, and when the captain sees him he nearly threw a fit.

" 'That's the Jonah,' says he, 'that brought a *miah* on the ship. Throw him overboard,' says he, 'this instant.' Well, the crew made a drive for him, when all of a sudden, what do you think that dog did? He made for the wreck of the bridge, where no one could follow him, and without paying the slightest attention to any one of the crew, he puts his two front paws on the gunwale and he begins to bark-bark, bark-bark like blue blazes. 'Stop!' says the captain. 'That dog have sense. He smell land.' 'Oh, then,' says I, 'if that's so, for God's sake turn the ship about, or we'll be run ashore and smashed to a cocked-hat.' 'No!' says the captain. 'That dog smells a port. I'll make for it.' Well, the crew prayed and beseeched him; they went down on their two bended knees, and they begged and implored him not to lead them on the rocks. No! He had his way. And to make a long story short, we turned her to larboard. On and on we went for hours, and all of a sudden the fog lifted, and the evening sun came out."

The four listeners looked at their glasses reflectively. Below in the dusty street of Rathkeale a cat was washing his face, and enjoying the last faint warmth of the afterglow.

"Where were we?" roared Johno, so that they all jumped, and even the cat paused for a second to look about him.

"Odessa, maybe?" ventured Johnny.

"Is it telling a story I am?" asked Johno scornfully. "How far do you want the smell of the poor ould dog to go? Is it across the Dardanelles, in and out among the islands of the Aegean, up the Bosphorus, and half across the Black Sea. Odessa? Odessa, indeed!"

"Well, where, then?" challenges the policeman.

"Malaga! And we could smell it ourselves. I can smell it now. The wine casks scenting the air. Yerrah, sure, that dog was brought up on drink! He could smell it five miles away."

Johno lowered his own well-earned drink, and challenged them with his eye to contradict him.

"He was a great dog," said the policeman dryly.

"What happened him?" asked Julie.

"The captain wouldn't part with that dog after that for a thousand pounds. He fed him at his own table. He made his bed in his own cabin. He almost slept with him. He adored that dog, as if it was his son. Why," sighed Johno happily, as he poured out another Guinness, "he called him Paddy, he was so gone on him."

He was the same everywhere, so that although he stayed in the town for no more than two weeks he became before he left the most welcome visitor to any pub; in fact, after a night of him, the topers would look in eagerly where they had spent the night before in the hope of finding him there again. Even Wintermann came one night to Well Lane specially to hear him, and had to admit to Johnny as they walked back up the hill that "That fellow would make a good raconteur, if he only had the education."

2

But by the beginning of the second week, the sailor was seen less often in the pubs of Rathkeale. Instead, with Leo, he spent the sunny days taking long walks over the fields by the river towards Newbridge, or on the white dusty road to Cappagh, or to see the reeded lakes twinkling among the commons, cooling the air on the hottest days. For in Johno at last the Fenian found somebody who was as ready as himself to spend hours arguing over a Land Act, or a Finance Bill, or Fenianism, or the Land League, or—a favourite subject of his—the number of Coercion Acts passed by the British Parliament since 1603. That, when they returned home, set them poring over the *History of Ireland* for hours, and they would leave it only through the doors of sleep. It all delighted the old man, but it meant that Julie saw very little of her son—her days empty, and her nights dull and tiresome, the table covered with Leo's books and papers, and no talk or "fun" in the house at all.

Leo took him one day, Johno insisted on it, to see Ahill and Foxehall and Bawnrea and the hill, far away, of Knockaderry. They walked out beyond the castle where the pikes had been hammered before 'sixty-seven, and they surveyed the plain from a small rise in the road. Leo pointed out the faint white of Bawnrea, where he had been born, and where his brother Phil now lived with his young wife and children. Farther east he pointed with his stick to the hill below Knockaderry, and on its slope the dark bulk of Foxehall. As James had cut down all the remaining trees the place was even more than ever like a barrack, bare against the furzy hill.

"And below there by the river—you can't see it, but you can see the bog following it to the west—that's where your aunt was born, and Bid Keene that's walking with that policeman. Her sister is there now with Nicholas O'Donnell and old Mag, their mother."

It was a windy, sunless day, with that endless bank of roof moving inward from the Shannon and the sea.

"I see, begob," said Johno. "A bleak place!"

The old man shook his head.

"It's rich land out there, once you leave the bog. Rich, heavy land. You'd only need to scratch it, and 'twould yield."

"That Foxehall is a big house."

"It's not a house," said Leo, holding his hat from the wind with his hand. "It's a mansion."

"And yours," said Johno curiously, "by law and right."

"Maybe it is. By rights, maybe it is. Though not by the law. Ah! I never was made for a farm," he sighed. "I never had any heart in it."

"It'll be yours again," encouraged Johno.

The old man turned away to the south.

"I could have kept it if I wanted it," he said. "There's Ballingarry," he pointed, and began again to tell about the night they climbed the hill to attack the police hut in 'sixty-seven.

"I never go there," he said—throwing his hand back to the Dee. "They don't want to see me there. They think I squandered my substance for nothing at all."

His eyes were lost on the distant hill. Faintly on its crown they could see a little church spire and a couple of houses. They turned homeward. What they must have talked of on that return journey one can now only guess, and what they talked of again, just as earnestly, in the little shop that night. The following morning they started early to walk to Ballingarry. They were going, Leo explained to Julie, to see if the old police hut was there still.

"Have a look for me at Cassidy's pub," said Julie with a wan smile.

"We'll do more than have a look there," laughed Johno, as they turned from the door.

They were not back for dinner, and they were not back at tea-time. It became dark, and yet they did not return. The town was asleep before they arrived home, to find Julie and Johnny and Bid all anxiously waiting for them. The old man was exhausted, and he kept on saying to Johnny that that walk was too much for an old lad of sixty, and even Johno was so tired that he did not sleep for hours.

As a result, in the middle of the night as he lay turning over and hither in his bed, he heard Leo's bare feet pattering up and down the creaking stairs to Julie's room behind the wall at his ear, and as he lay awake for a long time after that, he could hear his aunt whispering tearfully to herself —easily heard through the wooden partition.

"O Jesus, Mary, and Joseph, comfort me, and tell me what will I do. Oh, what will I do? Oh, what will I do?"

She kept on saying that over and over again for hour after hour.

"Oh, what will I do? Oh, what will I do? Jesus, Mary, and Joseph, comfort me, and tell me what will I do? Oh, what will I do?"

He fell asleep listening to her, wondering miserably to himself what could be the matter. In the morning he had forgotten all about it, and she gave him his breakfast as if nothing had happened.

That was to be his last day in Rathkeale, and he spent it going to and fro among the pubs, scattering his last few shillings, saving barely enough to take him to his ship, and

to buy a bottle of port for the farewell jollifications. Johnny
and Bid came and they all sat about the table, but there
was no dozen bottles of stout on the red plush tonight. To
set them going he opened the bottle of port, and pranced
up gaily with a song.

"What about a bottle of stout now, Auntie Julie? Drink!
The wine of life! The gift of the grape!" And he bellowed
out in his best engine-room voice:

> "O liquor of life why do I love you so?
> In all my misfortunes you laid me down low
> And yet I'll ne'er believe you're my foe,
>   Until I wake up in the morning.

"That's a bar from the *Cock of Saint Barry's*. Why don't
ye smile, damn ye?

> "Tattered and torn you've made my coat.
> I haven't a cravat to cover my throat.
> But I pardon you all, my sparkling doat,
>   Until my head wakes up in the morning.

"Out with the liquor, Uncle Leo!"

But his father, shamed to his last and uttermost shame,
sat staring down at the floor with eyes that leaped once or
twice, beseechingly, towards his son.

"I'll get something," offered Bid, with a gay smile.

"And I'll come, too," said Johnny, who understood the
situation thoroughly.

"Ah! It's a great song," cried Johno, floundering on stupidly, and trying vainly to guess what was wrong. And
there's the other song, too, *The Drunkard's Address to the
Bottle*:

> "Come here my friend and companion the
>   bottle,

For now I have in my fist a wattle,
Many a time and oft you did throttle,
My pocket and me, my thundering rogue.

"I'll crack your neck where the poison ran,
I'll crush your sides like a battering ram,
Too often I've lain in the gutter because
of your dram,
That deceived my pocket and me, you
thundering rogue.

"Yes, the Cock was a lad, for the pen all right. Not a poet,
you know. A versifier, I'd call him. A bit of an ould cod if
the truth was to be told! But a hand with the pen, still and
all. Listen to this wan:

"If I haven't a penny in my purse tonight,
And through my threadbare coat comes rain
and light,
Well do I know who laid that blight,
On my pocket and me—you thundering rogue.

"What do you think of that, uncle?"
"There's meaning in it," faltered Leo.
"Isn't it a good wan, auntie? Listen to it:

"If I'm broken and bankrupt, a sorry sight,
My cupboard bare—"

With a choking sob Julie rose, and almost ran from the
room. Before anything else could be said Johnny and Bid
were back, and they planked down their twelve bottles with
a clatter of fun-making; but here Leo rose, and with one
look at the bottles took his hat and went out, and the three
were left alone.
"What is up with ye all?" implored Johno.
"Where's Julie?" asked Bid.

"She's gone into her room. What the hell is wrong, will anyone tell me?"

The fun died out of the lovers, and Bid ran off to comfort her sister. The two men looked at one another, and with a sigh Johnny went to the drawer of the little sideboard to search for the corkscrew.

"I don't see, for the life of me," he said, "why that old fellow wouldn't work for a bit, and bring in a bit of money to the house. But he'll have to now, then, for it looks to me," he went on, with a slowness that maddened Johno, as he arranged the twelve bottles in a neat row on the table, "it really seems to me, that they have come to the end of their credit at last."

Suddenly Johno recalled Julie's moaning prayer during the previous night.

"Do you mean to say," he asked, "they're as poor as that?"

"Poor?" gasped Johnny, as he pulled at a cork. "Did you say poor?"

"Yes, poor! What makes them so poor? Don't they make anything with the shop? What about the dressmaking? I see my aunt working day and night at it."

"They do," gasped Johnny. "They make some small bit. But—"

The cork shot out suddenly, and the froth poured over the black neck of the bottle.

"That's," went on Johnny with a sly wink, "the way the money goes. And out pops the weasel."

He poured the liquor carefully into the glass and handed it to Johno with a meaningful look. Johno took the glass stupidly, still glaring his question at the policeman.

"That," gasped Johnny over another cork, "was a good verse you had about our friend and companion the bottle. But you said it in the wrong shop this time."

"My uncle doesn't drink like that," cried Johno angrily.

Johnny raised his glass, as he had seen the inspector do

to himself at Mount Massey. At the same time, he jerked his head ever so sligthly towards Julie's room.

"Blasht yeh," said Johno with venom, as he laid down the glass and went out of the house in search of his uncle.

Left to himself Johnny drank his glass in peace. Then his eye lit on the sailor's bag, leaning against the end of the sofa, ready to have the last few objects thrust into it in the morning. He went over and sat on the sofa by it, and with his glass in his right hand, he dived his left into the bag with curiosity, feeling down among the soft clothes and recognizing by the feel, a hairbrush, a razor in its case, a pair of boots. Then he came on a box. Many times his fingers felt about that box, and yet he could not guess what it contained. Taking every risk of being detected, he put down his glass and dived with his two hands and dragged it up. It was a neat mahogany case, with brass hinges and two brass clasps. Heart beating, ears cocked for the slightest noise outside, he opened it. One glance was enough. With a gasp of surprise he closed it again, and shoved it back where he had found it, pressed down the clothes about it, and with his ears red from excitement and his hand trembling he returned to the table and his unfinished drink.

After a few minutes he threw back the liquor, went out to Julie's door, and tapped for Bid. She came to him, her face filled with misery, wet with her own tears, and wet from the cheeks of her sister.

"I suppose I might as well go away, Bid?" he suggested. "I think I should leave you to Julie tonight."

"Do, Johnny. I'm sorry the way things happened."

"Good night so, Bid."

They kissed, and he went down the dark stairs and out into the quiet street. He strode so swiftly along the street and up the hill to the barracks that he was panting when he arrived there. In the dormitory he drew out a couple of sheets of foolscap, laid beside them his razor and rubber for the inevitable mistakes, wiped his round ruler carefully in his chamois leather, got a new *N* pen, and uncorked his bottle of ink. Then, after loosening his collar-hook and his belt, he began with many preliminary flourishes of the wrist the ancient formula of policeman and spy the world over: "I respectfully beg to report . . .

"This man," he wrote painfully, "purports to be the nephew of the Fenian Leo Donnel, but I have reliable information to the effect that he is in reality his son, born illegitimately to him by the woman who is now his wife, approximately twenty-one years ago. Proceeding at an early hour yesterday morning in the direction of the railway station of Rathkeale I observed these two parties embarking on the eight forty-five train for Limerick. On making due inquiries I discovered that they had both taken third-class one-day return tickets to Foynes, via Ballingrane. Proceeding to the house of the parties in question I discovered that they were actually supposed to be walking to Ballingarry, ten miles away in the opposite direction. Thereupon I deemed it my duty to telephone at once, with the permission of my head constable, to the head constable at Foynes, in order to have due observations made on the movements of these suspicious characters. Later in the evening I proceeded to the house of the suspect party, and awaited his return. This occurred at nine twenty-five, which is exactly ten minutes after the arrival of the last train from Limerick and Ballingrane. I observed that both parties in their conversation purported to have spent the entire day at Ballingarry and were both, especially the older man, Donnel, quite exhausted.

"On the following day I proceeded on my bicycle to Ballingarry and made inquiries as to the parties in question, but failed to find any corroboration for their mendacious statements that they had been there all the previous day.

"That evening (the 24th inst.) I had an opportunity of examining the travelling paraphenalia of the man John O'Donnell. In his bag I discovered a box of foreign-looking appearance, and on opening it discovered that it contained two nickel-plated revolvers of the bulldog pattern, apparently bran-new."

(The phrase brand-new was too much for Johnny—he had connected it with "flour, meal, and bran.")

"Carefully depositing the objects in the position in which I found them, I left the house. The man John O'Donnell will depart from here on Saturday morning for his ship which is situated at Limerick, where it has been taking cargo aboard and undergoing minor repairs during the past two weeks. It will sail from Limerick at the high tide on Saturday night and proceed to Cork, thence proceeding to Hamburg (Germany) in due course.

"I enclose three letters which I happened to find in the house of the man Leo Donnel. I respectfully suggest that the letter referring to the black pants is a code."

With a serious face Johnny read over what he had written, and then with a flourish he signed it. He added the word "constable." Finally, he put his letter and numerals, B123—his number that marked his place for life in "the Force."

Having addressed and sealed it he went with it to the post office and pushed it through the slit, feeling with his hand carefully after it had disappeared so as to be sure it was safely fallen into the box. Then he strode on to the chapel to say a few prayers before retiring to bed. As he rubbed his hands over his prayers—a kind of gesture of embarrassment and humility in the presence of his Redeemer—he could not help looking at his coat sleeve many times. It was almost half an hour before he realized that, after all, the gold stripes were not yet there. He renewed his prayers, his whispering voice wandering through the dark chapel like a supplicating moan. He prayed for Bid and for a happy married life. He prayed for his father and mother. When he left the chapel the cold night wind was blowing about the hill, and the whole town had gone indoors to their firesides or their sleep.

4

A Desperate Character

1

JOHNO's visit to the town had ruffled it like a stone flung into a pool. When he was gone, silence and quiet settled on the house in Well Lane once again—a deeper silence than ever before, since neither Bid nor Johnny came there as often as they used to. All their free hours were spent together, and the townspeople began to smile benevolently on them as they passed down the street, or turn away if they met them on the roads.

To Bid, too, calm had returned as the weeks passed by and no harm came to old Leo or to Julie; not, indeed, the old calm that was like a waking sleep, but a kind of troubled happiness, a ritual which was broken now and again by sorrow for her sister or by great joy in her love for her man.

So, after she had enjoyed one long summer's evening among the fields with Johnny, she felt she must go down and comfort her sister if she found her lonely or sorrowful, and she drew her lover with her. They found old Julie whirring away in her little workroom by the light of a guttering candle—she got little work now, nobody would trust her with it, and she could not afford the oil for a lamp. In the parlour, before a tiny spark of coal, sat Leo and Nicholas O'Donnell, poring over an old newspaper by the light of the fire, and arguing in low voices about some political meeting that occurred in Foynes fifteen or more years before. Johnny sat for a while beside the two old men, and when he went in to take Bid down to her shop and her bed, he found the two sisters in one another's arms, sitting in the dark, without sound.

"You ought to be going, Bid," warned Johnny.

She paid no heed to him; she did not even hear him.

"It's like the times long ago," she murmured to her sister, "when we used comfort wan another back in Ahill. We used to be sleeping with wan another, and our mother down by the well in the dark, and she thinking of Moll or Katie or Joanna gone that day from us beyond the sea."

"Ah, let me alone!" whispered Julie, and they heard her breath come trembling with tears.

"Oh, wisha, Bid," she murmured, "what is before us at all? What's before us, and what can I do?"

Johnny left them together, and went back to the door of the little parlour. There the two men were still arguing over their tattered paper. He heard the stairs creaking with the damp. It was a long while before he heard Bid stirring. She came out and asked him for twopence, and when he gave them to her she went back to her sister. Then she returned, and he led her down into the street and home.

" 'Tis to buy a candle or two, Johnny," she explained.

He said nothing.

"She's miserably lonely, Johnny," she said then. "When Nicholas comes he do take Leo from her, and they do nothing but talk all day and all night."

Still he said nothing.

"And now," she went on, "there's Leo going away from her for a week."

"Is he now," asked Johnny.

"Aye! Off with Nicholas to some meetings around Limerick, he is."

He held her hand. He wanted to kiss her, here in the dark hallway of Madigan's.

"Himself and his meetings," she muttered. "Making a gom of himself in Foynes and Tarbert and Newcastle."

"Foynes?" said Johnny with sudden interest.

"Aye! They're making for there in the morning! The poor girl. I do rage against him."

"I'll be saying good night, now, Bid," he said.

She kissed him, and ran up the stairs. He went back to the barracks, and once again he wrote to his inspector. Wintermann was eating his fried steak for supper—he was going on night-duty. The small leggings were on his feet, his great black coat was tight under his chin; a piece of onion clung to his lower lip, and the tea drops shone on his red moustache.

"Is it writing an epistle to another girl you do be?" he mocked.

"Ah, no!" countered Johnny. "It's an official affair. Would you post it for me as you go out?"

"I will, then."

He put on his helmet and buckled his belt. He hitched the baton around his hip, and slipped a small bottle of whisky into his pocket, with a wink at the cook.

"I hope we have no more of that thunder and lightning in the firmament," he said, as he took the letter.

His small red eyes scanned the address. He looked up at Johnny, who was wiping his ruler, but he said nothing. Then he slipped it between two buttons into his breast and went out. Under the gas lamp at the gate outside he read the address again. He felt the flap with his thumb. Still moist, it lifted easily. He heard steps behind him, and his comrade for the night joined him. He put the letter into his pocket, and the two marched slowly down the hill into the town.

Not until the late moon was up did he get a chance of reading it. Making a simple excuse, he clambered over the loose wall by the gas-works, and striding through the nettles he turned the corner of an old cow-shed. In a moment he had rejoined his companion, and the two resumed their circuit of the sleeping town. Sometimes they stood in a doorway to avoid a shower, holding their capes out with their hands to prevent the drops from falling on their polished boots.

"The stars," said Wintermann, "are aloft. Wouldn't you think it was the spring was there?"

2

It was about twenty-four hours later, the moon embedded in the clouds, that the bulk of a steamship moved up the great width of the Shannon, guiding herself by the red and green lights of the buoys sliding past, ignoring and ignored by the sleeping lime-white cottages and the mansions whose faint lights glinted on either bank. The roll of the Atlantic was behind, and the smooth waters of the estuary received her gently, as a lover might receive his beloved into his arms, safe from the surge of the sea. Occasional drops of winter pricked the smooth inky water all about her. A froth of waves hissed perpetually out from her prows. The bridge tinkled "dead slow," as the lights of Foynes drew near. She swung about the Reeve's lighthouse and lay across the stream. Her anchor fell with a rumble, and all her engines stopped a few moments later. She would lie there, "asleep on her iron," until the lighters from Limerick took enough cargo out of her to let her sail up the shallows to the quays.

As the boat was lowered to take the pilot ashore, nobody noticed a dinghy pulling swiftly and silently out of the dark on the opposite or port side; or the barrel-round figure of the second engineer deftly lowering overboard a long heavy package wrapped in brown canvas. It had given Johno a great deal of trouble to smuggle that bundle aboard the *Clarissa Ratcliffe*. He could not believe that he had got rid of it so easily, and for several minutes after the bundle was taken from him below and the tail of the rope splashed into the water, he kept looking into the dark after the dwindling boat. Then he slipped back into the engine-room.

At the prow of the dinghy old Nicholas O'Donnell, in his yellow oilskins like some top-heavy figurehead, was peering across at the wooded shore on the Mount Trenchard side of the river. Behind him Old Tom Mulcaire was pulling heavily on the oars, but it was a younger man whom they called Jerry who was really sending the boat through the water. He had red hair. The peak of his cap pointed to heaven. He spat as he rowed. After a quarter of an hour they stopped for a rest. All they could hear was the faint rattle of a winch from the ship. They pulled again, and now they were so near the Clare shore that they could see the clear bulk of Cahircon House among its trees and the small pier standing like a box in the tide, and the little wooden shanty surmounting it and the moon glinting on the panes of glass. They halted again, and now they could hear no sound at all. Suddenly from Foynes Island there came the cry of a lost gull and a splash of water.

"Chrisht!" hissed Old Tom. "I'm in a shweat through."

"Let me have a pull," said Nicholas.

As they exchanged places their heavy breathing resounded in the soft air.

They pulled on until they had put Foynes Island between them and the lighthouse, and they faced diagonally across the river for the Limerick shore. A half-mile down-river they halted for the last time.

"Lave us divide them," said Tom Mulcaire. "It might be better if we had to separate, and no one of us could carry that bundle by ourselves."

Nicholas ripped the cord with his penknife, and the three

of them crouched over the bundle as he and Old Tom tore away the canvas wrappings. Meanwhile the boat drifted with the river.

"He has more cord and cloth about them," muttered Nicholas, "than'd bury a corpse."

"He's right," said the young man Jerry. "It keeps the damp out."

"Look!" cried Nicholas, as the shape of the rifles appeared through the canvas.

"Hurrah!" shouted Old Tom in his excitement. "We have them."

In fear, the two other men clutched him. As they raised their heads to look about, they saw they had drifted near shore.

"We'd best pull out," said Jerry.

"We'd best separate them first," said Nicholas.

"Then make a divide of them, and hurry," said Jerry. They tore away the remaining wrappings. The dark barrels caught the edge of the moon. A light rain began to fall as they wrapped the rifles two by two. Then they suddenly became aware of a looming mass over their heads, and they saw the cliff, the leaning pines, the fibrous earth. They heard the waves on the beach. At the same instant a crashing through the woods—a cry—a gunshot bursting the silence.

They only knew afterwards that they scrambled madly over one another to the oars, while the boat rocked wildly and shipped gallons over the gunwale. They had a dull memory of shouts from the shore to halt, and more shots and bullets spitting into the water about them. They rowed so madly, that when they were out in the middle of the river again Old Tom collapsed over the oars, so suddenly that they thought he had been wounded, and Jerry could do nothing but lie back on the thwart with his heart striking on his ribs, and his shoulders heaving up with his breath. But they could not rest long—they knew the police were on their track. They could no longer see the shore. They argued between them for so long that they were drenched to the skin before they noticed the sudden fall of rain. In the end, they decided to try to make the mouth of the Fergus, and get on the deserted sloblands where the bog road leads out to Cratloe and Limerick.

All the night they stole along by the Clare shore, feeling for the mouth of the Fergus. In the dark it was a hopeless search, zigzagging back and forth among the islands.

" 'Tis there," argued Nicholas. "That's Church Island."

" 'Tis not," argued Old Tom. "A lot you know about it. That's the mainland. We'll row this way."

They almost fought about it in the end. They had been hours rowing. "God, this night," spat Old Tom in a fury. "What blashted me to come out with such gomawks? Don't you know anything at all, you? Where have you us brought? I swear to the good God we're back where we were."

At that point Jerry spoke. He had a split palate, and it was hard to know what he said.

"The tide is out," he said quietly, very quietly.

He said "clyde." He had lost his cap, and the rain had streaked his hair on his cheeks until it was like blood.

"Phwat matter?" growled Nicholas.

"If we're cluck on the mud!" warned Jerry.

"I'll row no more," cried Tom Mulcaire, and he flung down his oar.

But when Nicholas leaned for it, he took it up again, and they rowed wearily on. They rowed for two hours more. Then the storm burst on them.

When Leo Donnel fired his first shot, it was to warn the men in the boat. Then he fired at the dark figures trampling heavily through the undergrowth. The shot halted them, and they began to reply, but wildly, and shooting out into the dark river. Under cover of their shots he scrambled away through the briers and the brambles out on the road, without his hat, mud-stained, one leg of his trousers ripped to the knee; and so off west, behind the hedge, to where he had left his trap in an open field. Whatever other mistake he had or had not made, that, at least, had been a piece of cunning; a field was the last place the peelers would have searched for it. The road to Foynes was closed to him; it was even doubtful if the police did not also hold the road to the west, but he must chance that. He led the nag through the gate, and then mounting to his place, with his pistol cocked on his lap, first trotted her, and, when he thought he was out of earshot, galloped her hell-for-leather through the dark to Loughill cross-roads; that would lead him south about behind Foynes. Not until he had covered about six miles of those overgrown side-roads did he let her fall into a slow, panting walk, or his mind cool and his attention relax from the road behind him.

But he could not think clearly, his mind still in a turmoil from that unexpected rush of blackcoats through the wood, all his plans ruined. He was free of the police for the moment, but he could not tell how much they knew, and as he tried to decide whether or not to enter Rathkeale before the morning, again and again his mind would wander and probe for the man who had discovered him this time; and he would wonder whether they were waiting for him in Rathkeale, or whether they had caught Nicholas and the others in the boat, and so again back to, "How much did they know?"—until he could think of nothing but to keep moving from Foynes, and some foolish, wild plan forming in his stupid head to make for Ahill, and pretend he had been there all the while since he left Rathkeale.

Quite suddenly he realized that the rain had been beating into him for the past half-hour; at his feet the rump of his horse shone, and the brass fittings on the harness were dim with wet. As suddenly the rain ceased, and he found himself on a small rise, quite dry and dusty, with the nag halted and blowing. A flick of the whip and she creaked on another few yards and halted again. He drew out his great silver watch and saw that it was turned one o'clock. Far away behind him to the north he saw clearly the circling rays of a lighthouse on the Shannon; but as he looked, it became obscured by the rain sweeping across it. That was about the time when the three men on the river were losing their way among the islands at the Fergus mouth, avoiding the shallows and dreading the falling tide. He jerked on the jaded nag again, and after another mile or so of slow going he came to an estate wall, with the five-fingered fronds dripping into the sticky road and the great trunks thrusting out the bulging wall. This place seemed familiar to him, but not until he came to the little lodge, with its peaked windows dark and shining, did he recognize where he was. Another half-mile, and he was passing between the rain-soaked cabins of Ardagh. From that on, he could have found his way as easily as if he were crossing from the door of Foxehall to the road. Indeed, if there had been a light in one of its windows, he could have seen Foxehall across the bogs and the river.

He turned east. At this rate of going he might be able to enter Rathkeale before dawn, and again he began to debate with himself whether he ought not to wait until some word came to him from the other three. The mare decided for him. She had already been in and out of Limerick in the morning to fetch Jerry Haugh and Old Tom, and since then he had made her do a hard twenty. While he was losing and finding the thread of his arguments, she had been moving and stopping and moving again, wearily, patiently, faithfully. Now she stopped dead. Her head drooped. He whipped her under the belly and encouraged her to move on, but she did not stir. She sank on her knees in the mud, and he rolled, tumbling over her haunches, into the road. Cursing her, he began to unloose her harness, and after nearly half an hour he managed to haul the trap backward so that she was clear of the shafts. But for all his lashing and tugging and pulling and cursing, rise she would not. She laid her head in a pool of water, and her sides heaved with exhaustion. He hauled the trap to the side of the road, piled the harness into it, and undoing one end of the reins from the bit tied the other to a thorn root in the ditch, so that if she rose of her own accord she could not stray. Wiping the thicker mud from his clothes he crossed the ditch into the fields and made his way towards the river path, south of the Deel. He must either borrow a horse in Ahill or stay there for the night.

It was now pitch dark. The clouds had covered the moon completely, and, by the time he came to the Reens bridge, he sat on a tufted bank by the water-side and knew there was no hope of making Rathkeale that night. A long white house, just off the road, tempted him. Browne used to live there, and he might lend him a horse? But he drove on, waking the ducks clustered under the hedge by the slimy pond as he stumbled over the loose stones and the river gravel. The rain had ceased, but there was a low threatening wind in the trees, and in spite of it the air was heavy and warm, as if he were near a volcano. His mind was now in that state when one half of it seems drugged and the attention is gone wholly to sleep. He walked mechanically, and if the sky had not suddenly blazed and the thunder crashed around his head, he might have gone stumbling on until he came to the very edge of the town. Dazed by the light, he stopped and looked about him. There was not a light in a single house in the wide plain, and when he looked northward he saw, not the moving twinkle on the Shannon, but the white hands of the lightning waving all along the horizon, a racing quicksilver that shattered the bowl of the night-sky. Far away over Clare the thunder rumbled in response to that flashing, and still about him, as if it were a living thing, the low wind murmured through the bushes and the wild grass of the bogs. The downpour began.

He realized that he had passed the turning to Ahill, and even the boreen to Bawnrea. Ahead of him was the ruin of the Foxehall lodge. He strode forward to it and stood for shelter in the doorway. But at his back the rain and wind, now chill and stormy, drove down between the roofless walls. He ran out into the avenue and scouted along and along for a tree, but James O'Donnell had not left a tree standing, and he was half-way up the drive before he found a blasted bush—a stark, dark, berry-bare haw. There he crouched, with the rain whispering through the ragged claws that creaked and bowed over his back; in two minutes he was driven from it by the cupped drops that lashed his bare head and neck. Up and up the drive he stumbled. The sky blazed again, and he saw every field as clear as in the daylight—strangely clear, because he saw, or had time to see, no shadows, and all was livid and glittering for a moment. He was almost under the walls of the house, having, without knowing it, climbed up the long gradual slope on whose low summit Foxehall looked over the farms of the Deel. To his amazement one quarter of the face of the house, a surround of the two eastern windows, and the door and the parapets of the step, shone lime-washed in the rain; and there, through the chinks of the shutters in those windows, gleamed two lines of yellow light. Mounting the steps he looked over the plain, south and east and west. Not a light anywhere—nothing but one great tree, the old chestnut below the house, blasting and bowing under the wind. A lightning flash lit the entire bog valley for him like a sudden sun, the arrows of the widespread rain, the blowing tree, the river glint among its hissing reeds below, the hills far away. As he wiped the rain from his dripping beard that clung to his chest, and tried with a sopping handkerchief to dry his eyes, his fury seized him to think of the three men driving over the storm of the Shannon in their open boat, his horse shivering where he had abandoned it on the road to the north, himself flying from the law. He almost forgot completely what he had come for south of the Deel. He hammered with his fists and his heels at the shining door behind him. But the deep thunder that followed the lightning drowned the puny noise, and still, pitilessly, the rain lashed him from head to foot. He raced swiftly to the side of the house where the old stabling used to be, and the well that his mother had filled, and the cobbled yard, and the arched gateways leading out to the orchards behind. He was thinking only that down there a sunken passage led the way to the servants' basement, the great kitchens and the larders and the cellars and the harness rooms, and so into the house. At the end of the passage he came on its door, worm-eaten, chained, and padlocked, with staples outside. Furiously he flung his body against the timbers, but though it swayed in for the length of the chain, and creaked and cracked under his shoulder, it held, and despite several mad rushes it still held. Muttering and complaining, he groped about outside the ruined coachhouse until he came on an axle-tree, rusted with the storms of a dozen winters, used now only to prop a door open. He staggered back with it to the servants' door, slipped it behind the chain, and with one jerk put the staples flying.

"I'll give a surprise," he muttered, "to somebody I know."

The great arched kitchens smelled damp, and the ground was greasy under his feet. The thunder was fainter here, but the lightning shot its white fire down through the barred basement slots, level with his eye, into the empty maw of the grate, where they once roasted half a cow or a whole sheep's carcass, and where a broken wheel lay now in its own hoop. Through the larders and the harness room he came on the stairs, and so behind the hallway. He heard a door creaking and feet shuffling, and a faint light reached him from somewhere to the right. Then he heard James calling (how old and weak his voice was):

"Who's there? What's that? Hi! How!" as if he thought it was a dog or a wandering pig. As he felt for the door into the hall and the front of the house, he could hear James shuffling about behind the wall, and then, through the serving-hole in the partition, he saw the brilliant light of his candle.

"Tiger!" called James. "Blasht you! Tiger!"

Donnel found the door and opened it, but now, as if they were playing a game with one another, James had gone about to the back. He saw the half-open door of what used to be the sitting-room, where he used to play the piano and see the daguerreotypes on the mantel and the epaulettes and the swords. He moved to it, and entered with a strange, wild grin. By the fire stood a woman, young, plump, fair-haired. She spoke to him over her shoulder.

"What is it?" she said.

As he did not reply she turned, and he saw her open blouse and her bare white bosom. She screamed, and James came shuffling back. The two brothers looked at one another. James was decrepit, aged, half-bald, as toothless as a child. He did not recognize his brother for a long time, for he was muddy and wet and hatless and rain-bedraggled. Lifting his candle in a firm hand, quietly and keenly he looked at him.

"Well?" said the Fenian.

Still the other looked him over, blinking his hanging lids to keep them back. Then his open mouth snapped to; he put down the candle and looked at the young woman and then back at his brother, trying to think out for himself what he wanted. At last he asked the question.

"What do you want here?"

The Fenian sat down weakly, and looked about him at the room that had been turned into a farm-house kitchen.

"I want a horse," he said briefly.

"I'll give you no horse."

Donnel pulled himself up, and his hand fell on his great-coat pocket with his pistol still in it. He drew it out. James looked at it.

"Give it to me," shouted the Fenian.

"Wasn't wan bout of jail enough for you?" taunted James.

The blood rushed into the face of the hunted man. He raised his pistol. At the same moment the woman swept some garment of hers at the candle, and the room went dark except for the gentle fire laving the ceiling. There was a crashing and a trembling moan, and then not a sound but the rain falling against the panes of glass outside and somebody panting heavily.

As the tide rose over the waters, all silent and grey and mist-covered, the three men were poling warily in shallow water. They were between two islands on the Fergus mouth. Then they felt the keel rubbing beneath them and they pushed madly. But they were held beneath as by a hand. The dim dark of the sky grew less and less, until they could see the hills of Clare over the far shore, and they could see over the edge of the mudbank on the other side the top of an old ruined abbey on one of the islands. The Limerick shore they could not see at all. With a curse, Old Tom flung his oar in the water. It floated gently out of sight. Nobody upbraided him. Then the rain began a gentle fall. That, at least, hid them from the fishermen's boats making down the Fergus towards the Shannon and the sea. Helpless, shivering, wondering if they could be seen from the shore, they sat without speaking.

"They'll watch the roads," said Tom, after a long while. They argued no longer.

"If we could wait until tonight's dark," suggested Nicholas.

All his body was shaking, and his teeth chattered.

"We'll khkake the khance when the gusk fallsh," commanded Jerry fiercely.

The old men said nothing. It was his turn now.

Of one thing they had never spoken all the night, and they did not speak of it now—the man who had betrayed them. They did not speak of it because only three other men knew of their plans—Frankie O'Donnell, John O'Donnell, and Leo Donnel. It could not be Johno, and it was well for him that it could not be, or they would have suspected him first of all—the late-comer, the stranger. Neither could it be Frankie, because Nicholas was Frankie's brother. As for Leo? It could not easily be Leo—it could hardly be Leo—it would be strange if it were Leo. . . . And there they paused. Leaning on their elbows, crouched against the side of the dinghy—Jerry had bailed it out—huddled in the prow of the dinghy they held their silence. But they all knew that when they reached Limerick the man they would want to see first of all was Leo Donnel.

Long before the sun began to redden the boat was floating again, and Jerry Haugh decided to make for the shore. The morning had cleared before noon, and their clothes had steamed on their bodies for hours, but they were still wet, and old Nicholas was unable to stir his cramped joints. He must get food and drink and sit by a fire, or get into bed at once. So they rowed easily over to the Point—they could see the *Clarissa Ratcliffe*, whose winches they had heard unloading her all day—and without difficulty they clambered ashore. The first thing they did was to set the dinghy adrift, so that when found it should not tell where they had landed. Then, tired as they were, they buried the six rifles in three different graves, under brambles and wild shrubs; it was never known that they were recovered, so that they are probably there to this day. Then they struggled as far as Hurler's Cross, Nicholas between the other two like a drunken man, and there he was put to bed in the house of a man who was some relation of Old Tom Mulcaire. There, a few days later, the police found him, but he was too ill to be moved, and actually he never left that house until he left it on the shoulders of his relations. At night the other two drove by Bunratty and Cratloe into Limerick. They stabled the horse, and walked to Frankie O'Donnell's in Clare Street. There was nobody there but the barman, and he did not know where Frankie was.

Upstairs they found Mrs. Frankie O'Donnell, a small, white-haired woman, whose chins rested on her chest, and who held her head as if it was fixed to her spine by iron. Over the red plush of the tablecloth she abused them.

"It's the like of ye," she cried at them, "that have nothing phwatever in the world to lose or gain, that gets dacent men like my husband into trouble. There never was a black mark against this house as long as Frankie O'Donnell has it. And to think I'd live to see peelers and sergeants and inspectors ravaging over my house! What call or licence have yeer like to be up and down with a dacent man like my man." It was clear that Frankie kept his affairs very much to himself, and that she resented it. "What call or licence have ye," she went on, "have ye to be in and out of this house at all? It isn't to bring custom, I'm sure."

She threw this sneer directly at Tom Mulcaire. He bowed his head to it. "This is a decent house," she cried, "and my man is a decent upright man, that never went against the law in any shape or form. What business the foolish man ever had to be up or down with yeer likes I'm sure I don't know. What do ye want?" she screamed.

"Where is he?" demanded Jerry.

"It's no business of yeers where he is. Take yer mark off my house. To think my man would have to be flying out of the town of Limerick with the torment of policemen plaguing the life out of him because of corner boys like the pair of ye!"

Then, her curiosity absolutely eating her inside out:

"What do ye want with him?"

"Where's Leo Donnel?" asked Old Tom.

She scanned the pair of them with her small eyes. She was like a tigress debating which of them to eat first.

It was as if they had robbed her of her mate.

"What should I know about Leo Donnel?"

"Well," cried Jerry, "if you won't tell us where Leo is, tell us where your husband is."

"I will not. I don't know where he is." She tossed her head at this.

She was torn between fear and the craving to know why her husband had taken to his heels.

"You know well where Leo Donnel is," charged Old Tom.

"I do," she snapped.

"Where is he?" the two asked together.

"He's in his skin!" she cried.

And with that, she swept open the door.

"Go out," she cried, "or I'll crewsht ye with the poker, ye lazy lumps of sin."

The two went hastily, almost expecting a blow from her as they went. They stumbled down the stairs, while she mocked at them from the landing.

"My bould hayros!" she said. "My gallant men! My raparees!"

Hurrying from her bitter mockery, they felt their way out the narrow hall and into the street. As they made their way, debating, down the quays to the stable where they left the nag, they saw the bulk of a great steamer approaching the docks, and they recognized the *Clarissa Ratcliffe*. She had been lightened sufficiently to let her make the high tide at the moon-rise. They hastened to the quay, only to find a couple of policemen waiting for her to moor.

"By dog!" said Old Tom, "they know everything."

When the gangway was run up they dared not approach. They stood in the shadows of a coal-yard gateway and watched the police climb aboard. When they returned, Johno was between them, his bag on his back. At a distance the two watchers followed them, and saw them enter the police station in Green Street. For an hour they waited out-side—for two hours—they waited until nearly midnight. Then Johno came out, alone. They followed him back to the ship, and on the quays they came up with him, one on each side.

"Well?" said Old Tom.

"Well, yourself?" said Johno.

"What did they say to you?" asked Tom.

"Who the divil might you be?" asked Johno.

He was clearly in a bad temper.

"That's all right," said Old Tom, and he held out his hand. The sailor took it, and, as he felt the peculiar grip, he relaxed. He held out his hand to the red-head, and the fingers closed on it significantly. Still, he was being cautious.

"What is it ye want, men?" he asked.

"Come back the stable," said Jerry. "This is no plake for a talk. Earsh have wallk."

Abreast they walked back from the quays, down a side street, across the main street of the town, along another nar-row street, and suddenly into a laneway, where there was a smell of manure and the burnt hooves of horses. Jerry un-locked a padlock, and they went in. The horse did not stir. They lit a candle, and leaning in the far corner of the stable the two told Johno what had happened them. But when he asked about his uncle they had nothing to say. They had never even approached the woods where he was to meet them with the car.

"We must make for Rathkeale," said Johno. "Them peelers know everything, but they couldn't hold me, and they won't be able to hold him or any of us."

"By dog, I hope 'tis thrue for you," said Old Tom. "Wan five years in Maryboro is enough for me."

So they tackled the horse and led the cart out into the street. Limerick was long since asleep, and as they cantered into George's Street and out past the cottages that marked the end of the town, the whole country-side was white with moonlight. Jerry drove, and Johno and Old Tom sat in the car—it was an old covered-car whose seats sloped down to the rear door and the step on the slant of the shafts. Through the open back Johno could see the hedges passing away behind them, and then a turn in the road blacked out the lights of Limerick.

Old Tom fell asleep after two miles of the road had gone. Then it was a succession of white cottages at intervals, and the endless hedges slipping past into the dark. When they arrived at Rathkeale it was nearly dawn. They found the little house dark and deserted. As they knocked, two night police approached, and one was Johnny Hussey. He told them that Leo Donnel was in hospital in Limerick with a gunshot wound, and his wife was gone to be near him. He was under arrest in the hospital, for he had himself fired at a party of police near Foynes.

"A very strange affair," said Johnny, and as he spoke he could not take his eyes off the sailor.

Old Tom Mulcaire or Jerry Haugh he did not know.

"And for why is he under arrest?" asked Johno.

"I tell you," said Johnny, "that he fired on the police. And it may be that he killed wan of them."

"That," said Johno, "is a terrible affair."

"And, for God's sake, tell us," said Tom Mulcaire, "why should he want to shoot the polis?"

The policeman stroked his jaw with the side of his black woollen glove.

"That will thranspire at the trial," he said. "It's a very strange affair entirely!" he added, and nudging his companion the two walked slowly away.

When they had rounded the corner, Old Tom spoke.

"Well," he said, "it's not Leo. And it's not Frankie, unless he'd betray his own brother. And it's not you, for you couldn't do it. And it's not me nor Jerry, for we know nothing about it. Then who gave us away?"

The sailor looked at him.

"It's common sense," he said. "The information came out of the house where it was planned."

And he looked up at the house before him.

"It wasn't Leo, and it wasn't his wife. Who else," he asked himself rather than them, "was in that house? There was me, and there was Bid Keene, and there was"—he paused—"there was Mister Johnny Hussey. That's common sense," he said again.

The others looked at him and were about to burst out in a torrent of argument, when he held up his hand.

"Time enough," he said. "I'm going to sleep."

"Sleep?" asked the red-head. "Where?"

For answer, Johno stepped into the box-like car and curled up in a corner. The two others looked at him for a moment, and then they too entered the car. Huddled together for warmth, they were all three soon asleep. Presently the horse grew weary of standing, and began to walk back the way he had come with his sleeping load. When they woke they found the streets of Limerick about them, and the horse on the pavement snapping greedily at the shrubs in a doctor's window-box.

3

Leo Donnel spent his third period of imprisonment in Maryboro Jail, a period of five years, for wounding with intent to kill. The jail rises above the centre of a small village, in a plain swelling so gently eastward to the Wicklow Mountains that one cannot see the slow undulation of the fields seeping upward like a tide. It was not so bad as Portland. The warders were Irishmen, and inside the walls the air was soft and kindly with faint field scents imprisoned in the tiny sun-motes and the smell of the boglands, and the turf smoke rising powerfully in the rain. He spent the greater part of his first year in the prison hospital under medical observation, and though his violence returned to him only occasionally after that, he was often there until he was released.

But as it was the winter of the year when he entered the jail, and the winter of his life, it was also the dead time of Ireland. Parnell was long since gone, and men squabbled for succession. Now and again, almost under the very windows of the jail, a political meeting would rage, with party-cries and loud words and tar barrels flaring in the dark, and a fife-and-drum band rattling through the hurly-burly that rose and fell, as he returned to his cell for the night and dozed into sleep. Once—so a warder told him—a speaker had pointed to the jail walls and spoke of the Irishmen who had suffered there; but as he had mentioned no name, it was plain to Donnel that he had either never been heard of in that part of Ireland or quickly forgotten. Out of pique, he asked the warder if anything at all ever happened in that town. "They had once," the warder replied, "hanged a man in the jail." "But, in the town—about the place?" asked Donnel.

"Yerrah, no!" the man replied. "It's a quiet place, thanks

be to God. Long ago, one time, there was a bad murder
done. But nobody remembers it now, only the song was
written about it:

> "In Maryboro town that day
> A dreadful deed was done.
> A wicked man he did enslave and slay
> A holy nun."

He could remember no more, so he locked the door and
clanked away on his rounds.

It made Donnel realize that he was islanded in that jail,
islanded in that concave plain of Ireland, no more thought
of than an old stone pillar in a field. He set himself to be a
good prisoner—to keep the rules, to do his tasks as well as
he could, to be free inside five years.

At first the old man comforted himself that those five
years would not be long in passing; after all, he had done
twice that in Portland. But he soon found that five years
are far more precious to a man of sixty than to a man of
twenty-seven. In Portland he had been able to look forward
to many years of life and good living. Now he was penniless, and his wife penniless; he had learnt to value time. Of
that threescore and ten, which is the span of a man's life,
he had only five withered years to look to. Little wonder if
he began again to turn back to the short, empty story of his
life, to weigh up the sense and wisdom of it—the first years
on his father's land, the second years in Foxehall before he
went to prison in 'sixty-seven, the third years when he made
a beggar of himself, the last years of his retreat in Rathkeale. Short and empty as it was he found enough in it to
occupy his mind month after month, and he asked for, and
got, permission to have sent in to him the stubby black-
covered note-book in which he had marked with such minute care the political events of his day, and a few other

items of special interest—as the date of Davitt's visit to him in Foxehall, or the dates of a few political meetings he had attended here and there in County Limerick, the date of Parnell's death and the date and hour of his funeral—that was entered in red ink and marked R.I.P. The last date of all was the arrival of his son in Rathkeale. He now decided to add every single event, even the tiniest, of the last, third, period of his life since his marriage. But he never even began. He would spend such long hours luxuriating in himself, that by the time he thought of setting something down it was time for some task or for sleep, and he would fall into either task or sleep, dreaming of the past.

He would sit, with his mouth slowly falling open, scratching the side of his lip with an idle finger, staring before him like a cow. There was one warder there, a rougher fellow than the others, who would steal open the grille in the door to watch him. Then suddenly he would make big eyes and a mouth like his prisoner, and say:

"Moo!"

Donnel would snap his mouth close and caress his lovely beard, and glare into a corner as if he had been considering something very deep, and would not be interrupted. But when the fellow was gone, his eyes would widen and he was enmeshed again.

"Oh!" he would say afterwards, "I had plenty to occupy my mind, plenty to ravel out, if I could only hold it and track it down." But he remembered what his mother used to say to him long ago, when she was in a temper with him: "You haven't the head, boy!" And from one side and another people confused him. Old Mag O'Donnell, his mother-in-law, wrote bitterly to him about her daughter. She told him he hadn't thought of his wife when he went gadding about the country at his mad capers. She told him he was the scapegoat of others, as he had always been. She told him that her brother Nicholas would be alive only for him. She reminded him how he had brought Nicholas into trouble before. Aye, and how well Frankie O'Donnell hadn't got into the path of danger. Yes, he had saved everybody else that night when he fired at the peelers in the wood, and it was to his credit—but had he saved his wife now, or had he spared his mother when he saved the country lads that night in 'sixty-seven? When he read that letter he tore it up into a hundred pieces, and he stamped on it and he spat on it. Then Bid wrote and comforted him, and told him how she was married to Johnny; and Johnny had his stripes at last; and they were going to live in Cork; and she told him how she had made Johnny speak up at the trial, and say that there was small harm in the prisoner, only he was led away by others. How he rubbed his hands over that letter; as if he were trying madly to knead it into a dust. And Johno wrote from Callao—he thought it best to make himself scarce after his uncle's arrest—and he praised him up to the skies, and said that when he was free they would have good days together, and many a long talk and an argument—and they would sit in the sun again in Well Lane, and throw stones at the bank cat used always be crouching after the chaffering sparrows; and they would take fine long walks out by the lakes, and go rowing on the river and collect the water-lilies, and bring them home to Julie. He wrote about Rio, and told how they had a great night there.

"We went into pubs and out of pubs, and the men offered me cigars and wine and all sorts of drink if I'd only sing, *Ould Ireland, You're Me Darling,* and recite *Parnell's Last Address to the Irish People:*

" 'Stand beside the man that stood where danger called as I stand by the country for which I have fought and suffered. . . .'

"And in the heel of the hunt, Leo, we were all inside the bloody clink, and the *vigilante* with his rifle in the window, and he saying that if we as much as opened our mouths. . . . 'Ah,' the crew shouted at him. 'Go away out of that, you foreign so-and-so,' they shouted at him. And I up, and I out with *The Lights of Limerick Town*. Do you know what that fellow did? He down with his rifle, and he shouts, 'Honomandeel!' says he, 'is that *The Lights of Limerick Town?* God Almighty,' says he, 'sure I'm from Ballyneety!' And he let us all out on the q.t., and he came aboard with us and signed on for the voyage. 'Where are ye going?' says he. 'Straight back to Tarbert,' says I. 'I'm with ye,' says he. The poor fellow, sure we won't see Ireland for another ten months, and there isn't a dirty name he haven't called me for the dousing he got around the Horn."

That letter comforted him for weeks. Then he was called out one day to the governor's room, and there was Julie—meek-eyed and terrified at the long journey and the size and silence of the jail. As he looked across the table at his wife's threadbare blue serge suit, and her old battered hat, and her greying hair, his head sank slowly like a drowing horse. He could think of nothing at all to say to her.

"I'm going to be living in Cork, now," Julie whispered after a while.

"Is it Cork you said?"

"Yes. Bid is taking me to live with her."

He raised his eyes and looked at her humbly. "If Bid was doing that for her, it was well she had a sister," he thought.

"Johno is going to send me help," she said.

"Is that so?" he asked.

"If Johno was doing that, it was as well for her," he was thinking, "that she had a son."

"Johno says he'd like to settle in Cork."

"Does he now?"

"He says he knows a Cork girl in Dublin that he'd like to marry."

"Is that so?" he said.

"Yes."

There was a pause while she tried to gather up her scraps of news.

"Bid have a baby," she said. "A boy."

"Ye'll be all together so," said Leo, and he began to bite his trembling fingers.

Then she looked timidly at the warder.

"You'll come to Cork, won't you, Leo? When—when—"

"To Cork?"

He fingered his check handkerchief, and began to fold its hem with meticulous care.

"Yes, sure," encouraged Julie. "As you say, we'll be all together. And sure, Johno knows Cork well."

He continued to fold his handkerchief, stumbling over what he had to say.

"Yes. It's a nice town. But, sure, I have nothing to do in Cork?"

"Ah! You'll be all right. Johno is a great lad, and he'll look after you."

"Look after me?"

The handkerchief was folded now into a roll, and mechanically he made a puppet out of it, and under cover of the table danced it up and down weakly on his lap.

"Yes," he murmured absently. "I need someone to look after me, now."

Fiercely he rolled up the handkerchief in a ball, and tore it to and fro in his hands.

"I'll write to you from Cork, Leo. And Johnny Hussey, they say, is going for a sergeant."

"Aye!"

There was a pause.

"We had a mission in Knockaderry last month."

He shot a glance at her. She was looking timidly at the warder.

"Are you left Rathkeale?" he asked quickly.

She blushed with shame at being found out.

"I—I had to, Leo."

"So the shop and house is gone?"

"It is, Leo."

She leaned forward and whispered.

"We all renewed our vows, Leo, and we took the pledge for life."

"That's well," he said. "That's well."

He said it uxoriously and condescendingly. Her reference to drink had suddenly restored his self-respect.

He began to fold his handkerchief again, thinking of his papers, but afraid to ask about them.

"Leo!"

She was leaning forward on the table, her face flushed with excitement. He looked into her eyes, and she put her two withered hands on his.

"We'll have a nice little house of our own again, Leo, won't we?"

But at that she made a wry mouth, and long tears began to roll down her face. At the sight all his manhood returned.

"Arrah! Don't cry, girl. There's no use in your crying. We've had hard times before now, Julie, and we went through them. We went through thick and thin."

"But we're old now, Leo," she sniffed, "and we've no one to turn to."

"Ah!" he rallied her. "I'm not so old as that. Don't be burying me," he laughed, "before I'm dead. Never fear. There's people that won't forget us. There's men won't forget me. They couldn't forget me after all I went through. After all I lost for the cause. Never fear, Julie. And Johno will give us a hand. I don't want much from him, or from anybody alive. I have lived my life without help from anybody, and I can end my life without help from anybody."

She tried to smile at her husband, and shoved her grey ribs up under her black hat.

"I have the machine, Leo," she smiled. "I kep' that. That's all I want to begin. And we'll have a little paper shop. Johno will give us ten or fifteen pounds to set us up in the world, and we'll have a little paper shop."

The brief fire died out of him. Into his scaled and bloodshot eyes a slow moisture crept in spite of himself.

"We will."

"I'll be on the look out for it," she promised.

"That's right."

They held each other's hands—two wrinkled, bony hands. After a while he spoke.

"We had our times, and we'll have them again."

"Please God," said Julie.

As they had no more to say, they kissed and parted. He returned to the oakum shed, and she sat for several hours in the railway station looking at the shining rails.

He buried his past; but with regret he saw it go, the fume and exhalation of his life that had drowsed him in Rathkeale and soothed him in his cell. It was like watching the sunball sinking slowly through a wood of a winter night, and he one wanderer whom it did not call to rest.

It was as well that he did not build too much on the past, for when his five years were up they took it from him as completely as they could. All through the dark of the night before they released him the rain had been falling on the prison roof and through the morning of the following day, so that in the evening as he was being driven from the jail gate to the railway the gentle springtime sun was warming the lush fields and the soaked trees with their leaves like fans that were so green and wet and dripping that they blinded with their colour. He could not speak to Johno, who was come to meet him. The very road, mud-thick, sent him up its limestone smell and its smell of cattle dung, and there was one place where the hawthorn simply smoked its odours through the air. He covered his eyes; and then the tang of the turf smoke from the cabins trailed through the air, and all but choked him as he gulped it down so close at hand.

"I'm sorry it's such a wet class of a night for your return," apologized Johno.

"Oh! Christ!" said the old man.

And there was such a sob in his voice that Johno fell quiet until they reached the station, with its empty platform and its truck rattling on the gravel, and its smell of dust in the gloom of the waiting-room.

In Cork he found that his son had rented him a little shop on the blind side of Tuckey Street where he was to sit all day long behind a high counter—nothing but his white crown showing when you entered the shop. There he sold papers, a few boiled sweets, segments of coarse plug tobacco, and from the glass case on top of the counter a hundred small and profitless objects—as collar studs, pious badges, pencil sharpeners, those odd little crosses through which one sees a microscopic view of Lourdes or Paris or the Sacred Heart, all these and a hundred such he sold—pins, erasers, small toys, laces, matches. And if somebody came in for one of them, he would search the jumble under the glass case a hundred times over rather than let his customers go. And if they did go without what they wanted, he would still be searching and jumbling for an hour after, cursing under his breath, because he had lost a penny or three-halfpence by his carelessness.

His shop became known as The Green Pike, because Johno had bought an old rusty pike with a broken pike-staff on Saturday in the Coalquay, and in spite of his uncle's protests painted it in green and gold and nailed it for a sign over the doors. And as the old man began again, from pure force of habit, to take in every political journal, squib, ballad, or sheet that came on the market, there came a time when never an hour of the day but his shop had somebody before the counter, and at night it would often be as crowded as a pub with the drainings of the political clubs. The young men entered under the pike with the same feeling as they entered under a cross, and they bought his papers and his cheap tobacco and his collar studs purely for the pleasure of hearing him talk, or even seeing him.

"Why!" Johnny cried repeatedly in disgust to his wife. "The place is never without half the corner boys of the town in it."

"Ah!" Johno would say, just as often, to his uncle. "You're becoming the centre of sedition."

At which Leo would look at him sideways, and say:

"I took nine and fourpence today. If this goes on, we'll be able to live on the shop."

"Of course it'll go on," Johno would roar. "The men of Ireland not to support you, is it? I'd like to see them."

The old fellow would nod and raise his eyes and smile.

"I said that very thing to Julie this day."

"The fact of the matter is," Johno would point out with the stem of his pipe, creasing his belly to lean over the counter to his uncle, "the fact of the matter is, there's not a schoolboy in Cork but knows what a Fenian looks like."

And he almost smashed the glass case with the thump he gave it.

"Ah!" snapped Leo. "Mind that glass, boy. You're too damn rough."

"Sorry, uncle, sorry!" poor Johno would mumble and mutter and gesture, with much jigging of his bullet head. Then, as if to erase his fault, he would rub his palms together, shove his hat on his poll, take his stick, and with a

salute as to a king, go out of the shop. He would walk
down the street at a roll, slapping his back with his
walking-stick, and pausing, as usual, after walking a deck-
length to survey the gulls in the sky. But under his breath
meanwhile, he chewed savagely:

"Bloody ould curmudgeon. Pah! Cross ould sod."

But he would walk on suddenly, with:

"Great bit of ould stuff all the same," saying it so loud
that the children would call him names, and the women
step on to the roadway for fear of his whirling stick.

The old man began, too, to make a bit of money in another way. Among the men who liked to visit him was
Jeremiah Haugh. Though he was a Limerick man he often
came on business to Cork, for he was now a bookmaker,
and attended every race-meeting in the park. Leo he sought
out for the sake of poor Nicholas O'Donnell and Old Tom
Mulcaire, and the first evening he came into the shop he
actually recited over the counter *The Devil's Address to the
Merchants of Limerick*. He was become sallow of face, with
faint red hair turning grey, and a mouth so tightly shut
that you could see nothing of his lips, and his small eyes
were always on the ground: he was what would be known
in a police report as a down-looking man. Even when he
did look up at you it was only by flashes, and then you saw
two small eyes set like buttons deep in his head. When he
spoke his words were so harsh and guttural because of his
split palate, that they were just like shells falling crisp from
the metal lips of a nut-cracker.

He did not talk much about old times, but that first evening he mentioned a certain night in 'ninety-eight when,
as he suggested with a sideward gesture and a wrinkle of a
smile, as if he had only heard it by rumour:

"The Henians hried to land some rifles at Foynes, wan't
clat the way of it?"

"Did they?" asked Leo cautiously.

The metal mouth almost smiled fully this time.

"Well, maybe 'hey didn't," he said, rising from the counter; and bidding good night, he left the shop.

But he was back the following night to ask if Donnel would mind taking in a bet for him from one of his customers during the week. It was, of course, illegal, but the Fenian did not trouble about that. The week after Haugh came again, and repeated the request, and then several men came with their wagers. By degrees it became a customary thing for the bookmaker to use the shop in this way, until in the end the two made an arrangement about it that brought in almost a pound a week in commission to The Green Pike. It enabled Donnel to dress himself as well as he had been dressed in Rathkeale, and soon he and his wife were able to live independently of Johno. Asking no more, they lived in content.

So, as he had been before, he became again a familiar figure that people would stop and look back on. Because of his height, his tall black hat, his pale face, and beard combed with care and sweeping his chest, they could see him long before they met him, and they liked to salute him, and receive his lordly salute in return. He was come at last to a place where the people knew nothing of him, except that he was a Fenian and had been in jail for several years for his beliefs. They looked at him, these quiet-going, inexperienced people of the half-rural streets of Cork, as if he were some hero left by the tide of another age.

The police, too, looked at him, whenever he passed them by, and at night they saw with suspicion the light glowing in the shutter-holes of his shop. Once Johnny Hussey actually paused to peep through those eyes of light. The old man was bent over a table covered by neatly overlapping newspapers and weeklies. For a minute or two the policeman watched his gestures.

"Counting something," he said sideways to his comrade.

"What?" asked the other gently.

With a half-smile Johnny stepped back, and as they walked away said:

"Bullets."

The other laughed. They halted in the dark patch between two gas lamps, their hands behind their backs as they rose and sank on their heels, and waited for the old man to leave his shop. He did so presently, and after surveying the shutters and rattling the door handle, walked towards them, swinging his stick jauntily. Rising and falling on their heels they watched him come, pass them by unseeing, and walk out of sight. They watched him with contempt, and when he was gone they looked at one another.

"I'll tell you what he was counting," said Johnny.

"What?" asked the other.

Johnny sneered.

"Three and thruppence three farthin's!"

They remained there, Johnny encouraging his companion to enjoy a surreptitious smoke. He did not smoke himself, but now and again he spat lightly, as if to show his indifference and contempt for the mass of men.

But when he had turned the corner old Leo halted, and peeped carefully around it to see if they were still watching him. Finding they were not, he gave a tiny sniff of contempt that just barely shook his stomach, and then walked away, stroking his beard with pleasure, or tapping his stick on the pavement, or occasionally putting it under his arm to rattle the pennies in his pocket that assured him he was independent of them and the world.

BOOK THREE

1898–1916

THE CITY

1

Simple Folk

1

THERE is one special day, perhaps one special hour, perhaps one isolated moment in every man's experience of a place that marks it in his memory for ever. So Leo Donnel had always thought of the plain of the Deel by that one day of his journey to Limerick, and of Limerick itself by that night when Old Tom Mulcaire sang him a land song over the Thomond Bridge. With Bid Hussey there were two such days that always spelled for her the endless antinomy of her life in Cork—the evening of a Saturday of terrible heat in June when her first child was born there, her first summer in the city, and the inexpressible calm and ease and rest of the following Sunday morning. All that Saturday evening the lace curtains were blowing in about the room, a little wind having sprung up blessedly from the river, blown from the harbour and the sea. The evening sky was dappled with warm pink and a soft fire burned on the gilt halo of the Virgin on the peak of the Palladian façade of Saint Mary's across the river, on the gull that stood perched on it, on the windows in the redbrick houses on either side, and on the clouds resting heavily on the roofs that climbed and clustered from the river's edge. Since morning, between her pangs, Bid had been looking out at that warm sky, all red, as if it reflected some mighty conflagration in the city, finding it, above all, irksome to lie there in the dying heat of the day. She was wishful for the cool of the night, and fearful of what it would bring, moaning in a low key of agony as each torturing stab warned her that her time was coming nearer and nearer. Then as the cool evening fell there were the white curtains billowing in to her and Julie trying to tame them: while still they floated in and waved their white hands across to the bed. In the street below the children were running and shrieking at their play, so that when Johno came in for his tea he was sent out to hunt them away, and then called in again because he made more noise himself in shouting at them. At last the dark came and in the heavenly rests between her pain she heard the last Saturday night sounds of the city, dim as if muted by sorrow for the end of the day, or as if the people had grown weary with the fading of the light and the ending of the week. Across the river width the houses were now toppling their little toy cubes of light into the darkness of the water beneath, and the quays were emptied, and the sky above the church and the houses behind the church grew dark and cold. Julie lit two candles on the altar on each side of the little flickering red globe and sat beside the bed, whispering quietly on her beads, watching Bid and watching with Bid the minute hand of the clock on the mantel creep upward through its twelve, or, as the night wore on, its ten, or its eight, or its seven spaces, whereupon she would lay down her beads and get ready to hold her fists under her sister's back to help her through the next pang.

In the next room Johno sat by the open window smoking his Uncle Leo's amber pipe, watching the ceaseless tremble of the lamps under the wind, watching the ferryboat row and row across the Lee, watching the corners of the slips by the sheep-dips where they washed the skins with their long iron pincers in the river, and where with nightfall the girls of the alleys made passionate love to their men, holding them tight in the darker darkness of the shawls. They did not

end their summer love even when Shannon tower struck its
eleven slow strokes; the quarter, and they did not move;
the half, the three-quarters, and they were still there. But
when midnight rang out the river with its endless noise and
ripple was deserted. Beside Johno was his wife, Jill, rocking
her own child to sleep, swaying gently on her hips to the
rhythm of the cradle and gazing vacantly up at the moon's
vain struggle in the sky.

Towards one o'clock two heavy-footed figures in long
black clothes and with heavy round helmets on their heads
came and stood beneath the window, and Johnny spoke
anxiously with uplifted head. Then he entered and sat in
his greatcoat beside Johno, with Wintermann sitting by
Jill. From the decanter they drank whisky, and then
Johnny went in to his wife and Julie came and sat in his
place. The men smoked in silence, and all looked at the
far quay, now white under the moon and the lamps. Then
Wintermann began to read the stars for them, and he
showed them how to find the Stella Polaris, as he called the
North Star.

"The Persians," he said, "thought that that star held all
the stars by the hand."

"Wisha, give us a look at that," said Julie, craning.

"There it is—by the corner of the window. Look at it!
Up there by the cobweb."

Julie slapped her thigh, and Jill laughed at her.

"Bad cess from you," cried Julie. "How well you'd be
shaming me!"

"Will you look, though?" from Wintermann.

"I'm looking," snapped Johno.

"That wan," said Wintermann, with his arm through
the window.

"What one?"

"The one by the cobweb," cried Wintermann, bringing
his head near Johno's.

"Yes," said Wintermann shortly, tired of so much stupidity. "That's the very star."

"Aye!" said Johno. "It's a powerful star. I can see that."

Wintermann leaned on his elbows over the sill, and spat into the empty street. He looked up and about the sky again, his red eyes peering, smoothening his foxy moustache with his fingers.

"I don't see Jupither at all," he muttered.

Julie filled his glass. He leaned back into the room to take it.

"Jupither is a great star, if you only knew it," he said to his glass of whisky.

He cocked his head on one side and, peering through his eyelashes at Julie, he said:

"Five hundred million miles from the sun. Now, what do you think of that?" he asked her.

"Yeh, codding us, you are," mocked Jill O'Donnell.

"It's no cod," asserted the policeman. "If I told you the number of years that wan takes to send his light down to us . . . you'd be amazed!"

"What *raimeish!*" cried Jill. "Don't I see its light now? And tomorrow night, I'll see it. What have you to say to that?"

Wintermann laid down his glass, and slipped his thumbs in his belt. He shook his head slowly and sadly at her.

"Ah!" he intoned. "Ignorance is a terrible thing in this world."

"Who are you calling ignorant?" she flared.

"Sssh!" warned Julie.

The moans next door were sharp and keen now.

"All right! All right!" pacified the policeman. "That star," he explained, "began to send its light down to us millions of years ago. Now!"

"*Cacamus!*" sniffed Jill, and paid no more heed to him. They sat silent. They were waiting to hear the next cry.

Presently Johnny came out and took a drink, and the two policemen went on their beat.

Just as the dawn broke, and they returned, they heard the woman hammer the mattress in the agony of the birth. Then as suddenly as sleep falls she was released from pain, and called out to her husband that it was a boy. They all laughed with joy, and drank its health.

"You'll be catching up with me, soon," said Johnny's friend.

He had two children himself, and a third on the way.

And then she awoke to the chapel bells ringing for the last mass. That waking she never forgot—with her baby suckling its first milk from her breast, and beside her, on the warm window-pane, the buzzing of a bluebottle's wings. For Cork on a Sunday morning can be very calm and very quiet, with the sun shining from his distant elevation above the harbour out of a clear sky, and the rain crowded away to the moist mountains of the west. Then the wind falls dead into the roof-filled valley, a little aerial plain of smoke-webbed roofs, a straggling geometry that ends in green fields on the farthest hills and sycamores domed faint and high against the sky.

Even Johno felt that calm. More than once, looking down over the chimneys from his attic window, he said the city was like a bouquet spread along the valley, and though Jill laughed at him for it, she liked to hear him say that; or to hear him say such a thing as:

"It's like an ould nun!"

"A nun, Johno?"

"Aye! An ould nun in a convent, mumbling away to herself. I don't know how to say it—but it reminds me of a nun. You know! It's old, and it's sort of crumbling away."

"Like a nun?" she laughed.

But Bid understood him. She had felt it like that on that Sunday after Denis was born, and felt it so on many a day

after, when her other children were already come. It always kept for her that sleepy calm of her first impressions—
a faintly tolling mantel clock in the next room, or a fly
humming between the blind and the glass. She felt it especially down the flowing river where it widens slowly between the levees and at last breaks out into loch after loch.
There it was more still than a perpetual dawn when the
ocean lifted up the levels to cover the sheen of mud and
the river bore on its salver the still-born clouds. There, below as well as above, they fell heavily, creamy in their
whiteness through the mercury of the water that held them
suspended as if in ice. On Sundays she and Denis would
watch the city folk gliding over that coloured surface on
their way to the pleasaunces of the harbour, their prows
snouted towards Ringaskiddy or Clash or the unnamed in-
lets beyond the bar. From the shore they heard their slow
singing, or the silver whistle of a piccolo accompanying in
its highest registers the invariably melancholic songs, the
singers lingering in chorus over the words, slow-moving as
their oars:

> "The dear old land,
> The grand old land,
> It's there I'd wish to be-e-e.
> My own homeland. . . ."

Sitting on the grassy bank she would watch them, looking over her spectacles that perched on her nostrils, her
Irish Messenger of the Sacred Heart idle on her lap, small
Denis beside her, and one hand out to sway the go-cart in
which were sleeping little Robert and baby Paul; until
(long-looked-for joy of the evening) they would go into
the little pinewood café with its white oilcloth-covered
tables, and there, in a dim corner, buy a pot of tea and
unfold the sandwiches brought from home—Denis, as he

unfolded them from the wrapper of yesterday's *Cork Examiner*, picking the clung paper from their pith, the transferred newsprint illegible in reverse. They finished with a packet of arrowroot biscuits—they were good for the stomach, his mother said, telling him that he and his brothers were brought up on arrowroot pandy and "Neaveseses Food" when they were small, and suckled for a year and a half before that to make them fine and strong. Then they would walk up to the castle, up the great heights as they appeared to him, and down the quarried road again to the sandy beach, and sit there with dangling legs for the rest of the evening, watching the tide recede until he could jump down on the quaking sand, where an hour ago the tide had lapped. Last of all, they would walk to the very end of the road where the old empty lamp-stand sagged over the water's edge, and look down the loch and pretend they could see the ocean. But the sun would sink with the sinking tide, and the chapel bell ring from the convent, and his mother hasten home for the evening devotions. As they went they would look across the stretch of mud, widening as the tide ebbed to a narrow-bound river-channel between mud and mud. They could not help for ever halting if the great side of a cross-channel steamer, flaming with coloured lamps and every porthole lit, towered over them with churning stern, or the returning excursionists in their launches or the poor shawled folk in their six-oared fishing boats came in view. Now they would all be singing in unison, their reserve swept away by the day on the sands, the bouncing sea, the paddling in the shallow rock-pools, the love-making in the rock-clefts, all so bright and so rare to the hill-up and hill-down of their city. As they went by, their voices floated clearly over the evening water and echoed above the glistening flats. The women held their arms close about their escorts; the children baled the boats; the men pulled the oars; the girls

waved their scarves and hailed the moving shore. They sang
loudly, swiftly, gaily—all of them a little drunken from
their day in the sun:

> "Fare thee well for I must leave thee,
> Do not let this parting grieve thee,
> But remember that the best of friends
>   must part—must pa-art,
> For I'll hang my harp on a weeping
>   willow tree,
> And may the world go well with thee,
> May the world go well with the-e-e-e!"

"Hurry on, Denis!" his mother would turn to say.

Heedless of them she herself would trundle the go-cart
before her, her eyes already fixed on the elevation of the
Host at the Benediction, her fingers already nibbling
through her several sets of beads in her pocket, her head
slanted and her eyes far away with an incipient melancholy,
that sad pleasure that always glows in the eyes of Irish
Catholics when they think or speak of God. The go-cart
packed in the corner of the tram they would roll homeward on its dark top, between orchard and orchard, big
country houses with lit chandeliers, green fields, and dim
lawn squares.

In the bright church the two, mother and son, would
kneel side by side, his eyes closing and closing, and she
irritating him with her constant pinching. He would keep
awake only when the organ boomed and the few voices,
salvaged from the Sunday, sang their swift litany, and the
altar-boy swung his sweet-scented thurible, clouding the
lights with its fume, because all that promised the end of
the service, promised home and supper and sleep. The
choir raced on and on:

"Mater sine labia concepta
Mater dolorosa
Mater Christi,
  O-ora, pro nobis . . .
Mater. . . ."

Then he was home and his mother was tucking him into
bed, and in the cool daylight he would fall into a drench-
ing sleep.

All that meant to Bid Hussey so many globules of lovely
memory falling cool as dew upon her, and the more
parched her mind and heart with the passage of the years,
the more precious they became—precious above all when she
felt at last that her best days were on the wing, and knew
then, as all men must know, though it be long years after
they have been gripped by it, the passage and the power
of time.

2

And they were great days for Johnny. He had set about
arranging his life to his heart's desire immediately he
was transferred to Cork. He had taken a house on Lavitt's
quay, over a pub, next door to the tall house over Wine's
furniture shop where Johno and his wife lived on the top
floors, and later on Leo was to live after his release.

He put on his door a set of brass numbers, and beneath
them a single brass plate bearing the word, HUSSEY. The
next thing he did was to buy a set of cut-glass decanters,
which he ordered Bid to keep constantly filled with the
best Paddy Flaherty three-star whisky, and the best Sandeman's five-star port, and the best old brown sherry, and she,
of her own thought, added willingly an imitation leather
satchel in tin, which she kept filled with the best assorted

Marsh's biscuits. Then, with Bid on his arm, he went next door into Wine's furniture shop and bought six "massive" gold-framed pictures: *The Stag at Bay; The Doctor's Story; His Majesty Edward the Seventh and Her Majesty Queen Alexandra in their Coronation Robes; His Holiness Pius the Tenth;* Constable's *Crossing the Brook;* and *Etna Erupting* (in red and silver tinsel) .

Other purchases were: Blackrock Castle, with a clock inset; an epergne, with pink and eau-de-Nil vases; a horse-hair sofa (that was like a hair shirt to sit on) ; four plush-covered chairs (with turned legs) ; a family album, brass-bound and brass-bolted (empty) ; a fire-screen, with views of Killarney; a cork linoleum; fire-irons, finished in brass.

They bought also a sideboard cupboard, of such weight and height that the legs and the pediment had to be sawn off before they could stand it upright in their little room. It bore the decanters and the tin satchel and the epergne, and a photograph of Bid and Johnny in wedding dress, with Bid's dress partly hidden by a fern, because she had torn it at the wedding breakfast at Rathkeale. They bought, too, all on the one day, tea-coloured curtains with scarlet satin ribbons, a white enamel spittoon, a tin coal-scuttle, and a fox's tail. When each one of these objects was in its place they locked the door, and never went in there again.

For all of them Johnny went into debt, not as much as thinking of asking for credit, but simply telling old Wine, with his greasy beard and his greasy paunch: "I am acting-sergeant Johnny Hussey, and you'll be all right for the money."

"Sure!" grinned Wine through his moist moustaches, an Irishized Jew—flattery blended with cunning. "There's no hurry, at all, at all. Any time at all, sergeant, dear!"

And he bowed them out as if they were Lord and Lady

Aberdeen. And so off to his beat, with Johnny and Bid trotting home, pale with worry, to cover sheets of notepaper trying to see if they would ever be able to pay their debts. The only result was that she never after that day wrote one cipher of them on paper—too terrified to see her worries before her. When the first of the month came she just put what Johnny gave her into her purse and scuttled off, here, there, and everywhere about the city, as she said to Denis, "To lighten the load."

And to his credit, Johnny gave her every penny he got. He scarcely ever drank a drop of drink, and he never bought a cigarette or smoked a pipe, or spent a shilling on his own amusement from the day he married her.

"What a foolish fellow that John O'Donnell is!" he used to encourage himself by saying. "Drinking his salary, and smoking like a chimney-stack from morning till night."

From his sofa, where he would be lying in his shirt-sleeves reading the evening paper, he would turn to his son Denis, bent over his school work at the kitchen table, his round fair head and his chubby cheeks warmed by the evening sun.

"Never smoke, boy!" he would advise. "Once a man indulges a habit he becomes a slave to it. Do you hear me?"

"Yes, father."

He would smack the paper with his hand then.

"I'm interrupting you. Go on with the good work, Denis. That's what will stand to you."

"Ah, sure, the boy is blinded with them books," Bid would raise her head from her darning to say. "And the daylight is gone, too!"

For a second Johnny would grow so red that his windpipe might be choked. His lips would move rapidly in the attempt to form words that had not yet clarified themselves in his brain. His eyes would dance with irritation. Then it would all pass in a long breath expelled with deliberate noise. It was the only thing that ever irritated him—for the rest of his days a quiet, apparently easy-going man.

For all Johnny's pleasure was in his ambitions for his two children. All he ever thought of was to bring them up respecting the law, and to make them look up to the respectable merchants of the city—his boundless world and their battle-field. He tried, above all, to instil into them the love and fear of the good God who made them, and at night he would kneel by his bed with them, one on each side, his braces a bifurcated tail sweeping the floor, his regulation woollen blue shirt rolled to his elbows, his hands clasped and raised at the level of his eyes towards the bright day in the dormer window. He would pray in a loud voice, that could be heard downstairs echoing through the landings and the lobbies:

"O dear, kind, and loving Jesus," he would intone—his voice falling and rising in supplication—"give all thy help to my poor wife, Bid, and give thy help to these my two poor little sons, Denis and Robert, that they may grow up in love and regard for Thee, dear sweet loving Jesus, and give them Thy help to raise themselves in the world, and to be good boys and good men. And have pity, O sweet Jesus, on me a sinner. Have mercy on my poor mother that is gone before me, and my poor father, and my brother Phil, and my sister Kate . . ."

Hearing his voice fall into a kind of private, secretive prayer, Bid would close the kitchen door, where she would be laying the range fire for the morning, and say to herself:

"The poor man, sure he's very good. If we only had enough to live on we'd be very happy. All of us together here, like Brown's cows."

But there is no man who does not crave some small secret corner hidden away from the too great intimacy of love, a last piece of his old private life kept intact. And it was so with Johnny. He had a box, a square mahogany box, which was always locked, and it became for Bid, within a few months of her marriage to him, her Blue-beard's chamber. She referred to it once after a race meeting, when she saw him go to it, and with his back to her open and shut it.

"I bet," she said insinuatingly, "there's a nice little *gwuall* of money in that box?"

He had just given her a share of his winnings and been kissed and hugged in return, but he turned on her with a black face and a scowl that terrified her.

"Mind your own business, woman," he growled.

She fell silent at once, and went about poking the range fire and preparing the tea. She never spoke of it again to him, though she often spoke of it to Denis, and he, abetting her inquisitiveness, shook it and rattled it; and he was for years trying to get the key of it unknown to his father, and when her debts were pressing her and she was afraid to tell him, and she had spent nights awake worrying over them, she would cry complainingly to the dark that he had money put away there, and was sending money secretly to his poor relations in Limerick. She would say it to Denis again and again—he became her confidant for all such matters, for, poor soul, she had to tell somebody, and they would often take down the box and try again and again with every key in the house to open it. But unopened it would go back on its shelf. He had no other possession in the world but his gold chain and his silver watch, and his one suit of plain clothes. He lived, for all his ambition, as simply as a monk.

"Sure," Bid would say to Denis. "Your father is the goodest man. He deserves to be happy, Denis, and I hope you'll do everything you can to make him happy. Won't you, boy?"

He would say warmly:

"I will that, mother."

And with a sigh, knowing the ways of children, she would hope for the best.

He was, certainly, a "good man," as the saying goes. He had joined the Holy Family Confraternity as soon as he came to Cork, and he went to communion every month. To his superiors he was a reliable policeman who would probably rise to become sergeant, and might even be a head constable. But Johnny knew better. One step up was all he ambitioned.

"Whatever I know, or don't know," he said to Bid when she built castles in the air for him, "I know my place."

And a favourite word of his when he heard of somebody rising too rapidly in the world, was:

"Rise aisy, aisy fall. That fellow will draw his horns in before the grass grows tall."

He would return then to his racing calendars and pay no more attention to her unless she pestered him, whereupon he would dash his book on the ground and stutter at her so long and loudly that she would raise her hands and rush to the window to draw it down.

"Hush, hush, hush, hush!" she would whisper. "Don't scandalize the childer. Don't draw the neighbours on us. Who do you think," she would say sternly, "might be passing but the D.I., or the canon, or Jimmy Cox, the alderman?"

Glaring at her, but impressed by that awful possibility, he would take up the book, and Bid would return by slow approaches to the incitements that had roused him.

3

But for Denis Hussey and Robert and the other little brothers that came trotting after him—Peter Paul and Francis Xavier and Michael John, and the whole long line of them, they were days happy over all. To Denis, unlike his mother, Cork was for ever remembered as a place of endless summer daylight, that cold Irish daylight without shadows or sun-square, faint-falling from a sky that in its whiteness is so like the night-sky before the sun has gone, and the dawn before it has risen, that they seemed to sleep through light into light, and had no memory of the darkness at all. Each picture that remained to them out of Cork was like those Flemish interiors, where one sees everything without knowing by what light it is seen. The smallest pictures and the most trivial were like that—as a childish playball rising and falling fountain-soft on an elastic, with little grains rattling the cardboard inside. When it rolled on the ground over the red tiles of the kitchen it cast no shadow, and when it rose and sank before the open window, the houses, and the river and roofs behind it, glowed through so cold and mild an atmosphere that they were themselves like a picture in a dark frame.

Down on the quays, he remembered as if it all happened on the same day, a huge brewery horse stood patiently by the kerb, two children running back and forth under his distent belly. The waters lapped the limestone quay walls within a few inches of the passing feet on the pavement, gulls floating backward on its flood, and little naked beggar boys plunged their yellow bodies into the water from the ferry steps up the quay. Denis watched them with his big childish eyes, awed by their daring, squeezing between a throng of grown men to look. A tramway-man clouted a little girl on the head with his cap for something she had said, and then somebody else shouted, "Police!" and all the dripping bodies scrambled for their clothes and ran naked down the quays, their little bellies moving as they ran. Then the quays were empty and the hills were empty, but he always remembered how, above them, a single cloud fell sideways through the blue like a crumbling tower.

Later that same day he found golden cardboard coins scattered on the dusty street, near the stage-door of the theatre, each bearing the imprint of Napoleon and Josephine, and, on the obverse, black words on a white surface. Soon he had collected a great pile of them, so high that he had to hold the column in his two hands. Great canvas scenes sidled down the wide stairs, and ballooned gently on the waiting dray. Palaces followed forests, and on the forests came more palaces, all in white and blue and gold. A gold chair sat on the lap of another gold chair, and a cannon, dribbling a bit of tattered canvas from its under lip, pointed its sullen, stupid snout at his window. A dull musk smell of dust floated down from the lobby where a queen and a king and soldiers and lovely girls passed rapidly by, their eyes richer than the darkness of a skull, their lips more scarlet than blood, their cheeks pale and yet glowing. Yellow lamps flickered in the darkest recesses, and through the gloom he saw a red patch of firebox, the green of a baize board, all suddenly shut out as a castellated wall sidled down and lay on all its companions like the last leaf of a book.

His flexible cylinder glinted under the sun, and the beggar boys, their hair plastered wet, were snuffling about him, begging him to share it out. Sorrowfully he gave some, intimidated by their raggedness and their bold air, until only a few miserable coins remained, and he ran home in desperation with what he had salvaged from his weak generosity. Spreading his white and gold coins on the table of the sitting-room, he heard his mother and his aunt in the kitchen. They seemed to be always talking in the kitchen, and he wondered they should not go out on such a blue-weather day. But tomorrow would be a Sunday, and perhaps they would take him down to the ocean to see the ships and the waves, and smell the salt sea.

He did go, much later, for a day by the sea to Youghal,

the train, barely caught, racing down by the river's edge to where the first loch opened by the mud flats. Here there was always a squawking of seagulls, brothers to those who sometimes woke him of mornings on the upper reaches of the river in the city's heart. As the train raced farther down he could see, by kneeling on the seat, the mirror of shining mud, broken by a dark blue salmon-shape of abandoned tide, dividing the reflection of Blackrock Castle with its thumb of a turret in its crown. He could see the quiet loch turning with the meander of the river under the sun's glare, see the anchored brig far away, like a toy boat— promise of the great open sea to which they were racing. Already he heard the first thunder of the waves on the beach, even before the train ceased to puff and groan and grind; saw the crowded dots promenading the grassy dome-top of the cliffs; and then with a tremor of his body—how high-strung the cursed gods had made him!—he felt the cold rush of the water round his bare limbs when he ran bravely into the roaring sea, and the old element laved him with its generous spume. Mother spread her white dress around her on the soft sand, so like dust the way it blew up into his eyes and sifted among the coarse grass above the mark of the sea-wrack. And mother opened the bottle of milk and the packages, and the tea, made while he dowsed in the good old sea. "Ah, God!" he was to say many a time after when he recalled such days. "It was right what Uncle Leo used to say out of Latin about the happiness you knew and the unhappiness it made you know, so that you might wish that you had never lived at all to enjoy the ways of the golden world."

4

Cork on a Sunday morning! It meant so much to all of them—to Leo and Johno and Jill and Julie in the house next door, living a life that was even simpler still. It was for them, too, a little city of monks and nuns and priests, and heavy moving clouds and Mass bells ringing and church towers belling over the preachers calling out to the packed crowds suppurating through the doors into the hot sun. If you had asked Johno in those days what Cork meant to him, he would have held you there until the dark. For it meant to him a thousand things—processions and meetings and outings, and then all the people he had met in his lifetime airing their Sunday clothes. Once he saw Gussy Roche, with his Hebraic beard and his shiny tall hat on the back of his poll, and his gold mayoral chain stretched across his paunch, importuned at the corner of Nelson's Place one Sunday morning before ten Mass by a beggar-man. He talked of that one moment for years. "I seen it with me own two eyes, I tell you, at the corner of Nelson's Place, one Sunday morning, before the ten Mass. He had his topper and his chain like always, and swinging away with his walking-stick, yellow malacca with a silver knob—and did he stop? I seen him do it, and I seen him many a time do the same thing. Never less than half a crown. Half a dollar, bejase, every time. I know he couldn't speak a speech to save his life. But he was a decent old skin, if there ever was one, as decent a man as ever walked the streets of Cork. I never seen him refuse the stretched hand—and always half a crown. He had a special pocket, I'm told, full of half-crowns. He couldn't speak, I know it—you needn't tell me. But he, I tell you what, he never disgraced the mayoralty, anyway. He was a patron of the arts. Fitzy, now! Well, think of Fitzy, and think of Gussy Roche. Would you put them on the one level with one another? Or Paddy Meade? Or Marketfield? Or Bronty? A pawnbroker, a dentist, and a bloody publican. Gussy was never a publican. He was a wine merchant. Fitzy? My God, Fitzy? 'So help me, God,' says Fitzy, 'the Pope laughed.' There he was, telling the corporation how he went on their behalf to see the Pope. 'A real plush curtain,' says he, 'a most expensive plush curtain'; and they drew it aside, and there, up on a big chair, was the Pope. 'And so help me, God,' says Fitzy . . . Fitzy? Fitzy? 'Take away them fiddle-faddles,' says he to Gussy Roche. 'I'd prefer to be looking at a head of cabbage.' Most expensive ornaments and curios they were, in glass and silver, from all over the world. Gussy had them arranged in a case in the school of art, and I often heard he'd take a couple of bottles of wine and a box of cigars in with him, and spend the night going over them. Fiddle-faddles, if you please! I'd prefer a head of cabbage! Make me mad, you will. He was a decent man, God rest his soul, and now, would you believe it, they have him up in the new cemetery, and the pissabeds growing out of his grave. Pushin' pissabeds. There you are, there you are. Don't talk to me about Fitzy. Don't talk to me, I say, don't talk to me. Don't talk to me about Fitzy, don't talk to me about him. Will you not talk to me? Will you not talk to me? Let him alone. Let him alone. Let the dead rest. Poor old Gussy, pushin' pissabeds, be Christ, pushin' pissabeds. And that's the end of them all! Where's Charles Steward, I ask you? Where is—many a time I attended him down the Cork Park of a Sunday, myself and Jim Hourigan—his name is on the national monument below—I attended him the last speech he ever gave in Cork. I was his bodyguard. . . ."

Aye! To him, too, she was a flower lying between the warm breasts of the hills, the sun colouring the patches of blue between the clouds, edging the buds of the chestnuts, lighting every roof and coign, every cranny of lane-way and river-bed, shooting under the wharves on the sea-green water, with its dust scum tangling the bobbing corks in the flood-tide refuse—a city sunshot from end to end, glittering from one hill-top field across the roofs to the distant other. He never thought of it but as bright and colourful, with the

sounds of Sunday merry-making or the indiscriminate flag-
gery of festivals, as when on that great mid-week Sunday
of Patrick's Day the procession emptied the side streets and
filled the city with the blare of its purling bands. He lived
for such sights—they never died with him. They might have
been there, then, for him alone, the National Foresters in
their green jackets and their white skin-tight knickers, and
their tasselled boots and their snow-white ostrich plumes
floating about the black banditti felt. Or the fire brigade,
all red and brass, helmets glittering in the sun; or the great
banners astride the rumbling lorries, each guarded by a foot
Forester holding the golden ropes, watching down as he
passed from river to river a double row of upturned faces
glowing with peasant pride at the Master Masons, the Far-
riers, the Bakers and Confectioners, the Brewery Workers,
all daffodil yellow and spring green, all white and gold.
The Lord Mayor and his councillors would come next, half-
hidden under his funny Napoleon-Wellington hat and his
cape and his fur and chain, and the city sword-bearer, high
up on the dicky, in his hussar's tea-cozy of beaver brown,
clasping the naked sword like a crucifix. Gussy would doff
his Wellington hat at every ten paces, and his aldermen and
councillors smiling at the cheers like roses falling all along
the way. After them the ex-mayor and the other ex-mayor,
the ex-aldermen and the other ex-aldermen, and the ex-
councillors, all squeezed into the hired victorias. Then the
school children singing hymns, and the confraternities
psalming, and, last of all, place of dishonour, fifty policemen in their black uniforms with their black helmets, and
their black rifle-barrels up to the sky.

"Look at them, Leo, look at them. Last week they were
at an eviction in Watergrasshill—a dam' hot reception they
got, the sons of bitches—boiling water from the upper
stories, and one bobby got his hand seared with a red-hot
poker. The w—s, I'd give ten years of my life to get into a

scrap with them. Look at them, will you, with their shining belts and their Martinis—load, present, fire! They'd do
it in a second if they got the order, and who thinks they
care if it's their own countrymen they're firing at? Look at
Head Flinn, will you? I hate that bastard as I hate the devil.
May God forgive me. And that ruffian, Philpot. I'd like to
see him downed some day. Oh! A low specimen. A low cur.
Opened a man's head last Sunday at one of William O.'s
meetings at Silverspring. What took him there? I'd like to
know that. They're spies as well as peelers. Spying on their
own, like we know who." (This in a deep whisper.) "Isn't
that the worst of all? Is there a country under the sun
where they'd let the police do the work of military? Royal
bloody-well Irish Constabulary! To see them there makes
my blood boil. It's a disgrace to the courage and patriotism
of our people. Aren't they the fellows that put William O.
into Galway Jail, and you into Maryboro? Are we never to
fling off this yoke, Leo? Are we never to be free of this gar-
rison of England? When I think what they did to O'Neill-
Crowley in Kilclooney wood!—what they did to you in
Portland and Maryboro!—what they're doing every day of
the month at evictions! By God, if we had freedom in the
morning we'd not need a single peeler. I swear they create
trouble, these fellows; they're paid to incite the people to
riot. The world knows we have the finest peasantry on the
face of the globe. And what are them doing day in and day
out, only blinding the world about us? Did you see the
London Times of last week, what it said about us? May
God forgive me, Leo, I think it's an insult to Saint Patrick
to have them there, and it's an insult to our patriot dead!
Come home, Leo, come home. For I can't bear the sight
and look of them!"

Processions, bands, meetings, burials, wakes, marriages
—he sought out everything that gave him chatter and noise
and excitement and people and porter; he turned that quiet

town into a great city, where a man grows old without notic-
ing it, a place where a man will turn suddenly to find the
night behind his back.

5

But Leo he could never draw with him into his excite-
ments. Instead Leo would draw him quietly home to sit in
the parlour and conspire in mockery of the family next
door, of the children's bowler hats, Johnny's decanters,
and his brass plate, Bid's "Jew-shop pictures." Leo scoffed
because he *knew* what a gentleman's house was like—
hadn't he owned one?—and Johno because he was a travelled man, and a read man, and an educated man, as he
put it himself, "a bloke with a bit of knowledge of the
world." Yet Johno, for all his cunning, was never as success-
ful in smoking the peeler as old Leo. He was too kind,
and he had not bitterness, or the reason for bitterness, that
made the old man go prowling around silently, thinking
out ways and means of making a fool of his enemy. He
would, indeed, deliberately visit the peeler with the intention of having a quiet laugh at his household, but if Bid
or Julie were there, gossiping about something that happened in the city, he would come away after a pleasant
night of small-talk, feeling, if anything, far more kindly
disposed to Johnny and his family than he had been before
the night began. Then Leo would incite him, and maybe
the night after he would stroll again, as if by way of no
harm, into the kitchen next door, the idea fixed in his
mind that he would prod at Johnny about, say, his pictures
or his brass plate. With his hat on his poll he would sit by
the range filling his pipe, coaxing the shreds between his
fingers with his little finger, much too cunning to as much
as glance at the policeman where he lay on the sofa, choos-

ing and perusing one after another from a pile of *Sporting Chronicles* stacked on the red-tiled floor beside him—a pile far higher than Leo's *Freeman's Journals* long ago. By the window Bid, helping Julie at some sewing; outside the soft rain perforating the silken Lee, and on the quay edge a file of lane children with their skirts over their heads stamping in the sooty pools; by the table Denis at his lessons; far away the hum and rattle of the city and the tiny docks; near at hand, louder than any, the hiss of the kettle.

Delighting in his own cleverness Johno would plan to approach the brass plate as by a series of concentric circles. But he was so garrulous, and they were of so wide a sweep at the beginning, that he would be still a long way from the centre by the time the talk was done and the victim gone.

"Damp class of weather," from Johno, "for the time of the year that's in it."

Johnny lays aside his paper, and loosens his braces for a chat.

"Aye!" he replies. " 'Tis that."

"It's very difficult," Johno went on that night, "to retain your equilibrium on a day of this sort. A man, now, as you know, is what you might call a mixture of humours—hot, cold, dry, and moist—that's a very ancient bit of knowledge. Not many knows it."

"Huh!" from Johnny.

"Why!" roared Johno (so suddenly and loudly that Bid started with fright and looked crossly at him). " 'What a piece of work is man! How noble in reason! How infinite in faculty! In form and moving, how express and admirable! In action, how like an angel!' "

He waved his pipe, so that the dust of the fill poured over the hearth. His voice sank to a groan.

" 'In apprehension, how like a god!' . . . Ah! The only two men that ever did Shakespeare rightly were poor Tyrrel and Barry Sullivan. Didn't I see Barry in Dublin at the old Queen's, and he giving it out of him? Aye, and the Patrick's Street fife-and-drum going to meet him at Kingstown to herald him into the city? What? He had the voice! He had the presence! He had the gift!"

Then, lost in his love of the actor and the play and the dramatist, he would completely forget Johnny and his brass plate; putting his pipe on the side of the range, where the edge of the heat slowly took its wood and charred it to a shell, he leaps into the centre of the kitchen, and recites for them, *Richard's Speech before Bosworth.*

"I'm Richard! Richard before Bosworth!"

Out of the kitchen with him in a rush, snatching a broom or a shawl. A wink from Johnny to his wife, and a knowing smile from Denis to see the wink. In with Johno, an absurd picture now, Johnny's night-helmet on his head, scarfed in Bid's tartan shawl, limping on the broom, his hat under the shawl for Crookback. He stares about him. Bid looks at him open-mouthed.

"*What's it o'clock?*" he growls at Denis. Denis blushes.

Whirling again he growls at Johnny, who looks up mildly at him.

> "*I will not sup tonight.*
> *Give me some ink and paper.*
> *What, is my beaver easier than it was?*
> *And all me armour laid into deh tent?*"

A whirl that sends the fringes of his shawl winging and curling through the air. His reply is like a shot:

> "*Yes, me liege, and all tings in readiness.*"

Not bothering to turn, he rants on:

"So, I am satisfied. Gimme a bowl o' wine.
I have not that alacrity of spirit
Nor cheer of mind that I was wont to have. . . ."

Maybe two hours later he would be walking along the street, slapping himself on the back with his stick, winking in pride of his own prowess. Then, with a blow of his fist on his forehead, remembers that he has forgotten all about the brass plate. For a second he curses at himself; then with a laugh at his own folly and the folly of man, he goes on his way, slapping his back with his stick and from time to time chuckling into a shop window at a tinsmith working, or a pig's head, or a row of watches on a string, until at last a pub door swallows him and he has found a new audience for the rest of the night.

It was Leo, on the other hand, who induced Johnny to buy a piano, and laughed afterwards for a month at the thought of a piano in a house where nobody could or ever would play it; and it was Johno who failed him when he came to scoff over it. Six policemen and Johno staggered upstairs with it—it was a Collard & Collard, with pale green silk behind its fretwork panels—and as it wound its way up the stairs to its room they hoisted it sideways, diagonally, and even perpendicularly, and at Johno's suggestion they removed two banisters on their way. When it was in place they all tried it with their forefingers, and Wintermann vamped a tune on it, and they all sat on the horsehair sofa in a row and stamped their feet in unison.

"Oh. That's a rare piece!" cried Johno. "A topping instrument."

Then Leo came in, and to their astonishment he sat down and played a couple of dance tunes on it, old waltz airs that he had learned when he was a child at the piano in Dicky Wilcox's in Honan's Quay. Looking at him curiously they applauded him until he played the piece from *Berenice*, and a couple of country songs he used play on Nicholas O'Donnell's flute for his mother.

They wiped the sweat from their arms and faces as he played, and emptied the decanters, and Bid had to race to the nearest pub for more whisky and more Sandeman's, while Johnny raged at her under his breath in the kitchen for disgracing him before the "decent men"—then returning affably to the parlour to keep the conversation going until she brought what he wittily called "swate refreshers."

"Ah!" he chirruped. "Music hath charms. 'She is far from the land, and she can't swim a stroke.' The bottle," he pointed out, "has three stars, like a sergeant's stripes."

"And what about Sandeman's?" called Wintermann. "With its five stars?"

He held up his five fingers.

"You should know that," mocked fat Flaherty, wiping his moist brow. "You, with your knowledge of astronomy."

"The chair of Cassiopeia!" cried Wintermann readily. "The chair of wisdom. That's what it is."

"Stop that cursing!" bantered Lyons, where he straddled one of the red plush chairs, and scratched his stomach.

"Come on, now," invited Johnny when the whisky came. "Silence is golden, and so is whisky. God helps those that helps themselves. But may God help those that I catch helping themselves!"

Then he laughed out loudly to assure them that he didn't mean a word of it, and to prove it, gave them double helpings. Downstairs Bid was making wry faces at Denis.

"Twelve and six," she was computing. "And four and six. . . . Oh!" she sighed. "There's a bill as long as me arm down at that pub."

She leaned on her elbow by the open window, and with the fingers of the other hand counted on the table. Denis stood by her, and held the moving fingers.

"Wisha, mother," he said. "Why do you be worrying like that? There's no earthly use in worrying like that?"

Then, suddenly, he laid a finger on her head, and cried: "Mother! I see a grey hair!"

And he laughed out at her, to joke her from her mood. She smiled and shook her head at him, and rising went to the kitchen sink and began to drink slowly from a cup of cold water. As she sipped the voices fell upstairs and there was a moment's silence, and then Wintermann's firm tenor rose and fell in an old song. She listened with a far-off look in her eyes:

"Oh! Often my thoughts and their fancies take flight
To the home of my childhood away,
And the days when my patriot fervour shone bright,
Ere I thought that those days would decay.
For my heart was as light as the wild winds that blow
Down the Mardyke through each elm tree
Where I sported and played in the green leafy shade
On the banks of my own lovely Lee."

All the eight voices rose to chorus the last two lines.

" 'Twas a beautiful land and the green isle of song
Ere her gems shed their light o'er the world.
When wrathful dogs came bearing ages of wrong
To the standard Saint Patrick unfurled.
Oh, would I were there with the friend I love best
And me bosom-fond partner with me.
I would roam o'er that shore and when weary would rest
On the banks of my own lovely Lee."

Again the chorus swelled—deep, heartfelt, almost proud.

"Oh! How oft in the springtime of laughter and song—
Shall I ever forget those sweet hours,
With the boys of my youth I rambled along
Through banks of lovely green flowers.

And then when the evening sun sinking to rest
Shed her golden light over the sea,
The maid with her lover the wild daisies caressed
On the banks of my own lovely Lee."

Bid herself hummed in the chorus this time.

"Oh! What joys would be mine ere life would decline
Like sand on the sea-beaten shore,
If the steel-feathered eagle, o'erspreading the line,
Brought tidings of freedom once more.
But now what remains for this poor strength to crave
But that my last crimson drop be for thee,
To sprinkle the grass o'er my forefathers' graves
On the banks of my own lovely Lee."

Again the refrain rose—sadly, slowly, in *rallentando* to its close:

"To sprinkle the grass o'er my forefathers' graves
On the banks of my o-o-own lovely Lee."

Upstairs they were applauding, hands and feet.
"Great!" roared Johno, carried away completely. "Magnificent!"

But Leo cocked his head to one side and peered suspiciously and curiously at Wintermann; and then he saw that Johnny was doing exactly the same thing.

"Look at the crowd gathering below!" said Wintermann, leaning back in his saddle to look askew through the open window.

With vanity he raised his voice once more, and they all trailed the refrain. Below, a line of loungers were standing by the chains of the river-side gazing up at the windows. In a rage at such an insult to his position Johnny went to the window and waved them away.

"Be off out of that!" he shouted at them, and seeing his

uniform they scattered, while he shut the window smartly.

Tears were choking Johno as he stood shaking Winter-mann heartily by the hand.

"Aye!" said Johnny. "A good song. But there's politics in it."

"Aye, then," agreed a red-faced policeman named Lahiffe. "And, mark my words," he went on, as he made to drain his glass, "we'll see a parliament one of these fine days in College Green."

"Here's to that day, then," cried Johno, lifting his glass. And once again Wintermann sprinkled their forefathers' graves by the banks of his lovely Lee. The rest raised their glasses, though a little feebly, and muttered a reply. Johnny and Leo alone sat silent. Suddenly their eyes met, swayed a little, fell apart, and glared at the ground.

To Leo's disgust, when they separated, Johno and Win-termann went out together, and when very late that night Johno came home at a rolling gait, his "uncle" would neither see him nor speak to him. But Johno was in no con-dition to be aware of anybody's anger with him. He cocked one wavering eye at his wife and then turning, strategically, to the wall, floated downward into a pit of blissful sleep. Small wonder if after that the old man washed his hands of his son, and began to plot his petty revenges by himself.

2

Interlude

Old Julie and old Leo were sitting on the green grass by the banks of the tumbling cascades at Blarney, the castle towering above them, Julie with her dress about her waist and her red petticoat under her behind, and her legs splayed out from her so that the buttoned boots stuck up like the legs of a dead crow to the sky. Leo had one duck leg under him, and he held in his lap the old tin flute that Nicholas O'Donnell gave him as a boy, sixty years ago, its metal covering yellowed by time, its stops enlarged by so long fingering. It murmured now and again as the wind sang through it. The other women were in a group about their children—Jill and Bid and little Katty Winter-mann.

"Oh! little Mrs. W., I'm sorry to trouble you," proposed Johnny, at his wittiest, offering a glass of lemonade.

He lowered the wet-circled tin tray and gave out the bottles to the children. They tore at the wire fastenings and made the corks explode their guns, and the froth ran down their chins, and their eyes watered when the soda caught their breath.

"Wipe the neck, Denis!" said Johnny.

"Whooh! Jasus!" profaned Manus O'Donnell, and ran from his mother's swift fist and small Josie Wintermann's disapproving mow.

" '*Oh!*' " chanted Johno, red-faced, turgid from draught stout, a swollen cock of pride and delight, " '*Limerick is beautiful, as everybody knows.*' Drink, me hearties! 'Rat-cliff! Bring me a bowl of wine within me tent! Richard is himself again.' "

They all laughed except Leo. He turned the old tin flute over and over between his fingers, and blinked into the glare of the endlessly glittering spume.

It was Johno's day out. To the quayside he had brought up a long wagonette and a sidecar—when the first mass bells were still ringing and the showers of the dawn were drying in patches. To the window he hallooed:

"Ahoy, there! All ready to cast off? Look at me equipage! Look at the brasses of it! Look at the mirrors! Look at the shine of it!"

His stick ran through his hand—eel-swift. He swept his hat through the air.

"There's joybells for you! Look at the polish of it!"

He aimed a friendly tap at the bottoms of the lane children that were aiming to climb on the rungs of the sidecar and rattling the brassy handle of the wagonette door. "Go away, ye buggers! Take the tip of my ear, but I'll lambaste ye if I lay me hand on ye! Avaunt! Quit me sight!"

The people of the quarter began to gather in their stiff blue serge. There was a man with a naval cap and no collar. There was a child with lemon-coloured shoes and a ruby dress. There was a small boy with scarlet stockings. The sun caught the first triangles of the gabled roofs, and all the rest of the quay was black shadow. The Lee flowed sweetly by, gurgling in time with the dying and farthest bells. Day was beginning to spread. The Cock and his wife and four children came around the corner. "Ahoy!" cried Johno. "All hands aboard!" The two policemen were in their plain clothes, and as always with policemen the top button only was buttoned, and their caps on their heads as straight as shakos. That made seven children and they were all jumping in the long car—except Denis and Robert Hussey, who stood like little gentlemen, in their bowler

hats, waiting to be invited to enter—until Johno marshalled
them so that he had Robert in the long car and Denis with
his back to the dicky of the sidecar and his legs dangling to
cover the licence number. Then they had argued and
argued about the division of the others because Johno
wanted to be with Leo and the flute on the sidecar, and
Julie wanted Leo to be in the wagonette, and Bid wanted
to be with her children, and Johnny didn't want to be with
Johno or with Leo or with Wintermann. There they were
dividing and sitting up and sitting down until Johnny lost
his temper completely and almost took his family indoors,
whereupon the two little gentlemen began to cry, and
Johnny to scold, and Julie to rail at Johno, and the crowd
cheering them all like mad. And at last, when they were
settled and ready to go, Johno got down again to inspect
the equipage until he drove the policemen into a thorough
fury.

"Sit up, for God's sake!" they stormed. "Sit up, and leave
us be off!"

"All right! I'm coming. But can't ye look pleasant? Damn
ye, will ye look happy? Look at 'em. Ye're like fellows got
out of their coffins to scratch themselves."

"Will ye sit up?" implored Johnny.

But now Johno had to make friends with the drivers, and
give them their instructions over and over again.

" 'Port!' says I," he said to the driver of the wagonette.
" 'Starboard,' says I. 'Port yer helm,' says I. 'Full speed
ahead,' says I. That's nautical lingo, and you don't understand it, you bloody landlubber. But, never mind. I'll direct
yeh!"

Up then with him on his perch, his hat on the back of his
head, a carnation in his lapel, his stick held high like a
mace.

"Music!" he ordered.

Johnny got down.

"Is this a procession?" he fumed.

"What's on you now?" raged Johno.

"Is it a circus?" stormed Johnny. "I'll have no fluteplaying through the public streets."

"Ah! Ye're a wet blanket. A killjoy! A pisaun! Play up there, Leo. Put giz into it. Full speed ahead."

Johnny lifted down his sons. He beckoned to his wife. They all looked timidly at him. Leo and Julie alone paid no attention. Like effigies at a waxwork they sat looking unseeingly before them. Age had fallen on them too soon, and the unutterable patience of the years. They did not even seem to see the lane children leaping up at them with the aimless chattering of little monkeys.

In the end they were all rearranged so as to divide the Husseys from the O'Donnells, and at a safe distance the sidecar followed the respectable wagonette. For two streets Johno kept complaining to the driver that it was a nice banjax if a fellow couldn't play his flute in the public street on the road to Blarney, and he blasted all the wet, sour, long faces in Cork. But suddenly he saw a friend on the pavement, and to the disgust of Mrs. Wintermann he began to bellow at him how he was married that morning and these were his children.

Soon the red chimney-stacks of Cork, clean with the cold furnaces of Sunday, shone like spires among the fainter church spires of the horizon, and the fields spread green on each side of the road, and the cattle moved with a slow, stately sink-a-pace through the gaps. The sun, invisible in its own fire, burned the air white about it, and they, far beneath, felt the warmth of the turning world. Even in old Julie and her husband the cold blood moved like the tides, and they rubbed their withered hands to draw the warmth inward.

"Music!" ordered Johno again.

The flute slid out of the breast pocket, and the old man's

pale fingers felt blindly for the stops. He blew gently into the mouthpiece, and the high register sent its longest, shrillest, most piercing note into the air, sank and trembled, and sank and wavered, and struck the key of Johno's throat for the *O!* Then down and down through that loud human cry into the meaningful *oft*, and so away, racing and rising and falling softly and freely through the memories of:

> ". . . the evening sun
> Sinking to . . ."

But there, perversely, the music soared.

"Too high!" roared Johno. "Do you want me to burst my palate?"

The flute sank from the old man's lips, and his fingers parted his moustaches. Then he began to play again, his eyes far away from the near fields that alone he could focus with his failing eyesight, and the dim blur of distant woods filling his pupils until they were as enlarged as if the eyes of a visionary.

The flute was more silver now in its tone and it echoed where they passed under a tunnel of trees, their wheels rolling soft and steadily in the dust. High across the hills they saw a big house, and farther on another house buried in the woods. Swaying with the car Leo looked ahead. He could see Johnny pointing with his stick to the two mansions. It was not hard to guess what he was saying to his children and his wife.

"Coroner Broome lives there, Denis. A nice man, oh, a real gentleman, and very high in the world he'll rise before he dies, or my name isn't Johnny Hussey. The judge always stays there when he comes to Limerick."

"Is he always guarded, sir?"

"Yes, of course he is, boy. Night and day, by armed sentries with busbees. And that house there is Colonel

Dobb's. He's another powerful gentleman, Denis. You'd see him driving his tandem, with his coachman beside him, into the races or the spring show."

Denis looked with wondering respect at the great block-house, while faintly behind them rose Johno's song and Leo's sad music:

"Ah! Then what remains for this poor strength to crave
But my last crimson drop be for thee
To sprinkle the grass on my forefathers' graves . . ."

The Lee itself they could now see by glimpses, and in the shallow gravelled stretches it cooled the very teats of the cattle. Through the thick leafy trees the smoke of a train evaporated. Presently they were in Blarney before a pub in the green square with white limewashed stones set in the grass to form the words *Céad Míle Fáilte*. Mrs. Wintermann was wiping her children's faces as they arrived—they had been devouring brown biscuits speckled with pink sugar. A local band, out for the day on an excursion like their own, was playing Verdi under the trees. In the castle grounds children were fighting in a grove for possession of a swing. So they sat by the river-edge, and Johnny, and Wintermann, and the master of ceremonies—Johno, were now bringing them lemonade before they should stand by the counter themselves and lower the cool crowned porter.

Against his will Leo was drawn by Johno to the bar, and the four men sat about a cross-legged table wet-franked by the bottoms of other topers' pint glasses, and with one dry island about a tin ash-tray bearing its trade-mark of the red triangle.

"Well, Leo!" called Johnny Hussey. "This is the weather we want, aye?"

"Yes." With his finger he scratched the table.

"What'll you have?" asked Johnny. " 'Age before youth,'

as the calf said to the cow at the slaughterhouse! Haw, haw!
Aye?"

"Yes."

Johno made a sour face and threw a sympathetic nod at
the peeler. The nod said, "Sour ould sugar. What's up now,
I wonder?"

"Give it a name, me hearty," he cried aloud to Leo. "A
Bass?"

"All right."

The word Bass was roared across the room at the bar-
maid. Haughtily she ignored the order. Johnny Hussey
seized Johno's arm—he did not want a scene about nothing.
He approached the girl with a bow, as politely as any
woman could wish. She smiled and bowed in return, as any
lady would under the circumstances.

"Yah!" scoffed Johno, and he sat down to study his
father's gloomy face, glaring at it under his eyebrows and
the tilt of his hat.

"Feeling all right, uncle?"

"Yes, of course," snapped Leo. "I'm feeling all right.
Why wouldn't I?"

"Oh, yes. I—yes—yes."

With his lower lip he made a secret face at the old man,
and winked at Wintermann.

But when Wintermann rose to help Johnny with the
drinks Leo leaned over swiftly to his son.

"Johno!" he whispered.

"Aye?"

The old man caught his son's fingers.

"Don't leave my side this afternoon," he said. "There's a
fellow out there I just saw trying to get in talk with me all
the morning since we came here. It's about business," he
explained. "I don't want to meet him."

"Why, no," said Johno, looking out on the green and
seeing nobody. "I'll keep by you. Is it money, Leo?"

"Yes, yes! It's a matter of a bit of money."

Before Johno could offer to help the peelers had returned, whereupon with a sudden burst of spirits the old man seized his ale and raised it to Johnny.

"Here's to you, my friend of men," he said, so heartily, that they all looked at him in surprise.

"And here's to you, my friend," he toasted Wintermann.

Humouring him they raised their glasses and drank slowly. Johno looked curiously over his glass at him, and from time to time glanced inquisitively out of the door to see the man they must avoid. Then Johnny began to make small talk, as any gentleman should.

"Well, now," he asked Wintermann, "is there anything new from the Curragh?"

"Is there anything new, yourself?"

"I didn't hear. Behan often sends me a word from the stables. But I didn't hear yet."

"Oh! You ruffian," joked Wintermann. "If there was itself you wouldn't tell me. What about Calderon for the June meeting?"

"Aye!" said Johnny cautiously. "There might be something in him."

And he pulled his moustaches wisely and raised his eyebrows at his beer. Leo leaned over to him.

"No good!" he said. "Take a tip from me. The Minstrel Boy is the thing to put your money on."

They looked at him sceptically.

"You know Haugh?" he asked.

"The bookie?" asked Wintermann.

"Yes," said Johnny, "I know him."

He stressed the "I" in a manner which would not have pleased Haugh.

"He's a great customer of mine," said Leo. "He comes in to me every week for his tobacco. He told me in confidence about the Minstrel Boy. I'm putting a quid on him."

Johno looked at his uncle in astonishment. A pound? Did the old man have as much as a pound to his name?

"Haugh is no fool," said Wintermann, and he looked at Johnny. "The Minstrel Boy?" he murmured. "There's a touch of class about that mount, all right. I don't know, though? Seven-year-old? I remember him. Scully up."

He looked at Leo; one joker looking at another. He was trying to sum him up.

"Who's training him?" asked Johnny. "Clifford? It is Clifford? Aye, begod, it is. I remember him now. No! Seven-year-old is all right on the flat. The Curragh is a swamp after the spring."

"What do you know about horses?" asked Johno tactlessly.

"What do I know?" cried Leo. "About horses?"

He swept his moustaches aside in sudden anger.

"Where do you think I was reared? I suppose you think I'm a city caffler like yourself? Be damned, but that's a good one. How many of ye here ever rode a horse at a fence? Eh? How many of ye ever did more than pull an old plough-horse through a furrow? And I"—he went on in rising fury as his past flowed in on him—"I that lived with horses, and my grandfather before me that trained horses—you're asking me to my face what do I—what do I—?"

He thrust his glass from him.

"Ye!" he scoffed. "Ye, with yeer bits of papers and yeer yellow books and yeer *Sporting Chronicles!* Be damned! A bloody good one! Here," he boasted, "I'll lay a pound to ten shillings to any one of ye, that the Minstrel Boy will be among the first three nags at the Curragh next week. Here!" he called more loudly, suddenly asserting himself. "Girl!"

His voice was arrogant, his call imperious. She hesitated a bare second, and then came hastening out to him.

"Give it a name, gentlemen!" he cried to them. "I want none of this wash!" he scorned at the weak ale. "A double whisky, missie, if you please. And the gentlemen will give their orders. If you please?" he waved his hand to the three.

Timidly they said what they would have. They had never seen him like this before. It would be hard for them. He had not behaved like this since, as a youth, he swaggered it in the pub of Knockaderry when he was throwing his eye at Julie Keene.

From his pocket he drew his wallet, and flicking it open he fluttered a pound note across the table. The band outside was playing the *William Tell* steeplechase. The sun was streaming through the windows, and where the red curtains dyed its light a warm glow fell on his cheeks. He snapped his fingers at them.

"Come, now!" he challenged. "Who'll take up my bet?"

"Ah! Sure, I know nothing about it at all," excused Johnny.

Leo smiled at him. Then the hairy hand of Johno shot out a five-shilling piece. Large as a plate, it rang on the table.

"I'll back you five bob, me ould cockalorum," he cried. "Five bob to ten bob. Is it a bet?"

Leo looked about slowly at his son. He smiled gently at him, approving his own blood. Then he pushed the crown piece away.

"I'm taking the bet," he said, as Johno opened his maw to protest.

"Ye're witnesses to it," roared Johno.

The policemen nodded uncomfortably. The drinks came, and Leo moved them, almost it was with grace, to each man. He raised his own glass of whisky, and bowed to them.

"Look out for that nag," he said. "You'll be sorry, when you see the result of the race."

Then, lowering his whisky in one steady stream back through the white circle of his mouth, he rose.

"I must go back to my wife," he said.

He took his stick and set his hat on his head. He was comically magnificent in the way he strutted from the bar. But Johnny was too humiliated to be able even to sneer at him.

"Bejay," said Johno. "He's an amazing ould cock. He must have been a fine lad when he was forty years younger. And there's fire in him yet," he added.

They said nothing. It was a phrase Johnny had heard before on a certain night in Mount Massey, and he had made it his business never to forget it. Wintermann was scratching the red triangle with a calculating air.

Repeatedly during the day Leo dragged Johno back into the bar, and before the cold of the evening had begun to empty the castle grounds and drive the men into the village pubs, the pair of them were well drunk. Then, at last, as Leo went out to get Julie and bring her into the snug for a glass of sherry before they returned home, Johno saw him, in the full middle of the green, talking with Jerry Haugh. Racing out of the pub he went to them, calling his uncle as if he were calling him to a train. To his surprise Leo waved him away, though weakly, and as if it were without volition, and when Johno halted in his tracks the pair moved away to a corner of the field. With a shrug Johno left them, and went back to his drinks. By the time Leo rejoined him the dusk was fallen and the pub closed, and he was standing miserably by the jamb of the door measuring spits against each other from the edge of the pavement out into the dust of the road. In silence they went searching for the rest of their party.

The Husseys were long since gone home. In the long car the other children were sitting or leaning crooked beside their mothers, half-asleep, their clothes tousled, their faces sticky with sweets and crumbed with bread and biscuit. Julie, too, was gone in the sidecar, so that Denis Hussey had to remain behind in the wagonette. With his stick and his neat bowler hat, he looked entirely out of place. Even as the three men staggered into the car it began to roll away, the driver eager to be home. The river was louder than ever in the dusk, and they saw the grass littered with pieces of paper where they could not see the grass itself. Rain-clouds were scudding over the trees beyond the falls, and the lights in the closed pub made the place look empty and desolate.

For a while, tradition not to be broken, the men sang the road home. Then the rain began to blow down on them, and the night shut in the land. It was no longer May but March, and the wind was cold about their heads. They fell silent. The children huddled against them, sheltered by the corner of a coat or two. Only the driver and young Denis and young Manus O'Donnell were awake when they were passing the houses of the great that Johnny Hussey had spoken of that morning. Through the dark mist the tall narrow windows glowed with the delicate light of dinner candles or silk-shaded lamps or leaping flames in the marble fireplaces. For his father's sake Manus spat at them. He nudged Denis at the same time.

"Watch here, boy!" he said. "Do you know who was living up there last month?"

"No."

"Judge Nixon," said Manus. "And he was the fellow that sent my uncle to Maryboro Jail."

There had been wonder in the other boy's eyes as he looked at the big houses; it changed to timidity and fear.

"Now, then," cried Manus to him, "you can be shaping up to them, if you like."

And another great spit went sailing into the dark past the coachman's lamps.

"If I was up there," said Manus, "I'd bust the ould sugar's windows for him."

As the lights faded into the mist and the trees finally wrapped them into night, Denis lowered his head and pretended to be asleep. He did not raise his eyes until they were halting on the quayside and they all got down, tired and dusty. Then, as he waited politely on the pavement for the old Donnel pair, he looked along the quay and saw a strange collection of men lined up by the water's edge. The dim lamplight barely reached the serration of heads and shoulders moving against the glint of the river—dark, sweeping, lampshot. Of them all he could discern only one lanky youth whose upflung face caught the lamplight and whose arms and hands fell from him like a gorilla. A command was shouted. The row stiffened. Another cry, and a spiked fence of rifles shot into the air. On the car young Manus stood up and cheered them with a wild battle-cry. Old Leo Donnel halted as he was stepping down from the car; behind him Johno halted; behind him Jill halted. A low growling command, and there was a grinding of feet on the cobbles.

Deliberately Donnel stepped to the ground and approached the dark double row. Manus raced ahead shouting. Johno came with Jill. Denis followed, lagging. And then when he saw them clearly he burned with shame to find them dressed in comical scraps of military uniform, a brown empty holster on a black belt, a wide hat that came down on a man's eyes and stuck out his ears, a cheap trouser-belt wound outside an overcoat, tight as a corset, and one who had not even a belt or a hat wore his cap back to front, like a coalheaver's shoulder-apron.

"God!" Denis groaned to Manus, as he looked at the absurd costumes. "They're disgracing us to the world."

"What?" cried Manus, and he faced about at once for a fight.

But Denis stepped away, saying under his breath as he looked again:

"Fooh! They have wooden guns!"

Another command was shouted through the dark, and the odd company shuffled and jostled, and got in one another's way. With a groan, almost of pain, Denis turned and ran home, grimacing like a person who has seen something mean or humiliating. "Bog-trotters," he called them, "corner-boys, blackguards." In and out of the darkness he ran, swifter and swifter, as if to leave pursuing shame behind. How awful if any English person saw them and said, "Are all the Irish like that?"

Once he had been in the Victoria barracks and seen the Sherwood Foresters on parade, their flag before them, their band playing, the colonel and his staff reviewing them. They had made him thrill, just as he used to every Saint Patrick's Day at the National Foresters in their white chamois breeches and their green coats, their ostrich feather plumes floating on the wind, and their horses cavorting about the street on their hind legs. In the barracks it was the thrill of the power and pomp of empire, and when at the end they played the anthem he had felt his blood run cold and the skin on the back of his neck shrivel up to have to stand to attention, his father stiff as a poker beside him, and everybody holding their hats in their hands. That was England—its age, its glory. Had a colour-sergeant tapped him on the shoulder at that moment and said, "What about it, sonny?"—he knew he would not have hesitated a second, if they would have had him. But this rout of the back quays of Cork shambling in the dark through their awkward paces in their rags of uniform! He had to lean against his door to recover from the sight of them, and for a week after he felt as humbled as if he had been caught doing something disgusting in the public street.

In the kitchen his father was on the sofa reading his

sporting paper, and his mother, who was just come back from the Benediction, laying the table for a cup of cocoa before they went to bed.

"Well?" asked Johnny. "Did the wild ones get home all right?"

"They're on the way, sir," said Denis.

"Nothing interesting to report?"

"No, sir."

He sat by the range and took off his boots and began to clean them for school in the morning.

"Hang up your Sunday coat neatly," warned Bid. "You won't get another for two years."

"Manus O'Donnell," said Denis as he polished the toe of the boot, "was talking like a blackguard all the way home."

His mother sniffed and said it was kind father for him. Nobody minded the word "blackguard"; that household used it every hour of the day. To the Husseys street hawkers, newsboys, militiamen, corner-boys were all black-guards, because they were, as Johnny once said, quoting Wintermann, "without pride of ancestry, hope of posterity, or desire for place."

"Go up," Johnny would say, "to the post office and get an evening paper from one of the little blackguards."

Or his mother would say to Robert:

"Don't be coming home from school with any of those little barefooted blackguards."

Or:

"There's a blackguard always standing by the pub—I'm sure he'd whitewash the kitchen for a pint or two."

They knew the way Manus had been talking, and they knew he would turn out like his father. And that meant he would in his time become a blackguard, too.

"It's time," said Bid, "we left this house. It's time we got away from the grand company we have up to our cheeks."

Not until the children were gone to sleep and Johnny lay beside his wife in the depths of the feather bed did he reply to that. He crossed his hands behind his head and, looking up at the still lightsome sky, said, as if to himself:

"Yes!"

"What yes?" asked Bid, who was sitting up in the bed tying her weak hair with a bit of grey wool.

"We must make a move."

"Oh!" Then she said, turning to look down at him: "I wish we could."

"Well, leave us move, then," he said, "in God's name."

"And where, in the name of Moses, will we move to?" she asked crossly; for now that it seemed as if she were really going to move she did not want to.

He looked at her, and then, turning his back to her, pulled the clothes about his shoulder.

"Go to sleep, woman," he ordered.

"If we could move!" she wished with an earnest whine as she snuggled up to him.

"What's to stop us?" he asked the wall before him.

"Wisha!" she cried. "What nonsense you talk! Where would we get as cheap a house, and as good a one?"

"There's fine houses," he said, "in Warren's Place."

With her fist she gave him an irritable nudge in the small of the back.

"We couldn't pay for such a house."

He shrugged his shoulders.

"Move in, woman!" he said.

And when she had moved away from him he arranged the clothes again about his back, and said finally:

"Go to sleep."

"But, Johnny," she insisted, "could we?"

"Ah!" he grumbled, and wriggled with irritation. "We could if you would take in lodgers. But go to sleep on it now. We can talk it over in the morning."

So he slept, and she remained awake—thinking over his plan.

He knew she would be.

For a year he had been thinking over it himself—planning how he could send Denis up to the Christian Brothers' College, to be given a gentleman's education. It wasn't alone that the boy might have a vocation and become a priest, or if he didn't Robert would (maybe), and if he did he wouldn't go out to Africa or charity like any poor boy, but up to Maynooth like Mr. Wall's son or the head constable's, and have a parish of his own some day in County Cork. But, even if they didn't have a vocation, the ordinary Brothers' school at the monastery was no fit place for his sons—up and down with little blackguards like Manus O'Donnell; learning no good for themselves. But there was only one way they could afford to do it. Bid must take a big house and keep lodgers there. If it wasn't quite respectable, there was no other way.

She said no more about it to him until she had spoken with her mother, and because both she and her mother dearly wanted a priest in the family, they agreed in the end.

"A priest in the house," said Mag, "is worth the skin off your two hands."

They could get cheap potatoes from the farm in Limerick, and cheap butter, and even the home-cured bacon. They could get the ground meal, and Bid could bake her own bread. They could get fresh eggs and cracked eggs and sour milk and buttermilk in a dozen places in the back lanes known to the city poor.

"The world knows it," Mag said. " '*Ta fiche slighe chun airgead do dheanamh, ach ni deanamh go cogailt'.*" (There's a score of ways for making money, but no way like saving it.)

So to Warren's Quay they went, and there her life wove itself out. She worked there for her children, six in all, not

one a daughter, and a daughter would have been more
help and comfort to her than three sons. As it was, she
must look forward to their going from her one by one, to
the priesthood with God's help, or in marriage, with the
help of some lassie that would reap the benefits of her
labour, while she would toil alone for the remnant of her
line to her end. Not that she minded or complained. As
old Mag used say, *"Ni fás go h-aois agus saothar a ghile."*
(There's no growth like the growth of age and work, my
brightness.) She passed from her middle years there so far
and so quickly that the lodgers and the shopkeepers about
began to speak of her as Mother Hussey, in that tone of
voice that men keep for women who no longer waken in
them either their love or sympathy or desire.

3

Rising in the World

1

ALMOST from her first night in that big house over the tinsmith's shop, Bid's voice sank into the minor key of a lamentation and a regret.

"Them were the days!" she would say to Denis (her confidant in all things now—the only one old enough to understand). "Ah! Them were the days, when I used to take ye down to Youghal for a Sunday, and bathe with ye in the surf beyond the railway station by the new bathing boxes. It was well to be me in them days, when you were an infant, and I used entice you down to the edge of the sea by promising that you need only paddle and not bathe at all. But you were always nervous-like, and used roar and bawl when I caught you up in my arms and doused you under the waves. Ah! I wouldn't have the courage to go now. I'd never stand the shock; and I'd be shivering and shaking in the box, trying to dry myself with the damp towels the woman would give me. God forgive us all our sins, there's nothing but dishonesty and trickery in the world, Denis. I lay my oath she used exchange the towels while my back was turned in the water, and if I got a dry one to begin, I'd be left with a damp one in the end, and the fine dry ones given to her pet cronies in the hotels that gave her a sweet smile and big money.

"And weren't they the days when Johnny used to take us down the Cork Park to the races, and make a few shillings on the horses and jockeys, and give me a share. And then we'd get away before the worst of the crowd and drive back in the first stream of cars, some coming, some going, up along the quays to see what time it was by Shandon. And there was the kettle boiling at home on the hob, by Maggie Danagher—never a better servant was there before or since, not like the sluts nowadays. And we'd sit down and make tay, watching the seagulls flying, and the fishermen tarring their nets, and the folk taking the evening air by the river. God be with the days gone by."

Then she would set to praising Johnny. Johnny was always the best of men—and still so. A good husband and a good father. None better. A man that never hurt the hair of a single head. No better man in the Force. The finest ever trod shoe leather. Too quiet he always was. . . .

"Look, and O then well I remember," she would say, "how the blackguard from Kerry drew the pistol at him outside the court-house in Limerick—the time of the land troubles. The police wore swords then, and Johnny didn't have the heart to draw his sword on him. Only for a man passing, that hit the ruffian's hand with a walking-stick, he was as dead as a door-nail. The laddo was tried after at the assizes, and got five years; he should be swung for it, the cripple! But Johnny was always a simple, poor man, letting himself in for trouble when others were cute enough to avoid it. How well it would be he that caught the red-hot poker at Watergrasshill, and pulled it! He had like to lose his hand by that token. Too quiet he was. Not on the prowl for summonses like other policemen, trying to catch a pub open on a Sunday. If he was, the girls in Madigan's wouldn't let him within a donkey's bray of the shop, and he courting me in Rathkeale."

And at that reference to her courtship she would laugh out, and twist her body almost at right-angles and blush with pleasure—for all her grey hairs and her years thick upon her. Small wonder that she should. When the happy days of her young marriage and motherhood were flown by, more fast and more silently than the opening buds of the rain-clouds of a summer day, what was there left to do but fall into a dream of the long ago?

"And look at me now. Up morning, noon, and night, my nose to the bloody grindstone. Look at me . . ."

She would burst into a rage at that and, struck by despair, end in tears, with her son looking sadly at her, wondering that a woman could be so weak, and so helpless, and so cowardly.

2

Yet for him, too, after they went to that house, all his daylit memories of Cork seemed to cloud and fade. The very first night in the house, as he and Robert and Peter Paul slept on the mattress on the bare floor—there was no time to make up the beds—he saw through the uncurtained, bare, unblinded windows, for the first time as it seemed to him, the cygnet moon as she floats among the fragments of the sky, dissolving their cold ice, breaking it into a million floes. Peter Paul and Robert at the tail of the bed, and he at the head, they paddled with their fingers on the floor, and he told them the bright nail-heads were phosphorescence, like the glimmering on mackerels in the dark. But he suddenly recollected black-beetles and spiders, and at that they all huddled together, with little Peter Paul crying in the middle. "In the middle for the golden fiddle," comforted Denis—and they slept there uneasily, fearful of what might crawl over their faces as they dreamed.

Then there were the lot of them crowding in the morning about the lighted range (still black and barely flickering) as they tied their boots in front of it, and Denis tied Michael John's bootees, because he was small yet and couldn't tie a bow-knot, and if it wasn't done for him he would make black knots, and then be hacking them at night with a knife, or, head sideways for fear his father should see him, tearing the boots over his heels, bursting the heelclicks and the insteps and the fangs. Then with a sweep of the tongs at their legs, their mother would suddenly scatter them from the fire, with:

"How, hup!"—as if they were calves in a field. "What fires ye want! What shicadures we have in ye. Up with the lark ye should be, or out at early Mass praying for yeer-selves. How do ye expect to get on without prayer? Prayer can move mountains. God promised it. 'Come to Me all ye that labour and are burthened, and I will refresh ye.'"

And when they were all about the table, burking at the porridge they didn't want, and whinging for the sup of tea and the bit of bread and jam that she would not give them, she would return to the attack.

"Oh! The rising generation. God look down on ye. 'The tepid and cold of heart,' says the Lord, 'I spit them out of My mouth.' Did you even make them say their prayers, Denis?"

"Yes, mother."

"Wisha, it's a wonder. Think of the poor Blessed Sacrament up there all alone in the cold tabernacle, and not wan of ye would go out to pay him a visit. Not even Denis, that wants all the help he can get to find a vocation. God help us, indeed. I suppose when I'm gone ye won't say a prayer for me, or go to Mass in Lent for my poor soul. Denis! Wipe Pether's nose."

"Mother, he can wipe it himself."

"Do as you're told, boy. Are you answering me back?"

A dull white handkerchief, rigid with sputum, creased with body heat, would chafe at the small nose button.

"Make him blow," his mother commands.

"Blow," says Denis to Peter Paul.

"Fooh!" he blows weakly, and then, complainingly:

"He's hurting me nose on me, mother."

"Be gentle, Denis!"

Out across the wide street they could see the southern branch of the Lee purling over the slime of its bed. Over the far wall a woman, tiny at that distance, flings with a hiss a bucket of refuse that flutters a small cloud of dust in the air. Then, a full quarter of a minute after she banged the bucket on the parapet, they heard the sound of the impact, clear in the morning air. A milk car goes rattling its brassy churn-covers beneath them, and the milkman like a charioteer on the low-hung step behind. The sun is rising to warm the city from end to end.

"Mother?"

"What is it, Denis?"

"Gimme a cup of tea, mother."

"Pig?"

"Gimme a cup of tea, please."

Rinsing her own cup round and round, she flings the slops into the ash-collector under the range. She pours him a half-cup, fills it with milk and holds it out, too sweet, too pale, too cold. His eager hand reaches for it, but she withholds it.

"Pig?"

"Thanks, mother."

"Yes, Robert?"

"What duty is me father on?"

"Half-past eight to three."

They look across the river at the hoarding by the butter factory. Beside it three or four policemen have already gathered for parade.

"There's me da coming," cries Peter Paul.

"How, hup!" she cries at that, and they rise and race for their school satchels.

"Come back here!"

Coldly and sternly she orders them, and they cringe back and stand by the table with hanging heads.

"In the name of the Father . . ."

They repeat it; the smallest, John Jo, can only say, "Name of deh fady," and when he says, "Hody Dost," they laugh their regular morning laugh, silenced at once by their mother's glare.

"We give Thee thanks," intones Bid in a rising and falling antiphon, to which they make echoing reply. "O almighty God, for all Thy benefits. Who livest and reignest. World without end. Amen."

At the corner of the street Denis always paused to look at the posters for the play at the Opera House. Now he looked with new interest, because from this on they would always be having some of the actors and actresses to stay with them—"pros." his mother called them.

"Act 1. The living-room of the Lumley-Browns' country house in Surrey. Morning.

"Act 2. The living-room of the Lumley-Browns' country house in Surrey. That night.

"Act 3. The living-room of the Lumley-Browns' country house in Surrey. The following afternoon.

"Direct from its phenomenal success at the Duke of York's Theatre, London. Wigs by Clarkson. Cigarettes by Morris. The piano in Act 2 has been lent by Piggots, Patrick Street."

Then along the quayside and about the bridge and up the hill to the Christian Brothers, at the North Monastery —a long tramp, and all the way his mind trying to remember the exceptions to the rule for Latin prepositions.

"A, ab, absque, coram, de . . . coram, de . . . coram, de . . ."

Brother Carty would crease his palm with the edge of the metre rule if he didn't know it. *"Coram, de . . ."* His steps pounded the rhythm into his head, and he couldn't get it out, all the way, up the hill, past the church, by Peacock Lane, through the gates, up the drive, *"Coram, de . . . coram, de . . ."* Even so early as it was, the chatter of the infants' school in Peacock Lane was like a hedge of starlings crowd-clamouring the sun. In a few minutes he, too, was among a chattering crowd waiting for the entrance of Brother Carty, whom they called Shaper, because he had such a swinging swagger when he walked, and all his gestures before the blackboard curved out from his wrists and shoulders with the bravura of a singer at the opera. Then from Latin to mathematics, and into French, and, the last sleepy, hungry hour before lunch, to Irish.

That they enjoyed, because a layman took it—a great giant of a countryman, whom somebody called Bwaola Moawara, because his Irish was slab and thunderous, as an organ with the loud stops out and trembling under its weight of sound. He had long hair, lips like leather, hands like boxing-gloves, and he taught them by shouting at them.

"Thaw shay moawarrr. Abairrr e! Open yeer mouths!"

And they all said it in chorus, as he shouted again and again.

"Open yeer mouths. *Thaw shay moawarrr! Thaw Shay moawarrr!"*

What a noise they made during that hour—one endless clamour of voices, over which Bwaola Moawara howled at them and clapped his flabby hands, and pointed now at this boy, now at that, like the conductor of an orchestra appealing to the brass and the percussion and the woodwind for a louder and a still louder forte into a thunderous *crescendo.*

"Thaw shay moawarr! Thaw shay moawarr! Thaw shay moawarr!"

Unwearied, like the neophytes of a wild sect, they rose to his fury, all forgetful of the gentle sun on the windows, and, far below the school, Cork spreading out her fields of slate, and, shining through the smoke, the Lee, as it went on its quiet way to the green banks and the tide-patterned sea and the rocks.

Out with them then, worked to a false life, dragging their skull-caps on their polls as they tore at the paper about their lunch-bread. There he would stand on one leg in the shadows of an ancient sycamore, working with his toe the draining of the water-tap where it serpented over the white cement to the central gully-trap. He would be picking there at his bread beside Josey Wintermann conscious of the coat his aunt had made for him last week—a thing made of his father's cast-off uniform, as hard as a board, and so stiff, like felt, that it stuck out about his seat like a bell. Looking down at the valley below him, he began to boast to Josey.

"We're in our new house. It has five stories."

Josey ate his bread, and snuffled. They always shared the first place in the class between them—one time he had it, then Josey beat him at algebra, and he had to step down; he would recover it for Irish, which he liked and learned quickly, but he would lose it again at French.

"We have real plush curtains in the hall," he boasted. "They're very valuable things to have."

Josey snuffled, and ate on. ("Mind him," his mother had warned. "He'd be picking out of you. He takes everything in, and tells it at home.")

"We have five bedrooms, now," he went on.

Josey said nothing. He dusted his coat carefully when he had finished his lunch, folded the paper bag that held it, and put it into his breast pocket.

"Ye're keeping lodgers," said Josey at last, as if he had been considering.

"Well, it's a kind of private hotel," evaded Denis.

Josey looked crooked at him, unbelieving.

"But they're lodgers, all the same," he insisted.

"All right. They are."

"Then the five bedrooms are for the lodgers," said Josey.

There was no reply to that; the Husseys would be sleeping in the attics.

"That's your father's uniform you have on," pointed out Josey with malice.

Denis blushed for shame.

"Who made it?" tormented Josey.

"My Aunt Julie, on the machine."

Josey looked it over, and then looked at him. He never smiled, but there was always a queer look in his eyes like a sneer. Years afterwards Denis heard he became a religious maniac.

For half an hour they played in the yard; then back to singing and drawing and drill and geometry. Then down, down, down into the city, whose noise and traffic, forgotten during the day, suddenly enveloped them and flowed about them, and deafened them after the quiet of the monastery fields, until they felt they were in the middle of the bustle of the world and the world's life.

At home the dinner was dried from being in the oven, and his brothers kept racing in and out from the street, and his father was asleep on the sofa, with a paper over his face to keep the flies away, and nobody must make any noise until he woke. After his dinner he would want to go playing in the streets like the other boys of the place, but he was always told that only little blackguards did that. Instead, he had to take Robert and Peter by the hand for a walk up Wellington's Road and down Saint Luke's, always the same walk, always at the same time, and always they had to call in to Saint Patrick's Church on the way and do the Stations of the Cross. Sometimes they had a halfpenny for sweets, and then they would debate for a long time outside Ma Marsh's in Coburg Street, and if there was an odd sweet it was divided with stern justice in three bits. Then lessons, tea, more lessons, supper, more lessons, bed, a dull circle of days.

Within a week he was sorry he had boasted to Josey Wintermann about the house. It filled from floor to attics with ladies in fur coats, fair-haired and beautiful, with scents flowing from them, and English accents that intimidated him because he had always thought of an English accent as belonging to rich and educated people only, like the D.I. or Canon Richey. If he passed one of these lovely ladies on the stairs, she would smile at him so sweetly and tip him on the cheek so kindly that all his body seemed to grow warm as under a blast of sun. Her furs would sweep past him, touching him like a leopard's skin, and her scent float about him like a veil. He had never before seen such loveliness or such gentleness. And when he stole into their rooms at night, where the musk of grease-paint and the dying staleness of cigarette smoke and personal odours still clung in the air, and fingered their silver travelling clocks, or their leather-framed photographs of their friends, he again felt that here was a gentleness and a grace and a comfort in life that he had never even suspected before. At their photographs of pretty ladies in skin-tight hose and fluffy skirts, with constricted waists and bare backs, he would gaze secretly for long spells, wondering where they came from out of the great width of England, and what London was like, where everyone, as the monks hinted now and again, lived sinful lives, and whether they were truly damned already on account of it, and what a sinful life was like. With the men, he read their books and respected them, and was even humbled by them if they were books like Shakespeare, or poetry, no matter by whom; and he derided them to himself and Robert if they only read cheap newspapers and novelettes with coloured covers, or professional papers like the *Stage* or the *Era* or the *Variety Performer*. But even these foreign papers he would examine as being part of the hidden, distant world he had only just begun to hear and dream of, his eyes clouding and the blood rising in his head when there were pages showing a naked lady, or his eyes racing swiftly through some story where there was an illustration that promised an immodest description. Always he looked at such things without moving them, so that if he heard his mother's step he could close the page and be looking at a chocolate box or a patent lock on a whisky bottle, or a gold-bound pen in a chased and figured silver chatelaine when she entered. From these rooms, redolent of rouge or in a powdery disarray, with their odour of patchouli or cheap lily-of-the-valley, or Turkish tobacco mingling with camphor and eyeblack and body-smell and lip-salve, he learned about a life that nobody ever spoke of, or spoke of only as the life of a world and of people whom he and his likes would, should, and need never know.

Usually he worked among a debris of teaware at one end of the kitchen table, with his smaller brothers crawling about his legs or sitting three in a row on the sofa, cowed by his mother's threatening fist as she hurried and scurried to and from the sink. In an excess of pity and self-reproach to come by her and, putting his arms about her waist, press her soft bare arm, and press his lips to her shoulder that was then just level with his mouth.

"Oh, Dinny!" her voice would tremble between weariness and affection. "Go to your books, boy. There's not a bit else will stand to you."

Her hands wring the iron-cloth, and shake with the stress on her muscles.

"Nothing but the bit of learning will stand to you, boy. I wished I had it when I was young. I was the brightest one of the class in Knockaderry."

Her voice is high and thin over the whistle of the tap.

"If my poor mother could only afford it, Master Daly would have made a teacher of me. Work hard, now, Dinny, and 'twill come easier on you when you're a man. Won't you, boy?"

"I will, mother."

"Do, son. And when you're grown, you'll support your poor father and mother, won't you?"

"Yes, mother."

"Run on and go to your lessons, son. Don't let me be disturbing you."

At last her day would be done, the children all in bed, and nothing remaining but supper at eleven, when the crowds would be heard tramping by, and the jarveys' voices shouting, and the motors hooting a slow way along the street. She would sit in those few hours of rest at the table opposite him, her spectacles about her ears, reading a pious book, her favourite *Messenger of the Sacred Heart*, or looking up the coming festivals in the calendar the friars gave her at the Third Order of Saint Francis. If he raised his eyes she motioned him to attend to his work, as his father would have done, a mild taskmaster, a sentry of his mind, a gentle dragon. Other times when he was in the middle of his work she would interrupt him with some such message as:

"Here, boy. Run across to the stage-door with this bowl of soup for poor little Miss Sylvester. The poor soul will appreciate a drink of my fine hot soup between the acts."

Exasperated, he rises, and with the steaming hot jug goes out into the summer street, back once more to the tepid, opiate atmosphere of those strange people who, for so brief and unreal a moment, have touched with their lives his life and his mother's, who have confused and clouded his brain with strange thoughts that, like the memory of a dream, pass and repass, fall away and rise without summons through his waking mind, caressing it and dulling it with their wraiths of fume.

With his jug between his palms he stands inside the great steel doors that divide the stage from the lobby, a small figure by the towering scene, lost in the dusty shadows outside the radiant limes. The air is thick with odours wafted in from the darkness of the auditorium, a dark corner of which he can see just beyond the proscenium. A man, dark-visaged, black-eyed, his cheeks powder-white, and his eyes larger than human with lampblack and mascara about the lashes, is lounging and lingering behind the set, ghostly against the lime-white brick wall at the apse of the stage, superb as a shade. But they are all of them no more than ghosts, all that pass him and look at him. So in another world they might look at a visitor from this, a glance and then away, as if they did not believe in what they saw, a small stranger spying on them where they live out their wild, passionate, terrible lives.

Overhead loops of ropes snake down out of the dark. Everybody speaks in a whisper, except where an actor invisible behind the screen is shouting out in the loudest of voices something about wine on the table. The boy veered over towards the front of the stage, and the loud voice became a man, who, as he shouted, flickered his eyes to his eyes for a second.

"I drank your wine, Margaret, in this house ten years ago. Do you think I have been happy all these years? Look at me, and answer."

Up in his box behind a sun of light, a human rubs his nose.

"Darling, take my hand and feel if it has grown cold?"

Another of the wandering shades comes and peers through him at the man who is speaking, and slouches away into the gloom. But he can feel the jug of soup hot between his palms, and the smell of soup in his nostrils.

"Good-bye, Hugh. Good-bye, for ever."

That is poor little Miss Sylvester. Here she comes, fluttering, a wild bird escaped, blushing, beautiful.

"Aow! Dearie. You are good! Good old mar! Pea soup! Mm!"

After that to return to an equation of ciphers or the equivalence of lines in a triangle, was to return not to a real task but to another fainter, vaguer miasma. Small wonder if he was so foolish as to say to his mother one spring night when she read from her calendar some notice of the coming of Lent, and spoke again of prayer and rising in the world:

"Mother, what will happen me when I grow up?"

"You will get a good job," she replied easily.

"And then?"

"You will get a better job."

"And then?"

"I suppose you will get married."

"And then?"

"You will have a family, God help you."

"And then?"

"I suppose you will die, God help us."

"And then?" he persisted excitedly.

"You will be buried," she said coldly.

"And then? And then?"

"You will go to heaven, with God's help, if you are a good boy."

She said this more warmly, thinking that this was what he was aiming at. But it was here he really wanted to begin. He paused.

"And then, mother?"

She clouted his forward ear.

"Attend to your work, boy."

Aggrieved, he turned with a pout from his pursuit of eternity. Nobody ever took him beyond that same point—death and then heaven . . . and then . . . ?

But there were some things so real as to leave their mark on him long after their time was passed and their weight removed, pitting his mind like a "dead man's pinch," still glowing blue on the white skin after sleep. Once Brother Carty had slashed his essay over and hither with his blue crayon, so cruelly that Denis removed the pages lest his father should see them; whereupon the monk gave him six on each palm the following day, and kept him in after school to rewrite the essay, exactly as it was in the first instance, that it might be slashed over and hither again. That evening he did not get home until nearly five o'clock, and his father was not asleep but seated by the window curtain, filled with apprehension for him; and his mother, who had been ill for the few days previous, lay upstairs in one of the idle bedrooms, trembling with fear, waiting for him to come in and explain himself. When he went up to her he found her before the fire in a basket arm-chair under several rugs, her face pale and hollowed. He tried to pass it off airily by saying he had been playing in the yard with Josey Wintermann, but she looked at him so reproachfully, and his father so contemptuously, that he knew they did not believe him, and he hated them and hated himself and hated the Shaper for taking so mean a revenge on him as this.

"I see," said his father sternly. "I find I must be after you. I'll go up tomorrow to the monastery, and find out what kept you late today."

The next day he saw him there in the yard, walking up and down with Brother Carty, while Bwaola Moawara howled at him to say, *"Thaw shay mor!"* All that day he was in a gloom of misery, and when he entered the house that afternoon he wished it would fall on him and blot him out.

His father was waiting in the kitchen.

"When your dinner is eaten, boy," he said, "come upstairs. Your mother, God help the poor woman, wants to talk to you. And it's a nice thing for us to be thinking of paying hard and dear for you, and you behaving like this behind our backs."

Then he was standing before his mother, and she was weeping up at him, and his father was sitting in a corner crying like a child between his palms. And before they had done with him he too was crying, even while he knew how comical the three of them were there crying for one another. That evening, as he stood weeping before them, he promised them all sorts of things if they would only let him go to the college as they had planned; he promised them everything they asked, and that night he worked without raising his eyes even once from his books. But in his heart he knew his promises would come to nothing, because they had wrung his pride dry, like water from a dish-cloth. They had shared, too, in his debasement; his mother's lamentations went on all through the night, while his father insisted on going tediously over his essay and asking him endless questions about his work, and he said Brother Carty was "a most awfully highly educated and cultured gentleman," and said that that was a very poor essay indeed, as anybody could see, and even his mother could do better, and explained how if he worked hard and passed the Civil Service he would be in with the highest of the land, and know secrets of "the financial affairs of the empire."

From that night he worked hard—but only to get away from his mother's tears, and his father's endless encouragement, and his cheap clothes, and his Sunday bowler hat that made the bare-footed newsboys call out rude names at him in the street while he passed on, red to the ears but with unturned head.

In that way, as when a bright day falls, the city he had known builded of light and loveliness sank before his eyes as into a pit. Dark and tawdry he saw it now, old and deformed, crutched with piles, scabrous, bulged as with a goitre, empty, dark, and, as if to torment him, he found, flickering in the recesses of his mind, bright images of the beauty he had lost, a torch walking with him through the dim, dusty streets of Cork. In the summer, when he was going to the college in the afternoons for extra work, he would wander by roundabout ways through the slums behind the cathedral, searching thirstily for some sign of the loveliness he had lost, searching for some scrap of real stateliness in this city where he might have to live out all his days. He would wait until the evening sunlight grew powderous with the bloom of night and the lane lamps hung among the trees like those bell-flowers that hold their light within their yellow cups. He would hope then to find that the very decay and crapulence of the ruined slums, with their tottering, crumbling walls, would feed him some real and lovely image that he could lay beside those images of his memory within his mind. But often as he wandered about the streeted hills of night-time Cork he always came home as hungry of heart as a child is hungry of belly when it has been suckling an empty dug through the night. One lane, and one only, he found, where the campanile of a church presbytery, built of small, weathered red bricks, rose slim and glittering in the sunset that poured through an archway, a narrow pinnacle of scarlet above the slum roofs below and about it. To that arched alley-way he returned again and again, his heart on fire if the rickety lamp that dangled from the keystone were lit for the night and shone on the limewash of the tunnel through which he saw his burning Tuscan tower. In certain later lights, too, and at certain tides, low lights and brimming neap tides, it was good to look up the river at the bastion hills darkening with the fall of the sun behind their grassy bulk. As he passed over the little bridge of the Lee, he would look up at that domed horizon and down at its reflection in the tide that lapped the highest steps of the slips and hid every limestone quoin. There in the tide, just at its equipoise, smooth between ebb and flow, the hills lay ponderous, and on them all the little roofs etched, steel-smooth, tinted, hard. Once, a motor-boat nosing its way down-river with smooth arrowy waves shivered that picture on the water into a maze of rippling light, but before he had even crossed his little bridge all was smooth again, and the dusk fallen over the water with its bloom as of a grape. Quickly then he would avert his eyes as from the ruin of all loveliness. He knew the magic was of the moment, and with the moment gone.

Even so faded all the luminous memories of his youth, and as if his day-time life was too empty or too tedious to be worth retaining, all his images from this on became nocturnal and lamp-lit. Still he kept wandering about the city, searching patiently for what had never been. He would deceive himself for a week with some such fragment out of that reliquary of decay, as a bellied shop window left by the nineteenth century; or an old slum rookery, once a gentleman's town house, standing like a jail out of a welter of roofs; or it was a church, that had actually been a city jail, now so black and ugly and unfitting in its conversion that its stones, its ancient purpose, its new tenant, would hold him for long spells of wonderment. He would stand under the bright leaves of a tree, lamp-lit from above, trying to form the lines of a verse:

"Enchantment of still waters when the world's asleep . . ."

No!

"Night's enchantment on this grey stone . . ."

No!

"Night, from this grey stone and Christ within
    Waiting the morning crucifixion,
    Pass that they bring out my Christ.
    For I and all these men
Would crucify my Christ with sin.

"Dawnlight, this cold prison-house wherein
    They keep Him locked until thy breath
    Dim the enchantment of still waters.
    Now fill the cold caves' brim,
Tolling for the death of sin.

"Wake, Christ, from thy cold sleep. . . ."

But, no! The sooty walls did not evoke it, and it dried like a well. Murdering in his heart the secret it knew, silencing all that told him his city had grown old, like all the beggarly towns of Ireland, without any of that tenderness of face or memory that is the sole recompense of age, he would return to his home, murmuring to his unborn child that it, too, must be with all beauty, still.

When he reached his attic he found the bed untouched since the previous night, still hollow with his body-shape. Even the little wick under its glass globe before the statue of the Sacred Heart was dying for lack of colza, and as it leaped and fell the room was alternately filled with dusk- and lamp-light. His brothers were already asleep as he crept into his bed, and presently his father came from setting the fires in the rooms, and for a while his prayers wandered through the house like a wind. Last of all his mother came, heavily, step by step, up the stairs. Then, almost immediately after, as it seemed to him, he heard Shandon strike four o'clock, and beyond the thin partition his mother's voice, low and trembling, in a prayer that at times became a cry and a sigh of pain. Outside, Cork, dumb with sleep, and over the slates a creeping wind. Far away he could hear on that wind a train chug-chugging out of the city, rumbling past the sleeping, mist-white fields and past the cabins that would be pale and unlit among the trees.

4

A Desperate Character

1

With such a house Johnny had ample excuse for going, at first occasionally, and by degrees more and more frequently, to sit the night out with Leo before the clear fire in the kitchen at Lavitt's Quay.

"You're best out of the way," Leo would say, offering him a chair.

"I'm best," he would laugh. "A woman's way is neither man's way nor God's way."

And as Wintermann, too, occasionally called in there for a smoke and a chat about the racing news, it soon became like the old days in Rathkeale, except that old purblind Mag took the place of Bid, and the quiet of Cork humming below them instead of the dead silence of Rathkeale. Also, they never talked politics now. Instead, assuming a kind of childish interest as in a game that he did not know, old Leo would take the papers of the day, and with Johnny and the Cock go over the programmes of forthcoming races. With an entirely aimless cunning he would pretend a senile delight in fingering the name of a horse or a trainer's name and look up, as with a daring hope, to say:

"Now, tell me, am I right? Boss Croker? Pale blue jacket and yellow cap? Is that right? What? Am I right?" he would cry if Johnny patronizingly nodded his head.

His finger would seek another name.

"Parkinson?" Leo would catechize himself solemnly.

"Bird's-eye blue cap? Yes? Jacket? Red spots on white ground. I'm getting on," he would chirrup when the experts smiled their approval.

Again the wandering finger.

"Slippery Sam. That's a horse, now, that I look to see doing something. Do you know? . . . Ah, but I can't repeat that."

"What is it?" Johnny would ask with apparently no more than a passing interest.

"Well, somebody I know. I'll mention his name. Frank Speaight—"

"The flour merchant?" from Wintermann.

"The very man. I happen to know he had a large bet on Slippery Sam the other day. For the Lincoln. That's tomorrow, isn't it? So it is, then. Don't ask me how I found out. Mind now—no talk. Just a bit of information of some interest to racing experts like yeerselves."

His quick eye would barely catch Johnny glancing at Wintermann, and then going off into space to do a mental calculation.

"Shah!" Wintermann would pass it off by saying, "I don't believe there's anything in it."

Then off with them over the columns of the paper, and not a word from Leo as they went through their little brown books for an hour of scarcely broken silence. Or, if they were not reading their racing-books, the two policemen had again their *Police Code* and their *Constabulary Guide,* with its thin paper appendices and supplements when a new Act of Parliament had to be explained to the Force. For Johnny was aiming to be a sergeant, and Wintermann was trying again to get the two stripes.

"Not," he explained privately to Leo, "that I have any desire for promotion or want to spend my life for ever and always rising by doing the good policeman, but the little family, you know. . . . I have to think of the little family

and the poor wife. Sure we have to educate them, whatever. We have to get them on—to help them to rise.
Sure, we have to do it—and there's no getting away from
it."

"Oh, get them on," agreed Leo. "Get them on. There's
nothing like the education."

"Nothing like it," asseverated Wintermann. "Nothing to
come up to the bit of education. *We* know that," he flattered.

The old man waved his ring fingers and glanced privately
at the peeler. Having nothing to say on politics now, he
was content to be as much a silent image as Julie or old
Mag. He was content to sit in their company, yawning and
poking a cinder back into the fire with his foot, or nodding
asleep until some word passed between his guests. Then he
would raise his eyelids and look idly at them over his shoulder, as like as not yawning again, when it proved to be no
more than a question about a subsection or the effect of a
new Act on an old law. Besides, his joke was maturing all
the time while he waited there tapping his feet on the floor.
For the two policemen were trying to outsit one another,
trying each to be the last to have a secret moment with him
in the dark hallway. Then out of the little pocket beneath
the belt, where they kept their money, the few shillings
would slip crookedly, without a chink, into his fist.

"Put that on Slippery Sam for me, like a good man," the
Cock would whisper, and press the old man's arm to indi-
cate his thanks and his wish for privacy.

"Would you mind," Johnny Hussey would say, more
condescendingly and more cautiously, "putting this on
Slippery Sam for Bid? She'd be obliged to you."

And he would add:

"It's her birthday, you see."

Or:

"She's saving up for Christmas, you know."

Or any such excuse that would prevent him from being under too much of a compliment "to the old divil." But even if the contest between the two peelers ended in stalemate and they had to depart together, Leo never failed to find on the next morning, under his shop door, a little envelope from one or the other of them with a pencilled note about putting "a small wager," and how very much obliged the sender was to him "for all the trouble."

He kept these billets with care. He entered the bet and the policemen's names in his clearest handwriting. He wrapped up the ledger in many folds of paper, and tied it about with the same length of string from year to year. Once Johno came into the shop when he was entering one of these bets, and impulsively Donnel beckoned him to his side about the edge of the counter. Page after page he turned, pointing triumphantly to these entries.

"I see," said Johno, without comprehension.

Angrily the old "divil" shut the book. Then he opened it again, and with a glance over his shoulder at the shop door, said:

"Rope? There's rope. Rope enough to hang any man."

He closed the book gently, and tied it up with care.

"Wouldn't it be a nice how-de-ye-do if the D.I. saw that book?" he asked with a small smile.

"Begor, you'd be ruined!" cried Johno.

"How many," snarled the aged man, "would be ruined with me?"

He held up the parcel and shook it lightly.

"I told you I'd get him. Didn't I?"

Johno rubbed his hands with embarrassment.

"Ah!" cried Donnel. "You're too soft. But, never mind," he added, "there's plenty of time. And plenty more rope yet before I've done with the pair of them."

And standing up he rattled his money in his pocket and smiled Johno out of the door.

2

They continued to meet in the house on Lavitt's Quay, even when the streets grew darker at night and raucous with soldiers teeming in the pubs and the lane-women drinking their ring-money with the sailors up from Queenstown. They sat and talked there as quietly as if Cork and the whole world were still calm and unmoved beneath and about them. Perhaps they turned more slowly to the racing pages, or Leo again began to glance through the Irish speeches at Westminster, or Julie might say, looking up from the great magnifying-glass through which she read the *Evening Echo:*

"Begobs, they'll take you yet, Johnny."

At which he would say manfully:

"And glad I'd be to go. I'd defend my little pension, any, way."

"You'd be the fool," she'd say, and advise him always to "Leave it to the young men, Johnny boy. Leave it to the young men, that have no ties."

"The young men?" he would cry, angered and hurt by the words. "The young men! What good is there in them, I ask you? Look at the way they're disgracing the country with their bloody Sinn Fein and their corner-boys of volunteers . . ."

Leo's raised hand would stop that kind of argument at once; or at most a word thrown sideways, like:

"Now, now, Johnny. Live, and let live."

Whereupon Johnny would look at him for a minute and then, muttering through his moustaches, turn with impatience to the sport news, away from all such troublesome matters as politics and wars. But that would be all; otherwise the same quiet hours, and Leo whistling under his breath and tapping his feet on the fender.

There came a time when even Johno sat with them, and then the old Rathkeale circle was almost complete. A few weeks before Denis had been looking out one Sunday morning from under the corner of the window curtain into Warren's Place, when suddenly he burst into a roar of laughter that made all his brothers and his mother join him to look where he pointed with outstretched hand. There was Johno, tubby, small, almost bow-legged, in his leather gaiters, a wideawake hat cocked on the side of his bullet head, a green uniform, and a brown belt shining about his belly, an old Martini rifle under his arm, and his moustaches waxed furiously—their Johno, glaring out of his two brown eyes with a desperate intention as he marched off sturdily to the Corn Market for a morning's drill. At once his Bid called him Kruger, and Kruger he was from that on. When Johnny heard of it he simply threw his eyes up to the ceiling, opened his mouth almightily, made a silent "Haw!" and pawed the air helplessly with his hands. But two Sundays after that Johno was sitting before the table in Lavitt's Quay, his *Infantry Training*, 1911, open before him, and Wintermann and Johnny eagerly explaining to him every point of drill that he found puzzling or difficult. With the broom they sloped arms for him. With a pencil and paper they described the mechanism of a rifle magazine.

"Oh!" he would pause to say: " 'Tis great. To find Irishmen all together again. Ah, but it's only one man could do it. Redmond, the Parnell of the age. A gentleman, and a leader. Isn't that a fact?" he would appeal to Johnny.

"It must be admitted," Johnny would agree, "that Mister Redmond is a gentleman beyond all manner of doubt."

"To see us," says Johno, "makes my blood warm. To see

us together as I saw for the first time last night, side by side, green coat and black coat, guarding the city's bridges. It's grand that Ireland should have soldiers of her own to protect her. Isn't it a fact? Isn't it true?"

" 'Tis true," from Johnny.

" 'Tis true," from Wintermann.

But Leo would tap the fender rapidly with his foot and say nothing. They would look at him in surprise and disapproval, and privately Johno would say to the peelers:

"He's too bitter. Sure, he should forgive and forget."

It was Johno who always had the latest and most terrible news for them. He would rush in with a long face, waving them away as if what he had to tell was too terrible to be imparted.

"Did ye hear what's after happening? Yerra, my heavens, it's awful. Don't ask me to talk about it. There's weeping and wailing up in Quarry Lane: every man-Jack of the Fourth Battalion of the Munsters is wiped out. There's not a house there but has a widow in it."

Or:

"Did ye hear what the Gerras are after doing? They're after torpedoing the poor old *Bandon*. My God, I crossed the Irish Sea in that vessel fifteen times. And did I ever think she'd be sent to the bottom by a submarine? Listen to it. There's poor Sixer Flynn—he was fireman on his first voyage when I was on my last. He's gone."

On his fingers he counts them.

"There's Cal Sullivan. He was the donkeyman. There's Murty Canty, the stevedore. Oh, it's a crying shame. It's a shame to send poor men like them to their deaths. And for what? For what?"

He would apostrophize them with the question.

"For the aggrandizement of a bloody war lord. And what satisfaction is it to that fellow in Berlin for to see innocent, poor men like them going to their deaths?"

Hearing the hullabaloo, old Mag would cock her head up in the air and ask:

"What's it about? What's the trouble with ye, now?"

"The *Bandon*, Mag," Johno would roar into her ear, "is after being sunk, and half Cork is drowned in her by the Germans."

"*Wirra na Grasht!*" she would sigh. "It's the end of the world."

"It's the end of the Germans," Johno would say. "The world won't stand for such a crime. Ireland will rise up again' them. Aggrandizement? I'd give him aggrandizement. I'd aggrandize his backside for him if I was near him."

But Leo would only tap the table with his fingers, and look impatiently at the clock.

"Leo!" Johno would appeal. "Don't you see it? Don't—"

The old man would rise.

"I have to go to a meeting," he might say.

And taking his hat and stick, and throwing a muttered word to Julie, he would go out into the evening air, leaving them all to look after him with anger in their eyes, except old Mag alone who would have taken up her beads to pray for the dead.

Down in the street the Fenian would tap on the pavement with his stick and then turn indecisively along the quays, looking now and again at Shandon if it was still bright enough to see the gilt face. Then along the Coalquay, where the vegetable refuse lay withering on the macadam, and the tiny fishscales shone on the pavement. Through the gates of the Clothes Market he could see the gloom of abandoned halls, the clothes hanging from invisible gibbets in the darkness, and far beyond the white arc of light under the arched gateway to another street. So across Daunt's Square, that queer sunken little pub gully, where the lights were bright in the snugs and the tobacco smoke curling through the open doors. Finally, along the shopping street that opened wide beyond, with the dusty trams rattling in from the country fields, and a few loungers standing before the sun-browned window-blinds of the big drapers' shops. But here he would wander up and down like a man killing time, or he would go about a block and come back where he began, like a man undecided where to go. Then, at last, he would disappear down a side street, always tapping the side-wall with his stick, as timidly as a blind man.

Once, as he made his slow way along the quays after dusk, he met Denis Hussey returning late from his evening classes at the college, and they leaned over the side-wall and talked for a while at the flowing tide. At first the boy was shy, and he scarcely heard his uncle. Then:

"So you're doing Latin verse?" he heard Leo say, as his stick swung idly between his hands over the water. "Hum? And you like Horace?"

"Well, ye-es. His verses are short," Denis agreed more readily.

"I used to like one of his poems. I've forgotten its name now. About Atlas the son of Mercury. . . . No. . . . It was—"

The old man could not remember. The boy looked up at Shandon, and at the figures of the worshippers mounting the steps of Saint Mary's and entering the dark porch of the aisle. High above the pediment a gull gleamed on the gold wire halo of the Virgin's head.

"No," said the old man again. "It was about a mountain outside Rome. Mount Soractus," he said triumphantly.

"That's the *Ode to Marcus*," said the boy:

"O Soractus thou art white with snow."

"That's right."
"I didn't know you did Latin, uncle."

"I did a lot of Latin." He scraped a lump of moss from a crevice. It fell into the tide, and floated away by the wall. "But I mostly forget it now. It's small use to you unless you were going to be a priest. Or, maybe, a doctor. Yes, or a chemist. I thought of being a priest once," he lied.

He was always lying nowadays, as if he thought it was the part of a cunning man to deceive about everything.

"Then I was going to be a doctor."

"You'd have to go to the university for that."

"I was planning to go to Dublin."

"That would be the College of Surgeons?" suggested Denis.

"I don't rightly know. I never went there."

He looked down the river, where the lights from a tram moved like molten fire across the smooth water.

"I was a wild fellow," he smiled back at Denis. "I was a harum-scarum. Ah, sure, I had no sense."

They were silent then.

"But I had a good time," he smiled.

"That was Limerick?" asked Denis.

"The city of Limerick. Of course, I was very wealthy when I was a young man. I had large estates."

Denis blushed, because he knew the old lad was lying to him.

"Have it while you're young, boy. For when you're old you can't enjoy it."

They were silent again.

"Of course—"

He paused.

"Of course, 'tis sad to look back at it. That's a thing, now, I learned when I was a boy," he said musingly. *"Boethius! Fuisse felix et non esse felix.* . . . What is it? *Fuisse felix et non nunc*—that's 'now'—*nunc non esse felix —hoc est.* . . . What is 'unhappy'?"

"Infelix."

"*Infel-ic-iss-imum!* Yes, *hoc est infel-ic-issimum omnium-er-rerum.* You know, I haven't a bad memory, after all. Do you understand that?"

"Yes. No."

"To be happy, and not to be happy later on, that is of all things the most unhappy thing. Do you see? To be looking back at your happiness when you've lost it. But I don't regret it. I spent what I had. I didn't count the cost of it. I squandered it."

He threw up his stick.

"I suppose I had no sense, you know."

Silence again.

"What else are you at?"

"Irish."

"I had great Irish once."

There it was, rising in its wraiths before him, the ancient past. A dim cabin with a flickering fir on the hearth, and in a corner Julie comforting the small baby. Then it fell into dust—a splinter of a tree out of the bog mould fell into a dust.

"*Cuir an casúr,*" he said, "*in lar an urlár agus tóg an billeog as an casóg.*"

"What does that mean?" asked Denis eagerly.

"It means anything you like," said Leo. "It's an old riddle."

"I heard it," said Denis. "Bwaola Moawara told it to us once, but he wouldn't give us the answer."

"Bwaola? Who is he?"

"Our Irish teacher," said Denis, smiling. "His real name is Peter Casey."

The old man drew himself up, and laughed through his beard.

"Big Lips!" he laughed. "That's damn good. And it's just like the fellow."

"Do you know him?" asked Denis.

"I know him well."

He looked across at Shandon.

"What time is it?" he asked.

"Half-past seven, uncle."

The half-strokes chimed. Doh, soh, la, te, doh.

"Good night, Denis," he said, and walked away.

3

The winter after that Johnny got his sergeant's stripe, and for the third and last time Denis failed to pass his examination for the Civil Service, and Wintermann failed to get his first promotion. In despair, Johnny set his son to try for the bank—the refuge of all dullards. Many times from that on the boy met his Uncle Leo of an evening walking along the quays—his days at the college were finished, and he was studying now at a crammer's in town. But the old man never stopped, and never' spoke to him except to say, "Good night, Denis," as they passed on their way. That winter and spring he heard no more of him, and as he began to meet him less and less often, and finally not at all, he had almost forgotten about him until one Saturday night in late April, as they were kneeling about the kitchen saying the rosary, a terrible rat-a-tat came at the hall door. There were no lodgers in the house because it was the last day of the Lent, so that they listened in surprise.

"Go on, mother," said Johnny. "That's only a runaway knock."

It came again, louder than before, and when Denis went down there was Wintermann asking for his father. He came back, and his father went down in his shirt and trousers, and then he came back with a serious face and a great air of importance, and began to buckle on his uniform.

"Go on, mother," he ordered. "Give out the rosary. I won't be back for a while."

"Wisha," asked Bid, from where she knelt over the back of a chair, "what trouble-the-house is here now?"

"Never mind, now."

"Will I wait up for you?" she called after him.

"Don't. I won't be back maybe until morning."

With frightened eyes his children looked after him, up from where they knelt at the sofa or with a reversed chair for a *prie-Dieu*. He came back for his pouch that contained the handcuffs.

"Glory be to God," wailed Bid. "What's wrong at all, and it Easter Sunday night, and we all aiming to go off together for a long walk and a day out, before the lodgers start pouring in on us again."

"Ach!" grumbled her husband. "It's some upset at the Bridewell. Attend to yeer prayers. I'll have my breakfast at the mess. Ye must go off tomorrow by yeerselves."

She was so troubled that she did not finish the decade, but sent them off to prayers and bed.

In the morning, after mass, Denis saw Manus hurrying past him home, and Manus gave him a black and hateful look. Then along the street he saw Jill O'Donnell and his Auntie Julie, clustering their heads together with his mother, but when he came up to them he was sent ahead to light the kitchen fire, and they were silent until he was out of earshot again. His father was at home before him, taking off his uniform.

"Tell your mother I'm gone to bed for a rest," he said.

But as he was on the first step of the stairs Bid came in, and from behind the kitchen door Denis listened to their low-spoken words. He heard his mother say:

"They were down with me at the door this minute."

A murmur was all he heard from his father.

"But where are they at all?" his mother said.

He did not hear what his father said or what his mother replied, but he then heard his father's voice again, clear this time:

"Julie knows where he is well enough."

"She says she doesn't know from Adam."

"Rubbish. And so does Jill O'Donnell."

"Wasn't I talking to the pair of them, and they—"

Just then his father gave a "Pouf!" of disbelief or disgust, and moved on up the stairs: the boy scurried from the door. That was all he heard until after dinner that day, when he was alone with his mother, and he asked her what was wrong—and she, being unhappy, told him freely.

"Oh!" she said with wearied disgust. "What, but trouble. It's Leo Donnel. They raided his shop last night to search it."

"But what could they find?"

"Whatever they found or didn't find, they found what had no right to be there, anyway."

He saw the dark, empty street, more deserted even than usual because of the Sunday, and the policemen with his father—the sergeant—in the middle of them, trying their skeleton keys on the green door of the paper shop, and probably, in the end, bursting in the lock. Then, by the light of their torches and Leo's candles, they would be rummaging for hours in the shop and the little lean-to shed at the back, hidden by the shutters and the closed door.

"And what happened to Leo?"

"Nobody knows that. They went off to Lavitt's Quay, to arrest him for what they found in his shop. But he was gone. And it was a nice thing for your poor father to have to do the like. And, lo and behold, John O'Donnell wasn't there either. Aren't they the hayros to be bringing sorrow and misfortune on their poor wives? But we knew the pair of them would give trouble. The bad drop must come out.

'Tis the poor wives I do have pity on, God look down on them—"

He did not hear what else she said. His mind was a racing quicksilver, hither and over the city, hill-up and hill-down, with that one image always before him of a plastered cement house where the two men sat in an upper room behind drawn blinds, below them the can-cluttered backyard, rust-brown, littered, a jakes door swinging in the wind and the clothes ballooning on the line, and in the street the children racing at their play and the dray horses lumbering slowly up the cobbled hill. He could not tell why that was the kind of refuge he gave them, but there they would be, hiding east or west on the fringes of the city's hills, and the police smelling them out nearer and nearer every hour. Or they were out beyond the market gardens and the butchers' fields, and the cattle markets and the last factories and the last hovels, on some one of those hill-peaks with the unfamiliar names, Hang Dod, Garranabraher, Pouladuff, Turner's Cross, Youghal Road, Bandon Hill—always on a height he fancied them, so that they might be able to see and envy the train in the far greenlit valley racing under its belching plume of smoke that followed it wherever it wound its way from the fume and prison smoke of the city.

"And wasn't it well," he heard his mother say, "that it was Wintermann was in the day-room that night, and saw the orders of the day handed in by the D.I., and came running to your father. My God, sure, the pair of them would be ruined if the police found any sign in the shop that they were betting horses with that old blackguard."

"And did my father hobble the books?"

"What's that you're saying, sir?" threatened his mother.

"I mean, was my father able to take the books?"

"I don't know what he did!" his mother snapped. "It's none of our business!"

The church bells began to ring together all over the city, for the Benediction.

"There's the Holy Trinity," she said. "Go out to the chapel."

"Can I have a penny for the plate?" he begged.

"You can go in the aisle," she said crossly. "It's for prayer you're going. God will see you as well in the free place as the other."

He took his cap sulkily, but for spite he did not enter the chapel. He passed along the church door, and went along the silent Sunday quay down towards Leo's shop. It looked just as it always did when closed, except that he noticed a splinter torn from the jamb, and on the paint of the door the straight channel of a jemmy or a crowbar. He looked at the little show-case by the door for a while, with its rosary beads strung on a wire and a sun-tanned, dog-eared cardboard sheet of gilt religious badges. So back to the quays by the two long main streets, where the only shop open was a fish and chip shop, and the only shop lighted for all their length an eating café, with nothing whatever in the window but a delf hen sitting on china eggs and a notice saying, "NEW LAID." In one narrow lane a crowd of lane children were playing, still brilliant in their Sunday scarlet or purple velvet, still bibbed and ruffed with starched collars, but their green stockings manacled their ankles and their noses streamed, and on the boys the college caps were grey with dust, and the gilt tassel on the crown crumpled and awry.

The river stank at low tide. He was glad to leave it and climb the hilly street, that at its steepest broke into steps. Up and up and every shop closed; then at the brow of the hill he saw the country beyond, spreading in a sea of dusk up to the yellow of sundown. He descended the long street towards those open fields and that last rim of light, with a tree or two on either side confronting him with their worm-

eaten suggestion of a boulevard in tatters. At the foot of
the hill a small chapel stood, islanded on a gravel bank
because subterranean streams flowed here to their conflu-
ence, and then dived again through the comb of a grating
into the sandstone earth. The narrow windows glowed
through their cheap enamel, and the organ hum stole out
on the cool air and mingled with the gurgle of the sewers.
He knew the place well, because he had often come there
after his evening lessons with Brother Carty, when he was
at the monastery, and he leaned over the wall and looked
at a lighted tram grinding to a halt on the side-road.

He was about to turn home when he saw a motor-car
standing by the kerb, down the farther road where it de-
bouched, through cement plastered villas, on the world of
fields and hedges. A familiar figure was clambering into it—
his Uncle Leo. For a moment the blood pounded into his
heart. Then he saw John O'Donnell. Another man climbed
in to the wheel, and he knew him, too—it was Jeremiah
Haugh, the bookmaker. A fourth man came out of the
house with a long and seemingly heavy parcel under his
arm, and he knew him, too. It was Bwaola Moawara. He
laid the parcel heavily in the back seat, and then got in beside it himself. Seeing him there with these hunted men he
ceased to be an uncouth clodhopper of an Irish teacher,
and became, of a sudden, large, ominous, powerful bodied
—a man to be feared. The door of the car crashed with a
tinny sound; the engine raced while Johno, the only one
who had not left the pavement, leaned forward to speak to
Leo. Then the car lurched away in a cloud of oil and smoke
and dust, with Johno looking after it, his stick held weakly
in the air.

He turned towards the chapel. He passed the watching
boy without seeing him. He walked up the hill, past the
flea-bitten trees. Only then did Denis move from the wall

and follow him. He followed him to the brow of the street, with Cork twinkling below in the valley. He followed him down to the stinking river-bed. Only there, on the bridge, did the sailor halt to look about him, and then his head was raised to the sky as if he could see anything but the night-clouds bellied with darkness and night-wind and rain, threatening to wash and flood the city before dawn. For a long time he hesitated on the hump of the bridge; twice he crossed and recrossed it from head to head, and at each halt he stood staring into the darkening bed below him. Shandon struck nine o'clock and Denis knew he should be returning home, but still Johno stood staring into the narrow channel, from time to time turning to look up-river or down-river, or at the sky, or along the quay. Perhaps he was waiting for somebody—perhaps he would return to the far valley and the house he had left. The old Moorish clock tower over their heads struck out its sweet ascendant chime, and still he would not move. Then, quite suddenly, he stepped out along the street, past the shop with the delf hen and the china eggs, along to the corner of the street where Leo's shop stood, past that, and on to the bridge of the southern branch of the river, where he halted once more and stood looking into that low channel with its pungent bed, doubly stinking here because it was the low tide that disclosed the refuse on its shores, and carried the bile of the brewery sewage perpetually spouting into it up-river.

It was quite late now, and from where he sheltered in a gateway, Denis watched him with impatience. If it were his Uncle Leo he knew that he would have run to him and whispered that the police had raided his shop and would arrest him if he went home, but when two night police walked towards the bridge he was merely curious to see if they recognized the wanted man, and he would not have cared if they laid their four hands on him when they reached the spot where he stood. But they looked at him, and passed him without a word.

Now there was no one in the entire street along the quays, or up the hill beyond, but himself and Johno, dead silence fallen on the city except where the river purled in its low bed, and in a house near by the velvet tones of a hall clock counted out eleven soft strokes. Johno might have been carved out of the stone of the bridge for all the movement he made. Denis felt a soft raindrop smite his cheek. A side-car came galloping along the street, and he recognized a night reporter clinging to the bars. He could wait no longer. Even as it was he knew, now, that he must tell his father that he had seen his Uncle Leo and Johno; no other story would excuse him. Walking across the street, he tapped the silent man on the arm.

"Johno."

He did not stir. A little louder the boy repeated it, and at that the man whirled about, with his two terrified eyes flashing at the boy.

"Johno! You mustn't go home. They'd arrest you."

The drops of rain thickened, falling heavily in great splashes out of a thunder sky. It was very still and warm, and Johno eased his collar as if to breathe freely.

"You mustn't go home," stuttered Denis. "My father would arrest you."

Suddenly Johno loosed his body, and raised his fist high in the sky as if to crash it down on the boy's head.

"Go home!" he roared into the silent night air. "Go home, you spy, and you son of a spy. Go home!"

There was a terrifying rattle of sobs in his voice as he shouted it; and he shouted it again and again, higher and higher until it became a shriek as of agony. In fright, the boy stared at him, not realizing that he had lifted the dam of a swelling flood.

"You spy, and you son of a spy! Go home! Go home!"

A window creaked upwards, and somebody called down to them. The boy turned and fled down the street, feeling it lengthen before him as if he were racing through a nightmare, hearing the man shouting behind his back as he raced, and he did not stop until he was almost at his own door.

When he knocked his father came down in his long night-shirt and peeped out at him, silently thrusting his grey moustaches and his tousled head between the jamb and edge of the door. He stared at him so long and fiercely without saying a word, that at last he had to beg to be allowed in.

"May I come in, sir?"

At that the door was banged in his face. Immediately it opened again.

"Why," cried his father, "should I let you in? Where have you been, you young blackguard, to this hour of the night?"

"I was talking to John O'Donnell."

His father looked down at him. He almost wished the door would be banged in his face again, and he would walk off to his Aunt Julie for the night with, maybe, his father running after him down the street, his white night-shirt, made of boiled flour-bags, flapping about his shins.

"Where did you see John O'Donnell?"

The door opened a little wider for this question, and his father's face took on a hard, sharp, almost cruel, look.

"In Blackpool."

"Are you telling me lies?" asked his father furiously. "And what business had you talking with the like of him? Come in, out of this," he ordered, flinging open the door.

Denis sidled into the hall; by the light of a candle standing before the hall mirror he saw his own face staring at him out of the dark.

"In the name of God," his father said—almost weeping with dismay at the thought—"do you mean to tell me—"

His voice fell lower and lower as he went on; he was almost pleading with his son now.

"Do you mean to tell me, boy, that you are up and down with these blackguards behind your father's back?"

"I am not. I saw Johno down in Blackpool, and I was curious to follow him. He went all along to the South Gate, and he waited there for hours and hours. Then he saw me and spoke to me, and I came home."

"And where is he now?" his father asked.

"I don't know. I suppose he's there yet. Or gone home."

His father opened the door. It was pouring rain.

"I don't believe a word you're telling me," he said. "I think you're a champion of a liar."

"I'm not a liar."

"We found you a liar before, about the time Brother Carty kept you in."

"I'm not a liar," he cried.

"You're up and down with these ruffians of Sinn Feiners," his father shouted, and his red-rimmed eyes widened with anger.

Again Denis found him comical—there in his long nightshirt with his tousled hair and his drooping moustaches. The light was switched on over their heads. On the landing his mother appeared with a coat over her night-dress, a candle in her hand, her greying hair in plaits on each side of her face, and they tied with bits of red flannel.

"Johnny!" she pleaded. "For God's sake be quiet. Come up to bed, Denis."

She came down a step or two, the flame of the candle shivering in her hand.

"Go up, you cur," shouted his father, and he made to strike him.

"If you strike me," the boy cried back, raising his own fist, "I'll hit you in the face."

"Denis!" his mother called. "Denis! Johnny! Be quiet. Come up out of that at once, Denis!"

She pattered down the brass stair-guards and took him by the arm. He hesitated, exulting in the look of amazement that covered his father's face.

"I would," he cried, while his mother dragged him up a step or two.

"By God!" said his father very quietly. "You are a brat and a scut. I don't know where you got the bad drop. Not from me, anyway."

"I'm not a liar, anyway," the boy cried. "I'm not a liar. I'm not a liar."

His mother kept pulling at him.

"Come up to bed, Denis!" she pleaded.

"Go up!" ordered his father, "before I knock that sneer off your little farthing of a face."

He turned, and went up two steps at a time. At the turn of the stairs he looked down at his father, blubbering at that insult.

"Whatever I am," he cried, "I'm not a spy! Though it was flung in my face tonight that I was the son of one."

He saw his father rush up the stairs, and his mother tearing at his night-shirt to hold him back. He laughed scornfully, terrified, delighted, horrified, hating himself for having said it, and yet glad he had said it. He bolted himself into his attic room and stood listening. Through the wide cracks about the jamb he saw his mother's candle-light move over the pale green rabbit-wood of the ceiling. Her bare feet made no sound. She tapped at his door, and in a weary voice she said:

"Denis?"

"Yes, mother."

He felt he could not bear to see or speak to her. There was a long pause. Then she said again:

"Denis."

"Yes, mother."

"Say your prayers, like a good boy."

"Yes mother."

"Good night, Denis."

"Good night, mother."

She pattered away. He listened, but his father did not follow. Then, as he was struggling out of his shirt, he heard the front door bang. The cold iron of the framework of the window seared his chest, as he looked down into the long street beyond the gutters. The arc lights of the main street lit the tall façades of the distant shops, and, on the hitherside of the street, the roofs and parapets were jet against that brilliant violet glow below and beyond them. He saw his father, in uniform, walking swiftly down the street, a fine martial figure. He heard his mother tapping the partition.

"Are you asleep, Denis?"

"No, mother."

"Is that your father, gone out?"

"Yes, mother."

"Where is he gone to?"

"I don't know, mother."

But he did know, and knowing, he did not sleep for hours.

4

When he awoke in the morning the city was already echoing with the sounds of cars racing out to the country for the holiday; a cornet was playing in the distance one of those slow tunes that, too far and too fleeting to be recognized, seemed to hum and echo in the air not so much with the dull boom of memory as with the deep internal trembling of a moment of vague *recueillement,* like those waves that never fall within a shell. At one moment it palpitated with the divinity of an aria from *Aida;* then it seemed to waver into *Dalilah;* and then an earlier, richer memory changed it into a medley of every melancholy air that had ever risen over the guttering of gas flares and the boom of a German brass band in the Mardyke of a summer afternoon:

> "But now thou'rt gone to yonder happy home,
> Gone with the day-star fading fair and slow,
> Thou'rt gone, my dearest, when I did love thee,
> When I did love thee, when I did love . . .
> The cold moonlight fading,
> The dews of dawnlight cooling,
> Slake, ah, dearest, the fires of the night;
> Thou'rt gone! Thou'rt g-o-one!"

Stretching himself out on his bed he touched with his raised finger the ceiling that sloped down behind his head to the eaves; it was already warm from the sun. Below his window he heard the childish voices of two children where they sat talking on the step of the pub door. It was pleasant to listen when their piercing voices floated up the narrow canyon of the side-street.

"Yoy! I'm going to be all alone in the house, by myself. Awl alone, by meself."

"Gor!"

"My aunt is going to Blarney. And my father is going to Crosshaven with my mudder. So I'll be awl alone in the empty house, by myself. Now, Foxer!"

"Gor!"

"You see, if I was to go to Blarney I wouldn't be back for the Benediction. And if I went to Crosser I wouldn't

be back, then, neither. So I have to stay awl alone in the
house, by meself. Now, Foxer?"

"Gor!"

"Well, so long now, Foxer, boy. I must answer the ten
mass for Father O'Flynn."

"Gor!"

In the kitchen his mother was standing over the pan of
rashers, and his brothers were racing in and out, getting
ready for their outing.

"Is my father in?" he asked his mother in a subdued
voice.

"Yes. He's gone to bed; he came in at five o'clock."

Her eyes were red from lack of sleep.

"Sit in to your breakfast. You can shave after. Robert
wants the enamel dish."

As she put the plate of rashers on the table before him,
she said:

"Johno was arrested last night."

He looked up at her and she looked down at him, and
with a sigh she turned away.

He was glad his father would not be with them; alone,
with his brothers and his mother, among the late, rich,
spring-time fields he might be able to forget for a while
all that had happened the night before. They would have
a quiet day all by themselves at Carrigrohane. Not even Jill
or Julie O'Donnell were coming; they would be poor company, anyway, on such a day—a sad pair left behind by the
emptying city. They would take the steam tram that ran all
the way beside the straight white road, so that from the
windows they could see the people walking on the path
and in the fields, and the side-cars rolling out to Blarney
and Coachford and to the pine woods at Saint Ann's. And
so it happened—a day of such warm spring weather that the
trees were already summer-thick, and the air sweet with the
thorn that snowed on every hedge.

Here by the castled rock, pine-clustered even on its perpendicular crags, the Lee flows so shallow that with their
stockings peeled they could all but cross it on foot; and the
rich land on either side spreads low and level on a fan of
land, a waving meadow-grass. Their mother loved that
stretch of river because it reminded her so of the Deel at
Castlematrix, and she had spoken to them so often of that
hidden corner of her Limerick that they, too, saw here not
one country-side but two, and filled it not with its own life
but with the life of her vanished youth. The castle high on
its cliff she compared to the towering mills, the tiny tram
chugging beneath it to the train to Kerry, the fields, so soft
and somnolent, were identical with the country about Rathkeale. Here, too, thick-leaved chestnuts grew out of high
grass, and cattle ambled in and out of their low shade or
stood whisking their tails in the shallow water; here, too,
even so early in the year, the cones of white blossom and red
blossom grew upward on candelabra branches; nothing
missing but reeds and rushes to lie flat on the river, streak-
ing its darkness and its deeps. To make the day still more
familiar and complete, she had the fancy to dress herself
in white with a black belt tying her waist and a wide straw
hat on her grey head; so that as she walked with Denis
along the hedges she gleamed under the shadows of the
clotted may above their heads. But when she spoke the
likeness faded, farther even than that to which it was so
nearly like.

"Denis," she chided, "you had no right to say such
things, son, to your poor father. He's only working for to
help us all on our way. And it's sinful, Denis. It's sinful,
boy. For, if you won't take the advice of your parents, whose
advice will you take? You won't quarrel with your father
again, Denis, boy, will you?"

What could he say but:

"No, mother."

"No, my son. He's the best poor man in all Ireland. I said, and I said it, and I said it again."

They were far from where the others scrambled together in a far corner of the field. Their voices rang and carried clearly to them, and when they fell silent the air grew suddenly alive with bird-song. The far banks wavered in the heat haze, and the upturned earth on the distant hills was a pale fallow under the burning sun.

"Poor old Julie," said his mother. "Look at my poor sister. She was as good a sister to me as ever any sister had. The last of them all, I might say. Look at the life she had. And look at her now, not even knowing where her husband is."

The boy thought of the road from Cork, and the car racing away into the darkness with Leo Donnel and Haugh and the Irish teacher.

"Sure, glory be to God, your father is the best of men. He never once gave me a harsh word since he married me."

"Don't worry yourself, mother. Everything will turn out all right in the end."

"Take example, Denis, for example teacheth. Take example by that foolish man, Leo Donnel. He got every chance, every benefit his mother could give him. And he ruined it all. Look at him. I could cry salt tears for the way he has that poor sister of mine. And is she a young girl that could bear it?"

He was reaching up to pluck the white may, and she saw he was paying little heed to her.

"Run on, child. Run on and play with your brothers, for I'm poor company for you."

He clung to her arm, and watched her head lean slowly to one side and her eyes stare far away at the dim distance among the hills.

"I'll stay here with you, mother. I'd rather stay."

She disengaged his arm.

"Run on, Denis," she commanded. "I'll stay here and say my beads."

She found a cool place and sat there, and from her purse she drew a tangle of rosaries, and he turned and walked slowly across the fields.

But it was in the afternoon that the place grew loveliest of all, when the sky darkened and the sun was covered for the rest of the day. For these last hours the scattered sunlessness he had known as a child fell over the land again, and the thick trees glistened in their depths as with a green vapour of light. The very birds grew stifled, and the smoke of a far cottage could barely rise. Last of all, that peculiar spring-time softness that is too sparse to be called even a day-time dew began to float down invisibly through the air, cooling them in their exhaustion, and pricking after many hours each single grass blade with a diamond of rain. Still their mother sat far apart, easing her heart with prayer, while the smaller children lay under a hedge tumbled in sleep, drowsed and drenched like the cattle under a far chestnut ruminating with heavy lids.

Along the main road there rumbled a convoy of military lorries. He stood up to see them. They were always on the road these days, churning up the dust and back-firing. A Red Cross van brought up the rear. He counted them—four, six, eight. His mother came across to him, yawning out of her stomach with a loud sigh.

"Wisha," she sighed in the last breath of the yawn. "Will the war ever end? The poor wretches. I suppose they're off to the Front."

She looked about the fields.

"What a shame the day was spoiled by that mist. I'm dying for a cup of tea."

She yawned again.

"Gather up them things, Denis. It's time we went for the train."

The small children were cross with sleep and the heat and chase of the day, and they stood about scratching and shaking themselves.

"Look at the way they have the sugar spilt," said the mother. "Ah! It's easy known yeer not in England—little sugar ye'd have then."

With a spoon she gathered it and put it into a measure of paper. Then, each with a basket or a parcel, they trailed off down to the river's edge, where the water flowed sullen and leaden without sparkle or life, and so brushed their way through the shoots of the hedges to the long foot-high platform under the beetle of the rock. There they waited for an hour, legs dangling heavily, wishful they were at home at their tea in the cool of the kitchen. The side-cars were all now rolling back to the city, and every horse nodded under a draggle of greenery. Then the train clanked in under its waving bell, and they scrambled for their seats, and the children leaned on one another's shoulders like a pack of cards, so sound asleep when they drew up in the corrugated iron shed of the terminus that they could hardly drag their small, dusty legs home. The streets were strangely empty, and in the distance they thought they heard the sound of cheering, but with all their thoughts on rest and the end of the day they heeded nothing until their mother was turning the key in the hall door.

"Now," she said cheerfully, "for a pot of tay, and a happy family about the board."

The raced up the stairs, refreshed by having ended the journey. There on the sofa lay their father, a great white bandage on his head and a patch of blood oozing through it.

"My God above!" cried Bid. "What has happened?"

He looked up seriously at her and them: they stood about him in a frightened, frozen flock. With solemn eyes he looked at Denis.

"A nice thing," he said in a very low voice. "A very nice thing. I thought I'd never see ye home."

"Johnny!" she appealed to him. "What is it? Is it Leo?"

"It is," he said bitterly. "But he's finished now, the ruffian."

"Oh! Poor Julie! Is he dead?" she whispered in terror.

Weakly he moved a finger; his head he dared not stir.

"It would be better for him," he said.

"The brave Sinn Feiners," he said, "are out in Dublin. They're shooting the people in the streets. There's troops pouring in from England, and the whole city is in flames."

Bid blessed herself.

"And your head?"

"There's riots in the streets all the afternoon. Didn't ye meet any of it? Sure, the military are out in pickets all over Cork."

Standing by the window, Denis looked into the strangely empty street. He saw the wide street of a city in flames. About it distant cannonading. Rifles cracked ceaselessly. In that long street, wide and noble, empty from end to end, glowing under the perpetual sunset of its own fire, men crouched behind the high, barricaded windows, and glinted down the hot rifle barrels that barked and plunged by their cheeks at every trigger-pull. And there among them was Leo Donnel, with Haugh and Peter Casey; an old man, white-bearded, his pale cheeks and his long face lit by the city's doom. For a long time he heard nothing behind him in the kitchen. Then his father was saying:

"Out there in the Place," he was saying, "the clodhoppers, forming fours and unforming them again, forming and unforming for hours. Damn the bit else they could do. And then the police scattered them. And then the corner-boys got the news from Dublin, and they began flinging stones at the police. So there's running and racing and firing of shots the whole day long."

As they would in a thunder-storm, the children crowded together suddenly when a shot echoed across the quays.

"What's that?" cried Bid, looking at the opposite window.

Turning to it, Denis saw the running flocks halting at the corner beneath, crying:

"They're coming."

In the far corner of the square a scattered body of police appeared, shielding their heads with their uplifted hands and racing blindly, yellow batons shining in the sun, at the disappearing mob. A dozen fellows waited a little after the main crowd, flinging stones slingwise about the shoulder and grasping their coats across their stomachs to leave the catapult arm free. One man in their midst held a little revolver, trying vainly to make it fire. When it cracked, they cheered and ran. Under the window their feet galloped on the hardened street, and after the sound had grown faint the trampling of the police rushed past beneath. All evening there was the same distant shouting, and as they drank their tea (away from the window for safety), an occasional rattle of musketry. As it grew dark the streets quietened, though double rows of police stood armed against the farthest wall of the square, great black-coated, black-helmeted men, waiting to be called if the rioting began again.

As he sat by the window looking at them, brooding over what he had heard, his heart swelling and swelling with his secret thoughts, his father suddenly asked him if he had anything to do with these hooligans in Dublin. With mock politeness he begged his father's pardon, but he didn't catch the last epithet in his father's sentence. Between them both stood his mother, and she besought them both, for the sake of the head wound, not to cause disturbance tonight. From the couch his father poured out his bitter scorn on the dirty blackguards, with their bloody Sinn Fein, the cowards who wouldn't come out in the open like men. By God, his son wasn't going to have anything to do with these blackguards. He'd see to that.

"By Chrisht, don't talk to me, woman. Let me alone, will you?"

He sat up on his couch in his bitter anger, while his wife besought him with hushed whispering entreaty not to raise his voice, or all the street would hear them.

"No son of mine will disgrace me with his bloody Sinn Fein. By God Almighty, have I served in the Force for twenty-five years, and never had an occasion to have a single black mark up against me—for that brat to come against me, and my pension in sight? Aye, and promotion, maybe, to head constable waiting for me?"

"Hush, hush. Listen. Speak easy, will you? Speak easy. Speak easy."

"God damn the lousy pack of country hooligans. There isn't a man among them. A low, uneducated pack from the bogs. Where's your breeding, boy?" he sobbed. "I've served near twenty-five years in the Force, and I've never mixed with the level of people you seem to go around with."

"I go around with no one."

"God save Ireland! Oh, then, wisha, what do you expect these fellows to do for Ireland, will you tell me that?"

He put his palms together and looked up to heaven.

"May God bless England! May God and His Holy Mother bless her this night. England has only to withdraw her hand from this country in the morning, and we'd be crawling to her on our bended knees in a week."

Dublin in flames, fiery with its own murder, and that old man fighting there under the crumbling roofs.

"We wouldn't. What has she ever done for us but bleed us to death? What about the famine and black 'forty-seven?"

"Oh! You show your ignorance. What did England do: only save us from starvation? And little we deserved it."

"Save us from starvation! Ha!"

From some hidden well of memory all the stored hate of centuries jetted into his mind—words fallen from his mother, spoken even by his father, by the monks, by his school companions, read in his history, they fountained in him like the blood that surges to the head and blinds the eyes with rage.

"That's a good one," he mocked. "Save us from starvation! And what did they do to my own grandmother, that had to sweat and tear on a rack-rented farm for her ten children? To your own mother, and to my mother here, that had a hard and cruel life in Limerick when she was young? Who did that?"

He thrust his face down into his father's face. "Who did it? Who did it? Who but the English landlords? What did they do to Leo Donnel, but throw him into jail three times because he dared to rise against them?"

His father staggered to his feet, pale with rage.

"Leo Donnel is a common criminal and nothing else, and he'll suffer for it. I put him into jail before, and I'll put him into jail again."

The children were shrinking, all pale, to the sides of the kitchen. A dim rattle of rifle fire echoed in a distant street.

"You put him into jail?"

"Denis! Johnny! Denis!"

"So that's what Johno meant by calling me the son of a spy? You put him into jail, and you're proud of it. You spy on your own uncle?"

"Silence, boy!" his father cried.

"And now he's fighting up there in Dublin—"

His father struck him across the face. Then the red smear on his bandage began to spread, and he staggered. The boy held his hand to his face; tears of rage came into his eyes.

"You spy!" he choked. "You spy on your own people."

His father sank weakly on the lounge.

"Get out!" he commanded. "Get out!"

The boy ran from the kitchen, shutting his ears to his mother's cry. Even as he hammered down the brass stair-guards he heard her calling him, and over her voice his father's voice moaning and crying like a woman. When the door banged behind him he found the streets still faintly lightsome and quite empty. He raced down to the quays, and they too were empty except very far away, below the bridges, the dark figures, small as insects, of police marching in scattered formation along the roadway. He ran along towards Lavitt's Quay, seeing over his flying shoulder an armoured car go lumbering down the main open street of the city. Panting, he reached his uncle's house and knocked wildly. He heard the steps coming slowly down, and Jill O'Donnell opened the door.

"Let me in. Let me in for the night."

She opened the door.

"What ails you, boy?" she asked.

"My father has me turned out."

The crackle of rifles away down some back street made them blink with their eyes as if the dust of the powder were blinding them; they were not yet accustomed to the sound of bullets.

"Come in," she cried.

She closed the door behind him.

"For God's sake, why did he turn you out?" she asked, inside the cold hallway.

"Because I stood up for my Uncle Leo. Because I stood up for the men in Dublin. Because I called him a spy."

"Denis," she chided him. "You had no right to say that. Sure ye all have to live together."

"I won't go back," he said. "I won't go back."

"Come upstairs," she beckoned.

They went up quietly; there was old Auntie Julie, fat

and hairy-faced and big-chested, before the parlour fire. He sat by the fire listening to Jill telling his aunt what he had already said to her. Julie looked at him.

"Johno told us," she said, "what you did last night on the South Gate bridge."

"I told him he'd be arrested," he said.

"You did your best for him, boy."

"He had to come home," his wife said moodily. "Or else go to Dublin to the rising. And he'd be there, too," she said proudly, "if it wasn't that Leo persuaded him against it, for my sake and the sake of Manus."

"Where is Manus?"

"He's out gathering news about the rising. He thought he might get word about Leo. Is there many on the streets?"

"There's not a soul out."

They heard a stick being hammered on the floor over their heads.

"Come up to your grandmother," said Jill. "She heard your knock."

The old woman—she was ninety-eight—lay in her bed, from which she had not stirred now for over a year. As they entered she felt the air with her rheumaticky stump of a hand, every inch of it brown, mottled, and finely wrinkled.

"Who's that?" she mumbled, as she felt about her in the darkness. The fading day still lit the room.

"It's young Denis Hussey," said Jill. "He had a fight with his father about Leo and the rising in Dublin. And his father hunted him."

"Give me your hand," said the old woman. *"T'rom do lauv."*

The boy held out his hand, and felt her caressing it between her warm, soft old fingers.

"Is this Denis Hussey?"

"Yes, grandmother."

As he grew accustomed to the dim light he saw the wisps of white hair growing from her chin, and the scalp that had hardly any hair on it at all. Her face was shrivelled to a small apple. Her eyelids were not quite closed, but the pupils did not shine, and as she lay there they seemed to peer at the ceiling. Continually she caressed his palms with fingers that were softer than velvet, and more warm.

"So, it's that way?" she said. *"Do cuireag ar an mohar hu?* I'm praying, Dinny. I'm praying for the men in Dublin. 'Twas folly. It was folly for them to go there. But I never blamed Leo Donnel for what he did in 'sixty-seven, Dinny. So I won't blame him now. It's only of Julie I'm thinking, Dinny. *An ghirrse vocht!"*

"She'll be all right, Mag," said Jill. "We'll see to that. Johno will never see her want."

"I did my besht for her. *Ni 'eadhainn a huille.* I could do no more."

"She'll not want, mother," said Jill O'Donnell.

"Wirra na grawst," sighed the old woman. "It was madness to go into danger. Madness. They'll be killed out. They're always killed. England is too strong for us. It was folly. The poor wretches. I'm praying for them, Denis."

Her fingers worked excitedly on his palm.

"The poor wretches, they'll be killed out."

He tried to comfort her.

"They can defend themselves, grandmother."

"The poor wretches," she mumbled. "They'll be killed out."

"Say your prayers now, Mag," said Jill. "We'll leave you. I must run down to Bid and tell her Denis is safe. She'll be worrying about the boy."

"Wisha! *Do cuireag ar an mohar thu?* The poor lad. Good-bye, now, Dinny, boy. I'll be praying for ye all."

Gently he disengaged his hand and, turning, saw Jill beckon him to the door. Together they stole from the darkening room. Through the lobby window Shandon raising its black finger against the last ray of day, and far away a faint, faint crackling of rifle fire.

And then came its still fainter echo over the pale city, under its pale sky, listening and holding its breath in a silence of fear.